MY
LIFE WITH
DARWIN

MY LIFE WITH DARWIN

MOLLY BEST TINSLEY

Houghton Mifflin Company

BOSTON

.·.·.·.

1991

Library of Congress Cataloging-in-Publication Data

Tinsley, Molly Best.
My life with Darwin : a novel / by Molly Best Tinsley.
p.   cm.
ISBN 0-395-57785-3
I. Title.
PS3570.I57M8   1991
813'.54—dc20   90-25129
CIP

Book design by Anne Chalmers

Printed in the United States of America

DOH   10   9   8   7   6   5   4   3   2   1

For William and Evelyn Best

MY
LIFE WITH
DARWIN

PROLOGUE

THE BLACK-BOUND BOOK is about the size of an open hand. Inside, my father's plain, upright script announces that it is January 5, 1949, and we have arrived in Macuma, Ecuador. The mountains are behind us, and all around, the infinite greens of the Oriente. We thank God and Shell Oil for the usable landing strip and for the remnants we find of a settlement — three crumbling concrete slabs and the rusted tin privy. The river at this point is pure enough, though swollen with the rains, which pound furiously all afternoon.

The next day my father and his friend Hobby erect a roof over the largest remaining foundation. My mother, Grace, and Hobby's wife, Thelma, set up the kitchen. On the next, we all make friends with the gentle Quichua who wander in from their nearby village. They bring gifts of plantain; they wear cotton clothing of sorts. They are no strangers to God's Word, which has been brought to them once a month from the Principle Mission downriver. It is a pleasant first meeting, of which I have only the vaguest memory, though I become the center of attention by virtue of my white-blond curly hair.

More than three weeks pass, peaceful, industrious weeks, but also vigilant, edged with suspense. We are watching for signs of the Janca. Documents back in the States called them natural killers. *An embarrassment,* admits the government of Ecuador. *A costly stumbling block to the essential production of rubber and oil.* "What better creatures," my father asks, "to prove Christ's redeeming Word?"

A week later my father and Hobby argue. The waiting has gotten on Hobby's nerves; he's pushing to put up a fence, something with barbed wire. My father would rather try it without one. They arrive at a compromise plan. Hobby starts on the fence while my father takes off each morning in his patched-up Piper and follows every branch of the river looking for trails, clearings, thatched roofs, dead fires. "Our Father has called me," he writes, "to carry the Gospel where Christ has never been named before. Sooner or later I will find these Janca, and from that moment on they're marked men!"

On February 21, not far from a flooded tributary of the Tiwano, my father spots a break in the tree cover and a broad, flattened cone of thatch. This I think I remember: great rejoicing out at the landing strip when he returned; the adults jumping about, cheering; me getting into the spirit, running around and yelling with abandon, then all at once being swept off my feet, plunked onto my knees, and sternly shushed, while my father began a prayer that went on and on, even when the sky cracked open and rain poured down on us, kneeling, heads bowed, in the mud.

After that Hobby gives up his fence — the Janca are beyond striking range — and joins my father in the air. Almost daily they fly over the village and with proud precision drop gifts right in the center of its clearing — gaudy, useless things, like ribbons, lengths of porcelain beads, and toys, and also illustrated pages from the Bible. Soon they engineer a way to lower more valuable offerings in a basket while circling slowly above the village — tin pots, matches, a machete. The third week in March, they find manioc bread in the basket when they pull it up, and precious strips of dried meat. They decide it is time to move closer.

April 1: They are ready to take the plane in. The rains have abated and there is a promising sandbar, growing wider every day, where the Tiwano forks off into Janca land. There is no time for my father to write anything the next day, the day they leave, but I remember standing with my mother and Hobby's wife and all the good Quichua Indians who had established themselves as part of our household; we stood and waved the plane out of sight, a yellow X shrinking into the deep blue sky. There was a hollow place in my chest that knew they would be gone too long.

Easter comes and goes. My father is a voice over the radio. He is waiting, keeping busy, building a platform six feet above the riverbank in an ironwood tree with strips of rippled tin for a roof. He tinkers with the plane — he has to keep sand out of the landing gear — while Hobby meditates neck-deep in the river to escape the relentless gnats. And there are signs. Animal noises, glimpses of movement, the sensation of being watched. My father is gallant words penciled on a page: "I feel the Lord's Will in this. How could I ever rest in peace with the knowledge of all these creatures wandering outside His Kingdom, ignorant and lost?"

On April 11 comes the answer to his prayers — three Janca walk out of the forest and into the camp. They wear nothing but strings around their bellies and ankles. They talk nonstop in a language my father cannot understand, though he thought he was prepared to. They seem friendly enough, like children, curious about everything, though when Hobby offers to daub a little bug juice on the shoulders of one of the Indians, for they are pocked with bites, he jumps away and bares his teeth. They turn down a second taste of beans, spit my father's warm tea into the sand, and then, as abruptly as they came, disappear behind the screen of trees.

The next day they return. All they want to do is gawk at the plane. One keeps rubbing the front of his body against its wings and murmuring something that sounds like a question. My father figures maybe he'd like to go up, gives him a shirt, and, by shivering and holding himself, tries to show it is cold in the sky. Finally he lets my father help him put the shirt on and climbs into the cockpit. As they take off, my father looks over at him and he seems to be smiling, or maybe squinting because of the sun. My father follows the river a way and then veers off over the forest, heading for the spot they have been dropping all the peace offerings on. Pretty soon there it is, and the folks below see them and turn their faces up and wave their arms. Maybe they are expecting another gift. They seem to make my father's passenger a little nervous. He keeps looking down, then looking back at my father, who smiles and nods. He looks at his own hand almost as if he's never seen it before, then he puts it outside the craft and forces it up and down against the rushing air. Suddenly he stands up, gives a strange cry, and shows every sign of jumping. My father has to grab him by the back of his shirt and yank him down. It is all my father can do to hang on to him until the clearing is out of sight.

What was he thinking? my father wonders afterward as he prays for help in understanding these creatures. All three Janca vanish again after the bad landing, which my father expects knocked his new friend around more than he liked, for he scrambled over the side and was off with his buddies while the prop was still spinning. Hobby went after them, but only halfheartedly; he lost them in minutes. The one left a trail of vomit, poor soul.

Thirty years afterward, I know my father's story is all but over, the pages are numbered. But he is sure the Janca will come back, sure they have understood that he and Hobby mean friendship — and he radios the wives in Macuma, where we celebrate by singing "Open Heaven's Glory Gates." After that he prays all evening for the Janca to bring others when they return; he falls asleep with the certainty he will be answered.

>> .·. <<

I am Hannah Charles, my father's only child. I am trying to begin where his writing runs out, where the warped pages are blank except for water stains. I am looking for something that isn't here — not in this book, not in these layers of yellowed news clippings, pictures, the *Life* magazine photo-story, cruelly focused: here we have my father's plane torn apart; here, the riverbank from several angles, littered with clothing, cans, a square of corrugated tin; the search party with rifles in late-afternoon silhouette; a wall of trees; then the swollen seat of my father's pants, the only part of him visible in the shallow water, a Janca lance jutting like a rigid tail. Wrapped around its handle, the caption tells us, is one of the Gospel tracts he had scattered over the jungle from the air. When we were first married, it was this last picture that my husband, Darwin, could not erase from his mind. *How could I not love you,* he used to ask me, *when your dad died of a spear up his ass?*

1

·   ·

·

LAST NIGHT WE CELEBRATED our first-born Jeremy's thir-
teenth birthday, against his wishes. He didn't want a cake or
presents, he'd announced that afternoon. In his unreliable voice
he implied that he has outgrown such things — just money would
be fine. He is two weeks into eighth grade and wants to begin
saving for a car. It would give him something positive to think
about, he says, when he walks the three miles home after deten-
tion for skipping showers in P.E., or when the kids at the bus stop
are calling him Germy and fighting not to sit next to him.

"It seems to me," I said, "you could use a little boost right now
from your family. Isn't that more important than money?"

His mouth went into a sullen set he held all through dinner,
even while chewing, until Darwin handed him the matches to
light the candles. Maybe he didn't want a silly cake, tiered and
decorated to resemble a coiled king cobra, but he does like to
strike matches, make that small flame spurt and spread. He per-
formed the job slowly, half entranced, while Darwin reached
back and slowly turned down the dimmer on the lights.

There the six of us were, gathered in by the darkness, shadowy
gray except for Jeremy on my right, whose bottom-lit face looked
slightly startled, whose eyes shone with candles. On my left,
unusually silent, was Matthew, our middle boy, difficult and
handsome, and beside him, our daughter, Rachel, in whom Darwin's compulsive extroversion shows up softened, as personal
charm. We count on her not to continue whatever Matthew tries

to start. Though youngest, she is also our authority on the current styles, which she tends to confuse with normalcy. Across from her, Benjamin knelt in his seat in order to see better. Born one month premature, he has always been small for his age; he tries to make up for it with speed and agility. I wished then that I could touch all of them at once, draw them to me in a single embrace — even, no, especially Darwin, my husband, who seemed so far away at the other end of the table. He had taken his glasses off, but his deep-set eyes were lost in gloom. Was he conceding that I had been right to insist on this moment together, that it was good for all of us?

Benjamin started singing "Happy Birthday" in his high, nasal whine. Our voices strained for a measure to reach his key, then split off into more comfortable ones. Matthew, jealous boy, scrapped the tune completely and made his own loud invention of high and low extremes.

Jeremy gave the candles a long blast, Matthew claimed he saw his spit land on the cake, Rachel gagged and said she didn't care for any. Benjamin flipped the bright light overhead back on and then scrambled up one side of the kitchen door frame like a telephone man on a pole and dropped to the floor with a crash. (Sometimes he wedges himself straight-legged at the top of the doorway, his sneakers against one side of the molding, his back against the other. He can eat a whole meal that way, seated above us in midair.) "From each according to his ability," Darwin mused, and briefly met my eyes. He had felt the moment also, I was sure, until we were halfway into our cake and he announced he had to go out for a while.

"In the middle of Jeremy's party?" I said.

"It's all right," Jeremy said hoarsely. "I never asked for one of these prehistoric productions in the first place."

"I don't mean this minute," Darwin said. "Later."

Now. Later. Off and on for years. Does it matter? Again I decide not. I used to go with him in the beginning, Jeremy strapped to my back. There were SDS meetings, a move to unionize the campus food services, there were the ill-fated Young Scientists for Marx. Idiots for Ideology, Darwin calls them now: the

Bad Old Days. Then Matthew arrived and I stayed home. That was all right; I wanted Matthew. And tiny Benjamin and finally Rachel. I probably would have borne others, year after year, hoping with each to deliver myself into virtue, if Darwin had not had the operation. Sometimes when we're all together, like last night, it's as if the perfect souls of all those unconceived children are hovering over us, humming some secret that we will never hear.

"Where're you going?" Matthew asked, troublemaker, and asked again when he got no reply.

"To see some friends," Darwin said. The younger children looked at me as if my face would tell them what this meant. But I have not met these new friends; they are a post-Revolution crowd. They have a lot to learn, Darwin said last week. They look up to him, he added with a dismissive sigh. They are in the midst of designing a social experiment with themselves as guinea pigs. I raised my eyebrows at the children and shrugged.

Darwin shoved himself up from his end of the table with a groan. "OK, I saw that," he said. "Just tell me, somebody, when did it start?"

"That is a good question," I said.

"Don't think I don't catch your little signals. You've gotten to all of them, haven't you?" He gave a backhand sweep as if to brush the children away. "Behind my back."

I have learned to wait for him to settle down. Meanwhile Jeremy was frantically opening and smacking closed the fat, hardcover text on herpetology (his birthday present from all of us) in coded protest: *Jeremy to Dad, Jeremy to Dad, no she hasn't, she has not gotten to me.*

"I know what you're thinking," Darwin said. He yanked up his jeans by the belt and slid them back and forth on his vanished waist, his way of scratching himself. "I've got no one to blame but myself. Well, you're right. I should have caught on a long time ago." He stomped into the kitchen.

"I guess that means it's later," I said to the children with a laugh. We were used to Darwin's walkouts, his one-man demonstrations. But the three youngest were looking at me anxiously — three pairs of Darwin's brown-black eyes full of questions — while Jeremy stared glumly at the muck of cake crumbs and melted ice cream on his plate. He is the one with my unfortunate face, freckled from weak chin to hairline, my blond, almost frizzy hair, my pale eyes. *How's my Jeremy?* I still ask when he gets home from school. Yet last night I felt him pulling away from me and toward Darwin, wishing Darwin would walk back in the room; or, more likely, wishing that he, Jeremy, had the courage to get up and join him in the kitchen, where he was throwing plates around daring something to break. Finally Jeremy lifted himself another segment of the devil's food snake from the central platter.

"Why don't you ask the rest of us if we'd like seconds," I said, and while he suffered the boredom of cutting his brothers slices, I offered to tell them the story of Grandfather Worden. They have heard it I don't know how many times, often on special occasions; it is a sort of ritual, and I thought they needed something to distract them from their father's fuss, and also to keep them from excusing themselves from the table and walking away. "When I was a child," I began.

"You know you play right into your mother's hands," Darwin said to me, standing framed in the doorway. He is out of proportion, his head too big for his narrow shoulders, his brow too high and wide for the rest of his head.

"I can't not tell them," I said.

"And why not?"

"What else do I have to give them? They don't want my advice anymore." Benjamin slid out of his chair and draped his arms around my neck. No one else would meet my eyes.

"Why do you have to give them anything? Why can't you let them be." He hasn't forgiven history for casting him aside in the late sixties, for stomping on all his beliefs.

"When I was a baby," I repeated. This was *my* story, I thought. Its ragged ironies hurt me once; I had every right, no, it was an obligation, to weave them into something proud. "My mother and father picked up everything they owned, which wasn't much, and moved to South America." Darwin was gone. "Someone told my parents about this tribe of savage Indians living deep in the Amazon jungle, which had never been seen by anyone who survived to tell."

Pausing for effect, I leaned down and set my cake plate on the floor beside Underdog's squat yellow snout. His amber eyes opened, there was a slight rotation of the head, and the tongue began licking.

"Every once in a while, at night, these Indians came out of the jungle and attacked the peaceful tribes along the edge. Sometimes they killed people," I went on, dreading the glance I couldn't not steal at Matthew, whose eyes had gone remote, dreamy. I had his attention, anyway. Someday the true moral of the story will take hold in his mind; the violence will wither away. "My parents and two friends of theirs thought maybe if they could find them and talk to them, they could get them to change their ways."

"A-a-a-ah-men-n-n," sang Darwin from upstairs.

"They gathered up presents, and they fixed up this little yellow plane —"

"What presents?" Benjamin wanted to know, and when I said, "Bright buttons, tin cooking pots, salt," he looked across to Jeremy, hoping his idol would share his amusement — some presents! But Jeremy was busy moving chocolate icing around in his mouth, his mind elsewhere. He was still trying to figure out what he should have done, could have done, to get his father to summon him to his side. His distraction annoyed me. It was *his* birthday, after all, a sort of passage. He especially should appreciate these blood links to the extraordinary, whatever their price.

"And machetes," Matthew reminded me sternly.

"Oh yes, machetes," I had to admit. What Matthew wouldn't do for a machete; and where would the rest of us be if he had one? "They're very handy for cutting trails. Then the two men flew the little plane over the jungle until they saw the main hut of these Indians. For a couple of weeks they dropped presents into the clearing, until my father was pretty sure they had made friends. And then very carefully he landed his plane along the river."

"They should of took guns," Matthew said.

"If the Indians saw a gun," I reminded him, "they might be frightened and never come. So my father and his friend just built themselves a little treehouse and waited.

"Then one morning, lo and behold, three Indian men dropped in for a visit, and they weren't wearing a stitch except for these things like cork they'd forced through their earlobes."

"Balsa wood," said Rachel, with the calm confidence of one whose answers are always right, while Benjamin smirked at some private vision of male nakedness. Rachel's own lobes glint with tiny gold shells. She presented Darwin and me with a petition signed by the sixty-four members of her mooncrater at school, to persuade us to permit, and pay for, the piercing.

"The Indians stayed all day, and my father tried to talk to them and learn their names. Toward evening they disappeared back into the jungle. But my father was happy."

Darwin was making as much noise as he could descending the stairs, singing, "I come to deliver the message, the message of redemption, redemption through the blood . . ." He stopped on the dining room threshold and pretended surprise that we were all looking at him. His body was encased in a royal blue leotard, brightened by baggy red trunks, a red and black S across the chest. He exuded the ripe, smoky smell of grass. "Well, what do you guys think?" He raised the old black athletic bag he was carrying. "I've got my cape in here."

Jeremy suspended chewing though his mouth was full and his fork already loaded with the next bite. Under dragged himself up onto his spindly legs and gave his master's crotch an apathetic sniff. The rest of us just looked him up and down, from the determination of his grayish jaw to his worn-heeled boots turned up at the toes like a jester's.

"Are you going outside like that?" I asked.

"Does everyone know who I am?"

"Superman," yelled Benjamin. He popped away from me,

raced round the table, out to the kitchen and back, and then rammed into Darwin's paunch with his head.

Darwin couldn't hide his pleasure. "This is just the first part of the surprise."

"What's the second part?" Benjamin asked, hanging on his father's flexed bicep, legs kicking wildly.

"You look like you're wearing a big red Pamper," Rachel said matter-of-factly.

"There are a lot more than two parts," Darwin said, ruffling forward Rachel's perfectly blown-back hair with his free hand. He sounded out of breath. "But they'll come later. You guys all have to bear with me." He took off his glasses. From under his heavy brow, his dark eyes pulled at me, pleaded with me not to look so distant, skeptical. "Hannie," he said, "this has possibilities. I know it seems crazy, but it's legitimized craziness. You've got to understand. The sky's the limit."

"Is everyone wearing a costume?" I asked. "Why are you wearing that costume?"

"Look, I promise to get you guys in on this as soon as there's something to get in on."

Promises, possibilities — he has not spoken those words in years. This is not the Darwin whose idea of a family outing was to cruise the riot corridor, declaring it was the only place around D.C. that felt real. Who spends every other night stoned, watching "Star Trek" reruns on TV and talking back to commercials.

Jeremy was smacking his book again; the air crackled with its plea: *Take me with you now, maybe I'm fat, maybe I'm getting boobs like a girl's, maybe I can't leave my zits alone, but take me with you now.* His abject eagerness worried me. He is having a difficult enough time as it is, without falling for some fantasy of Darwin's, who obviously has no place to take a son, has nothing to get any of us in on except the figments of his own erratic need.

"Are you coming back?"

My question took me completely by surprise; I didn't hear what I'd said until he snapped, "Of course I'm coming back. What do you think I am?"

"We don't have to fight," I said. "You can just go."

His tone softened, got almost plaintive. "Let me tell you, it's weird to have a little energy for a change. It's like I put this suit on and I really do feel like doing things, leaping tall buildings, whatever. Maybe it's stupid . . ."

"If you're going to go, go," I said. What did he want from me? It wasn't fair of him to stand there that way, so obviously and surprisingly eager, alive, yet out of reach.

"Then comes the part about the war party," Matthew said, impatient.

"I know I'm going to have to pay for this," Darwin said.

"I said it's OK. I'm not mad."

"I know you're not," he said. "You're great. I meant I'm not going to feel high like this forever. I wonder how far down I'll have to go." His eyes dropped to his sloping chest; he adjusted his posture. "Do I look too stupid?"

"Just go," I said, suddenly forgiving him, every flaw of his body blatant in bright blue. I could see him marching into D.C., forging a trail through gray-suited bureaucrats, savoring their shock.

"Bye," said Rachel, walking over and wrapping her arms around him, calmly enduring his pressing her face into his stomach.

"You still didn't tell us about the war party," Matthew insisted.

I nodded — to Matthew, to Darwin, to myself. *It's coming next, I love you, things will turn out all right, they always have.* Still nodding, I said, "The next morning before dawn the Indians did come back." I made my voice move evenly across the moments when Darwin's mass slid from the edge of sight, when the front door thumped shut. "A war party with spears."

"Yeah," said Matthew.

"You shouldn't gloat like that, Matthew. My father didn't have a chance. On the edge of the jungle," I went on, as if Matthew were to blame for this, "my mother was trying to radio them, but she couldn't get through. Then a rescue team marched into the jungle and up the riverbed and found them and buried them."

"The rescue team carried carbines," Matthew said, impervious.

"You didn't tell about the storm," Rachel said politely. "You know, when the sun disappeared. And the scavenger beetles." She always seemed to float off on her own little cloud whenever I told the story, yet she never forgot a single detail.

"One night the rescue party heard all these noises," Matthew volunteered, "and they were Indian signals except they sounded like a bunch of jaguars, so they fired their carbines in the air, and those noises sure stopped."

Jeremy restoked his mouth.

"Next time," I said flatly, because something was wrong. Missing was the surge of pride I have always felt in bringing the children unscathed across such dangerous terrain. What *was* the point of that story? What am I really doing every time I tell it but killing my father once more? Matthew, our prodigy in violence, must have known this, may have even guessed at the box I put back on the top shelf in the laundry room, the pictures I'd rather not think about, will never allow the children to see. What am I trying to prove? That I wouldn't have preferred my father alive?

A little shaky, I launched into the happy ending: how everyone admired my father for trying, how Grandma Grace received a letter of sympathy from Bess Truman, and, best of all, how several months after the bodies were buried a pair of Indian women from the killer tribe walked out of the jungle and into the Mission, and Grandma Grace made friends with them and learned their language, and how one day they invited her to return with them to the jungle and become part of the tribe, and joyfully she accepted. "Of course she took me with her," I concluded, "and that's where I lived until I was about Jeremy's age."

I looked over at him expectantly. Ever since he was very young he has taken it upon himself to round out the story with the question "And there was no more killing?" "And there was no more killing," I always reassure him.

But he was hunched over another piece of cake, chewing ruefully. Again I felt a flare of annoyance. Why couldn't he play his part? He was too sensitive, sinking into himself that way when events didn't go exactly as he thought they should.

"Are you going to eat the rest of that cake all by yourself?" I asked him. The color rose behind his freckles, and he tried to glare at me. "Oh, Jeremy," I said, but he looked away. "I guess I can't say anything without hurting your feelings."

"You didn't hurt my feelings," he said. "My feelings are basically fine. I don't need any more boosts, either. You couldn't boost a flea. Do you think I care what your prehistoric father did?"

Do you think I care about them? I hate them, he has said about the kids at the bus stop, the kids who laugh at him in the showers, P.E. teachers. He is going through a stage, I tell him, one everyone goes through. Not him, he says, he's not going through anything anyone else has gone through. He's getting to be just like his father.

>> .·. <<

I must think of some way to say this to Jeremy: That story is just a story, compiled from old words I heard around me. Maybe it's a trick I play on myself, maybe I shouldn't try to play it on you. I was upset last night, and maybe I didn't understand whatever it was you were feeling, because it got all mixed up with something that began happening a long time ago, one morning in the Mission kitchen when my mother's radio went silent. More and more urgently she turned the dials, and the wife of my father's partner asked if she had tried this, if she had done that. Perched on a stool at the short, rough table my father had built for me, I knew something was wrong. And it got worse when the women gave up and became very calm and began murmuring things about God's Will. *We are not to cry,* my mother announced later. *He's gone far away to heaven,* she said to me. *You are not to cry for him. He is happier there.*

All I remember then is that for days, weeks, no time passed, and there was no escape from this dark blur except into an awful longing, a longing for a glimpse of him so sharp and real that my child's mind kept assuming it would have to be fulfilled. Couldn't they call him on the radio? I asked my mother. *No.* Couldn't he come for a visit? *No.* But couldn't Jesus help him come, hold his hand so he wouldn't fall? *No. Never. No.*

Maybe that would have been too much truth, Jeremy, for one night. So I told you to come off it, and I'm sorry for that. I told you to have a little pride in who you were. I criticized you for not saying something to your father, for just sitting there moping and cringing. I'm sorry for that too, but you know, I never, ever feel I can apologize to you enough. And when you seemed on the verge of tears, I said, "For heaven's sake, Jeremy, he'll be back. You know he always comes back."

Maybe I was kidding us both.

2

My mother refused to leave Ecuador after my father was cut down by the Janca. She asked to be flown over the muddy grave in the bend of the river where he was buried. She peered down through the small round window, then drew me across her lap to look too. There was nothing to see. "He was worthy of his homegoing," she said, and I construed that to mean he would be back at Macuma by the time we had returned there.

In the following days I watched for him everywhere that I could picture him — at the kitchen table in our pair of rooms, talking on the radio, napping on his cot, or sitting under the thatched awning out front, drinking tea with his friend Hobby. I could see him in the shower he'd rigged up out back against the wall of the house, the middle of his body and his feet bright white from always being covered, and then that strange dark pouch between his legs I had to try not to stare at. I could see him in the shadows of the oven-hot tin workshed, repairing a part for his plane. He was always working on that plane, in it, under it, climbing all over it; now the plane was gone too. There was nothing to do but settle down and wait for it to come buzzing into the strip of sky above the empty runway, which I must have sneaked off to check ten times a day.

My mother taught the Quichua children in her Mission school; every night at dusk she took a slow, deliberate walk beyond the brand-new fence topped with barbed wire, down to the end of the dirt road, where it narrowed to a crease in the grasses and then vanished behind a dark green wall of ironwood and palm. She just stood there and stared at that barrier, where the territory of the other Indians, the Janca, began. I watched from our doorway, heart beating, wondering if maybe she'd heard from God that my father would return on foot. But she always came back to the compound alone — slowly, deliberately, with that slight hitch in her stride, up the road, locking the chain-link gate behind her for the night. If I asked her a question, all I got for an answer was a sidelong unfocused look, as if she had heard a voice but couldn't figure out where it was coming from.

Then one morning my mother was presenting some Bible story to the row of smaller children sitting against the back wall of the schoolroom. "It won't hurt for you to hear this again," she always told me, but I wasn't allowed to answer the questions she posed as she went along, or ask my own more interesting ones. "There's nothing worse than a showoff," she warned. A group of older girls at a squat table fiddled with the abacus my father had made of bamboo and palm nuts. The older boys in the corner were behaving, copying verses from the Sermon on the Mount onto tiny slates, phrase by phrase, holding each one up for my mother to read, then erasing it to make room for the next. Having learned the consequences of disturbing the monotonous order my mother loved, I just sat and resented her. I was too bored even to daydream. Then my eyes wandered to the open end of the schoolroom, and there like dark ghosts stood two women.

They had nothing on but a film of gray dust, against which their nipples shone like polished blue-brown stones. No taller than the older children, they stood utterly still, on sinewy shins, full lips slack and slightly parted. My heart beat loudly with the suspense. It seemed to me they had understood the situation at a glance and were smiling patiently. That is how I remember one of them, Nimu, the woman who became my Janca nurse — her wordless understanding, that probable smile.

Two of our girls looked up at the same time and gave a frightened cry. My mother turned on her low stool, her skirt folded under her knees. One of the strangers emitted a string of alien sounds. All the girls at the table stumbled up and huddled with the littler children against the wall. The boys tried to stand straight and stick out their chests and chins while they inched together in a tight clump, clutching their slates in front of them like shields. "Ye are the salt of the earth," my mother read as she pushed one fist against the earthen floor and raised herself to her feet. "Cross the *t* in *salt*, Tapuy."

My mother seemed so tall to me that the two visitors, one on the other's shoulders, would not even reach her waist. As she rose, the surge of delight I'd felt in these little strangers toppled into fear of her and her enormous size and strength, the way her sleepy eyes and calm, deliberate crossing of the room betrayed no surprise. Even when her broad hand touched their dusty skin, when with a slight quaver in the voice she said slowly, gently, "Welcome to our Mission, I have been waiting for you," I felt afraid.

>> .·. <<

Nimu. How little my children know about her, beyond her wonderful stories, the ones in which things change into other things — water into women into trees into fire and then somehow back into water. Stories of jaguars fathering men, boas that talk. Yet day by day she loved and cared for me and the children of the tribe. She was always there, you smelled her and touched her, beside her you felt safe. That was Nimu.

When she first came to the Mission she brought only one story, and she needed to tell it over and over, in Janca and pantomime, soon interspersed with bits of English. She couldn't tell it enough. It began with the attack by her people on the two white men and their wood-bee, which is what the Indians called the little yellow plane. (It had been most abused, its canvas torn from its framework, the landing gear battered with stones, the seats gouged and the stuffing scattered.) Her story ended in trembling grief over the fighting that divided her people afterward.

Nimu's brother, headman of the tribe, had been the elder in the party of three who greeted the white men. He knew the two men had come as friends, that they carried no spears, and he was very angry at Jiwaro for gathering a band of younger, rash warriors to return to the river the following dawn and spear them. He ordered each youth to surrender a handful of arrows as punishment for so foolishly destroying the creature from whose body had dropped many gifts. But Jiwaro was the young man who had gone up in the plane with my father, and he was certain the wood-bee had been a trick of the evil ones. Hadn't it tried to carry him away forever from his blood kin? Hadn't they all been foolish in accepting those cursed offerings from the sky?

Backed by his friends, Jiwaro then declared that Nimu's brother had struck some treacherous bargain with the evil spirits and the white men, and speared him. Jiwaro survived the inevitable reprisals, but soon the whole tribe had split into sides, and every night there were spearings. Women and children too were speared. That was why Nimu and her daughter had escaped to the Mission. They did not wish to be speared.

Months later, they begged my mother to return with them to their village. I rode strapped to Nimu's back; my mother carried clothing, books, new gifts. As we stepped into the clearing, naked women and children pressed in on us, peering, touching my hair, hands, bare legs, whimpering some endless unanimous complaint. Nimu shifted from one foot to the other as she listened, then explained to my mother in broken English what she had just learned, her story's sad epilogue: It was safe now in the village of my father's killers. All but a handful of men had speared one another and been buried. The few surviving husbands and brothers had fled upriver, Jiwaro among them. The women bade us welcome to the lost place, the village of tears.

They had so little to offer us, which deepened their sorrow. The meat feasts, the contests of wrestling, chest-pounding, dancing, the days themselves, had all been organized by the men. In the absence of men to fell trees and cut brush, the gardens were shrinking, failing. But it would be peaceful, we would be safe. My mother, of course, needed no such assurances. She was probably even disappointed that the mission she'd prepared for had become less risky, the old way of life she had come to defeat had already half defeated itself. I think she, like my father, would have preferred to gamble everything on the irresistible force of God's Word.

For me those first months were a wretched confusion of dark, odorous flesh, inedible food, the choking smell of smoke. The insects bit right through our repellents and kept me scratching constantly, while my mother swabbed on the Mercurochrome and said prayers against infection. I dreaded going to the bathroom. My mother had requested a private place for us, a short inroad into the forest right beside our separate shelter, and I was soon expected to go there by myself, fight my way through brush and vines that seemed to grow back over my path behind me, watch for snakes, and manage my clothes, often with Janca children chasing in, thin-shanked, pot-bellied, stolidly ignoring my pleas for them to go away.

Maybe if I endured all this, I thought, my father would come back to earth. My mother still firmly denied the possibility — my father was more than satisfied in heaven. Then the rains came, and the sandbar where he had landed was swept away.

And so Nimu became my salvation. My mother was busy from first light to last, helping erect a separate shelter for God's House, visiting the half-dozen tribal families who lived under different wedges of the one round roof in the main shelter, and learning the complex links and ancestries that caused them to call so many Sister or Mother or Daughter. She mastered more of their words, taught ours, and carefully prepared the ground for His.

There must have been some agreement finally that Nimu would keep me with her. At first I shrank from the nearness, the unavoidable touch of her woman's body, its hovering breath. I was fighting the loss of a father, the loss of a home with four walls and a floor: I was dead set on mistrusting anything that felt like consolation. But Nimu's comfort was steady. She scolded the other children for poking me and grabbing at the shift my mother made me pull over my head every morning. She gave me the slinky backbones of fish to play with, caught butterflies in her cupped hands and then, close to my face, set them free. She taught me to chant, to dance the children's dance, to speak and understand the words children need to speak and understand in order to play — *You can't do this, You can't find me, Mine.* Several times a day she took me with her on the trail that wound around the edge of the garden, and braced my thighs with her hands while I relieved myself.

By the time the rains abated, I could hold my own among the village children. I was allowed to play beyond the clearing with them, clambering over the giant roots of trees, looking for orchids and bright ruffles of fungi and signs of wild bees. We collected monkey bones and made ourselves rattling body ornaments; they showed me how to roll the fire stick between my hands. Nimu's grandnephew wove me a headdress of toucan feathers, with one tall heron feather in back.

A whole other world unfolded alongside that scheduled world of my mother's, defined by "God's purpose and plan" (which He relayed to her more or less on demand), that world of wrong and right, of marching forward and falling back. For after the hypnotic prayer, the blend of deliberate voices, once the seductive promises had been respoken and the moment of chilly awe passed, where were you but adrift on the eddies of Nimu's daily care?

Not that it was all pleasure. Forest spirits bedeviled Nimu's world. They came at night to suck blood, leaving black and blue marks on the skin. Their deputies, the insects, were merciless, and the sting of a scorpion or rayfish or giant ant could make a child sick for days. When we children disobeyed (and there was often no discernible logic to this judgment), Nimu herself thrashed us with nettles. It was a painful, long-lasting punishment, but there were times I invited it, even craved it, because I wanted to cry. Crying fascinated me; it was my mother's taboo. When I did it, I watched myself doing it, hoping to remember later how I'd gotten going. But I could never find my way back to sufficient pain without Nimu's help.

Once my mother caught Nimu in the act of whipping me. I was howling with all my heart, and she must have recognized the sound, must have come running in alarm. Stumbling over baskets and clay pots and children, she barged into the center of the round house, which was open to the sky, tore the clump of stems from Nimu's hand, and raised her own in furious disbelief, a fist so tight it trembled. "No!" she screamed. "Must not, bad, no, no!" Then she realized that Nimu was terrified; maybe she saw the shadow of her own arm lifted like a hammer, her body twice the size of the cringing Indian's. She lowered her hand, softened her voice, remembered patience.

Still sniveling in little spasms, I dried my face on my shift and tried to fade back into the ring of playmates who had gathered to gawk. I was ashamed of my mother in front of them, and ashamed of myself in front of her. Nimu hung her head, nodding it minutely though I could see she'd decided not to understand a word of my mother's lecture on alternative disciplines that spared the body and edified the spirit. After that the whippings occurred in the dark recesses of the hut, under the low-sloping thatch, and we children learned to clamp our teeth on the sound. Her mind on higher things, my mother never noticed the occasional welts on my thighs, and I did what I could to hide them. The last thing I wanted was to be sentenced to spend my days in God's House, apart from Nimu, copying Scripture or pretending to pray.

Nimu was magic. We children knew that. On the mud floor under her hammock was a pile of smooth stones. Sometimes she chose one and rubbed it with her callused thumb while she told us about the land of mountains where the river began, or the flats by the sea where it ended, places she could never have seen. Sometimes the older children stayed awake nights and spied on her hammock, and sometimes they caught her sneaking away. When she returned, they accused her of making deals with the spirits to carry her off; otherwise, how could she know so much about other worlds? Where would she have found such special stones? She gave them her loose, gap-toothed smile and told them that she had simply gone out to relieve herself. "The stones are from our river," she always insisted. "Everything is here, in the river, in the stones."

This boundless world of Nimu's my mother tucked into a corner of her own. My mother never seemed to notice that her world was just as peripheral to Nimu. There were small collisions, like the matter of nettles, after which life in both resumed, smoothly remeshed. Firm to herself, my mother never pushed too hard on Nimu; and Nimu could yield without yielding. But as I grew older, it got harder and harder to shuttle between them. I resented my mother's teachings, the way the children vied for her approval, flaunted their crude mastery of the Bible as they might flaunt the tip of a monkey tail tossed them by one of the women back from a good hunt.

"God died on a tree," one might say loftily.

"His good blood dripped, dripped. It washed my heart clean," said another.

"I live well. *My* heart is not black."

"God says you must not spear," preached one boy to another. "If you tell another to spear, it is sin."

After morning school, the clearing was loud with their preening, and after evening prayers, at the broad entrance to the round house, the Janca lounged around my mother, picking lice from one another's scalps, captivated by her stories, into which she often wove a familiar name from the tribe. She held them all, even Nimu, who offered refinements in Janca whenever my mother paused. Afterward the woman my mother had featured would retell the story to anyone who would listen, as though she alone had grasped the proper truth.

I hated it when Nimu gave in to my mother like this. I knew all the stories backward and thought my mother was sneaky to stick those names in. But what really made me angry was my mother's confidence. She thought she knew everything about the village, she thought she had everything under control, when really the only truth she ever knew was the strength of her own faith and her own discipline, which she blindly saw everywhere. (It still is all she knows and all she needs.) She didn't understand, for instance, why the Indians were unnerved by the story of Lazarus, one of her favorites, why many of them got up and walked off into the darkness when she told it. And she didn't try to understand. She just continued with it, speaking away her own perplexity while they squirmed and muttered uneasily and I rolled my eyes up in scorn. There was no point in my explaining to her that the Janca could not forget the Great Feud. Among themselves they still told and retold its story, which amounted to a chronology of spearings about as long as the *begat*s in Genesis. They preferred to think of their spear-happy relatives as permanently buried, the food of worms. They were alarmed at the prospect of them rising from the dead. They had no desire to give up their peace and security for the sake of some miracle. Of course, Nimu knew this. But I guess she didn't see the point in explaining either.

3

A BOX ADDRESSED TO JEREMY arrived in yesterday afternoon's parcel post. It was about a foot and a half square and six
inches high, with small holes punched in its cardboard sides.
Through the holes you could see newsprint. It was mailed from
Ecuador, obviously my mother's doing. As each of the younger
children came in from school, we lifted the box and gently shook
it, but the contents were packed too tight to shift or rattle. It was
fairly heavy, a promising sort of weight that made Benjamin
widen his eyes with surprise.

"I'm guessing it's fruit," I said. Wouldn't an export company
in Quito pack boxes of exotic fruit to be sent as gifts? I told the
children about the refreshing *yarina* and the peachlike *omuyama*.

Rachel said it was too heavy for fruit; it almost felt like it was
filled with dirt.

"Why would Grandma Grace send Jeremy a box of dirt for his
birthday?" I asked.

Matthew thought maybe because Jeremy was a nerd; Rachel
seemed to consider that possibility as she pulled her fat pink
comb from the leg pocket of her painter's pants and gave her hair
two needless flips.

The truth is, the children hardly know my mother. She speaks
to them on the phone at Christmas and Easter; some years she
remembers birthdays on time, some years she doesn't, and her
packages arrive, as this one did, a week or two afterward. For the

last nine years she has lived in western Pennsylvania, helping out her uncle Samuel, the headmaster of New Progress Christian School, as his sight and hearing began to fail. Under his administration, and I suspect in spite of it, the place has expanded from a sort of last resort for the adolescent children of missionaries to a thriving day school, a popular alternative to the county's public facilities, which teach ungodly things like sex education and new math.

Two years ago Samuel's left leg was amputated because of diabetes, and he had to retire. The Church put up a two-bedroom prefab house for him on a corner of the school property. And there the two of them are — my mother has never learned to drive — and here we are. We rely on phone calls, the first Sunday of every month. The reason we don't drive there is that they don't really want to see us, not if "us" includes Darwin. He and my mother fight about everything. Besides, I spent the most horrible years of my life as a student at that school; of the two friends I made there, Roger and Valerie Wells, one killed himself, while the other has tried to in more subtle ways — thank God, without success. I get physically sick at the thought of going back.

Jeremy slouched in through the doorway and tried to pretend he didn't notice the package on the kitchen table or that we had gathered to watch what he would do with it. His Husky Boy pants were cinched above his waist, as usual, and his T-shirt was splotched with sweat. A faintly sour smell made Rachel ask when he planned on using the special birthday stick of Old Spice she had given him. I pushed the box in his direction, told him it was for him, handed him a knife to cut the string. He opened it inefficiently, still feigning indifference. Inside the ring of crumpled newspaper were the folds of a burlap sack. He groped around for the neck, tried to bunch the extra cloth out of the way. Then I caught a glimpse of something like a round of slack painted hose. Right away I recognized it, with that warm sort of shock that accompanies coincidence. Jeremy's face struggled with disbelief. He rested a hand tentatively on one of the coils and gave it the slightest caress; then his face brightened with pure delight.

It was just as he'd expected — only the ignorant could call that slimy.

"What is it?" the others were asking. Underdog's muzzle pulsed with sniffing.

"Is it alive?" he asked me.

"What do you think?" I asked him back.

"I can't see. What is it?" came the chorus.

"It's a snake," Jeremy said, his voice covering an octave. "It's a live snake." He was panting. "It's a boa constrictor."

He began walking in a tight circle, his arms held stiff and close to his sides, announcing, "I have in my possession a live snake. *I* have my own snake." Benjamin careened around the kitchen to show he shared his big brother's excitement, Under barked, Rachel got no attention for her screams of "Oh, gross," and Matthew looked truly afraid.

"I wonder how long it is," Jeremy said, "if we stretched it out."

"You can't take it out of that bag," said Matthew, putting up his fists.

"Can I?" Jeremy turned a face up to me that I hadn't seen in months — unselfconscious, all bleak nonchalance dropped, as if he were willing again to be loved.

There was a piece of paper tucked between sack and box: "Care of Your Boa Snake, or Anaconda," in Spanish, English, German, and what looked like Japanese. "It doesn't bite," I noted.

"Of course it doesn't bite," Jeremy said, his body sort of jerking with impatience. "It *constricts* its victims."

"But it prefers live food."

"It prefers live food," repeated Jeremy, nodding vigorously.

"And warm temperatures."

He kept nodding. "And warm temperatures."

"Well, it's certainly warm enough today," I said gamely, and had just plunged my hands into the sack when we were all engulfed by a familiar, near-paralyzing roar. Our townhouse in Sugarland lies only ten miles from Dulles International Airport, and every other afternoon for the past three years the new supersonic airplane has arrived from Europe along a path directly over us. Every other day the noise builds defiantly, shouts, *To hell with your windows and dishes, your peace and quiet*. At its peak, if you're not careful, the noise can lift you right past common sense to panic, when you almost imagine the plane headed right for your trembling roof. Unless of course you are thirteen and about to unveil your heart's desire.

While the rest of us waited, breath held, for the thunder to pass, Jeremy kept working the burlap away from the coils and nudged me and nodded at me until finally I lifted the awkward supple weight so he could shove the wrappings aside, and there it lay across my hands, in what seemed now like utter silence — coils of the finest texture, beautifully marked with black and gold.

Rachel doubled over in a spurt of unconvincing giggles, Under's hackles rose, Matthew shrank back against the wall. Almost too slowly to be perceived, the creature curled itself down my arm, reaching my hand with a foot of length to spare. Its head hooked up, sleepy-eyed. The children stared as if gagged and the dog kept up his steady low growl. "It seems friendly," I said.

"Can I?" Jeremy held out his freckled arm. I took hold of his hand. It was sticky, moist, still a child's hand; he didn't notice how tightly he was gripping mine, he was so absorbed with the snake's slow progress across the juncture. I set aside the thought that it was my mother of all people who had sent us this creature, my mother who was giving me this glimpse of my old Jeremy. Maybe the giver is not the cause of a gift, but just a convenient intermediary. I did have the urge to remind Jeremy, *If it weren't for that prehistoric grandfather you say you don't care about . . .* But something sealed my lips, and the urge passed. Then finally the snake had eased most of itself onto Jeremy, and I had to let go. I stepped back and beheld him in its loose embrace. He raised his arms as it eased over and around them, and his eyes teared up with a fearful joy — as if he were showing us something he had just unburied, and it was the most precious treasure in the world.

>> .·. <<

"Why don't *you* get the job downtown," Darwin called out to me, "and ride the Sugarland Commuter Association bus with all the poor suckers who moved to the boonies to improve the quality of life for their families?" He reminds me of a wild boar, crashing into a clearing, trying to attack in all directions at once. "And I'll stay home and fight for everything that sounds like a good cause, except late in the afternoon I'll want to wander down to the tennis courts and mingle with those charming ladies in the short skirts. And as the first buses rumble in, I'll be sure to give a dainty wave to all the downtrodden sons of bitches inside with their pale faces pressed to the windows."

No hello, just the latest version of the speech he likes to polish on his hour's ride home. His jacket bunched under one arm, he snapped his loose tie at the giant philodendron in the front hall and then at the spider plant, mother of all my spider plants, that hangs upstairs in the skylit landing. (Darwin calls them all Venus's-flytraps — the ferns and ivies in the north windows, the spiders in the south. He especially resents my avocadoes, whose fat seeds sprout infallibly, propped with toothpicks in jars. The top branches of the one in the living room are spreading now off the ceiling; its main stem has roughened into bark.)

Yes, I feel guilty. Not because his shirt was missing a middle button or because of his trousers, which always ride so far below his waist that their wide hems drag and fray. He cultivates that bedraggled look; it's his way of asserting that he is a scientist, not a government bureaucrat. At the Center for Environmental Control they all wear lab coats and have more important things to attend to, keeping track of domestic radiation, than one another's appearance. Darwin just designed and built a robot to test microwave ovens. The robot opens the door, closes the door, sets the timer for one minute, waits for the buzz, then repeats the cycle. That way ten years of wear and tear can be crammed into two months.

I feel guilty because Darwin says his job is doing the same thing to him — ten years of setting alarms and getting on and off buses, of gulping cups of coffee at hour intervals, have aged him a lifetime. This is the fourth year Rachel has been in school all day. When am I going to make some money? When am I going to start carrying some of the economic burden for this family?

I *am* taking courses, I remind him; I'm not exactly sure how many credits I have, but soon I'll be qualified to teach. He reminds me how much time I spend on Womancenter, which I founded in a storefront here on Sugarland Plaza in 1973. The U.N. had proclaimed it International Women's Year, which inspired a cigarette company to get together with a cosmetics company and channel portions of their PR budgets into a fund for the liberation of women. When the year ended, so did our little grant from them. Now the center sells homemade baked goods to support its walk-in resources and crisis counseling.

I wrangled a reduced rate on the property out of Sugarland's marketing chief, and I assembled a board of directors and organized the volunteer staff. After that I should have backed off, Darwin says. I have to let other people take more responsibility. He says I run Womancenter the way I run the children, trying to solve every problem, feel every feeling, monitor every breath.

He is being a little dramatic, as usual. Valerie Wells is the one who takes on the male power structure — she gives legal advice, handles job and credit discrimination, leads consciousness-raising groups, and counsels individuals. Of course, I have to support Valerie when she needs it. I'm the one who appointed her acting director, and I don't want to see her burn out. Officially, though, I stick to simple, practical matters, like keeping the rent paid and the plants watered and the air fragrant with brewing coffee and fresh breads.

Darwin has been burning out for years now, and I feel guilty about it the same way I've been chilly these last September nights, but, half dreaming, can't muster the will to get up and get a blanket.

This evening I assembled the children around me and called up the stairs, "We've got a surprise for you."

Darwin reappeared on the landing in socks, a T-shirt, and

BVD's. "Wait a minute, wait a minute," he said. "I've got a surprise for you guys."

"Remember," I asked, "when we couldn't imagine why anyone would want *three* and a half baths in a townhouse?" (The reason I pushed for us to move to this planned community in the first place was because it promised natural preserves, "open" schools, a racial and economic mix. I have always felt a little tricked to discover how much it traffics in luxury.)

"Remember when I said the Superman business had prospects?" asked Darwin.

"You go first," I said.

He was buckling on his oldest, softest Levi's. "It's nothing," he said. He gave each foot an elegant little kick forward before placing it on the next step down. "Just that Children's Hospital bought our proposal to come and cheer up their patients once a month."

The children and I made noises of approval; he gave a deep bow, showing the bald spot under his tangled hair.

"Do we get to wear costumes?" Benjamin asked.

"Not this time," Darwin said. "I mean, you guys'll have to sit this first one out." There were sounds of indignation. "Look, they wanted us to give them an exact list of everyone in the group. It's a hospital. They can't let just anyone wander in."

Jeremy cleared his throat and then stammered, "You did imply that we would be part of the group."

Darwin colored. I could see him feeling around for his trusty anger in order to get through this awkwardness. I didn't want him to lash out at Jeremy, who was so happy that afternoon. "We will be eventually," I said. "But you wouldn't want to go to Children's Hospital anyway. The patients are all kids your own age. It would be too depressing."

"That's right," Darwin said, and after a silence, he added, "This business is going to take time. You guys have to be patient." His audience was easing away, slipping back down to the basement. "You know what we're calling ourselves? The Retired and Tired Superheroes. R-A-T-S. It was my idea."

He tugged at his belt and looked at me, alone in front of him.

"Great," he said. "Here I stand on the threshold of my midlife crisis and no one gives a damn. I'm supposed to put food on the table and a roof over your heads" — I reached up and put my hand over his mouth — "and if I can't be nice, I'm supposed to keep my mouth shut. You realize I'm a money object?"

I wiped my wet palm down the front of his shirt. "They were waiting all afternoon for you to get home," I said. "They have something to show you."

His face went blank. "Where?" He began moving down the stairs in the direction of their voices. I stood behind him as he looked in on them gathered around the tub in the basement bathroom. "What's that?" he asked. Jeremy explained that it was the screen from the large window in the family room. No, it had not fallen out, he had simply disengaged it from its track. Why? Because it fit perfectly over the tub and with books piled at each corner it made a cage. And why did they need a cage?

"For my boa constrictor." The magic words burst from Jeremy, caused him to jump up. I think he would have started his odd, stiff-armed dance if there had been the space.

Darwin leaned over the kneeling children, peered through the screen, and muttered, "Jesus Christ." Then he didn't give us another word.

"Well," I said finally. "What do you think?"

"I think there's no way those books are going to keep that thing from crawling right out of the tub."

Breaking into little panicky moans, Matthew hopped up and squeezed between his father and me.

"It's only a temporary arrangement," Jeremy explained.

"And we're keeping the door closed, Matthew. For heaven's sake, Matthew!" He was pushing at me, pulling on my clothes.

"I take it you didn't find this creature in one of Sugarland's widely advertised manmade lakes or on an award-winning landscaped walkway?"

"Dad," Jeremy said tolerantly, "there aren't any boa constrictors in North America."

"My mother had it sent from Quito, for Jeremy's birthday."

"Your mother?"

"She knows Jeremy is into snakes."

Darwin shook his head in disbelief. "She must have run out of that *New Testament in Pictures*. Maybe we should send her back half a dozen."

"I wish I'd thought of it," I said.

"Smuggling the serpent into Utopia," Darwin said. "Hey, I like that. Maybe those shock treatments did your mother some good. Maybe she's signed a pact with the Prince of Darkness. Maybe it's a plot to overthrow 'Capitalism with a Conscience,' this Sugarland of redwood decks and Weber grills and Sierra Club calendars, this land of sold-out activists and *Consumer Reports* subscribers and tennis greenhorns. And cleaning women — don't forget cleaning women. Why else would you include subsidized housing, if not to guarantee a captive supply of cleaning women? Maybe your old lady knows something we don't know. Maybe —"

"I suspect she does, Darwin," I said.

I resent my mother. I can't not, after what she has done. And yet, against Darwin I always defend her, grant her more than she deserves. Well, I will grant Darwin this: he likes that snake, and not in spite of but because of its unexpected source. Hard-core depressive though he sometimes is, he can't resist a surprise. He traps himself in his own relentless logic but celebrates like a pardoned killer if it breaks down.

In the golden age of his innocence he got his kicks from theoretical physics. For whole days at a time he could actually feel his continuity with everything else, the hilarious lightness of his material body, knowing that under intense magnification it came and went, lived and died and sprang to life again, an expression of pure and spontaneous energy. I remember years ago when we were making love for only the third or fourth time and he recalled this happy interlude for me. As he did, his tone wavered between wistful and self-deprecating — this vision of atomic magic was such a thing of the past even then, an undergraduate wild-goose chase, a pleasant evasion of what he had come to decide was the only pertinent reality: History.

Holding him then and listening to him, I was flooded with

sadness; it creeps up on me even now. I knew about belonging and still feeling free, about feeling more than a body and yet less. I knew about living almost without effort, but with enough awareness that the mind too can enjoy the ease. I had learned these harmonies when I became a Janca child, and like Darwin's dancing particles they are figments of the past.

4

· ·

·

THE SUMMER I TURNED THIRTEEN, my mother decided to fly me back to the States to enroll in Samuel's school, New Progress Christian. "You're not to think there is anything wrong with you," she said, referring to the fact that I had awakened that morning to find streaks of blood on my thighs.

About the blood I was pleased. It meant I had risen to a higher, more demanding order of life, which I knew I could handle. I could understand that my mother's first concern might be about practical difficulties — Janca taboos, the simple matter of supplies. I could not understand why she was so quick to give in to them. "God will help us," I said, kneeling beside her in our hut, trying to imitate the fervor with which she so often spoke those words. Did the suggestion sound facetious, as everything was beginning to, on my adolescent tongue? Couldn't she see that I was more than willing to spend certain days in the cozy women's hut beside the garden, with its densely thatched walls? Why couldn't this God of hers manage to help us take care of a few more sanitary napkins every month? Desperate, I got sullen: "What if God tells me I belong here?" Wouldn't it make sense for Him to reveal to *me* the infinitesimal spot in his purpose and plan which I occupied?

My mother stood up and replaced her Bible in its tin. Despite the tight-fitting lid, its frail pages were edged and spotted with black mold. "It's time," she said. The struggle to remain composed always turned her cold and severe. "It's time we considered the welfare of your soul."

"No," I said. Dared. What did I have to lose?

Her sun-bleached brows rose and then relaxed into her expression of patient endurance, its lines etched darker by the soot from steady fires.

"It's something else, isn't it," I said.

"Isn't what?"

I hung my head and fumed — she, who knew everything, was supposed to tell me, not me tell her, the somewhat unbelievable things I was in the process of figuring out. "I don't know."

She started across the clearing for the round house. Back when the men ran the village, this main hut was burned down on a regular basis and its perfect replica rebuilt near a freshly cleared garden. But now the same hut over eight years had gotten crooked and unshapely, acquiring odd offshoots and annexes, because the women preferred to repair it, one area of thatch at a time, and were always inventing little improvements. "After your breakfast," my mother declared to the world in front of her, "there will be time to talk this through."

At my age, my mother had contracted polio, spent months alone in the hospital, survived. Afterward, to cancel the pathos of a limp, she had mastered the slow, deliberate stride I was hating now as I watched it from behind, that stride and that broad, stubborn back.

I took several steps after her. "It's Bai," I called. "I know it's Bai." Bai was the granddaughter of Nimu's brother, the man whose trust in my father and Hobby had made him Jiwaro's third victim. Bai was not much older than I was, but she had just given birth to a son. What a deliriously happy event that was — welcoming the first of the New Family, a child unscarred by the horrors of the Great Feud. And there I was, right in the midst of the women encouraging Bai's labor, as the girl straddled the special hammock beside the women's hut and gripped the vines strung over her head. We chanted and clapped and drew long, loud breaths. We held each other and bore down when Bai did, and we all made the sound of bearing down. But I missed the crowning, the finale. I had wanted to hear that first cry, witness the strange spectacle of one body turning into two. But my mother came after me — she knew just where to look — and plowed through us, dragged me out and away by the arm. "What's the matter?" I kept pleading. "I wasn't getting in the way." But she waved off all questions as though she were about to break into guilty tears.

"Bai is married," my mother called back over her shoulder this morning. A pair of young women ran out from the round hut to flank her arrival. I hated the large, freckled hands that descended to rest on their dark heads.

I stretched myself out on her bamboo pallet under the slanting thatch and stared up into its brown fringes and folds, where there were always things moving — insects, lizards, never a puff of breeze. Leaving Nimu, my mother, the village, was so inconceivable to me that before long I decided that my mother had mentioned it only as a sort of threatening alternative to the new conditions she was about to lay down for my behavior. Fine. I would be good. I would never again let what she called my "selfish quest for amusement" interfere with our higher mission.

I thought of the babies that would begin to fill the bodies of Bai and her friends, then their laps, their lives. I felt perfectly capable of motherhood. I was already taller than any girl or boy in the village, and I figured that if I had a baby my breasts would be sure to grow. Briefly I let myself imagine what you did to start a baby, and it was like a stone thrown into the pool of my body, sending out ripples along all my nerves. Kaewi, Nimu's grandnephew, had nudged me away from the girls' group again the other day, pulled my ear down to his wide grin — would I like to come with him to see the alligator? And again I had followed him, not to the river but into a web of subtle paths beyond the fallow manioc plot, where he finally pushed me to the ground and lay beside me, nuzzled my face and neck until we were both gluey with sweat, fumbled heroically with my clothing, touched my naked skin with his hand, touched me, so much cloth interfering, while I lay drenched without the strength to give help, as if drugged by his thick, ripe smell. It was not just my appetite for amusement he whetted; I awoke to a fierce curiosity. I knew I would go with him, go further, whenever he asked. My stubborn mother would never understand. If she hadn't exactly told me, it was easy to guess what she had in mind: my body was to remain the irrelevant yet exclusive temple of my soul. She would set stringent rules, I would have to break them. So. I was not going to be good, I was going to pretend to be good.

In the distance she was making her way back across the clearing already shimmering with heat. She carried a bark tray of banana drink, mashed manioc, and, since it didn't interest her that Janca women refused fish while menstruating, a piece of charred fish. She sat beside me on the bamboo bed and watched me gulp the food, stopping at the fish.

She pointed at it with a wagging finger.

"No," I said. "Not now."

"That silly business," she said, breaking off a piece in her hand and holding it in front of my face. "Now is when you need it. The iron."

I turned my head away as though revulsed. "I'm not a child anymore," I said. In my mind I was a Janca woman.

She put the fish in her own mouth. "There will be nothing else for breakfast," she said. That was the old rule by which she had trained me to appreciate Indian food. She continued to break off and consume pieces of the blackened flesh, pausing between bites to see if I had changed my mind. I paid no attention. When she had finished, she gazed out into the trees and said, "Maybe it would be best for me to work here today."

That brought me back to where we were. I had better stay alert now, guess what she was getting at, and stay one beat ahead. "We can do the Dictionary," I offered. She flinched with surprise. The Dictionary was one of her cures for the wild freedom that infected me when allowed to run with the Janca children for more than two days at a time. I hated doing the Dictionary — the monotony, my friends shouting in the distance — but it was important now to show my mother how useful, how indispensable, how good, I, child or woman, could still be.

So we sat each on one end of the plank table and with thick pencils began copying Janca words from a ragged notebook onto cards, filing the cards alphabetically in another tin box, long and narrow with a tight lid. Twice my mother put her pencil down and looked over at me, whereupon I became the picture of diligence, suspending work just long enough to throw her a cheery smile.

A yodeling call interrupted us. It was Nimu, trundling toward the hut. "Where Hannie is? Where Hannie?" she wanted to know.

"Hannie's here with me," my mother said.

Nimu peered into our shelter. "You have sickness?" She took quick, sniffing breaths, and then her black eyes searched my face.

I looked away. My mother shook her head. "I need Hannie to help me today."

"Soon my children beat jungle today," Nimu said. Every week or so the young Jancas walked the perimeter of the clearing with large sticks and shells, chopping back the invasive vegetation. "Jungle getting bad."

"But this is important too," my mother said. "See" — she held up a card — "we save Janca words."

"Paper smell," Nimu scolded, moving on. "White people like paper so much."

When Nimu was gone, my mother put down her pencil for the third time and said, as though she had just decided, "Nimu should wear the dress I gave her." (Nimu preferred to roll the dress into a ball and carry it with her during the day like a talisman.) I continued copying — the Janca word for *climb* went into the box. It was the same word as for *fall,* the difference captured only by the voice. "God tells us to cover our bodies," my mother said. She spoke slowly, trying to hide her reluctance the way her slow stride concealed her limp.

I listened, as always, several sentences ahead. Might she possibly be about to bring up that subject, which she had never spoken of before? For long minutes there was nothing to hear but bird sounds and monkey chatter and the purposeless calling back and forth of the tribe, for the pleasure of making noise.

"It is natural and right between husband and wife," she said finally. Her sunburned neck flushed darker.

"What is?" I tried to sound innocent, knowing full well.

"That union," she said. "Blessed by the sacrament of matrimony." Matrimony: My mother read from God's Book. After that Bai's hammock was carried by her howling family over to the area of her young man's.

"What union?" I had to hear what my mother would say; I was hungry to talk about what I had seen and overheard, what I had figured out. Particularly now. It was my own future I wanted to discuss. I was full of questions that could not find words.

"Of man and wife. That is why Bai had her baby."

"Why?"

"And the others will have their babies."

"Bai's stomach sure was sticking out at the wedding," I blurted. "It's still sort of wrinkly, and her *kauki* are so full of milk they hurt all the time."

"Hannah," my mother said. Then after a pause she added, "I'm afraid you have worn out your welcome with Giti's family." Giti was the mother of Bai's new husband, the fifteen-year-old Naemwi, one of seven male children who had escaped the spear during the Great Feud. Giti was compulsively generous, submissive, apologetic: she could never forgive herself for being the older sister of Jiwaro.

"Giti didn't say that. She always says I have come well under her roof. And Bai says that when I'm there, Naemwi keeps his hands off her *kauki*."

My mother's eyes clouded in that strange way that said I had gone too far. She reached for a blank card and scanned the notebook page for the next word.

"I must radio the Principle Mission this afternoon," she announced. "They will contact Samuel."

A grinding pain attacked my belly. Pressing hard on the pencil, I gave everything I had to copying the Janca for *foot itch*.

"I must tell them we'll be coming sometime this month."

>> ∴ <<

In the days that followed, my last-ditch strategy was to block all thought of leaving the tribe, to behave perfectly but as though nothing had changed, to hope that my mother would forget.

On Sunday night two weeks later, the tribe assembled as usual outside the round house to hear her speak about God's Book. Bai lay in a hammock slung near the open end of the hut, her baby sprawled on her breast. I sat below her on the packed earth, teasing a giant lightning bug with my cupped hands, wondering why when I opened my hands it made no effort to fly away.

"We can all be helpers of Jesus," my mother was saying. "If we help Jesus we will be strong against sickness and evil spirits. He gives us great power."

"Then we fight the upriver people," a voice called out from the knot of boys, to be met with murmuring assent. There were always rumors that the exiled warriors were gathering behind Jiwaro's deadly spear beyond the horizon.

"No," my mother said. "Someday we will teach the upriver people of the Kingdom of Heaven. Jesus tells us to go among them as deer among jaguars. He tells us to be wise as the grandfather boa and gentle as a soft bird."

The prospect caused exclamations of disbelief.

"If we love Jesus, then we have no fear, and our souls are safe from spearing."

"Our souls fly well to the Kingdom of Heaven," remembered Giti out loud. The tribe stirred with approval. The boys began punching and pinching the one who had wrongly suggested fighting. The session was breaking up.

My mother's voice rose over the chatter. "Sometimes Jesus asks His helpers to love Him more than they love their mothers and fathers, more even than they love their sons and daughters."

Her words restored silence, a sullen, uncomfortable silence, for this claim of hers challenged their dearest value. Mothers reached for their children, though even the youngest were now solid nine- and ten-year-olds. Bai mashed her baby's face into her chest. I had guessed enough about what was coming to dread it, and had the oddest feeling that I was already fading into the warm night air.

"Once when Jesus was busy teaching God's Word," my mother

said slowly, solemnly, "His mother and brothers came to Him and said, 'Return with us, come well to our house, we are your family,' and Jesus said, 'My family are those who hear God's Word and help me do it.' "

In the silence that followed, the Indians struggled innocently with this story. Then my mother shifted to a cheerier voice, and got to her point. "Tonight, I will tell you our wonderful news: in three days' time the wood-bee comes to the Principle Mission downriver. And Hannie will begin her journey to her other home, in America."

There was the sound of many indrawn breaths and a single cry of protest, and Nimu's squat body arose. "Hannie's home over there," she said, pointing in the direction of our small hut.

"Hannie has family in America . . ."

I bowed my head and pressed my knees to my ears.

"Hannie's family here," Nimu said, jabbing a stiff hand at the tribe around her. "We hear God's Word, we are His helpers."

"My mother's brother in America is also God's helper," my mother began. I had seen the man once, on a visit to the States two years before. I remembered a broad chest, short bowlegs, and a carelessly composed face — crooked hairline, uneven eyebrows, and a lopsided smile. He had arranged our appearance on a radio program out of Harrisburg called "Wings of Prayer," after which people sent us money. I wished now that I really could disappear; I felt otherwise helpless against my mother's strength of will.

". . . white people must teach their children," my mother was saying, "just as there are things the Janca must teach their children."

I could smell Nimu beside me. "Hannie is my children," Nimu said simply. She crouched down: I threw my arms around her neck. A wave of murmuring rose from the tribe.

Above it my mother's warning again rang out. "He that loveth son or daughter more than me is not worthy of me." I heard her voice quaver, with exaltation, I assumed, with pride at knowing and being able to perform what was Right and Good. Then, stepping over the Indians reclining in her path, she took my limp arm and pulled me up, had actually to drag me through the dark to our hut. "And ye shall be hated of all men for my name's sake," she muttered to herself as she lurched along, but I heard.

"Yes, I hate you," I whispered, the second time louder than the first. The words sent blood to my arm, and I yanked it out of her grasp. "I hate you. I hate you." The words had a life of their own.

"Think not that I am come to send peace on earth," my mother countered with her own incantation. "I came not to send peace but a sword."

In our hut she turned away from me and began to prepare for sleep, managing as always to remove her clothes after she had slipped on her night shift. I stripped to the skin and flounced about naked as long as I could before putting on mine. "I hate clothes," I said, and flung aside the mosquito nets and flopped into my hammock so heavily that the thatch above us rained down a few bugs.

"And he that endureth to the end shall be saved."

"It's stupid to undress and dress at night and then undress and dress in the morning, and all they do is get dirty." I shifted my back to the inner hut and gazed out at the stars, at a grinning crescent moon. I heard the bamboo creak under my mother's weight, followed by the murmur of further prayer, absorbed gradually into the background music of tree toads honking, lizards singing, the scream of a preying cat — the sounds I had slept and awakened to for, it seemed, my whole life, steady as the smell of smoke. I simply couldn't imagine myself anywhere but where I was. I wondered what true silence would be like; I had never heard it. Nor had I felt winter. I tried to recall the cold things I had been taught at my great-uncle's — that white, frost-lined box, ice in glasses, water from the silver pipe, even the paste my mother made me put on my teeth. All were cold, always cold. I remembered, after our return to the village, my mother slipping into a rare spasm of longing: "If only there were a window to be opened somewhere, to let in one breath of fresh, cold air."

I heard but wouldn't hear my mother call my name.

"Listen to me, Hannah. Please." This was one of her rare voices, so plaintive, so tired.

I had to clench my teeth not to answer.

"Maybe if you don't think about it, Hannie," she said. Her voice caught between the syllables of my name. "It's a much harder thing to think about than do."

>> ∴ <<

But it was so hard to do, all I could do was pretend I wasn't doing it. And then forget it had been done.

Nimu came to our hut the next day to offer me two gifts. The first was her woman's belt — lengths of cotton twine braided and strung with shells to represent all her living relatives, by blood and marriage. Nimu's belt was almost a map of the whole tribe. The second gift was one of her special stones. That day she was wearing the yellowed cotton dress my mother had given her, which she bunched up to the waist before she squatted, beckoning me down to join her. She began to draw with a ragged nail on the earth around her toes, faint scratches, indecipherable.

"Remember we are not bad peoples," she said finally. "Remember we are not spear our friends." She always felt a deep, anxious remorse over the river attack on God's helpers, a feeling made worse by her own losses in the feuding that followed. No matter how often my mother repeated her version and its moral — the Janca had acted in primitive, unenlightened fear; Christ asks us to turn the other cheek — I knew there were days when Nimu thought maybe she, Nimu, should be dead too. "Remember Janca are beautiful peoples," Nimu continued, and began to recite what sounded like fragments from God's Book. At first I thought it was some sort of performance, that she wished also to be remembered as one who had learned my mother's lessons well. Then I realized Nimu was talking about the Kingdom of Heaven because she wanted to make plans to meet me there: she would wear this dress, I would wear the braided belt.

"That is too long a time," I told her. "I'm coming back sooner than that." Somehow I knew I wouldn't, but I spoke the words to calm myself.

Her mouth turned down, she curled out her lower lip, and shrugged — it was a look my mother always mistook for compliance. "Not so long," Nimu said. "In dry season we say it never rain." She began to count off the shells draped over my hand, name by name, the tips of her fingers stroking my palm, and I realized the last were names of the dead, two sons, her brother. Then she slipped the stone into my skirt pocket. "Kingdom of Heaven," she said, as if we could all be there tomorrow. "Remember."

"Yes," I promised, thinking, *What is it again that I am promising? I have already forgot.*

The following day we set off for the Principle Mission, me plodding numbly in my mother's footsteps, behind Naemwi for a guide. The rest of the village thronged in the rear, then fell away by twos and threes (I hardly noticed) once the trail had spilled them out along the bed of the river and the sun jumped higher in the sky. Nimu was the last to turn back: I remember her sudden tearless howl, the way she stopped in her tracks (I looked back once) and yanked her skirt up to cover her face.

Days later I let myself be lifted into the cockpit of a small plane. My mother looked up and waved, her eyes buried in the black shadow of a salute. In disbelief, I waved back. Why hadn't I run off into the jungle, found my own tribe, started my own school? Now it was too late.

In Quito, before the eyes of thousands, I was led into the belly of a large silver aircraft. I felt like a criminal, tears of shame clogged my throat; I thought, *I will never see or speak again.* Minutes later I was caught up in the tumult of revving engines, the massive backdrag of takeoff, the steady lift of the air under our ascent. Our course leveled, the noise calmed, and, to my surprise, so did I. Though I wouldn't have admitted it, I felt relieved. The terrible thing had happened, it was over, and here I still was. I looked down on umber mountains and, behind them, the green, woolly plain of the Oriente. Somewhere on its tangled surface I imagined my mother crawling like an ant from one clearing to another, and I stiffened with disdain — my mother was old and a widow, and here I was, young and strong, seeded with womanlife, flying into wide-open space. Soon, through wisps of cloud, the Gulf of Mexico was everywhere below. I,

Hannah, was going to have dozens of children when I grew up; I would populate a whole village with them, a village where no one ever had to promise the Kingdom of Heaven.

Somewhere along a slit of dry riverbed stood Nimu, who had almost succeeded in doing just that — Nimu, up to her knees by now in silt and sand, Nimu, who gave me the strength to think I could forget her, howling a grief as dry and inaudible as I have kept my own.

5

· ·
·

I GUESS IT IS NOT SURPRISING that I feel this pity for Jeremy's snake, dragged away from its home, packed onto a plane — another unwilling émigré from Ecuador. Day after day it has refused even to look at the gray pellets of official snake food that Jeremy bought for it at the fancy pet shop on the Plaza. Conrad, the young man who owns the shop, specializes in the exotic — iguanas, parrots, tarantulas, and an obscure rodent from Southeast Asia. Slender and blond, with the smooth pink skin of an angel, Conrad looks as if he evolved a little further than the rest of us from the chimpanzee that's not for sale in his front window. He never worries that business is slow; every morning he strolls two doors down to Womancenter for a bran muffin, Red Zinger tea, and a leisurely chat. He's got an MBA from UVA; he did a marketing survey; it predicted a sufficient population of Jeremys to sustain him by the time Sugarland was fully developed. There seems to be no end to the variety of snake supplies Conrad stocks, though he has not been able to tell any more than we have whether our miserable creature is male or female, so Jeremy has named it Either.

Meanwhile, I catch myself playing a silly game with Either: I walk into the family room pretending to forget it is there, then happen to glance in its direction. In that split second of contrived surprise I can almost conjure more — the humid echo of the forest, the winding trails around the garden, the caved-in men's hut where families of anacondas gathered — whole scenes spun around those coiled golden markings, once hardly noticed as I moved past.

It was Conrad's idea to try the frog — he thought maybe Either needed a little drama, the thrill of a life-and-death struggle, to whet its appetite. Jeremy brought the frog home in a tropical fish carton.

It was my idea to turn this into an educational experience, a lesson in nature. "Children," I called cheerily. "Matthew, Benjamin, Rachel." I love speaking those names; when I doodle, I decorate their first letters with flowers and feathers. "Anyone want to see Either get fed?" For all the times I have known exactly what Darwin or my mother or one of the children would do next, with Either I must have a blind spot.

In minutes, all including Underdog had assembled around the fine glass case Conrad is letting Jeremy buy in monthly installments. Jeremy lifted the screened lid and dumped in the frog. It hopped about experimentally while the idea of it traveled slowly toward the appropriate region in Either's brain. The idea of the snake came much more suddenly to the frog. It began to spring wildly, hitting the glass, the roof-screen. Then Either started to move. The frog emitted a series of shrieks or bleats, noises none of us ever knew a frog could make. Under began to howl in what sounded like sympathy. I looked over at Jeremy in alarm, wondering if we shouldn't stop this. He wouldn't meet my eyes but was beating his thighs with his fists. Well, how would we have managed to get the frog out of there anyway, and what could we do with it then except set it free in the woods, where it might survive only a little longer? Matthew had gone down on his knees, his eyes inches from the glass, and offered guttural encouragement to the snake.

"Cut that out," I shouted at Matthew. "Cut out that disgusting noise this minute." He looked up at me with a smile of strange triumph.

Rachel, who puts her stock in popularity and being nice to everyone — Rachel said haughtily, "I can't believe I hung up on Amanda to watch this." A minute more and she announced, "I'm not watching," and left. I would have liked to stop her, try to explain the complexities of what was going on, apologize. Sometimes I think I'd do anything for a sign from Rachel that I am a little bit important to her. Then I remember how angry I used to get at my own mother, and I have to let her go her own way.

The frog's noises went on, hopeless, pleading. Either's coils rippled and danced. I couldn't tell what was where. Benjamin looked so unhappy, so alone, I drew him to me, and we stood holding each other, staring into space, like survivors of some disastrous accident, until Jeremy said, with a quaver in his voice, "Either's finished. That's it."

It was the frog that was finished, though there still came a few faint last cries from inside the snake.

>> .·. <<

Darwin is sleeping with someone else. I know this, though of course he hasn't told me yet and I have no hard evidence, and because I haven't been told or offered evidence, I can live as if I don't know, or, the more demanding pretense, as if it weren't true. He isn't calling any more often, really, to say he has to stay late at work. The children and I haven't really been in bed any longer by the time he gets home. And it's hardly a new thing for him to keep to his side of the mattress and jump when accidentally touched.

I don't want to think about it. I let it happen in a curtained-off corner of my mind, and life goes on. I have the children: after Darwin's first innocent pleasure over baby Jeremy, I'm the one who practically willed the other three into existence over their father's doubts and fears. *It's not that I don't like kids,* he kept telling me. *It's that I do. Too much to force another one into this fucked-up world.*

But Darwin smells different. He comes home after midnight and I am still awake, and as he fumbles around undressing, I catch a whiff of something sweet as baby sweat mixed with the rougher odor of smoke. He kicks Under off his half of the bed and stretches out next to me with a groan, and I pretend to wake up then and summon the dog back to the space on my other side, along the edge. I want something to hang on to, his sour, doggy odor to breathe, because that other smell makes my throat ache.

"I don't see how you can let that bag of mange under the covers with you," Darwin says.

"It's easy," I tell him. "At least *he's* here." The blanket slides off the dog as Darwin turns away from me onto his side. I quiet myself by thinking that he will tell me about it when he is ready. But the smell is still coming at me in shrill waves. I'm afraid I will never fall asleep. "Anyway, you've always had a thing about Under."

"Right," he mutters. *"I've* always had a thing."

"Someone has to stick up for him," I say.

"So you said ten years ago, when you passed over all the friendly, smart-looking ones."

"He was too proud to save himself." He was a yellow fuzzy creature then, almost cute, but what caught me was his silence and composure. He seemed to be gazing at something above and beyond the yapping, slobbering throng.

"Another misfit," says Darwin, and punches his pillow into his ear.

>> .·. <<

We'd been married a little over a year; Darwin was still ostensibly studying physics at Penn State and managing to keep one jump ahead of his own politics. We brought Underdog home to our graduate student apartment — three rooms the size of closets. "Dog," Jeremy repeated, his first word. "One more mouth to feed," Darwin said. "I think you're trying to torture me."

Under turned out to be lacking a testicle, and the vet said that abnormality often correlated with erratic behavior. But you don't stop loving a pet the minute you find that out. If anything, you love him more, even when he can't seem to distinguish the newspapers laid down for him in the kitchen from other papers — lab books, class notes, political notices and manifestos — stashed in various corners. Even when he pees to death the rubber tree a friend gave you as a wedding present. But Darwin decided the smell bothered him. I swabbed Underdog's failures up with a paper towel. Darwin, who had always declared daily showers to be a bourgeois hang-up, who had defecated gleefully in the ashtray of the dean of students at Penn State, began following after me with a damp sponge and Mr. Clean.

After Matthew was born, we qualified for a larger unit on the first floor, and I hassled the university housing office until we got it. On the mid-September day that we moved our mattresses, books, bricks, and boards, even Darwin seemed cheerful — justice had prevailed at least on this small issue, we would have the greater space we deserved, fuck Chicago, fuck politics, he would turn over a new leaf, tend his own garden, smoke his own grass, study for his Ph.D. exams, get back into subatomic particles, enjoy his family. "Why not?" he asked me as we surveyed the empty, sunlit rooms. I remember slipping my hand through his arm just as Underdog, full-grown by then to the size of a medium suitcase, took one look at the freshly painted walls and lifted his leg.

Darwin exploded. "Oh no you don't, you son of a bitch!" he screamed. "You're not going to turn this one into a barnyard!" He kicked the dog out of the apartment and down the half flight of steps. With one sharp yelp Under scrambled upright and took off out the entry door, almost knocking over Jeremy on the stoop. After him stomped Darwin, still threatening, and after him, me, frightened, seeing it coming — the headlong flight into the street; the minibus, with rippling stripes of pink and green; a tall arc of dog crash-landing on concrete.

I knelt beside him where he moaned, tongue out and dragging on the pavement. There was no blood anywhere, but his hind legs lay straight back from his haunches, as though he were racing at high speed, and when I shifted him, front half and then rear onto an old sheet, they were limp. He was not to lift either leg again because the vet had to fuse them, straight and splayed about thirty degrees, at the hips.

So that is the story of Underdog and how he got his weird walk. The villain was Darwin, and Under had forgiven him even before he hit the pavement. And I have managed to make Darwin look heartless, when actually Darwin pleaded to help me carry the broken body to our old Opel, and for months afterward the sight of the dog in motion — the rear half of him can only rock from side to side — made Darwin slump with guilt.

As partial atonement he played the dutiful son on the phone with his mother and borrowed enough money to pay for the best in veterinary care. But late at night he'd want to go over the incident. We'd sip mugs of instant coffee until our ears rang, until sleep, once we'd climbed into bed, was out of the question. In fact we made love often during that time (hence Benjamin) — often but very gently, because Darwin had not yet recovered from Chicago. His ribs still ached when he yelled or laughed, his hair was still short at the crown around a raised scar, and if he dozed off, he'd wake up with a start, groaning under the sharp, sick weight of a boot in the groin. He said it wasn't the pain, though, that caused the nightmares. It was coming face to gas mask with men who had the force and desire to kill you, and realizing that everything you had done to lead up to this meeting was really play, a chain of wonderfully logical inventions, a game you loved because it made you feel alive and free. Whereas this was reality, and reality wanted you dead or in jail.

So as we lay awake those nights, I'd hold him and tell him over and over that after what he'd been through, he shouldn't blame himself for lashing out at Under. "Maybe I shouldn't," he'd say. "But I do."

>> ∴ <<

Darwin will tell me about it when he is ready, and when he is ready has always been when it is over. The times and places will get harder to arrange, the touch of the other's body will begin to feel like simple pressure, not fire. The captivation with some physical flaw — that was what often stirred Darwin's hunger: a visible scar or birthmark, an overbite, the bend of childhood scoliosis — the strangeness of that will wear off. In the past, you could also count on political loyalties to shift. For the women were mostly in the Movement, and the Movement was always changing its mind about where and how it was moving, who moved it, and whom it wanted to move.

When it was over, we'd discuss it. And Darwin would admit

that the former other woman had appeared to him as the embodiment of everything he was looking for, everything he ever needed, and you could tell that in his now-sober mood, he thought such looking and needing were slightly shameful, if not dead-end activities. Something had happened to him, he said; it was probably chemical, more hallucination than romance — he fell for a figment of his own imagination, and of course his stupid penis couldn't make those fine distinctions, it just did what it was designed to do. And I understood. Even though I still thought *he* was everything *I'd* ever needed, I understood. "The fucking itself never measured up to the anticipation," he said. "Never delivered on the promise."

"I don't know what you mean, 'promise,' " I would tell him, with either my pregnant belly to stroke or the down-soft hair of the child at my breast.

Other women in the Movement may have been sleeping with Darwin; but I was the one he had made the bond with, the only one having his children. I was the only one having anyone's children, for that matter. The women in the Movement served as ministers of birth control, all the while deploring the risks and inadequacies of each method. It was a favorite subject for discussion among them, that and the ravenous egotism of the men. When I began to show with Benjamin, they kept asking if I was still a Catholic or something. Darwin, exasperated, said I must love being pregnant more than I loved him. I could never see there was a difference.

>> ∴ <<

The book I am reading for Human Development II says it was some ancient philosopher's idea to limit the senses to five, that modern research has differentiated many more. Is one of these the inner brace (like your sense of balance, maybe) that locks you in time, keeps you moving forward, though blind, in your tracks? Because mine, whatever it is, is going, failing. It's getting harder and harder to look at one day at a time, pare the truth to single events, assign befores and afters. The room fills up with Darwin's women, faces clear as yesterday. He always told me who they were, told them I knew. We tried to think of ourselves as a team, pretend that the differences among us were minor — we all wore jeans and sandals and embroidered shirts of Guatemalan cotton from The Peasant Shop in town — so minor that jealousy would be petty, counterproductive. And we were making History — background social history, anyway.

Or if I gaze a moment too long at the children, their faces go soft and round, their bodies curl back into plump nakedness, I feel a cheek, a hand claiming my breast, the sting of milk letting down. And they complain that I am staring at them again; Rachel particularly, who takes every opportunity to study her own reflection wherever she finds it, begs me not to look at her like that. Rachel — the ultracivilized girl I might have been without the Janca in my past? I can't help wondering, is she happy that way?

Jeremy was in the kitchen when I got home from class this afternoon. An odd expression on his face prompted me to ask what he was up to. He went a little pale as he considered the question for a moment, then shook his head surely. Nothing, he wasn't up to anything I'd be interested in, he was just checking something.

What was he checking, was something broken, I asked. One of the appliances often is. Mysterious debris keeps the dishwasher from rinsing, a fallen spoon jams the disposal, a drain clogs somewhere in the bowels of the refrigerator and water seeps out across the floor.

Oh, no, nothing was broken, he said with great energy, glad to shift the subject.

Well, good, I said, and then we just looked at each other with more awkwardness than ever, like strangers, but too proud or maybe embarrassed to resort to one of those conventional exchanges that strangers can fall back on. Why is it getting so hard? Why is it so different? As I eyed him nervously, it seemed to me that his jaw began to square off and strengthen, his nose seemed to concentrate in a firm, thin ridge; had he grown taller, begun to shed his pudginess? "Jeremy," I blurted, desperately. "Do you know what? I think you're going to be a handsome man someday."

"Jeez, Mom, would you give me a break?" He straightened his shoulders. "You know I don't care about that stuff."

"I'll bet anything Grandfather Worden looked a lot like you when he was a kid." I can't explain what I was trying to tell him. It had just come to me, a flash more of hope than of recognition — that Jeremy would make his own unaccountable future, that there was some hidden plan for him. I meant it as a compliment, but of course he felt no such thing; all it did was plunge us back into the bitter tension of his birthday.

"Great," he said. "Thanks for the boost." And then, with uncanny timing, that cursed SST went over, and for once rescued us, its victims. The moment exploded harmlessly in its hideous roar: I gripped the back of a chair, grimacing; Jeremy got some further retort off his chest. I could see his lips move, but he didn't volunteer to repeat it when the noise began to recede, and I didn't ask.

As suddenly as the plane passed, he stopped being evasive. In a firm voice he informed me of his latest project, approved by Conrad. He opened the freezer door, took out a quart Tupperware container, and popped the lid. He tipped it toward me; there were three white mice curled around each other inside, their fur coated with frost. I took the container and jiggled it. The bodies chinked. "They defrost in an hour," Jeremy explained, "and if you wave and jerk one around by the tail, Either will think it's alive and go after it."

My heart sinks at the prospect of mice filling our freezer. Jeremy has bought, on credit, a large cage, an exercise wheel, and a supply of mouse treats, and plans to raise mice himself. "Isn't that a little cruel?" I asked him, thinking of all those tender pink snouts and pink tails. I probably should have known that a so-called innocent act of my mother's would lead to something like this: a family who has sworn off meat for reasons that include kindness to fellow creatures suddenly in the business of raising mice for slaughter.

"Freezing them first is merciful," Jeremy said in that future voice, without a hint of doubt.

>> .·. <<

At night I dream of the rain forest, tree trunks soaring to the broken, translucent canopy, a twisting trail sprinkled with light. The Tiwano is many rivers, Nimu reminds me. In the dry season it was a graceful curve of road, marked by smooth, sun-bleached stones. During the heaviest rains it swelled to a brown flood, swallowed its boundaries, promised nothing, and carried everything away.

I'LL NEVER FORGET the flight from Ecuador, the glimpses of sea and earth sliding by underneath me, through mist and wisps of cloud, more mysterious than any map, and then the shock of coming down and being whisked off to Samuel's school and being held there like a prisoner for life. For four years I waited for the day of release, weaving subversive plans out of stifled outrage and bits of hope.

My mother always assumed I would go to Warren Bible College on the plains of Kansas, where I could meet a good Christian man like my father. She had written to me from Ecuador to remind me of this, then had flown to the States to show up at New Progress a few weeks before graduation and remind me again.

Uncle Samuel was on her side, of course. A former chaplain in the Army Air Corps, he saw Stalin jamming his feet into Hitler's shoes long before the fools in Washington began to sound the alarm. (Literally *saw* — Samuel has visions.) Now Communism was spreading across university campuses nationwide, invisible but irresistible as the Asian flu, which the Communists probably invented. You could be brainwashed almost without your knowing it, and once you were brainwashed, you turned against your family and toward sinful practices — fornication and things worse than that. His mouth went dry at the warning, and he had to pop another lemon drop into it. "Stronger than you have succumbed," he told me, smacking his lips. My mother conjured up the image of gates clanging shut on Life Everlasting, she and my father forced to watch my exclusion with helpless out-stretched arms.

But as far as I was concerned, the gates had clanged shut years before, when she made me leave the tribe. I survived then; now I would enjoy the irony of her futile efforts to keep me in the fold, as she put it. "You started this whole thing," I told her, but she never saw the connection.

I was setting forth into the Valley of the Shadow: Penn State University. I had two new skirts and two sweaters, one pair of paper-stiff Sears and Roebuck jeans I'd coaxed out of my mother at the last minute. I had the small, flaking suitcase she'd bought for me in Quito and the unopened bottle of Tigress cologne my friend Valerie had stolen for me once when I'd dared her to steal. I mounted the steps of the Greyhound bus, slid into a window seat, and looked down on my mother: I could hardly believe the tears on her weathered cheeks. She hadn't cried the first time I left. Well, I couldn't feel anything but happy to get away from Samuel, that school, her even. I shoved the pane open and stretched an arm down to reach the hand she stretched up. "You won't know a soul, Hannie," she said. "You won't know a soul." For one second, that moment when the bus disconnected us, I thought maybe I was making a mistake. But after that I would never look back.

I had been attending classes for about a month when I noticed the head of a young man seated behind a folding table in a corner of the Student Union lobby. It was very large for his average body, the brow so prominent and high that the eyes behind wire-rimmed glasses seemed to squint under its weight. He didn't look like someone in graduate school. He looked about my age, maybe younger, half embarrassed and half amused by his own soft, scrubbed cheeks and wetly combed hair and the dark suit and tie he was wearing. He seemed to be the keeper of the big, redheaded man in rumpled overalls and workshirt sitting cross-legged on the table above him, who was doing all the talking. Through the smoke from a cigarette tucked into the corner of his mouth, that man was telling us how protected we were on campus from the horrors of reality, specifically Mississippi, where Negroes were living in danger we couldn't possibly imagine — they were being beaten and killed by night riders, bombed in their homes and churches.

The big one spoke quietly, hypnotically; the smaller kept glancing proudly up at him and then into the audience, his burdened eyes jumping out at you when you caught them head-on. The two were collecting money. All I had was the dime in my bookbag for the treat I allowed myself every afternoon — I loved Coca-Cola, had come to live for its almost painful sweetness, the way it flooded your mouth when you threw your head back and sucked at the bottle, even the taste afterward of the burps. It was my only indulgence, and I hoped Uncle Samuel would find it slightly sinful. With my hand wrapped around a slick, cold bottle of Coke, I could sit in the Union and stare at people and not feel alone.

I asked if there were other ways to help; Darwin Charles raised his dark eyes to mine and for a moment seemed to drop his public smile and really look at me. He saw that I had never heard any of these things before, yet somehow I understood them, somehow I knew about horror, I was one of the unprotected. Pain was everywhere, said his eyes, a global secret just now being brought to light. This very day, for the first time, from now on. He gave me a petition to sign in support of students in California, and then another condemning the "People's Betrayal" in Atlantic City. As I bent over to write, he spoke softly into my ear, something about fighting History, changing its course of oppression. I thought, "This is it. This is real life."

The redheaded man I wouldn't see again for months, but watching Darwin Charles became a habit. I began to think of him as an old friend. I mentioned him to my roommates as such, reporting the high points of his speeches as if we had had an intimate tête-à-tête. When the two of them went out together to their parties, I lay in bed imagining dates with Darwin. They all began with him walking up to me and asking for a drink of my Coke; they stalled before he could suggest anything Samuel or my mother would have disapproved of.

Week by week in real life, I noted the lengthening of his hair, the deterioration of his clothes. There were days when he looked exhausted, sometimes ill, but he was always there in the Union with his petitions and announcements of rallies, and his air of being slightly amused. He didn't recognize me again; there was no sequel to that one private moment. But I signed, I attended. The first time I heard the accusation *Commies* flung at a group that included me, my head spun with fear — gates everywhere dropped forever — and exultation — I was out at last.

What was I getting into? I opened the bottle of Tigress and daubed it on my neck. I kept preparing myself for a life of interesting depravity, but all I got was Darwin Charles at a distance, the sound of his voice — more ironic than impassioned, though always energetic — and my Coca-Cola to fill up the gray emptiness of late afternoons. He was not a natural orator; there were bursts of memorized eloquence connected by stretches of er's and um's so awkward that even his hecklers eased up. ("We are anti-anti-Communist," he kept telling them, "which doesn't make us Communists.") It was comforting to see my name tucked in the middle of a list, to feel my body enclosed by the crowd he managed to draw.

In midwinter we began to hear about Vietnam. American troops there had doubled, tripled, since Johnson took office. He was bombing innocent villages to hell. Darwin Charles was suddenly fluent with rage; I was drawn closer, I felt the spray of his spit when he spoke. It was betrayal by the liberals all over again. He was signing up bodies to fill three buses he'd chartered for Washington, D.C. Students around the country were organizing a demonstration to end the war. In large enough numbers, we would speak and be heard. We would take our stand against the system, he said, and this time History was on our side.

The breeding ground of stupidity, Uncle Samuel always called Washington. Stupidity was, he said, the one thing worse than sin because it fathers it. Darwin Charles thought the same way: it was government by back-room managers, deal makers, they needed to be dragged into the streets, have their noses rubbed in History. History was coming into his speeches more and more often — the stammering pauses were disappearing — and the word made me feel chilly and humble, because I never knew quite what he meant. I began to imagine a large, sacred animal, something like the jaguar among the Janca, an embodied spirit to be both worshiped and feared. History was coming down to earth — he pulled in his chin now when he said that word. We must give up Biography for History. (Biography nuzzled and clung like a friendly monkey.) Vietnam was a mangled piece of History, History coming off its leash.

So I went to Washington and marched to the Mall, vigorously singing "Ain't Gonna Make War No More" behind an impromptu trio of guitars. At some point there was a flurry of argument and the group around me broke away from the crowd, and I followed, spurred by their sense of urgency, half running to keep up. Then an arm reached out and hooked mine; there was an enormous door, a cool, domed lobby, the smell of something burning, and me in great excitement being driven along. All at once it hit me: *This is what History means* — the weight of the door, the curved height of the ceiling, bodies massed, chanting "Hell, no, we won't go." Then just as I caught on to the chant and joined in, a policeman dragged me out the door again.

Which is how I came to be sitting on the floor of a D.C. police station right next to Darwin Charles — typewriters clacking, phones ringing, his very white, damp forehead leaning into mine, its wire-framed glasses askew. "They've got nothing on me," he whispered loudly, so close his breath made me shut my eyes. "That was an old driver's license I torched." When I opened them, his curly dark head was on my shoulder.

Someone was probably pushing him from the other side, but he didn't seem to mind. For me the contact was almost too intense to bear. In my mind, this man was my only friend. It had been almost a year since I had felt a friendly touch — my mother; poor Roger, awkward with guilt; his sister, Valerie — and even those times came more as reminders of comfort than as comfort itself. I stared at the arm that went wild during speeches and rested now on my knee. It was pale and smooth as a child's.

I edged toward him until my whole side was against his, and he didn't seem to mind that either. I sniffed him; his smell was a little sour, smoky: it was all uncannily familiar. I wanted to taste his arm. I wanted to pull the others in our group in around me, I wanted to nestle against them, I wanted never to separate my flesh from theirs, couldn't possibly, any more than a molecule of water could will itself away from the stream.

When the charges were dismissed, Darwin said, "Stick with me," and I imagined telepathy. In a Greek restaurant on Pennsylvania Avenue we shared one souvlaki sandwich and bitter, mealy coffee. Then we went off to find the Potomac River. After the skimpy springtimes of western Pennsylvania, the city seemed a paradise, abloom with daffodils, grape hyacinth, exuberant forsythia, luminous in the twilight. I wanted to run up and down every street, read every sign, check every statue, see everything before night fell. I also wanted to walk arm in arm with Darwin, touching. Darwin kept stopping and stepping back to ask me questions. I had no way of knowing that was what he did with new people — ask personal questions, one after the other, compulsively, in the hope that mere information would create closeness; if it didn't, it was always leverage.

I assumed he was trying to figure out why I was so frantic and odd. Afraid of what he would make of the truth, I gave vague answers: I went to a small private school near Pittsburgh, my father died when I was a child, my mother was a sort of teacher. He riddled each meager fact with more questions, his own bizarre answers; he danced on the pavement until I smiled. I felt him nudging his way into my life; I found the company cozy. Without mentioning religion, I told him about Ecuador, and how good I felt today being in his group, how it was like being back in the tribe.

"Right on," he said. "We're like that, you know — joined together. You, me, this mailbox, the whole universe, it's all just resonance. I mean, distinctions like 'you' and 'me' imply boundaries that don't really exist." His glasses slid down his nose and he punched them back up. "When you think of it, all words do is name impressions. Hannah Worden, Hannah Worden, where is that fantastic concentration of subatomic undulation I call Hannah Worden?" His hands groped through the air and grabbed mine. He pressed one of my palms against his massive brow and sighed. "One of these days I've got to work out the political implications of all this. You know, I haven't cracked a physics book in a month. Anyway, fuck the war."

"Fuck the war," I repeated happily.

Later he wanted to know how my father died. We had come to rest on a bench in a tiny park. A bronze patriot loomed over us. "He was killed," I said. "He was killed trying to make friends with those Indians I told you about."

Darwin didn't understand.

I gave him my story in simple, shortened form. "It was sort of a mistake," I said. "I guess they got the wrong impression."

"Not the wrong impression, *their* impression. They're entitled to their own point of view."

"My mother calls it God's Will. She's religious."

"But you don't fall for that shit." The pressure was beginning already. Such a choice: one version of death or another.

I pulled forward the thick tail of my hair and smoothed it across my mouth. "I don't know," I mumbled. "In his case I don't know."

"Far out," he said, laughing.

"You know," I added, moving the hair out of the way for a moment, "you sort of remind me of him." Not in looks so much as in expression. Not him, of course, but a photograph of him, the one my mother sent away with the men from the newspapers, which returned in the next weeks fuzzy and multiplied, for me to fold and tear out again and again and store in the tin with the Bible: a man squinting confidently at the future, his mouth stretched more to dare than to show delight.

"Uh oh," Darwin said.

>> ∴∵ <<

I don't think History had anything to do with it. It was Biology that pulled me to Darwin, the mating instinct. I had to have him beside me. I had to see what our children would be like, blended of such opposites — large-boned versus small, fair versus dark, quiet versus excitable and loud. Biology left no room for choice, not even later when those random flarings of sexual chemistry started to pull him away.

We almost missed the bus back to school. Darwin dragged me with him to the rear and began negotiating a rearrangement that would allow us to sit together. There were halfhearted objections. Someone called him a lecher; he held his hands out palms up, as if collecting praise. "Every mass movement needs an asshole," he reminded them. "I'm doing you guys a favor." His persistence was exhilarating. He knew them all; he was president, I realized, of some big club. I was nobody, who only thought she recognized a face or two from the trip down. When I confided to him that Caucasian features tended to look the same to me, he stood up and announced it to the whole bus as mind-blowing.

"The guy you love to hate," he called himself as he welcomed me to the inside seat. Had he intuited already what combination would hold me like magic? I've often thought that Darwin and I read each other's minds but get things backward, or get the emphasis wrong, or something. We are always just missing.

At that moment I was wondering at my luck, remembering all the months I had watched the girls with drooping earrings and long flowing skirts, long flowing hair that they tossed for emphasis when they spoke. Girls with mothers and fathers and small brothers, who visited on weekends and took them out to expensive dinners in shining station wagons. All the months I had played poor Hannah. Maybe I was not as poor as I thought.

Just off the mark, Darwin put his mouth against my ear and said, "Too bad you're not loaded. They said this campus was crawling with rich girls from Philly, but I never meet them." He bumped my shoulder with his. "Just kidding. What's money anyway?"

"I'm not the person to ask," I said. "We didn't have it."

"You must have had something for the most anal-sadistic members of the group to hoard and manipulate and convert into power over the rest. There's got to be a medium of exchange."

"Machetes, then," I said. "Or maybe feathers."

"Christ, you're beautiful." He snapped his glasses shut with one hand while he held my chin with the other, fumbled them into the pocket of his shirt, and kissed me.

When he pulled back for breath, I said, "But no one collected them. They just cut trails with them."

I saw him struggle in the dark to produce a solemn face. "They didn't do it with a machete, did they?"

"Do what?"

"Your father. OK, I'm being crude. Why would it be important? Forget I asked."

"He was speared," I said generously. There had been no mistakes, I could accept everything that had ever happened to bring me to that moment. The weight of Darwin's arm across my shoulders, his confidential voice, the tangy smell of tired bodies and a rich, sweet smoke — call it History, Biology, or God's Will. Call it beautiful, because that was what Darwin had called me, beautiful, and I was just uncertain enough what beauty meant outside a Janca village that I believed him.

And I had no idea that Darwin wasn't very attractive himself. I was captivated by him. I liked the fine, bluish white texture of his skin, the salty, smoky smell of his clothes. His body turned out to be like nothing I had ever imagined, so pale, the muscles barely defined, covered with fine, dark hair. And I liked the way he made love to me the first time, in the room he rented above some professor's garage. We went there after a meeting, climbed the rickety outside stairs in the dark. He went in first, and from the doorway I watched him stumble around scooping up the dirty clothes scattered everywhere and dump the armload into the closet. Then he tore all but the bottom sheet from the bed and brushed and smoothed it from head to foot before he invited me to sit down. He had begun talking calmly but rapidly about something else — the astronauts walking in space, it was — and he continued as we began our tentative touching — the precious beauty of the earth from their vantage — continued even as he fitted himself into me — its perilous fragility — as if he wanted to help me over the embarrassment of what was going on. There was a flurry of motion and he was finished; I cradled him as he dozed, cheek on my breast.

By the following spring I was pregnant and what seemed the sweetest, clearest year of my life had passed. A year of trusting Darwin, sitting beside him at SDS meetings, head cocked, ear turned to his exhortations, taking the imprint of his mind, his manic catechism. I typed position papers, lettered posters, licked envelopes, begged money. I made coffee. I preserved and flaunted my naiveté for his novelty. I tried to do and say as often as possible those things that seemed to impress or arouse him. It turned him on when I didn't wear underpants, when I rolled his joints, when I screamed obscenities, the meanings of which I could hardly keep straight. Until finally he told me, as if joking, that it turned him on when I didn't try so hard to turn him on.

I hardly noticed what he called his "minor fuck-ups." There were meetings after meetings, he came hours late to see me, always forgot money. For my birthday he bought two tickets to a touring company production of *Man and Superman,* but he did it at the last minute, so we had to sit on opposite sides of the balcony. He was always letting some detail slip in order to express his distaste for them.

Now and then he'd remember a condom, digging the crumpled packet out of his jeans and setting it unopened beside the mattress with a baffled shrug. "We don't need to do that," I always told him, but when I announced I was pregnant, he looked at me curiously, as though there were questions he was thinking better of asking.

There was a hasty courthouse ceremony, and Darwin notified his draft board. My mother, who should have been used to giving me up by then — my mother claimed a broken heart.

7

· ·
·

THE NAME IS A BAD JOKE: Concorde. They should have
called it Chaos, coming in over at Dulles Airport, tearing through
our sky, rattling the plates in the kitchen cabinets, windows in
their metal frames, lungs against ribs. It is so loud you can't even
hear the curses you hurl up at it, the pleas for mercy. It makes you
stop whatever you are doing, draws you to the window for a
resentful glimpse of its white tapering body, the arched nose, the
taunting grace, as it climbs into the world above clouds, before
sound.

Outdoors in the cul-de-sac the innocent faces of the children
tip up, fingers point in the air. Except for Matthew, who dances
around laughing, they all grimace and hunch their shoulders to
their ears. I have decided to protest this nuisance officially. Three
years ago, before the airplane's maiden flight, an editorial in the
Post warned of illegal noise levels, potential damage to the ozone.
Now the officials at FAA are not answering my calls.

"It's nothing," Darwin says, "a non-issue."

"Are you speaking scientifically or as another bureaucrat?" I
ask. His own Center for Environmental Control has reported no
significant hazard.

"How about as someone who knows you're addicted to lost
causes and has watched you practically invent this one out of thin
air. I mean, who hasn't griped once or twice about the thing, but
why suddenly the big crusade?"

"Why not? I'm supposed to wait for God to appear in a dream?"

"Speaking of God," he says, "maybe now you can appreciate how those poor Indians felt when your old man started zooming in on *them*."

Last week I offered to buy Jeremy a special climbing branch for Either's cage if he would distribute fliers for me door to door. I composed this warning:

> DANGER : SST
> Nitrogen oxide emissions
> Ozone depletion
> Solar ultraviolet radiation
> Skin Cancer / Blindness
> Waste of precious fuel

At the bottom of the sheet I announced a meeting to discuss these issues. I made a huge pot of tea and baked two dozen muffins filled with pecans and chopped apricots, but only one woman came — my next-door neighbor Yvonne, who humors me mostly, I suspect, because I am white.

"You just kick me out if I'm bothering you," she said as she cuddled into her purple mohair sweater, confident that she could sit all day at any kitchen table in Sugarland and never be asked to leave, because she is black. She wears a turban over her straightened hair, plucks out her eyebrows and pencils in sleek, disdainful replacements. I try to be exactly who Yvonne expects.

Consider the irrevocable damage to our environment, I urged. Consider our children's children. We've got to do something to stop it — write our representatives, go out to the airport and picket the terminal, lie down on the runway. I had prepared my voice for a vaster audience. It sounded like a parody of itself.

"I don't feature getting in the way of any airplane," she said, pulling a long cigarette from her sweater pocket and waving it around unlit. "Besides, I was telling Thomas just the other day, isn't it sort of pretty, sort of mysterious, hanging up there in the sky?"

Did she know it consumed four times as much fuel per passenger? I asked. And only the very rich and big business could afford the fare.

Was that the truth? she asked — why, that was like her husband Thomas' Mercedes, which cost him a bundle and takes another small fortune to run, but then that's what he wanted.

But they were taking more than their fair share, I said.

Well, she guessed people were allowed to spend what they earned however they wanted, weren't they? She took a big bite of a muffin and told me how tasty it was.

I couldn't find the energy to say anything else. I didn't feel like trying to argue with her. I am getting tired of it. I know people think I'm too extreme, too intense, too contentious, even Darwin, though he knows how far he has to push before I will give in and actually fight. Whether you have the last word or whether you give it up, you always feel terrible afterward, sort of up in the air, all alone. There is no such thing as two people talking *through* their differences, no coming out on the other side *together*. One never says to the other, *You know, you are right, thank you for showing me the truth, my life will be better, happier, for it, we will be friends forever.*

Never, Mother.

>> .·. <<

An idle remark by Asst. Prof. of Hum. Dev. Theodore Balch, last year's Outstanding Teacher on campus, who invites his students to call him simply Theo: The senses serve us not by letting things in but by shutting things out. If we were to perceive all that was happening in a given moment, we would go insane. Or at least get nothing done.

"Do you know," I told him after class, "that is the first thing you have said that sounds logical? All that other stuff, about hanging on to penises or losing them, getting them mixed up with feces" — I ticked items off on my fingers — "boys building towers in honor of them and girls designing circles to enclose them — I don't know *what* to say about all that."

Though he is younger than I am, his hair in front is getting thin and wispy like Darwin's. Long on the sides, it thickens into a reddish beard that makes him look a little biblical, prophetic. But where you expect flowing robes, a coat of many colors, there is pastel oxford cloth, a necktie striped sedately, tan pants. He is always smiling faintly — I think it is the curve his mouth makes at rest — while his round blue eyes look sort of dazed or resigned. He is known for being laid back, for still keeping the sixties' faith in relevance and human potential, and for being particularly supportive of older women, mothers returning to school. He struck his favorite pose, the fingers of one hand tucked in the pocket of his pants, and said, "It's just the beginning of the semester, Hannah. By midterms the puzzle of early childhood sexuality will all fit together."

"What the Janca children do . . ." I said. "I mean, *their* favorite pastime is decorating their bodies."

"Janca children?" he asked, poise jarred. "Who are they?"

"The Janca are a tribe of Indians in the Amazon rain forest. I was raised among them."

For a split second I saw his eyes roll up, as if to plead with someone above me, *Is this a crazy woman? Why do I always have to get the crazy ones in my class?* But it was the truth, I wasn't crazy. I told him I didn't remember any of us thinking or pretending something was a penis when it wasn't, and did he think that might have been because the Janca wore nothing to cover their penises, unless you counted tying the tips up with penis bands, so they were in full view of everyone, all the time? Wouldn't that habit of dress, or undress, I asked, tend to cut down on some of the confusion anyway?

With relief, I saw that he was taking me seriously; his tenseness relaxed to curiosity, even warmth — here was the man who had so often gone on record claiming that older students have much more to offer, he would rather teach them any day. "What an unusual experience for you," he said, and I thought, he really did have a nice face, what you could see of it above the beard — a fine, straight nose, high cheekbones — though all along the hairline there were patches of pink, chapped skin.

"Not really," I said. "It was just the way things were. Things got unusual when they sent me back to the States." He stopped and thought about this, that all-accepting smile on his face, and I confess the question crossed my mind: How do men and women do it? Who asks whom, and what do you say? *Would you like to see the alligator?* suggested Kaewi. *Would you like to kiss me?* I asked Roger, my hands already on his skinny shoulders. *Let's fuck,* said Darwin after he adjourned the meeting. But there were signals beforehand, things leading up. And something I have almost forgotten, call it hallucination, call it desire.

"Of course," Theo was saying, "I can imagine the dissonance. You might be interested to know, by the way, that the literature makes a great deal out of the anxiety caused in small children by exposure to the father's adult penis, because of the comparisons that must necessarily follow."

"But there were no fathers," I said. Inspired by his blue gaze, steady but vague, I told him a detailed story of my father's death and the Great Feud.

As I spoke, he pulled gently at different parts of his beard, as if he expected to find a spot that hurt. "Age five, you say." His fingers pulled and pulled, then another burst. "According to the literature, the basic groundwork is all but established by then."

"Groundwork?"

"Of the self."

"The self." I felt myself flush. "You mean me."

"More accurately, the structures that define you. They were already in place before all that happened. Or virtually so. The loss of your father at that age, however, must have left certain things up in the air."

I agreed reluctantly. These assertions of his, unaccompanied by suitable emotion, were somehow twisting the truth. "As I was saying," I said, "we children turned everything we could find around the village into a body ornament of some kind, or else into something we could smear right on our skin. We had all shades of green, and there was one plant that bled purple. We got white and yellow dust from butterfly wings, and black from charred sticks. There were berries, gray mud, orange mud. I guess we got a little carried away with mud when the season turned wet. We used to scoop out holes along the riverbank and sort of wallow in it."

Theo's smile deepened mischievously. "You must have some idea at this point of what the literature makes of children playing with mud."

"We weren't doing *that*," I said.

"Not consciously you weren't." He put his hand out as if to touch my arm, but didn't, and then just held it there, warding me off. "You know, I think your experience has been highly unusual, whether you do or not. I'd like to hear more."

I'm not sure why all at once I disliked him and vowed to myself that he would never hear another word. He was the one who was up in the air, releasing his little theoretical bombs one by one, completely uninterested in his target. Of course my experience was unusual. It was in his hands that it seemed to turn flat, run-of-the-mill. What if I told him that the older children re-membered the Janca custom of live burial, which my mother had put a firm stop to, and we were playing at that — allowing our bodies to be covered with sodden clay until we couldn't lie dead another minute, then leaping up, flinging it all away, plunging into the warm river to rinse ourselves back to life?

How unusual, he would probably say, pulling at his beard. *Thank God the literature knows all about that. Tell me more.*

>> ∴ <<

Matthew pushed a girl off the parallel bars in the school play-ground. She was practicing something gymnastic called forward cherry drops. According to Matthew, she and her friends have formed a club called the Nadias, and no one else can use the parallel bars during recess because the Nadias are too busy show-ing off. That is no reason to push her, I tell him, echoing teacher, principal, school counselor, grasping at no-reasons because the reasons are too hard to figure. The girl landed on her shoulder and snapped her collarbone. This isn't the first incident, his teacher told me ominously; we've just been lucky up until now.

Matthew has been ordered by the county to see a child psychologist. In the school office, a list of them was folded into my hand. *A fairly long list,* I assured myself as I drove home in numb disbelief. *We are not the only ones.*

"Do you want to tell me what happened?" I had to say something to him, but what? I felt so ashamed of him, of us. He knew. He slumped against the passenger door and didn't move an eyelash.

We pulled up in front of the house and sat. "Why did you push her, Matthew?" I asked. His body stiffened. He looked out his window, sharp chin thrust forward. "Why would you deliberately hurt someone?" I wanted to shake him, deliberately hurt him. "Why? That is what I will never understand. Why?"

He didn't answer. I had started to open the car door when he made a gagging sound and buried his face in his hands. "They didn't need the stupid rescue squad," he said. "She could of walked. She just wanted to make sure they put me in jail."

Then I realized he didn't know why any more than I did.

I told him no one would put him in jail, he said he didn't care if they did, I said I could see how terrible he felt. "Don't tell anyone," he said. I reminded him that Rachel and Benjamin had probably witnessed the incident. (Rachel is probably a Nadia herself, heaven forbid. She thrives on groups as much as Darwin does, and she is one of the brigade of Sugarland girls who take gymnastics once a week, which is how she discovered she was double-jointed. She can force grotesque positions from her wrists and fingers, do the splits, bend herself in half backward, and draw her head through her ankles. This special talent, along with her general niceness, is what got her, a lowly fourth-grader, elected vice president of Salyut Crater, which includes fifth- and sixth-graders, from which poor Matthew has now been exiled.) "I mean," he explained before we got out of the car, "don't tell anyone about me."

And what did that mean, what does he know that he thinks I know too? Or what does he know that I thought he didn't? It seems a little odd that he should assume jail when Darwin has never mentioned to the children the fact that his father died serving a one-year sentence for fraud. Actually I don't know much more than that myself. Alvin Charles was an accountant popular with small businessmen — owners of laundromats, frozen custard stands, auto body shops — and he was flexible. He could turn his back on thousands of dollars in gross income, he could work around inflated overhead figures, invented losses. In return — Darwin has never been able to figure out what his father got in return. "Maybe they put pressure on him," I have suggested. "Maybe they threatened to harm his family." But the subject is closed for discussion or speculation. Nothing will move Darwin to forgive him. His old man was either stupid or a coward. Best forgotten. Unforgettable.

So all morning I've been thinking about Matthew, and how we say things like *my own flesh and blood,* choosing to forget how many others' have mingled in the lottery. Who is he? I picture his face, so familiar it might as well never have changed since infancy, Darwin's eyes and coloring, that chin we can find no precedent for; his boy smell; the slightly crisp feel of his curly hair. Is it all a deception, is there something hidden, dangerous?

He is in my arms, not even a day old. He is sucking vigorously, and I can feel the rush of my milk. "Doesn't this make you believe," I ask Darwin, "just for a little while anyway, that perfection is possible?"

Slouched in the chair at the foot of our bed, he wants to know how I can be so irresponsibly naive as to talk about perfection at a time like this. On the TV screen mounted high in the corner, Robert Kennedy's funeral train crawls south through Philadelphia, Baltimore, toward Arlington Cemetery. Darwin turned on the set the minute he arrived. He can't not watch. "Do you think you can raise a child outside history?" he demands. "Do you think the contamination doesn't touch everyone, everywhere?"

The child in my arms is all I know, all I need. "I only said 'possible.' I just meant I can't help feeling hopeful."

"Hope!" he says, popping to his feet. "What do you mean, 'hopeful'?" He grabs the bed frame near my feet and jerks it back and forth for emphasis.

Matthew clamps harder on my nipple as we ride. "That hurts my stitches," I say.

Darwin sinks back into the chair and mutters something like, "If he's very lucky, he'll make it to eighteen, at which time they'll draft him and give him an M-16."

I remember that the Janca were careful around Bai's new baby for weeks, speaking only pleasant words, lest a curse enter the baby's soul through an ear. But maybe Darwin was right — how could we have kept all the anger and panic and grief of that summer from infiltrating Matthew, born the very night his father's last hope died?

It was all the more ruinous for Darwin because he was so sure he hadn't fallen for Kennedy, so sure he thought RFK was just another slick liberal, tied to the system that kept him in the cushy style to which he was accustomed. Darwin and his people had no use for political whores; they had made their break with negotiated reform, they were set for confrontation, violence. But I knew that in Darwin's heart he was hoping. Hoping that Revolution could still mean just being a creative pain in the ass, hoping that Kennedy would get elected and turn into the big brother they all needed, someone they could talk to, and no one would have to get hurt. And now all that was wiped away, and everyone was furious and terrified. There was meeting after long distance phone call after meeting; they argued whether to participate in a memorial service, whether to demonstrate and what for or against. As if they thought these decisions were matters of life and death. A bunch of us were gathered around the black and white television in our apartment. "Robert Kennedy's dead? So what else is new?" said Darwin's friend, mentor, idol — the red-headed Clark, returned alive from the war in Mississippi. "So what?" he asked, and broke into inconsolable tears. That was when I noticed the first contraction. I excused myself from the confusion and drove myself to the hospital, where I pushed Matthew into it.

>> .˙. <<

This was a bad time to try to discuss Matthew with Darwin. He is still reeling from his humiliation this past weekend at Children's Hospital, where the RATS were commissioned to perform a series of skits in the open short-term wards, for kids recovering from tonsillectomies and hernias and reset bones. If these went well, their contract might be extended to more critical audiences — accident victims and transplant recipients, patients with riskier surgeries. And beyond them Darwin's real objective faintly glowed — children with terminal illnesses. He wanted desperately to perform for dying children, to bring them pleasure, see them laugh. He is still planning on doing conventions, large parties, maybe weddings. He is convinced they can sell themselves to a society of corporate lawyers and government bureaucrats as custodians of the Spirit of Play. But if he could establish credibility with the hospitals, in the children's wings, that would be the RATS' spiritual raison d'être.

And then, in the midst of their first opportunity, Spiderman betrayed him, betrayed all the RATS, by trying to break into the pharmacy in Pediatric Oncology. He had heard rumors of the perfect drug, administered to children during chemotherapy to lessen anxiety and nausea, purported to cause a sort of massive emotional amnesia. It didn't just lift you out of time but drew you back through it to the clear, pure beginning where there was only innocence and trust and possibility.

He was caught tampering with a combination lock inside the pharmacy; he said the door was open and he was trying to find something for a hangover. No charges were filed, but the RATS were banished, and Darwin was furious. So what if it sounded like a good high, how could anything be worth jeopardizing the future of the group? He asked Spiderman to turn in his costume; Spiderman pleaded for a second chance.

"Where does he think I'm going to find a second chance like that?" Darwin asked me. "That was our first and last." Spiderman has allies, notably Miss Piggy, whose wealthy father created the Regenesis Foundation, which offers support to various grassroots liberal enterprises. We are still in the middle of this crisis —

on top of which Darwin's tights and trunks have given him a raging case of jock itch — and I had to break the news to him about Matthew.

His first reaction was to accuse everyone of overreacting to a random accident.

"The school is talking about a *history* of aggressive behavior," I told him. Let the magic word remind us of what we are up against, the inauspicious hour of Matthew's birth.

"It's these goddamn suburbs," Darwin said, too far gone to be subtle about his scratching. "We live in houses with identical floor plans, and our kids are supposed to join soccer teams and walk the balance beam, and if they don't there's something wrong with them."

"You know what maybe started it?" I said. "I think it started when he didn't get into Gifted and Talented. After we made such a big deal about Jeremy getting in."

"*We* didn't make the big deal," Darwin said. "And Matthew's been different since the day he was born. He would have been a big hit twenty-five years ago in Yonkers. He could have walked to school with me, and maybe I wouldn't have gotten the shit beat out of me every third day. Look, Matthew's Matthew."

"I don't know," I said. "Maybe we've been wrong not to discourage that tough-guy business. I think it's all an act." Maybe no one else sees that when he talks tough, the sound of his words seems a split second ahead of his moving mouth. He reminds me of TV when it's not coming in right and the image gets blurred by its own skin, shimmering a fraction of an inch off.

I make the appointment, regardless of Darwin's objections. I explain the situation to Matthew, that he will have to try to talk to someone about why he has been bullying other kids. I search his eyes for some hidden danger. He just stares at me, silently, darkly, and I see the fear on his face pushed away by pride and then the pride slips into doubt — as if he has just glimpsed something dangerous and hidden in me.

>> ∴ <<

The temperature dropped to cold last night. I woke up before dawn with a stiff neck and went from floor to floor, room to room, pulling down windows.

I dread this lonely season; as silly as it sounds, the first cold snap always comes like punishment, makes me feel tentative, tense, as if I had something to hide. This is Darwin's season. He loves winter, hardly feels the cold. In winter he gets back at me for July and August, when he claims I try to kill him by turning off the air conditioner and opening up the house during the day.

I have a sort of premonition that I'm not going to make it this time — the freezing, the shortening of daylight, will be too much. It's like that child's fable: there is famine ahead and I have forgotten to store up reserves. The house closed up for winter feels like an oversize, very thin shell that could collapse any minute on Underdog and me. And on Either, who is pining for the tropics and seems intent on sleeping itself to death. Jeremy has had to learn to pry open the snake's jaws while it dozes and wedge a softened mouse deep in its throat.

Jeremy, my unhappy one, a gifted and talented mind lost now in the muddle of a stubborn body, all sudden bulges, pores, glands, and fringes of hair. "Jeremy," I say, "do you know anything about this?"

"Anything about what, Mom?" he asks. He has developed a kind of speech disorder, repeats as many of your words as he can — echolalia, I think it's called. He is looking right at the paper towel I am holding under his nose; on it are two apparently used condoms.

"Under threw these up today on the kitchen floor," I tell him.

"Oh, those," he says, a flush rising under his freckles.

"What can you say about them?"

"What do you want me to say about them?"

"Jeremy," I almost shriek, "don't do this to me!"

"Do what to you, Mom?"

"I've got a right to know what's going on."

"Jeez, Mom, control yourself, it's no big deal. I've got a right to know what one of these devices looks like." He makes himself meet my gaze, mouth pursed with a sense of justice.

Why two? Why do they look used? What in heaven's name are you doing using two of them? I can hear the questions bounce around in my mind. It isn't my voice, it is my mother asking, and then Uncle Samuel chimes in, *I've got you there!* And then I remember a boy named Rich, so long ago there are only pieces of him left — a green satin jacket, a powerfully sweet smell, the softness on his upper lip — and all of Samuel's cold, crazy rules almost palpably breaking. After that there was Roger, whom I didn't exactly love but came to hate passionately, for being awkward and homely and the boy right under my nose, the one I could have. I could cry now when I remember how we felt our way along the contours of pleasure, certain that we had found something, though Samuel had worked hard to twist it beyond recognition. I *should* cry, because it was life we found in that horrible, dead place, and now I think we have both lost it — Roger, absolutely, forever; as for myself, I don't know. Something quickens at the glimpse of Jeremy's fumbling hunger; something remembers what he is daring to hope.

"Well, you don't have to put them in the trash," I say, "where the dog can get them."

8
.   .
   .

THE REVEREND SAMUEL J. HARNED, my great-uncle, is a
broken man: by his own sonorous admission, "broken in the
service of Christ." An army chaplain, he was a vigorous bachelor
of forty when the United States declared war on Germany, and
he pulled every string he could to accompany the first flight
squadrons to Britain. There he held daily services for the avia-
tors, leading them in prayer, consecrating their missions. They
were the picture of Christian manhood, all muscle and taut skin
and fearlessness, yet ready to bow their heads in humility as soon
as Samuel said *Let us pray.* Whenever one of them didn't come
back, Samuel helped the others rejoice that God had called His
hero home.

But the end of the war brought strange rumors, intimations of
hell on earth. Samuel prepared for higher combat. He contacted
the Red Cross, was right behind the British troops who liberated
the camp at Bergen-Belsen after the Nazis deserted it. Dozens of
skeletal bodies had already wandered out onto the roads to die.
Others were stacked like felled trees in the prison yard. The smell
he has never been able to forget; it was strong enough to taste.
Nor can he forget the woman who stumbled up to him, her eyes
sunken, lost, and handed him a small bundle. He thanked her
with a gallant bow, having always had the reflexes of a gentle-
man. Then he opened the filthy cloth and found it contained
an infant, stiff and gray. He called out to the woman to wait,
took several steps without direction, he had to give it back, but

she had vanished among the other prisoners. They all looked alike.

He realized he could put the bundle down anywhere, yet it entered his mind that perhaps the child wasn't dead, or wouldn't be as long as he cradled it like a living one. He doesn't know where such a thought could have come from and why he put up such resistance when a nurse tried to tear the baby from his arms. Afterward he worried terribly about the incident, still does. He is sure it was a sign.

This is Samuel's story, which I heard often during those four years I boarded at his school, a time I try to forget, which rises vague but alive now, pulling me back. He never spoke to me except to give strict advice or else reprimand, and in either case it never took him long to shift into autobiography. When the bombs dropped on Japan, Samuel was back in the States: they had confined him to a hospital in Texas for veterans who needed to rest their nerves. They didn't seem to understand that the problem was not in Samuel's nerves but in Eastern Europe. He began having nightmares — crazy things like Joseph Stalin goose-stepping west in Hitler's mustache, or Roosevelt returning from the dead as a red-nosed clown with an air horn. It was the absurdity of his visions that terrified him. The war had been a satanic joke. When he was alone during the day, he heard the sound of relentless laughter.

Then, because they decided he needed permanent peace and quiet, he was a civilian, pastor of a rural parish in Illinois. That was worse. Nothing but rainfall and the price of grain and hogs to make news, nothing to distract him from his growing conviction of apocalypse. The malignancy of Communism had surely ushered in the last stage of depravity on earth; end-time was near. The farmers got tired of his ranting. They worked hard all week, and I imagine they wanted a little encouragement on Sundays. Samuel was shunted off to New Progress Christian, where his pessimism combined with the military training might be profitably utilized, to extinguish the erratic fires of youth.

As for his students, we were pretty easily extinguished. We didn't know what to make of him, but then, we never expected to. We saw in him the image of the God we had each been raised on, whose purpose and plan was to be obeyed rather than understood. And Samuel was not obviously unkind. He never raised his voice, and when he corrected or punished one of us, he seemed to suffer more than we did. We learned to bend with his shifting moods. When he raved about the boat we were all in together, blindly drifting past Communist conspiracy toward the Niagara of World War III, we tried not to look bored. And then he sat for days in his darkened office, silenced by self-pity and guilt, as though he alone were responsible for everything. He did have his ashtray full of hard candies beside him, but we all knew they brought no pleasure — they served only to keep him from losing his voice. He looked so sad and pathetic then that we all felt sorry for him and answered extra questions in our workbooks in hopes of pleasing him. *What hazardous medical treatment was prescribed by the ignorant ancient Egyptians?* Answering always in complete sentences, we wrote, *The ignorant ancient Egyptians prescribed that human excrement mixed with milk be applied to lesions. Such treatment, it is now known, can result in serious infection.*

I say "we," though for over a year everyone more or less ignored me. I was Jeremy's age, and winter came and never passed, and I searched every corner of the school and property for something I could not have put in words, I only knew I never found it. Not in the stone farmhouse, its drafty rooms furnished with scavenged castoffs, smelling of whatever was happening in the kitchen — beans scorching, milk spilling and going sour in hidden corners, potatoes and lumps of strange, pale meat boiling and boiling. The chairs in the Main Room circled an upright console radio permanently set to one station in West Virginia, C. W. Burpo's Bible Institute of the Air. The boys slept in a frame barracks in the rear, the girls in horrid, precarious bunks in the attic.

There was nothing I sought in the prefab aluminum classroom out back, a setting for failure, humiliation. I was behind everyone else in mathematics because I didn't know my multiplication tables; I garbled my daily verses; why hadn't my mother taught me to memorize? Didn't my mother realize memory was the cornerstone to learning? Nor in the hillside garden plot in the shape of a cross, to which we lugged barrow after barrow of compost, from which we forced such rewards as broccoli, Swiss chard, and spinach in the spring. Once a month, at any hour, life was disturbed by a siren scream, and everyone assembled outside, and Reverend Samuel marched us to the bomb shelter. One by one we filed down the concrete steps, knelt and rested our foreheads on the concrete floor, folded our hands over the backs of our necks. We weren't to look up, but I caught glimpses of ceiling-high shelves of Spam and tuna fish, a toilet in the corner, the rifle on the rack over the heavy steel door. Nothing there either.

When they weren't ignoring me, the other students treated me distantly, with the same vague guilt I see today in my neighbors when they talk to the women who clean their houses. I guess I served a useful purpose — I kept Samuel busy, I made the other students look good. We were expected to work silently and independently at our desks. If we encountered a problem we couldn't solve, we were to signal Reverend Samuel by erecting a tiny American flag in a hole at the corner of our desk. I forgot these rules so often you would think I was being deliberately difficult. I stood up without authorization, moved around, spoke out, made loud noises as I studied. As soon as Samuel corrected me, I realized how bad I must have seemed, but I could never guess right beforehand. It was all so hopeless. I longed for someone to take pity on me, I'm sure I tried to act as pitiable as I could — but pity wasn't an authorized response at New Progress.

Then one day I was reading along in the workbook "What Did Genesis Say?" about the difference between the Bible and the pagan polytheism when I began to realize it was talking about Nimu, Nimu whom I had avoided all thoughts of, except to write at the end of each of my letters to my mother, *Tell Nimu I say Go well*. I made myself think of something else as I wrote the name, hardly pressing on the pen, because I didn't want to remember or picture anything.

Now as I read I began to hear a voice in my mind. It gathered conviction from the words on the page, then took off on its own, launched into one of the musical stories, half Janca, half English, that had lulled me to sleep on drowsy afternoons — how the earth began when the moon cracked in two like an egg, and then the part that was to remain the moon spilled rain on the part that was to become the earth, and from the first drops of water rose women, and from later drops came fish, birds, and monkeys, plaintain, manioc, and trees. I must have closed my eyes to listen, because as Nimu spoke, it was as if she'd slipped into the room and stood in front of me. Or else I was the one who'd slipped, back in time to the village, and I was seeing Nimu the way she appeared that final day in her uncrumpled dress, dark, bright-eyed, mouth stretched in a gap-toothed smile. It was so wonderful to see her, I remember feeling such joy and relief, did I really just imagine the whole thing? Why did that voice have to fade, that woman? My mind grabbed frantically at details — teeth, wide-cut bangs, hanging breasts — but they fell apart. I called her name out loud and broke into sobs.

At the head of the class Samuel cleared his throat. "You haven't forgotten the signal for assistance?"

I shook my head wetly. The rest of the class bowed low over their desks so they could stare without seeming to.

"What is it, then?"

I didn't answer but cried harder. It was a grief so pure at that moment that it needed no causes to feed off. The girl next to me handed across a clump of tissues but I shrugged it away. Let the tears run from my eyes and nose — I had kept them in too long, and now I would bathe in them.

Samuel held his position on the small platform at the front of the room. "Are you ill? You may be excused to go back to your bunk. Stop in the kitchen on your way. Ask Mrs. Dietz for —"

Without really willing it, I stood so abruptly that my chair went over backward, hitting the concrete floor with a loud crack. "I just had a vision." The announcement came out between gasps for breath.

My classmates groaned in unison. "Hannah," Samuel said with a sigh, "I doubt you had a vision. A gloomy thought, maybe. Some say those are Satan's tools. Please pick up your chair."

"It was a vision," I said more firmly, very much aware of the curious looks I was getting. "With voices. Like in the Bible. Well, one voice, Nimu's voice. I saw her clear as day. She was sort of whispering things." And then I told them Nimu's story. When I had finished, all shifted their secret gaze from me to Samuel.

He cleared his throat again and dryly smacked his lips. Then he shuffled over to his desk, opened the drawer, and fumbled something into his mouth. "The Lord be praised," he said finally, slurring the words a bit, the candy clicking against his teeth. "He has stirred Hannah's memories of the South American Indians in order to provide us with a fine example of heathen ignorance. We in turn must appreciate to the fullest how illogical and incomplete it is as an account of creation. The origin of the male, for example, is a glaring omission."

"That's the second part," I said. And there had been a third and a fourth part, there were always new parts, not always consistent with the old. "When the son of the moon came down and stole a woman, the moon punished him by biting him in the stomach. Then where each drop of his blood fell on the earth, a man rose up. The blood fell thickest over Janca land, and there the fiercest men grew." (Grew and fought and vanished finally, all of them, to become the food for worms — yet Nimu never mentioned the Janca's legendary fierceness without her voice going hoarse with pride.)

After the others left the classroom, Samuel sucked candy and lectured me, on and on — it was not what I'd said but the way I'd said it; I was more than welcome to give testimony of primitive ignorance, but I must learn to recognize the appropriate time and to control my feelings, if I wanted people to understand what I was saying; claims of visions were not to be made lightly; indeed they brought a burden of responsibility, sacrifice, even exile. Visions were not to be confused with simple influxes of strong feeling. He spoke from his own prophetic experience, which had been lonely and thankless. No one realized, for example, that this upstart hothouse-flower Kennedy was taking us a big step closer to disaster. That Khrushchev was a man possessed by the Devil, you could tell by his eyes.

When he said this, I happened to look at his own eyes, almost hidden in the folds of their sockets, and they were strange, entranced. I thought, *He is talking to someone else, not me.* And then it dawned on me how negligible my place was in his world, he hardly cared about me; for all his instructions and prohibitions, he didn't really know I existed, much less care what I did. *Beware,* he said, *Berlin,* and Nimu gave me one last glimpse of her grin. I could feel the chuckling sound of it in my own throat. After long months of empty motions, of following orders, and, when there were no orders, of putting one foot in front of the other because I saw nowhere else to put it, Nimu told me not to worry about Samuel, Samuel couldn't reach me, wouldn't even try.

He had finished talking, he was staring at me, and after a minute I could see that he remembered who I was. "You haven't heard a thing I've said, have you?" he said.

I thought, *You've got that backward.* I thought, *I am free to do what I want, if I can just figure out what that is.*

>> ∴ <<

My whole first year I had waited to be chosen. Barb, Girl Guardian, who slept in the bunk beside me, was chosen every week automatically, and she always appointed Valerie, who was next oldest and sang to Jesus off and on during the night in a furry soprano, to be Auxiliary Girl. Saturdays after lunch, I watched the two of them tie woolen scarves taut under their chins, button coats, pull on gloves, with a sort of sublime resignation. Far be it from them to show any eagerness or curiosity over a supply run into the town of New Progress; they were too busy building character, polishing self-surrender. With the same air they forced themselves to be helpful to me, to give me the benefit of their moral teachings: right to latch the door of the stall in the bathroom, wrong to stand and watch the flush until the level of fresh, lovely water stopped rising. From posture to bedmaking to washing and hanging out clothes, every moment in every day presented a choice between purity and impurity. In those days Valerie couldn't even think what a slouch or a wrinkle or a spot might lead to, the thought itself was too risky. Her kind words never sounded kind.

Barb and James, Boy Commander, kept order among the younger students privileged to go with them, shushing spontaneity, while they waited for my great-uncle to bring the reconditioned mini-schoolbus around. Every Saturday I was there, trying to edge my way into the group, trying to snag Barb's or Val's eyes as they picked their team, but terrified that I might succeed. Much as I wanted to go with them, I was afraid of being allowed beyond that plot of rocks and gullies, yellow grass and leafless trees. I had been trapped so long. I had to keep reminding myself that I hadn't soared over two continents and an ocean for nothing. I couldn't stop here. I had to keep pushing forward.

How many weeks did I stand on the porch and watch the olive-drab bus jounce down the pitted drive, between the two piles of rock, fallen pillars, at its foot? When my eyes lost it at the bend in the road, my mind propelled it on across the only terrain I knew — a jungle mission, the jumbled streets of Quito, a blur of airstrips, the sudden dark blocks of Pittsburgh. Then, faint with fear and longing, I brought it onto a flat, straight road, desert to either side, and ahead a town such as Jesus saw nestled in his donkey's path on Palm Sunday — a bubble of bright blue sky and flocks of tiny houses, white as the stuff they were calling bread.

Finally, in the fall of my second year, I stood in the open door of Samuel's office. "Is that you, Hannah?" he said, glancing up from the account book on the oak desk in front of him. His squint was greenly shadowed by a visor, above which his yellow-white hair stuck up in a fringe. He plucked a red sourball from his ashtray. "Is it the milk again?" He sounded wary, as he always did when addressing me, in case I intended to make some special claim on him, based on our common blood.

"No sir," I said, though my stomach still balked at that unfamiliar liquid and routinely threw it up after a meal.

"That's a stubborn system of yours," he said. "Remember what the Bible says about milk and the Promised Land."

"Yes sir." My eyes roved the room. The seat of the one armchair was stacked with newspapers, books were stuck every which way on the shelves — the clutter stirred a little hope. On the side wall were two photographs, a large sepia portrait and a glossy black and white with scribbles in one corner. In one year I had heard more than I'd ever wanted to know about William Jennings Bryan and Joseph McCarthy, two Christians who dragged victory from the jaws of defeat, who had to lose to prove they were right. A slick Sears and Roebuck catalogue sat like temptation on a littered table. I had glimpsed its pages twice since I arrived — toys beyond the imagination, plaid shirts and dresses, things with ruffles, ribbons, sparkling jewelry, adult bodies modeling underwear. From such possibilities Samuel ordered my clothing: stiff corduroy jumpers, a dark pleated skirt, blouses with short, flappy sleeves, and a navy blue orlon sweater.

"I was wondering," I said, "if next time could be my turn to go in the bus." I met his blinking eyes and looked away.

"To go in the bus." He sighed, took off his eyeshade, and ran a hand through his unruly hair. "There are doubts in my mind, you know, that you are ready for such a trip, that there aren't more productive ways for you to spend that time."

"Valerie showed me the trick of times nines," I said. "And I can almost do Genesis four."

"It isn't your accomplishments, Hannah, or the lack thereof. It's how strongly you wish to go."

"Very much, sir," I said.

He tucked the candy into one cheek so it stuck out like a small tumor. "Exactly. A sure sign that you aren't ready. My concern is the shock. You know what perfectly good milk does to your mortal body. Think what the wickedness of the world could do to your immortal soul."

"I can't stay here forever."

He resumed sucking, appeared to concede that point. "Well, it isn't a joyride, you understand. It's one of many duties the students of this school must help with of necessity. I'm not a young man," he added, pulling his collar away from his jowls. "My strength is gone."

"Yes sir." A new word, *joyride*. Despite his disclaimer, it sounded promising.

Samuel picked up his pen, dipped it in the inkwell, and began to write again in the ledger in front of him. I waited for a while without moving, then pulled a lump of tissues from my jumper pocket and blew my nose.

"Nine times six?" Samuel asked, pen poised above the page.

"Fifty-six," I said.

"Fifty-four," he said, scratching in the figure. Then he added, as though he needed this further answer for his accounts, "You know your mother is a stubborn, foolish woman?"

There had been times I'd thought this, certainly, yet I felt uneasy nodding my head.

"I expect she thinks she's saving the world by converting a few ignorant Indians. All she's really doing is drifting more and more out of touch. What's going on down there anyway, all that nonsense about moon-cracking?"

"I can do all the other nines," I said.

"I always liked your mother. She was a sensible young Christian lady until she met your father. He's the one that gave her that hero complex. That's what I call it, anyway. You know, he had us fooled for some time. I have always admired a man with energy, fiber, who doesn't shirk the tough responsibilities, as long as he isn't going off halfcocked, as long as he's acting in a good cause. But your father was a loose gun. He had his own ideas. Instead of falling to his knees the way he should have every day of his life and offering thanks that he missed the War, he had to find one somewhere else."

My blood rose. "That's your idea, looking for a war," I said. "He was trying to make friends." In Janca, the word for *friend* was the word for *sibling;* at New Progress, it seemed, there was no word at all.

"He was living in a daydream." His eyes rolled up at me under their heavy lids. For once he wasn't squinting. "He had to be a hero. So he did whatever he darn pleased and called it the cause of Christ. Do you understand what I'm saying?"

"I was not listening," I said quietly.

"You never do, Hannah. Which is why I doubt you should be allowed to leave the school."

I decided I had never seen a face as ugly as my great-uncle's. His skin made me think of chewed manioc, with darker pink blotches and grizzled patches of stubble. The corners of his mouth plunged in deep creases that were always wet. "You're jealous of him," I said. The story of my father has never been negotiable.

Samuel tried to moisten his thin lips with a dry tongue. "I know that if I asked you to apologize for that remark, you would."

I looked at my shoes, hateful, heavy, heel-barking oxfords.

"You will please pick up that Bible from the top shelf. As of this moment you are allowed to skip over the names and ages in Genesis four and five. You will begin reading chapter six, verse five: *And God saw that the wickedness of man was great in the earth . . .*"

Outside the funnel of light from Samuel's lamp, I read, dim verse by dim verse.

"Exactly," Samuel said when I had droned to the chapter's end. "Now look at me. *It repented the Lord that He had made man on earth.* That was when the earth was brand-new, life was simple. Think how He must feel now. Why did He repent the creation? Because *the earth also was corrupt before God, and the earth was filled with . . .*"

"I don't remember," I said when I realized he meant me to complete the reason.

"Violence, Hannah, violence. *And God looked upon the earth, and behold, it was . . . ?*"

"Corrupt?"

"Exactly. For all flesh had corrupted His way upon the earth. You will remember this next week when we go into town."

>> ∴ <<

The first time I went, Uncle Samuel expected some lapses in execution. He had been more than willing to make allowances for my inexperience, he said, the shock to my sheltered senses.

But he never dreamed that one person could make as much trouble as I had, he told me with a long-suffering sigh once we were back at the school. It seemed that I'd robbed everyone of the satisfaction of a cleanly accomplished mission, I'd made everyone regret bringing me along. Ah, but his plaint meant nothing, it was too late for guilt. I had been out in the world.

How could I walk in line, in step, when there were animals to touch, strange sights to take in? "Look, everyone," I kept calling, "look over there": a row of shrubs clipped into spheres, someone's bright socks, a kid on roller skates, dummies in store windows. "Hurry up, Hannah," came the reply. "That's nothing." It had never occurred to me to doubt that the school and its rocky plot had been created by a God who looked like Samuel, a God whose moody exploits I was memorizing in Genesis. Or that the jungle in Ecuador had fallen from the fertile moon. But what was I to make of kids my own age cruising the square in cars, windows down despite the cold, spilling loud music, jamming traffic as they braked and shouted at loitering friends? They clustered outside the Palace Theater holding hands, laughing easily at everything. One boy had opened his jacket and wrapped a girl in it with him. Head tucked under his chin, she stood blissfully dozing. What was that buttery smell in their vicinity? "Popcorn," Valerie whispered in the voice she used to name sins. Uncle Samuel tapped the glass cases displaying movie posters as he shuffled past. "Eyes front," he barked, and we kids filed stiffly behind him.

Then he stopped abruptly — cocked an ear and shook his stubbled jowls at some overheard profanity — but we kids kept marching and bumped up against him, into one another. We realigned ourselves to the sound of hoarse laughter, the question "How're your little sheepies, Dad?" A knot of boys in front of Star Trophies made bleating noises. In the window behind them, statues of all sizes gleamed silver and gold.

"Sheep-eyes," one of them called me when I couldn't stop staring. "Lookit sheep-eyes over there."

Why shouldn't I smile at them? One of them smiled back, spilling smoke from his mouth, and turned away. Its faint smell

pricked my nostrils, mingled mysteriously with the smell of flowers. Across the back of his shiny green jacket an arc of white
letters said KNIGHTS.

"Catch up, Hannah," Valerie hissed. She dropped back and
tugged me into forward motion, but I still craned my head, still
looked those boys up and down. "For the umpty-umpth time,
you can't just stop whenever. It isn't right."

Since I had proclaimed my vision, Valerie, now a senior, was
turning more of her peculiar attention on me than I really wanted.
She was imposing beyond her years, with square shoulders and
a large bosom over which she kept her arms crossed most of the
time like an annoyed parent. Except for a stiff clump of bangs,
she pulled her hair back from her face in two barrettes, tight
enough to lift the skin around her temples, which made the angry
angle of her brows and her solidly dark eyes look even angrier.
Often at night, she informed me haughtily, she herself saw Jesus
Christ floating over the foot of her bunk, naked except for that
cloth you-know-where. I was high-waisted like her, she said, and
it was much better, purer, to be high-waisted than low-waisted.
She went out of her way now to stand or sit next to me, to ask
me questions. She seemed to be waiting for me to say some
particular thing. I had no idea what that might be, nor did I
know, if I happened to say it accidentally, what Valerie would do.

Now Uncle Samuel checked his watch and chopped the air
with one hand, and Valerie dragged me into Brockett's Drug
Store, jingling the bells on the door. She raced straight to the
pharmacy in back, dropped off the slips of paper for Samuel's
pills, and whispered something to Mrs. Brockett, who disappeared behind a dun curtain and returned with a large bag sta-
pled shut around a large box. When I asked what it was, Valerie
flushed and giggled emptily. As soon as Mrs. Brockett went back
behind the counter, Valerie pulled me over to the book and magazine rack and reached down a paperback. On the cover there
was a jungle clearing, except the trunks of the trees were dark
purple and their foliage light purple and a clean, pinkish man and
woman half dressed in civilized clothes lay among the flowers on
the forest floor. He was shirtless and on the verge of licking her

arched neck. Her dress had slid from her shoulders and barely covered her breasts; she seemed in the midst of a painful dream.

"*Velvet Chains,*" I read slowly. "*First he took her body — then he stole her heart.*" I looked at Valerie in alarm, but she was watching me the same way.

"That is a book of sin," Valerie said, her usual authoritative tone failing her. She flipped it open, riffled some pages. "*She had never dreamed a man could make her feel so alive,*" she read in a loud whisper. "*The Raven was her enemy — yet he was the one for whom her body had been created.*" I drew a loud, involuntary breath. "What's the matter?" Valerie asked nervously.

"Nothing," I said, but it was the word *body,* there a second time — the very sound of it seemed to expose a secret.

"It's terrible, isn't it?" Valerie wasn't sure. "Look, it says *devil.* Isn't that terrible? *Before his devilishly handsome smile, she lost all feeling of right and wrong.*" Her voice seemed to give out as she read. "Right there, *devil.* There." She was stroking the page with her finger. Then she added, more firmly, "Some people," and gave the word on the page an angry jab.

"Let's keep this one," I said, plucking the book out of her hands.

"Hannah," said Valerie, with practiced horror. "That's a wicked thing, we shouldn't even be looking at it, I haven't got any extra money, he gave me just enough."

"She's not ever going to read it." I tipped my head at Mrs. Brockett, who was spraying a blue fluid on the glass countertop and scrubbing round and round with a rag. "She's got all these others, doesn't she?"

"It doesn't belong —"

"We'll bring it back next week." The book disappeared into the pocket of my coat.

"You have to pay for things, they'll put us in jail, Reverend Samuel will get —"

Her objections were cut short by Dr. Brockett rattling a bunch of little bags and calling from his window, "You want these now or next year?"

"Yes sir," Valerie said. "Now, sir." She handed me the big box and nudged me toward the door. Mrs. Brockett was already figuring things up on the register, adding in three bags of butterscotch drops without Valerie's having to request them. When Mrs. Brockett didn't ask whether there would be anything else, Valerie didn't have to lie.

"Nine minutes, twenty-seven and three-tenths seconds," Reverend Samuel said as we stumbled out onto the pavement. "I will assume there is a reasonable explanation for the delay?" His eyes under their heavy lids glanced at me. I hunched down behind the box.

"Yes sir," Valerie said.

"Shall I assume it does not require any action on my part?"

"No sir," Valerie said, "I mean, yes sir. Yes, it does not."

"Well done, Guardian," Reverend Samuel said, and the reconstituted squad marched forward.

"You should never, never have," Valerie whispered sidelong to me. We were bringing up the rear.

"You wanted to read it too," I said.

"I never wanted any such thing."

"Why can't we read it if we're curious?" I ventured a glance at Valerie's profile. The eyebrow began in a furious clump on the bridge of her nose, then rose in a sharp, straight dart to her hairline. "You're curious too, I can tell."

"I said I'd look after you because I felt sorry for you, because I thought you were so ignorant, but now I can see that I've been wasting my time. You're nothing but a wicked liar."

"Oh, I see," I said, groping. "You wanted me to get one you haven't already peeked at."

We have since laughed about this day, though we never mention the irony, slightly painful, that over the years we have reversed our roles. Slightly painful to discover that you have moved away from what you thought was your self, left it behind, forfeited. But when you think about it, where else is there to move but away? Space is curved, Darwin says. Maybe away bends back.

Her virtue offended, Valerie shoved me hard, knocking me off balance and the box out of my arms. I picked it up again and glared at her, but she turned away a blank, innocent face and walked very fast to catch up with the others, who were crossing the street to the center of the square where the flagpole rose above two bronze plaques etched with the names of the sons of New Progress killed in World War II and Korea. I stood where I was, biting back the urge to scream Janca curses at her and never tell her what they meant — child of monkey incest, rotten fish head. Who did she think she was? My one vision was better than all her silly ones put together. Did she think I was going to come scrambling after her? I wasn't ever going back to the school. I would hide out somewhere, get lost.

I took a couple of steps in the opposite direction but was brought up short by my own reflection in the window of a dry cleaner's. I was shocked at how ugly I was. Pale, frizzy hair twisted into two lumpy braids, large, pale mouth, freckles, no eyelashes. And I hadn't realized until that moment quite how ugly my clothes were — the sleeves and bottom hem of the secondhand coat were too short; the jumper hung below it, leaving a few inches of skinny ankles and navy blue socks before the heavy brown shoes. Now that I knew girls my age wore skirts that stood out like the roofs of round huts, or tight ones that made them swivel as they walked, or blue jeans cuffed under the knee, bright scarves knotted tight at their necks, lipstick; now that I knew they wore supple slippers that made their feet look tiny and light, and clutched little purses, not big brown boxes — I had to draw the obvious conclusion. No one else on the square looked as hideous as I did.

My pride and courage shriveled. I hadn't *felt* so ugly, but I couldn't deny what I saw. I began trudging in what I thought was the direction of the bus, then stopped, then started again. What choice did I have? As I wavered, I noticed a woman coming toward me with an air of purpose. She had on a bright red coat, and a long fuzzy scarf was draped around her head. In front of her, in what looked like a little chair on wheels, she pushed a bundled-up baby. For a moment I forgot my gloomy fate, pretended for a moment the woman was approaching me especially. Janca babies clung to their mothers' breasts and backs like little monkeys. This mother thrust her baby out to the world as a wonder, an accomplishment. Her eyes and skin were bright from the cold; she walked briskly and seemed to smile at me as she turned the corner and passed — surely that was a smile, an invitation.

I followed her along one edge of the square and down a side street, a steep hill, where she had to slow and pull back on the rolling baby. First she and then I crossed the bridge over a creekbed — there were empty lots between squat buildings now — then we turned left into a road that ran along a field of tall brown grass, edged with rusty fence and rows of weathered benches built up like steps. Beyond that, the sidewalk ended and the woman swung the baby out into the road and, since there were no cars in sight, pushed it right down the center. I tried to follow more subtly now, because I was in plain view, but the woman never seemed to notice me.

She had begun to skip behind her stroller, skip in slow, graceless motion, and sing. Then she started to run and make the stroller swerve to left and right, and above its clatter I thought I could hear the baby squealing with joy. Way ahead of me she turned down another road, and by the time I reached that corner, she must have turned again or vanished, stroller and all, into one of the small, flat houses.

I didn't know where I was; back came the sickening knowledge of who I was, how ugly I looked. There was nothing to do but find the bus, accept where I belonged, never ask to leave the school again. But when I imagined the pained speech I would hear from Uncle Samuel and Valerie's fierce contempt, I couldn't move. Daylight had begun to fade; my hands and feet were freezing. I started to walk back and stopped next to some rotted scaffolding that had been bleachers. *I won't ask whether you are sorry for what you have done, I know you are,* I heard Samuel say as I slumped on the lowest bench. *But I'm not,* I thought, *I'm not sorry, and I haven't done anything wrong.* As I sat there, staring into the field, the protest swelled to a grand scale — I had never in my life done anything wrong. That was why I felt so miserable: I was the most falsely accused, unjustly ugly person on earth.

Then I remembered the book. I set aside the box I'd been hugging, dug the book out of my pocket, opened it to Chapter One.

It began, as I suppose many of those books do, with a cold, damp night and dense fog billowing along deserted cobblestone streets. There was the sound of horse's hooves in the darkness, and then silence, and then a tall shrouded figure emerging from the shadows outside a lighted house, the elegant house of a haughty lady, a beautiful lady, and I had never read anything like that before. I made myself stop; my hunger to read on was almost unbearable. That was when I heard the shrieky whistle. I twisted around and behind me, through the bleacher, saw slices of boy. Were they calling to me? Had they even seen me? Should I stand up and wave? I didn't know what to do, so I slouched down over my book and pulled the box closer.

"Baah, baah," one of them called, and the other two took it up in different keys. I decided then that we sort of knew each other. I raised my head and baahed back.

They came around the bleachers and stood in front of me, loose-jointed, shifting weight from one foot to the other. There was a tall one with a large, bent nose and hair that stuck up like a scrub brush; a short one shaved to the scalp, with little light gray eyes. Behind them, I recognized the shiny green jacket, the dark, wet hair.

"Whatcha doing?" the tall one asked, lifting one leg and sitting astride my bench.

"Waiting for the moon," I answered. It was the way Janca invited conversation.

"Looks to me like you're reading," the tall one said with a game laugh. "My name's Chuck." He stuck one hand right at my chest. I raised mine to block his but he grabbed and shook it. "Cold hands, warm heart," he said. When I tried to pull it back, he shook it some more, a little harder; then he let go and laughed again. "This guy's Marty and that one's Rich." I tucked my hands under my arms. "You a good reader? Rich is a good reader." He reached over and lifted the book from my lap. Then he whistled. "Jee-sus, would you get this? *Velvet Chains.*" He turned back to me. "I thought you Holy Rollers were, you know, big on morals. This is trash. Where'd you get trash like this?"

"I was just curious," I said, haughtily. "It isn't wrong to be curious. And besides, it's not your business."

"Hey, no big deal," Chuck said, patting my hand. "You and me can be friends. You like this stuff? *The gleam in his golden eyes made her blood flash like quicksilver through her veins?* What can I say?"

"I never saw golden eyes on anyone," said Rich in the green jacket. His cheeks and forehead were purplish with acne, and his front teeth grew at an angle that he tried to hide with his upper lip when he talked. "Except maybe a hound dog." He wasn't trying to be funny. I liked him. I felt sorry for his teeth and skin.

"What's quicksilver?" Marty asked.

"It's like Spanish fly." Chuck looked hard at me. "Pretty hot stuff you got here. What's your name, anyway?"

"Sheep-eyes," I said.

"Shit," he said, and it was the first time I'd heard the word. "No harm intended."

"Really it's just Hannah," I said.

Marty began strumming an invisible guitar. "Hannie had a baby, cain't work no more," he sang, keeping time with his pelvis. Rich punched the top of his arm hard.

"*When he bent his head and captured her lips,* what's this say, Ameba?" He held the book out to Rich, pointing.

"Amber," said Rich, trying to look matter-of-fact.

"What's that mean?"

"It's her name," I said.

"So Ameba *felt her senses ripple like a tidal wave.*" He looked from Rich to Marty. "Hey, why don't you guys get lost?" He pulled himself closer to me along the bench so that I was sitting between his knees.

"Baah, baah," said Marty.

"Chuck," Rich said.

"Shove off, guys. We want to be alone."

"I don't want to be alone," I said.

"You know what I mean," Chuck said, and slipped his hand between two of the buttons of my coat. With a surge of disbelief, I knew exactly. I looked down curiously at the motion of his hand hidden against my chest. It felt hard and cold, but insistent. Maybe I wasn't as hideous and out of place as I thought.

"She doesn't want to, Chuck," Rich said. Marty had removed himself to the field. He was jogging around imaginary bases.

"Yes I do." I braced myself for flashing blood and rippling senses.

"You do?" Chuck said, surprised. "How 'bout we go somewhere private . . ."

"Him too," I said. Rich's cheeks flushed a darker purple.

"Him too?" Chuck was astonished. He cleared his throat, then leaned forward and stuck his mouth onto mine. I tensed with the shock. His tongue pushed against my lips while his palm scrubbed my chest. All I could picture was Mrs. Brockett, whose book I clutched like a hand, as she scrubbed her counter. And I was cold; I couldn't stop shivering. Chuck drew back, looked at Rich with a triumphant laugh, asked me, "Still say him too?"

In answer, I shook off his hands and wiped his kiss off on the sleeve of my coat. Then I walked over to Rich. He was no taller than I was. There was dark hair on his slightly protruding upper lip, and he smelled like flowers. "I'm cold," I told him between chattering teeth. "I want to get away from here."

He didn't laugh at me. He reached out and patted my shoulder. I stopped shaking, my jaws relaxed, I felt inspired. "Do you want to go on a joyride?" I was sure all at once that that was the right question to ask.

But he looked confused, and so I took a step toward him and my lips touched his lips, chapped and dry, edged with that soft hair. I touched a little harder, and he returned the pressure, shuffled closer, so that I could feel him up and down my body, which began to go warm and weak — for a moment enthralled by its own blind vision of another place, hot and dry, the chaff of a dormant garden. Neither of us moved, we just stood there touching. My heart thumped as if afraid.

"Oh, that's cute," Chuck said. "So that's how you Holy Rollers kiss. Whatchou got in here, anyway? More dirty books?" He grabbed the package I'd left on the bench and tore open the top of the bag. "Jee-sus," he said. "Just my luck." With one loud rip he unveiled the box. "You can forget everything, Rich, she's got the curse."

Rich stepped away and let the cold rush back through me. "What curse?" I asked.

"What curse, she says. We're taking off, Rich."

"What is that, anyway?" I asked. "What's in that box?"

"Now she's Miss Innocent." He pushed on the dotted line and pulled back the top. "This ring any bells?"

"Oh," I said, taken aback. "I didn't know what . . . Those are just things." Why did I feel such embarrassment? My mother had said, *You are not to think there is anything wrong with you,* but the next time it happened I was thousands of miles away, alone, doubled over with cramps in a cold toilet stall. Those things — they looked like giant bandages. Last year Barb and now Valerie, disdainful Girl Guardians, issued them on request, one at a time.

"We know what they are," Chuck said. "Hey, Marty," he yelled, "know what this is?"

Marty stopped between third base and home, readied his hands to catch. Chuck took a couple of steps, arched back, then hurled the pad. It went a few yards and dropped in the grass, a blinding, artificial white.

"Stop it," I cried, without conviction. Janca women didn't use those things; I wasn't sure exactly what they did instead. "The moon is resting," they said, to explain their disappearances into the women's hut. Janca men, before the Great Feud when there *were* Janca men, could not have strong spears around women's blood.

Chuck had taken out another one, tied the ends together to turn it into a wad, and headed for the field. He threw and it flew sharply off to one side. "Too bad we don't have a bat," he called.

I edged a little closer to Rich, but with a pleading look he backed away. "Those guys are big jerk-offs," he said.

Marty was singing about the joys of a ballgame, running, leaping, diving, to field the white aimless missiles Chuck flung with loud, fake laughs from home plate. They littered the ground. Rich was watching his own foot kick a bare spot in the grass.

So I made a quick lunge and grabbed him, and pressed one desperate kiss on the edge of his mouth. Then I let go and turned my back on all of them and started to walk away. I didn't know where I would go now — I would just keep walking until I couldn't take another step.

"Hannah. Hannah Worden."

I heard my name called out behind me.

"Jee-sus!" Chuck yelled. He went bounding past, laughing and shouting back over his shoulder, "Party's over, you guys, take off."

When I turned around, Marty and Rich looked small and silly running into the outfield in different directions. A block away the olive-drab bus was creeping toward me, close to the curb. Valerie marched ahead of it, calling my name.

I tried to act happy to see her. I tried to act as if I had been conscientiously looking everywhere for the bus.

"I saw you kissing him," Valerie hissed first thing after I climbed on board. "That's wicked, wicked. Do you want to have a baby?"

>> ∴ <<

In the village of tears, having babies had become a dying art. During the first months after my mother and I entered the half-empty village, a handful of babies were born posthumously, but for years after that there were none. Nothing to set against the remembered terror and grief of the Great Feud but my mother's strange promises on behalf of God, the Great Father. Nothing until girls not much older than I was began to spend certain days in the women's hut, and boys began to tie their foreskins closed with thin strips of palm.

One afternoon as my mother and I lay resting in our hut, we heard shouts and loud laughter, and there was Nimu, her mouth stretched in the widest grin, leading Bai, and behind them, skipping and clapping hands and singing to the heavens, the rest of the tribe. Last of all trudged young Naemwi, posture downcast to hide his pleasure and pride — he had fathered the child that was causing Bai's body to swell, causing this whole parade to our shelter, where Nimu asked my mother to perform the marriage ceremony. "This my prayer," Nimu kept saying, stroking Bai's abdomen. "God's Will be done."

"God's Will be done, indeed," my mother said. To me she said later, "You are not to bother Bai anymore. She and Naemwi have other responsibilities now, difficult changes to adjust to." She made it sound grim, but Bai and Naemwi seemed not to appreciate the seriousness of their fate. They were always nuzzling or play-fighting or laughing, never louder than when they caught us children spying on their love.

Finally, though, Bai had to carry her distended belly in the brace of her own hands and began to prefer spending her day in a hammock in her mother-in-law's corner of the main hut. And Naemwi took up a forlorn post in the yard of the deserted Men's House. Once the center of importance in the clearing, it had now more or less collapsed in on itself. The children had gotten lazy about keeping the jungle cut back around it, allowing the undergrowth to take it over from the rear and weave a perfect habitat for snakes. The focus of the village was now on the other side of the clearing, where God's House adjoined my mother's school. Except for that one day when all of a sudden the women were running, popping from the forest around the clearing, letting go their backloads of firewood, bare soles thudding down the paths to the garden, all converging on the yard of the women's hut, where they pushed us curious children out of the way and ducked behind a bark-cloth screen, from which strange noises were coming. I took a deep breath and ducked after them.

There hung Bai, naked, swollen, eyes clenched, mouth stretched wide, clutching two vine-ropes slung between posts over her head. At shortening intervals she let her body go into a squat, let the springy vines bob her up and down, matched her moans to this rhythm. *Nange*, grinding, the women called this — an old word with a new meaning: it also named what you did with your teeth to contain sorrow or rage. The women moaned with her, added their strength to hers. And I added mine, from deep in my throat. Deeper. Bursting with the energy of shock, of sudden knowledge, of wonder, I held back nothing. Then my mother's hand was around my arm and I was outside, being marched down the path, across the deserted clearing to our hut. The urgent rhythms that had filled me, surrounded me, sounded more orderly across the increasing distance, almost playful, like the background for a song.

I didn't know, of course, that that day was the beginning of the end, and that in a matter of only months, time would run out on me and distance multiply beyond conception and I would wake up one morning in Samuel's school in the States. My mother said it was for my spiritual welfare, but it always felt like punishment — for pushing myself in where I didn't belong, with Nimu.

Do you want to have a baby? asked Valerie, Girl Guardian of New Progress Christian, as though speaking of a dreaded disease. I guess I should have thanked her. In the time I had spent trying to adjust to that place, stumbling this way and fumbling that way, I had almost forgot.

9
.   .
.

NOW MATTHEW HATES ME. He eyes me sidelong, his shoulders tensed, like a cowed animal. "This wasn't my idea," I remind him each time I drive him to the office of Dr. Dooley Clement, Child Psychologist, on Sugarland Plaza. "I didn't push whatshername." Eyes down, we march across the expanse of herringbone brick, swerving to avoid the weathered-wood planters with their faded petunias set randomly about. I tell myself that as an adult I should be above feeling ashamed, but I don't want to look up and catch Conrad spying on us over the shoulder of the catatonic chimpanzee in his window, or Valerie waving curiously from Womancenter across the way.

Matthew gives me glaring, hateful looks and silence as he sits in the waiting room, arms folded across his chest. Dr. Clement shares this space with Sugarland's sports podiatrist; on the wall opposite us is a diagram of a gigantic foot, all its hundreds of bones labeled, along with its tendons, its muscles, an esoteric tangle of fine print, and for a moment I pretend we are here because Matthew's problem is only pigeon toes or fallen arches. Then comes that awful moment when he jerks himself out of his seat and disappears without a backward glance behind Dr. Dooley Clement's bright yellow soundproof door.

I don't blame Matthew for being sullen anymore. It is horrible spending an hour alone with this man, though I'm sure he is perfectly nice as a person, unimposing, gentle. He has asked us to call him just Dooley. He wears faded dashikis and worn-out running shoes and one of those monkish haircuts that looks as if it were shaped by a bowl. He smiles apologetically but helplessly whenever an awkward silence descends, leaving it to you to think of something else to say. It's worse when he does choose to speak, because he stammers and you have to pretend not to notice. Pleasantness, sincerity, freeze on your face, and you think you cannot stand another minute of this — each at the other's mercy.

Dooley doesn't tell you things, he *shares* them. He doesn't ask you things, he requests input. On the day Darwin and I were supposed to give him input on Matthew, at the last moment Darwin couldn't leave work early enough, and I had to go give it by myself. Everything in the inner office looked wishful and new — at one end a small red table and yellow chairs, two blue vinyl beanbag cushions, a dollhouse, white shelves along one wall neatly lined with dolls, guns, trucks, blocks; at the other, two chairs of what smelled like leather and chrome. The contrast with his shabby clothes made me skeptical. Maybe he had taken out enormous loans to pay for all this equipment. Maybe we were his first and only clients.

Why didn't I begin at the beginning, Dooley suggested, as he relaxed into one of the leather chairs and waved me into the smaller, simpler version opposite. Between us on a round white table were a folder and a fresh box of Kleenex. The beginning. Beginning there wasn't a simple proposition. Already I felt defensive as Samuel's visions crossed my mind, and then Darwin's father's crime, my mother's breakdown, Darwin's dope, all the incurable stuff that runs in our family. Then I remembered little things: how when I fed Matthew he seemed to hold himself apart; how he made his body stiff when we tried to hug him; how he hardly ever smiled. Jeremy at that age smiled shyly whenever you met his eyes. Matthew smiled only at loud noises. When Darwin turned the Rolling Stones up as high as the speakers would go, he gurgled and grinned.

"Matthew has never been an easy child," I had to admit. "He will say or do anything to get attention, like ride his bigwheels down a flight of apartment steps and hairline-fracture his skull.

He has smuggled war toys into our home, and sometimes when he can't have his own way he threatens to blow our heads off."

I paused to see how Dooley would react. He grasped a lever on the side of his chair and shifted it into a semirecline. We were only ten minutes into the hour. He gazed at me benignly, almost slyly, as if he knew I had something amazing to tell him, though I hadn't quite come up with it yet. "I know Matthew doesn't really mean that," I said — asked. "He says those things too deliberately." Dooley raised an eyebrow. "Darwin says he's just pulling my chain."

"Why does he say 'just'?" Dooley stammered, but to prove I hadn't noticed his halting speech, I changed the subject.

"My chair doesn't have one of those levers."

"Would you like to discuss trading places?" he asked.

"That's all right," I said. "You're comfortable."

"If you're uncomfortable," he said.

I guessed I wasn't. "I see you have plenty of war toys," I said. "I suppose those are the first things Matthew goes for." Dooley smiled, affirming nothing. He seemed to be waiting for me to drop *the* clue, the one that would let him blame all of Matthew's problems on me. And the funny thing is, part of me wished I could, and wished he would, because then I wouldn't have to talk anymore, I could go home, and everything would be simple. I could change. He would tell me how and I would be more than willing to do it. I have had enough of sudden switches, random leaps. I wouldn't mind a few deliberate, planned changes.

"I love Matthew," I blurted out. "I swear I can see something underneath his troublemaking, some fear or something. But I can't get to it. He's not a happy child, I know, but I can't reach him. And I do love him."

Then Dooley Clement looked me right in the eyes and said, "There isn't a doubt in my mind about that," and I was so grateful the words began pouring out of me, about how it was when Matthew was born, and I saw the first breath of air enter those tiny lungs that had never tried air before. "With Jeremy they knocked me out, but with Matthew I saw everything from the very first moment. They laid him on me, all mucky and purple, and cut us apart — him screaming and me thinking, *He is so alive and brand-new,* so purely new, for a moment it seemed almost as if perfection were possible. If we were very, very wise and careful, I thought, maybe he could be the perfect child.

"Don't you see" — I wanted to step up onto that little white pedestal of a table and tower over him until I was sure he did — "we did want Matthew; we were happy to have him. The mistakes, whatever you decide they are, must have come later."

Dooley gazed at me dumbly. He didn't seem to understand. Finally he said, "Mistakes aren't really the issue here. Neither is perfection."

"I just meant there are so many ways a child can be hurt, damaged, and we don't even realize. You know, with Rachel, I delivered in a tub of warm water. You've probably heard of it. The room is dimly lit and they play soft lullabies. The doctor eased her gently out of me, brought her up through this reddish cloud to the surface. She gasped once — maybe she was surprised at the air rushing into her — but she never cried. She is nine years old now, and very calm and secure. She is so secure she frightens me."

"Hannah, Hannah," the doctor said. "No one is accusing you of trying to damage anybody. But we need to figure out how all your kindest intentions can best help Matthew."

"It must seem silly to you, and extravagant, all this fuss over one child who's just a little mixed up, when a million children suffer and die every day."

"Does it seem silly to you?"

"My children are very important to me." My voice broke on the word *important,* it was such an understatement. "Maybe too important. Whenever I feel depressed, I picture the four of them lined up by height, three smiles and then Matthew, of course, making some gruesome face. Or I write their names over and over in fancy scripts until I realize I don't regret anything. On my deathbed I want to be able to say I don't regret anything, that my life has taken the only shape it could have."

"Deathbed?" His features twisted to get out that stubborn word. "Isn't your focus a little long-range?"

"I don't let myself forget that my life could end at any moment, as suddenly as my father's did, and I worry about mine not being, I don't know, as worthy as his was." Finally. I flushed to have spoken out loud what I must have gone over in my mind so many times, and hardly known it, like a memorized prayer. And then he asked me if I wanted to tell him what that was all about, and I flushed again, anticipating the pleasure of telling my extraordinary story, of filling up the remaining half hour so entertainingly and safely. "You did say begin at the beginning," I reminded him almost playfully. As I launched into it, I thought, *I am home free.*

Twenty minutes later the little red light was flashing on Dooley's telephone; he began to get that distraught look of someone who is listening only for a convenient place to interrupt. So I closed dramatically, with my mother striking out into the jungle to win over the souls of her husband's murderers.

"Darwin says I take life too fucking seriously for the suburbs," I said by way of epilogue. I was thinking, *Thank goodness Darwin didn't come; he would have made me nervous.* He would have said my story had nothing to do with anything, it was self-indulgence. I should have been talking about Matthew.

"And how are things," Dooley asked, "between you and Darwin?"

"It has been a while since Darwin and I even touched." I didn't realize for a minute what I'd said. When I was reciting my story, my mind had drifted back to Rachel, how beautiful it was when she was born, but sad also because Darwin had been to see a urologist and I knew she would have to be our last.

"How long?" he asked.

"I'm no good at time," I said, then caught myself, caught him. "I don't see what that has to do with Matthew's hitting. I don't see whose business that is but mine and Darwin's. What I meant to say was that Darwin and I disagree on how to handle Matthew. When I try to discipline him, Darwin says I'm ruining his

identity. I should let him be a free spirit. When something happens to our rose-covered cottage and we all wind up on the street,
Darwin says, he's putting his money on Matthew."

Dooley shifted himself upright and set his Adidas gently on the
carpet. "This Darwin sounds pretty serious himself."

>> ∴ <<

A family falling apart, that's what we are, that's what Dr. Dooley
Clement was trying to tell me. I don't know what to do, I have
failed — everywhere there are signs I have tried to deny. I need to
confide in someone, a close friend, that I am worried. I want at
least to discuss this, I want to make resolutions out loud I will
have to keep. I consider picking up the phone and dialing the
Womancenter hotline, disguising my voice. I could become just
another woman fed up with husband, children, life, toying with
desperate acts. And let Valerie, unmarried, childless, like a priest-
ess, talk me into something practical — legal advice, a support
group, financial planning. But I can't do it. I can't bring myself
to show her such weakness. I am the one who saved *her,* got her
to the hospital when she almost died, got her off the street, invented the job for her at Womancenter, the only job there that
pays. Her stability now is tenuous. She finds it boring. There are
too many days when the peace and quiet allows her to remember
too much, think too hard. "Is this all there is?" she often asks me
out of the clear blue. "You are healthy," I tell her, "relaxed and
independent; you're helping other people." "Well," she says, "if
you can do it, I can do it," as though "it" were the same for both
of us. She must never find out that I can't.

No, the only one to tell, my only friend really, is Darwin. The
irony of that hurts — he's the one who's out of reach, out of
touch, the one with whom such confidences aren't possible.

I tried to tell him the night after my appointment with Dooley
that I was worried, that he didn't seem like part of the family
anymore, he was always jumping up and running.

"Don't say it," he interrupted. "Don't take this away from me,
Hannah. For the first time in years, I've got ideas in my head
again, and the future doesn't look like a blank. And I'm not

running anywhere. I mean, I'm not your father. Maybe that's the problem. You're disappointed because I've given up on trying to save the world. But the other side is, I'm not going to leave you either."

"How can you say that?" I asked. "You are always leaving." Hadn't he left the dinner table two hours before to answer the phone and stayed on it almost ever since, first to Spiderman, then to Miss Piggy, who, by virtue of her father's connections, keeps dangling the possibility of a small role for the RATS in the presidential campaign next year, plus maybe a little exposure on national television during the Democratic Convention? Then it was back to Spiderman to negotiate the conditions for his return, then a call to a friend of King Kong's, who has contacts in the D.C. public affairs office and thought he could line up a gig for the RATS at the Old Post Office on New Year's Eve.

"If that's what you call leaving," he said, starting up the stairs.

I followed him into our bathroom, where he dropped the lid of the toilet, sat down, and started rolling a joint. "Well," I asked, "when should I reschedule the appointment you missed today with Dooley?"

"Who the hell is Dooley?"

"Matthew's doctor — Dooley Clement."

"Don't bother," he said.

"He's really a knowledgeable man." In fact Dooley's piecemeal knowledge of us makes me a little nervous, now that the relief of blurting things out has passed. "It's important for Matthew, Darwin. His problem stems from a lot of different issues, and they all have to be sorted out before meaningful treatment can begin."

"You've bought the whole thing, haven't you?" Darwin took his first deep hit. "The trouble is, I don't *believe* in Matthew's problem. I have no desire to neutralize his energy, I don't care if he never turns the other cheek, and" — he began to let the smoke seep out — "I wish you'd take that religious impulse you got from your mother and dump it once and for all, because I can see you beginning to glom onto this business of personality reconstruction as your latest pie in the sky."

Silence, in which we each went over his speech point by point.

Then with a deep sigh he stood up and offered his sweetest, most modest smile — I could see he was pleased, almost expecting applause, but I was choking on objections. "We are talking about Matthew's antisocial behavior, which really, Darwin, has nothing to do with my mother. I'm tired of you dragging my parents into everything."

He hitched his rump up onto the vanity counter. "I'll stop when you stop."

"It's because you're ashamed of your own father."

"Did Doctor Doolittle tell you that?"

"Maybe you don't want to think Matthew might be headed in the very same direction."

"Ah, the Charles legacy. A recessive gene for jail. At least Matthew's nobody's fool, thank God for that." With his body folded in on itself, shoulders hunched over, one elbow on his crossed knees propping the joint mouth-high, he toked nonstop.

"Your father wasn't a fool."

"You could have fooled me."

"I wonder how the children see you?" My hand on his shoulder, I felt him go so still his breathing stopped. "Why don't you let Jeremy and Matthew go with you some weekend?"

He sat up straight. "Impossible."

"I think they need you."

He brushed the remark off like a compliment.

"We could find them costumes."

"It isn't that."

What is it, then? The words clamored to be spoken. Darwin was braced for them. "Anyway," I said, "it isn't very pleasant, making one-sided intimate conversation with this Dooley person. He just sits there and acts like he knows everything. You're not going to weasel out of taking your turn."

Another silence, to let the tension relax, appraise my seriousness. Then a slack smile spread across Darwin's face, a look of someone in on all the mischief in the world. It was his farewell smile; he was on his way to wonderland.

I wasn't going to be left. "I don't imagine you've got anything to hide."

Darwin tried to blink himself sober. "What a charmingly bourgeois thing to say."

"Do you?"

"Other than my love affair with the weed?"

"Funny you should talk about it that way. I think Dooley thinks our sex life has something to do with Matthew's hitting."

Darwin jumped as if startled, then began to yawn endlessly.

"Something is wrong," I said, and the admission out loud almost toppled me. I clutched the door frame. Not out there in the world, but right in the middle of my family, something was wrong.

"Don't listen to him," Darwin said. "Think about how long we've been together versus how long you've known this guy."

"What's going on?"

"Nothing's going on. Nothing. God, that's it in a nutshell. Nothing's going on."

"I'm not talking about the big philosophical picture. I'm talking about you and me."

"I knew this shrink business was a mistake." He staggered as he slid onto his feet. "Mind if I take a leak?"

I refused to back out of the doorway. "It's funny," I said, "the way every time we talk it turns into the same old wrangle."

"It's called 'Get Daddy,' " Darwin says, to the tune of his falling pee. "It's the game I let myself in for as soon as we started having kids. I mean, when you blame your old man the way I do, you've got to figure it's just a matter of time before your own boys turn and put the finger on you."

"Nobody's putting the finger on anyone, Darwin. I know it feels that way, but that's not the point." I wished we could invent new words, or find some whole new world where nothing had been named and begin all over again.

He'd zipped his fly, flushed the toilet, and now he stood with his back to me, head bowed. "You didn't use to care what I did."

"I can see how you would think that."

"It's not like I snuck around and hid things from you, Hannah. You've always known, and you've never said a word."

"What did you expect me to say? It was your choice. Do you

think I want to tell you what to do? So you can lump me in with all the other bad guys in the world who are out to get everything you have?"

He turned to face me so close all I could focus on was one of his eyes, bloodshot in the depths of its socket. "Maybe when we all stop inflicting pain, Matthew will," he whispered.

"When do I inflict pain? I mean, intentionally."

He said again, "Maybe when we all stop."

And then I was brushing my teeth, and I heard the front door open and close, followed by the snort of the Bus's failing muffler. I thought, *What if this time he's gone forever?* and my face in the mirror surprised me with a sort of sneer, then bowed to spit — as if warning me that it could never be that easy.

Of course he was back within the hour, tromping in and up the stairs so carelessly I was afraid he would wake Rachel, the iffiest sleeper, letting fall a cascade of hangers in our closet, leaving on lights in the hall, our bathroom, then sinking onto the foot of the bed, where he sat passing his head from one hand to the other. I peered up over the bedclothes and asked what was the matter.

"You know, when I was Matthew's age," he said, "I tried to change my name to Bear."

He has told me his father cursed him with the name Darwin not to be witty but because he wanted something people would recognize and remember. Success in the business world or even politics could hinge on such a name. His father's name, Alvin Charles, might have done him in if one of his baseball teammates in high school hadn't happened to shorten it to Big Al, which stuck.

"Why Bear?" I asked last night, and it was as if we hadn't just fought, or maybe it was because we had and it was time for diplomacy, for cultural exchange.

"I thought it sounded like someone big and gruff, like my old man. Can you believe it? There was actually a moment in my life when I wanted to be like the guy? I guess I got the idea from my mother. She worshiped him, mostly because he'd let her reform him. He used to go drinking every night with his buddies until she came along and shook her dainty little finger and warned him, *Lips that touch liquor will never touch mine.* Turned him into a steady provider, a devoted husband who gave her Whitman samplers and roses on anniversaries, in return for which she gave him loud kisses and called him a big bear of a man.

"Anyway, when I started junior high, I went to work persuading the teachers my name was Bear. But the kids kept right on calling me Darwin, among other choice epithets, and then I'd forget to answer if someone happened to call me Bear and the project just sort of got abandoned." Under must have heard the wistfulness in Darwin's voice, for he plunged clumsily off the bed, lurched around to his master's side, and settled a comforting muzzle on his knee.

"So you did look up to your father," I said, trying to sound both indifferent and receptive — whatever mix would keep him talking — while I reached down and pulled Under back to my side, before he could change the subject and go off on the dog's shortcomings. "I think it's pretty normal, Darwin. It's where Jeremy and Matthew are now."

Darwin's boots hit the floor with two clunks, then still in his clothes he stretched out on the bed. After a while he said sleepily, "He used to sit in his big brown LazyBoy and talk down the long slope of his belly at you, slow and stern. He had this long, droopy nose, with a deep double pleat at the bridge, and this long upper lip, which made him look like he was about to sentence you to hard labor for all the nasty thoughts he read in your mind. No such luck. All he really wanted to do was give advice, one mundane platitude after another. Like *If at first you don't succeed,* like *Cheaters never win.*"

I pushed myself up on one arm to look at him. He looked back at me, and it was too dark to read expressions, but he knew he'd told enough for me to understand.

"All I've got to do," he continued, turning his face to the wall, "is think something fatherly and this shadow looms up out of nowhere. His words start to come out of me in his voice. I don't get it, Hannah. He was a nothing, or almost a nothing. He should have passed through this world without leaving a mark. Why couldn't he have? One glob of protoplasm stuck in the middle of a lot of other globs he called friends. They were always phoning him, he always came up with new jokes for them, asked after their families. The phone was right next to his chair. Six feet away was one of the first TVs in Yonkers. *A man's home is his castle,* he'd say, settling back to watch 'Zorro' and 'The Cisco Kid.' *You know, son,* he'd say, *I live like a king.* The asshole."

I waited, intrigued by these glimpses, knowing better than to ask for more. ("Go ahead, give the old knife a twist," Darwin told me a long time ago when we heard that two former Penn State comrades were going to prison and I'd asked him innocently what prison was like.) I could feel him struggling, clutching at silence, but it is hard to stop remembering once it starts.

"The only reason I ever went to visit him was my mother," Darwin muttered finally, as if I was dragging it out of him. *"You've got to forgive and forget,* she told me every fucking time I turned around, until I thought maybe I'd better see him, maybe it was some procedure she knew about that would change things back the way they were." Then Darwin told me about getting on the bus for upstate with all the wives and so-called sisters his mother had warned him about, not one of them good enough for her even to speak to. It was right about this same time of year, he said, but unseasonably warm and rainy so there was this eerie white fog, and he still remembers the way it floated over the valleys, swallowing up scenery, because it seemed symbolic or something. Inside the bus the women chattered and argued and sang.

After they were checked in, Darwin went one way to be frisked and the women went another, and then there was some unlocking and locking of heavy doors by guards who acted, Darwin said, as if they had the fate of the world dangling from their key rings. And then he was stepping into a little screen cage, and on the other side of a table was his father.

Alvin Charles had lost weight. Everything sagged miserably — eyelids, cheeks, shoulders, paunch — except his hands, which rose as if offering some gift when he saw Darwin. The guard parried the move with an arm, shook his head. There must be no contact, no chance for the visitor to pass a file or a switchblade or cyanide.

Then his father smiled, and Darwin saw he'd lost a tooth, not a front one, but almost, and the dark gap made Darwin sick. His father had always been proud of his teeth; they were proof of his attention to detail.

Things were going as well as could be expected; his father had just a few small complaints — boiled coffee, powdered potatoes, no fresh fruit. He might have been describing a disappointing restaurant. Darwin's parents used to make a hobby of going to ritzy restaurants and finding fault — a chipped plate, a spot on the tablecloth, brown edges on the lettuce, too much ice in the water or not enough. The subtler the detail, the better. Sometimes the management took something off the bill.

Alvin Charles's only serious problem with prison life was the lack of time or privacy for a man to move his bowels satisfactorily. He thought maybe he'd write a letter about that. Didn't prisoners have a right to healthy elimination? He gave Darwin a feeble wink. "I'm afraid I wouldn't recommend Green Haven to my friends," he said.

"Maybe you ought to," Darwin said. He couldn't stand it that his father's attitude seemed no different, that he didn't see how radically things had changed. He should have been hating those friends and hating himself. "Your so-called friends should be in here with you."

"I don't begrudge it," his father said. "No reason why half a dozen should suffer if one can pay the price."

"There is if half a dozen broke the law," Darwin said, who had believed till then in objective good and objective bad, and that the latter was something that happened once in a while in a world clearly governed by the former. You might break the law, but it knit right back together in time to mete out just punishment and inspire contrition.

"They've got families," his father said.

"And you don't?"

"Sometimes I wonder," his father said, looking down at the floor. "Every Sunday up till now, to be exact."

"What do you expect?" Darwin started to shout. "I've still got to go to school every day. Everyone knows. They all stare at me, they're wondering what it's like having a criminal for a father, they're wondering how I can stand it, they're waiting for me to break."

Alvin Charles raised his eyebrows but kept on looking down.

"You don't have any idea what you've done to us," Darwin said.

His father sat up straight, then leaned across the table. The guard stiffened. "I put everything in your mother's name," Alvin Charles whispered indignantly.

In our room last night Darwin got up from the bed and started fumbling around in the closet for another joint. "All I wanted was some moral intensity," he said. "I used to fantasize that he did it out of a grandiose plan for me, or that Mother needed some life-or-death operation and he did it for her. I was so fucking young. All he'd ever say was, he did it because *they* were his friends. Then he said, *If you're only coming here to condemn me, son, I'd just as soon you didn't come at all.*" Darwin straightened and smoothed a joint. "Drained the energy right out of me. I told him that was the first thing he'd said that made sense."

I was sitting cross-legged on the bed, and I lifted my arms to Darwin in a gesture as hopeless as Alvin Charles's had been blindly, maddeningly hopeful when Darwin first stepped into that visitor's cage. "Please," I said. Darwin didn't move. "Please, don't smoke," I said.

"What are you talking about, 'don't smoke'?"

"For once, don't. Let me do something." I had no idea what. I thought of all the silly ways I once managed to clear the angry film from his eyes, to bring the brightness back — how he liked me to steal little presents for him; how it used to turn him on that I could pee so easily outdoors, behind a tree, in an alley; how I used to whisper all sorts of colorful Indian threats to his penis.

"Look," he said now, "there is an eagle-eyed guard who will vouch for the fact that I never passed my old man anything, and we made our peace. I had nothing to do with the fact that his blood pressure spiked into the two hundreds and killed him in a month."

I shoved Under off my lap and onto the floor. Darwin froze as I crossed the room to him, but I took his arm and led him to sit beside me on the bed.

"You know what I think?" He stared straight ahead but gripped my hand. "I think he did it to punish me. He figured that if he hung on, survived his sentence, lived on for twenty or thirty years, that one year would just kind of shrink to nothing. People would forget, my pride would heal. So instead he had to die in jail. The obituary had to slip it in: in lieu of flowers, donations to a college fund for the sons of the inmates of Green Haven State Prison. *Convicted criminal* just stuck there at the end of his life, getting more important, growing out of control." He stubbed the unlit joint into a saucer by the bed and mustered a smile. "That's History for you."

10

DARWIN CALLED TO SAY he would be only a little late getting home, and would we please hold dinner for him. The surprise of that has unsettled me, put me on guard. What do these things mean — Darwin remembering his father, Darwin thanking me afterward (for what, he isn't sure), Darwin raising my hand to his lips and kissing it before he turns over and falls asleep? How close is he going to come this time before he pulls back? If he and I ever do find ourselves on new ground, will we be able to tell it is new and step gently, and not trample it into more of the same? I have put aside my book for Human Development, *Obedience Reconsidered: The Moral Growth of the Child.* It annoys me that the literature, as Theo calls it, can't make up its mind whether we have an inborn tendency toward justice or whether we need to control one another with threats of physical pain. Where are the answers? I am baking extra bread, a rough, dark sprouted wheat — two loaves for Womancenter, two for us.

I dig the heels of my hands into the grainy dough. Punch it, flatten it. Fold and dig again. I could eat a good half of this mound uncooked, compelled by its smell of yeast. Let it rise inside me, fill me up. In the family room downstairs Either languishes loosely coiled in the glass box on which Jeremy is spending an unhealthy percentage of his income. The special branch is wired upright in one corner — Conrad is sure a tree snake needs the hint of a tree — but Either ignores it. Next to the case, a plug-in radiator whose heat we cannot afford runs constantly. Under snoozes here during the day, his cozy hearth, but for Either, poor creature, it's not enough, it's not Ecuador, nothing like it, I know. Its silver skin has faded to dull gray, its golden markings to a dirty mustard. Its eyes, rarely open, look remote and cloudy. Such a simple, concentrated body. That first week we couldn't tear ourselves away from it; its slow assertion entranced us, frightened us a little, proof of life beyond the clutter of arms and legs. Now it seems helpless as an amputee. Meanwhile, in the storage room the mouse cage swarms with a first generation of offspring, busy chewing up newspaper and fighting to race around in the treadwheel. Jeremy has frozen some mice in plastic sandwich bags. He calls it harvesting.

From where I stand at the kitchen counter I can see the loop of stiff twine and dusty shells dangling in the window beside the front door. Nimu's gift. I remember the day I tore the storage room apart to find it — pawed through boxes of infant clothes, physics books, yellowed stationery from my mother with a different Bible verse on each sheet, gifts from Darwin's mother, Avon aftershave and body lotion. I never did come across the special stone.

I had just gotten back from a Pittsburgh hospital where a Dr. Rodeheaver, a man half my mother's size who wore starched shirts and vests, had decided that electroshock therapy was the only way to make her forget whatever it was that depressed her so mysteriously, whatever it was that had caused her to push away from the dinner table at New Progress and run outside into the subfreezing dark with Boy Commander in pursuit. When he brought her back and turned her over to Samuel, she threw herself onto her bed and writhed like a snake. The simile was Samuel's, "just like a forked snake" — each time he repeated it, he had to fumble for a cough drop to control his pleasure and disbelief. Whatever my mother may have forgotten because of the treatments — my face at first, the existence of my children, the deprivations of life at New Progress, to which she kept pleading to be returned — she remembered Nimu, kept coming back to her, muttering crazily vague accusations, calling her names.

Before that trip to Pittsburgh, it had been years since I'd really thought about Nimu. Afterward, I searched my memory so urgently that it went dead, blank. No visions. Hanging the belt was all I could think of to do, a desperate attempt to restore her and protect myself maybe against this thing that was happening to my mother, that made no sense. If only I could have conjured up the tough, upturned hands of that final morning — the hands, the arms, that bothersome dress, too tight around the middle, hastily, crookedly pulled on, and the denseness of the body inside it. And now — if she could just show herself to me once more the way she did in that chilly classroom in New Progress, where bodies watched each other suspiciously, called out stiff answers across expanses of cold, empty space. She seemed to rise right out of the concrete floor that once, out of the emptiness, offering me the whole palpable world.

It was the Devil playing with my mind, Samuel said; then he changed and called it a lesson in something from God. I still claim that it was her, Nimu, that for a moment the combined strength of her love and my need had cut away thousands of miles. But she is dead now. She has been dead for years.

To me, those thousands of miles away, the death had seemed sudden. *I saw it all coming,* my mother wrote. *Something was bound to happen. It was only a matter of time.*

When the men ruled, the Janca had moved every few years to find fresh soil for their gardens. They set fire to the round hut and rebuilt it in a new spot that they'd hacked and burned clear. The first year we were with the tribe, my mother taught the stricken women about compost, and it was probably that as much as God's Word that saved them. They dug everything they could back into the soil — forest debris, the unused parts of vegetables, animal blood and bones, the endless ashes from their fires — everything but human waste, where my mother drew the line. And the gardens prospered, and the women started to feel secure in that one spot.

But in the year I left the tribe, all that changed. It was during the dry season, and two children apparently wandered farther than they were supposed to down the riverbed and found a flash-light battery stuck in the hardening mud. They thought it a most extraordinary treasure. Nimu slapped it from their hands and, though my mother tried to explain to her what it was, rolled it up in a large leaf and returned it to the Tiwano, where she gouged a deep hole in the exposed bank and buried it. Then a few days later one of the women came running back from the garden in a panic, swearing she'd heard in the distance a strange roar, even harsher than the white man's wood-bee.

A very sad time, came the wire from my mother, the reason I had to cancel my plans to return that first summer to visit the tribe, the reason my mother could not fly to the States to see me. With great sadness the Janca had folded up and strung together all the belongings they could carry, and trekked for two long, hot days up the river. No one could bring herself to set a torch to the precious round hut they had to leave behind.

It was hard labor, clearing the new ground, and as much as the women wished for the safety of the deeper forest, they had to settle where the trees were younger, more shallow-rooted, less dense. Rather than attempt the vaulting open thatch of the old hut, they wove a tight ring of small, individual roofs. So I suppose it was inevitable that near the end of my second winter at New Progress the tribe was found. It was still the rainy season, and even the carrier from the Principle Mission hadn't been seen for months, when three strange men marched into the sodden village one morning, claiming it was a good-will visit — a government anthropologist, an official of the Ecuadorian State Petroleum Company, both armed with pistols, and their sheepish guide.

In all good will, they explained that the tribe needed to move to a spot downriver again, far downriver, near Macuma, where the forest had been cleared, right next to the village of the Qui-chua. The government, which needed all the land the Janca had called theirs, would help them construct larger, stronger huts, and they would have access to a government-run school, a gro-cery store, a medical facility.

Nimu and the other women turned to my mother, their eyes trusting her to decide. She knew there was no choice. Knew it would be of no importance to these men that the Janca were happy in her school, healthy on their diet of manioc and plantain, monkey and fish. They had everything they needed. The only illness for which they had no remedy was the slight case of the sniffles the petroleum official brought with him. Nimu was not the only one who caught it and took sick during the hike to the new clearing, where there was a government clinic, which none of them could trust enough to visit. Many of the tribe suffered for weeks with fever and coughing, but Nimu was too old to regather her strength. She lay in her hammock and let her lungs fill up. Within two months she was dead.

Terribly unfortunate circumstances, my mother went on from the new village. *This has caused quite a disruption in our lives. Though we rejoice for Nimu, for she is with our Father in heaven, three of the boys are acting strange. I write "boys" out of habit; they are young men now, of course. Naemwi and recently Kaewi are fathers, and the third is soon to be. They blame the White Men for bringing an evil spirit. At night they have their own fire apart and persuade the younger ones, as well as certain no-good fellows from the Quichua, to sit with them and whisper plans to hunt the White Man down and spear him. It is best that you stay with Samuel again this summer. I will try to visit during the month of July.*

I read the news over again, waiting to feel the grief I thought I should feel. Mail from the new village was only slightly faster and more reliable than it had been in the days when it came through the Principle Mission, and the letter had taken almost a month to reach me. For almost a month I had been addressing complaints and promises to Nimu when no one else was around, the living woman who had made her appearance in Samuel's classroom, who still could listen and inspire. The idea of death in relation to her just didn't register.

Besides, it was late spring when she died, and I had spent the whole long winter pining for a boy in a green satin jacket and fighting my indefinite restriction to the school. For several Saturdays after my trip to town, a car with a powerful engine blasted up the drive around midnight, the driver leaned on the horn, and from rolled-down windows the cry went up, "Hannie, we want sheep-eyes Hannie." Uncle Samuel finally shuffled into the police station and signed papers making such night quests a crime.

As the days lengthened and warmed and the spinach and chard came into leaf, I became aware that there were other boys besides the mysterious Rich — eleven of them were lined up right in front of me. None was as worthy of my fascination and energy, maybe, but they were all ridiculously available. Maybe they weren't as sophisticated as the boys in town, but hadn't I learned a thing or two about that? I knew I liked kissing. Again and again that winter I had dreamed myself back into kissing Rich, felt again that lift along my nerves, almost like fear, like standing dizzy on the verge of some unknown spell. And it seemed reasonable to conclude that boys liked kissing me. It hadn't seemed to bother Chuck or Rich that I wasn't beautiful; in fact, it had been kissing that made me begin to think maybe I was a little bit. My hair was finally long enough to pull back from a center part into a rubber band. When my uncle wasn't around, I liked to make it swing from side to side as I walked, the way I had seen girls do that long-lost day in town.

I cannot remember exactly when or why I first approached Valerie's brother, Roger, a skinny, prim tenth-grader like me. With very narrow shoulders and head and the mandatory boys' haircut — close-shaved around the ears, above which his light orange curls sprang up incorrigibly — he looked a little like a flower on a stem. "Would you like to kiss me?" I asked him one afternoon in the back hall. "No, I would not," he replied, offended, but I grabbed him anyway, and he resisted hardly at all. Soon we were meeting in the aluminum barn on chilly afternoons, on the back seat of the schoolbus, clouding all the windows around us with our breath.

I didn't ask any questions the first time Valerie arrived with Roger. She had been avoiding me since the supply run when I had let her and everyone else down, but now she made no mention of wickedness or sin. Instead she said she would be standing guard because Roger was her brother. Then she sat way up front in the driver's seat and practiced with the clutch and the gear shift, simulating the sounds of acceleration with her throat. After a short time she got up and swung her way back, calling out, "Last stop, everyone out."

Roger and I looked up, puzzled — we had barely begun.

"I am protecting your reputation because it's my brother." She always spoke without inflection, at an even pace, to make her nonsense sound like inarguable common sense. At night she sang imploringly to Jesus.

At the following session Valerie let us fumble a little longer; at the one after that, she took the next-to-last seat and pretended not to watch. Somehow I understood, although she could never admit it, that I was teaching her something, some knowledge I possessed the way other kids possessed physical coordination or a good memory, by chance. In between these lessons, in a slow monotone Valerie told me pieces of her past. Her mother had died of a viper bite in East Africa, and Valerie, barely nine years old, had assumed full care of little Roger and helped her father run the dispensary. Then her father had succumbed to sleeping sickness, and the three had been shipped back to the States like failures, her father to a Home in Ohio, she and Roger to foster parents so strict that Samuel's school was heaven afterward. Valerie bore up well through each of these hardships: that was her refrain, that was what she'd become known for. She used to take a bus once a month to visit her father at the Home, and then one day he didn't recognize her. She dropped to her knees beside his bed and recited the Lord's Prayer. He began waving his arms as if to bat the words out of the air, and knocked the water in a pitcher on his nightstand all over her. She was sure the Devil had taken over his body. She didn't know how she was able to bear up under that, but she had.

Poor Valerie. It didn't occur to me to sympathize with her, for she herself didn't. We compared our stories and judged them equally extraordinary, equal in dramatic suffering. On that basis our stuttering friendship resumed. And actually we all thought her story was already moving toward the happy ending when she would graduate and go off to Warren Bible College on full scholarship, the pride of Samuel's school — though there was that one afternoon it faltered, when I might have caught a glimpse of the truth to come.

My affair with Roger lasted until the night he had to be taken by ambulance to the hospital emergency room in town. He was running a high fever, and his testicles were engorged to the point of pain, even danger. They had been too intensely stimulated without release.

Though I think he guessed I was a key figure in this disruption, Uncle Samuel took full responsibility himself. Maybe he had not been as clear as he could have been about certain issues, and early the next morning he called the student body together to address any confusion we might be harboring about what was right for Christian boys and girls and what was wrong, for the Bible was clear on these matters.

"The Lord be praised for one thing," he told us. "The act of fornication did not actually take place. Now what exactly does fornication mean?" He looked out over a classroom of bowed heads. We knew he preferred to answer his own questions, and in the cold, pale light, he began a methodical presentation of the anatomical facts of reproduction. I listened avidly — it was not kissing that caused babies, as Valerie had threatened and I myself secretly hoped; it was this other complexity, which kept calling up images of what I had seen spying with the younger Janca children on Bai and Naemwi. I understood then what Roger and I had been groping toward (and how close I had come with Kaewi). The physical procedure struck me as a bit bizarre, but I had had a taste of lust and trusted that it would sustain me in strange territory. The others sat in wide-eyed shock at the words spilling from Uncle Samuel once he got started. He described positions as if giving a lesson in military strategy. He didn't even pause to prime himself with candy, and having lost its saliva over the years, his mouth kept sticking on words like *genital* and *sperm*.

"But fornication is not the immediate danger, oh no," Samuel went on with increasing energy. "The enemy is too smart to leave it to such an awkward, inconvenient act as that. He has trickier ways to ambush our souls. What about harmless touching — a caress here, a friendly hug there — what could possibly be wrong with that? you ask in all innocence. And the answer is, Nothing, in and of itself, if you could stop there. *If.* But the flesh is stubborn. The next thing you know you're wheedling a little kiss, an innocent peck on the cheek, nothing in and of itself, except that" — his voice deepened triumphantly — "the next thing you know you've got one mouth glued to another mouth, including tongues." (That last word he forced in two disgusted syllables.) He went into the perils of petting, from cause to effect, the inevitable downward path. For once when his eyes glazed and he forgot his original point to go rambling off into his own associations, his students, though embarrassed, secretly urged him on. There were the hungry women of Britain, throwing themselves half naked at the American servicemen; there were the farmers' daughters in Illinois. Though none of us dared move a muscle, our bodies yearned, mouths watered.

When I think of it now, it could have been this fluky revolution at New Progress that made me so optimistic — so blindly optimistic, Darwin says — about social change. Roger came home from the hospital a sort of hero. And because Valerie insisted to everyone that *I* was innocent and had had no contact with her brother, that she had witnessed nothing unusual between us, everyone knew it had to have been me who had almost slipped into sin, and after that I could kiss any boy I wanted.

An eye sharper than my uncle's might have noticed the boys and girls gliding into pairs, letting hands brush, glances meet. Soon the schoolbus in the barn was more popular than C. W. Burpo's Bible Institute in the Main Room. Everyone was careful to avoid the terrible act of fornication, now that we knew exactly what it was. We teased ourselves instead with the easier and forgivable misdemeanors Samuel had proposed to us. Except that now we also understood the importance of release. Oh God, those afternoons come back to me and I want to exult, cheer for the frenzy of touch and then that utterly private giving in to the still-not-quite-known. That strange pleasure-pain our bodies just past childhood could not quite believe. We had to try it again and again, to make sure. Driving the bus on Saturdays, Reverend Samuel seemed not to recognize or even notice the sour, bleachy smell of spilled boy.

>> .·. <<

I am thirty-three now, I have had four babies, it is only sex. A twelve-second spasm, Darwin says, triggered by certain stimuli to the anatomy. There are books with diagrams, owner's manuals, anyone can do it, everyone does it, you can do it yourself, the women's magazines recommend that, but for some reason, as with tickling and back-scratching, it's not the same.

Valerie held out the longest against temptation, but it was no more than holding out; she didn't judge or fight back. She often sat as self-appointed monitor in the bus, watching the others with a tense fascination. One day she asked me if I would kiss her. "Because we're friends," she droned, "and it's not as wicked as kissing boys."

I said yes without hesitation. She had accompanied Roger and me in the bus so many times that she tended to merge in my mind with him, with kissing — it was all in the family. And I was the acknowledged expert.

"I guess I just need a little help getting started," she said with a flat laugh as I sat down beside her on her bunk. I waited. She fidgeted, blushed, her breathing got loud. Her scornful eyebrows knit above her nose and she said angrily, "Well, aren't you going to show me?"

"You just do it," I said. "There's nothing to show."

All of a sudden Valerie moaned and started twisting her hands. "I can't," she said. "I don't know how."

"Everyone knows how." I wasn't going to make it easy for her. "Think about all those books you peek at in the drugstore," I said, settling an old debt. "Then you'll remember."

"I don't read them. I'm too afraid."

I softened. "Think about when you were little."

"I can't. I don't know how. You do it. Nobody ever kissed me. I think it's wicked. I never kissed anyone. Not even when Mama died. After she was dead, they said, *Now you can kiss her goodbye.* So Roger went first and then me." She took her hands away from her eyes and looked at me, stricken. "It was awful. She was so stiff and a funny color, I didn't want my mouth to touch her. And someone said, *We ought to drop the lid now, she's started to smell.*" Her head fell forward with a shudder. "I tried to tell them I hadn't done it yet, but Father said, *That is enough.*"

I took her by the shoulders and tried to shake her head upright. She kept crumpling. Finally I planted a kiss on her forehead, at the hairline. "There," I said. "Easy as pie." She looked up and I caught her cheek with another kiss. She flinched, and turned the other one, which I kissed. "Now you try it," I said. "Lick your lips first, then sort of dry them on the back of your hand." Valerie was leaning toward me. "Try not to spit" was my final advice before our mouths touched.

Valerie looked stunned. After a few seconds she threw herself back on the bed and drew a deep sigh. "That was a kiss," she said. A short laugh escaped her. "I did it. We were kissing." She had a clump of sheet in each fist, she looked frightened. "I did it, I did it, I did it." She beat the mattress three times for emphasis.

I patted the back of one clenched hand. *"Masa masawi,"* I promised, the words Nimu used to chant over and over as she gathered me into her arms and stroked and kissed away crankiness, frustration, even the tears that she herself had released with her nettle whips; words I no longer murmur to my own children, since in one way or another they have all managed to lug their problems and struggles beyond a mother's comfort, or at least to think they have. *Masa masawi,* my mother wrote on one of her index cards. *Literal: your heart will be heartened. Idiom: your life will improve.* "Masa masawi" — words of a dead woman, they come back to me now with the sting of tears. I wish I could feel her frank, unconditional embrace one more time.

I touched Valerie's hair, her face, I loosened her grip on the sheet and stroked her hand. Her eyes had gone blank, as if fol-

lowing my touch around her body from the inside, expecting it
to hurt, not believing it hadn't. It was as if we had slipped out of
time, shed all its fine stories, decorations, and instead of the
highest-ranking Girl Guardian and self-appointed handmaiden
of Christ, I held an injured child.

11

. .
.

"M-MATTHEW DID SOME good w-work today," Dooley says
as he releases him into my custody. Matthew stiffens his mouth
against a smile.

"I can't wait to see it," I say, trying to hide my skepticism. It
seems too good to be true. He has been a terror to everyone all
week, but worst to himself. The other night I caught him by the
bare arm on his way from bedroom to bath. Where some men
have tattoos, Matthew now has a cross, two deep scratches risen
to welts on his skin. "Who did this to you?" I asked. "How did
this happen?" I pulled his elfin chin around to face me. "I was just
fooling with Jeremy's compass," he said, deliberately vacating his
eyes. "What do you mean, fooling?" I demanded. He flushed a
little and shrugged. "I put it back." Now outside Dooley's office
his eyes are red and puffy from crying.

"Well, it's not something you can hang on the refrigerator, is
it, Matthew?" Dooley winks at him and the boy gives a liquid
sniff and looks away. I wonder how this man can act so cheerful
with us, unless Matthew is not telling him the truth. "But I venture to guess you will see some results of it one of these days.
What do you think, Matthew?"

Matthew bolts for the Bus.

"And how're things going with Darwin?" Dooley asks, turning
his good humor on me.

"Oh, I'm working on him," I lie, thinking that that is the

good-humored thing to say, then feeling that it is an awful thing to admit — it sounds so inconsiderate, relentless. Dooley nods as though I have confirmed something he has thought all along. *Tell me what it is,* I want to say. *Tell me what to do.* But my pride stops me. Darwin and I will manage. For now, we are breathing very carefully amidst the fallout of the other night, waiting to see what will remain when it disperses. He has been coming home for dinner every evening, dinner and the inevitable challenge from Matthew. I guess it is foolish of me to keep hoping that a meal together can be nice — Matthew is bound to talk about matters slimy or intestinal, and Rachel, to put down her fork and flee the table gagging. Maybe they're even in cahoots. You can tell she basks in our pleading, "But Rachel, you're too thin." She lets Darwin coax her back into her seat, but she refuses the rest of her meal. I think she's as proud of being thin as she is of being so flexible. In a leotard, that limber backbone of hers sticks out like a string of small cysts.

After dinner Darwin has been watching television with Benjamin and Rachel. The other night, when Matthew went into a rage because they wouldn't turn to "Tales of the Dark Beyond," Darwin carried him upstairs to his room firmly, though looking a little perplexed, almost scared. Matthew flailed all the way, then fought to get past his father and out the door again, so that Darwin finally had to hold it shut from the outside, whereupon Matthew began throwing himself against it and screaming. It was I who gave in first, worrying out loud that he would hurt himself. So Darwin shrugged and opened the door, and Matthew charged into him with such ferocity that it was all Darwin could do to buckle up and drop his hands to his groin.

We have been staying up later than I am used to, watching the eleven o'clock news — Ronald Reagan is gathering his forces; Cambodians wander hollow-eyed and starving; security for the pope's visit gridlocks downtown D.C. We even laugh together at Jane Fonda in her new salon grandly breaking a bottle of champagne over the steel plates of a body-building machine; at Jerry Falwell and his road show — Jesus was no sissy, he preaches, fist raised, to the multitudes in Harrisburg. (Nor is Uncle Samuel the eccentric of New Progress anymore. Having revised his predictions of impending doom in favor of a nation of Christian soldiers born again, he has been appointed patriotism consultant for the town's upcoming centennial celebration. A guest sermon of his, "Life Is a Boomerang," is in great demand.) I can look over at Darwin and laugh at all that. "Why shouldn't I?" I ask him when it is obvious what he is thinking. "I don't see my father as anything like that man." "You don't?" he asks back with exaggerated concern. "Let's not start," I say, and he bows his head in assent.

When there is nothing left to watch we go up to bed together, and lie down side by side, and say good night politely. In the silence I can almost hear him thinking, *Reach for me; make the first move this one more time, and I won't push you away.* But I feel so heavy and tired, so certain these friendly relations won't last. Once I put my hand on his chest and felt him stiffen, begin to control his breathing, then I began to think about my breathing, until pretty soon I had to take my hand back, before we both passed out from lack of air.

"If Darwin gets in to see you," I tell Dooley now as he holds open the door for me to leave, "I wouldn't ask him that question about sex."

"What question about sex?" he asks.

"It's funny, in the beginning Darwin and I used to talk about it all the time — you know, what he wanted, and what I wanted, what it'd been like, who was doing it with whom, how and when and where. Everyone we knew talked about it, maybe because we needed to stop thinking about all that violence and death going on. Now we both find the subject sort of embarrassing."

On the way home in the car Matthew asks me if I believe in ghosts. "No," I answer, my mind divided between the muffler, which is getting ominously loud, and the question Dooley never asked. A minute later I started hedging that denial. "It depends on what you mean by ghosts, Matthew."

"I believe in 'em," he says. He is psyching himself up for tonight, Halloween, when he will put on a hideous rubber mask, with a bloody eye socket, scars, and bad teeth, wrap the rest of himself in a sheet, and probably terrorize all the younger children he can.

"I believe the spirits of people who have died can live on in the hearts and minds of their loved ones." He has heard this deliberate, instructive tone of mine before. He fixes his eyes on something ahead, follows it all the way back over his right shoulder as we drive past, repeats the process. "I almost believe that those spirits live on without the loved ones, but certainly not floating around with arms and legs and stuff, and certainly not trying to frighten people and make them miserable — why would they want to do that?" He gives no sign of listening. "But maybe they connect up with each other into one humongous spirit —"

"Am I Grandfather Worden's loved one?" Matthew interrupts.

"Of course. We all are."

"Even if he never saw me? How can he love me when he doesn't even know me?"

"But he does," I blurt out. "I'm sure he does." Matthew is looking at me quizzically, sidelong. "I guess it's just a feeling I have, Matthew."

"Well, I didn't ever know *him*. Why does he have to live on in me?"

"I've wished like anything he could have lived to see you children and you could have known him. When you get down to it, I've wished like anything *I* could have known him. I never really did, you know." I feel my eyes smarting, my son staring at me with a puzzled frown. "I'm really being silly now. I should be more careful driving, I'll run us right off the road."

We pull up finally in front of our door, but neither of us moves to get out. At the same moment we sigh and turn each other's way. Matthew looks strained, as if he is listening to something far away that he must work to translate. Finally, solemnly, he tells me, "The ghost of Grandfather Worden is in my mind."

I don't dare ask him what he means, because it's clear he is sharing with me exactly what he knows. "I'm not surprised," I say, pulling him over into a quick one-armed hug that he doesn't encourage or resist. "He's pretty much all around us, isn't he?"

"And he's mad," Matthew says.

That surprises me. "Why is he mad?"

"He says maybe because those Indians wiped him out and he didn't even do anything to them. He wasn't even carrying a gun or anything, and they wiped him out." The tension rises in his voice. "It wasn't fair."

Matthew has never before shown anything but a sort of visceral yet detached fascination with his grandfather's fate. For a moment I am speechless. "My father knew that might happen, Matthew, if he did what he did. It was sort of all right with him. I mean, he was willing to take that chance."

Matthew shakes his head hard. "He didn't know. He says he knows now, but now it's too late."

Another surprise, and for a moment Matthew's utter certainty unbalances me. I get a jumbled glimpse of my father flailing against his attackers. For a split second I catch the sound of stone ripping through flesh, cruel cheers, a cry of pain. It all flashes through my mind so fast, all at once, as though it has been ready, waiting. And my first reaction is to yell at Matthew — how can he say such things, make up such ridiculous stories? He has tried and tried and finally found my vulnerable spot, figured the precise angle of assault. But the worried, almost doomed expression on his face stops me; this possibility he has somehow stumbled on has disturbed him as much as it disturbs me. He is vulnerable too. And I'm actually relieved to set aside my own confusion and grope for something to make him feel better. A child should not look so hopeless.

"You know, Matthew, nothing you can do will ever change what happened. Whatever happened . . . happened."

"I wasn't even there," he pleads. "He doesn't even know me."

"I know you weren't. Me neither. I think it was just a terrible thing that happened to Grandfather." My eyes are smarting again; I open the car door decisively. "But there's nothing we can do about it, except for I guess feeling sorry." I realize that's the last thing in the world I've ever wanted to do.

"I do feel sorry," Matthew says, his voice hitching and his

lower lip turning out and down. "I told Dooley I feel sorry, and I told Grandfather Worden too." He starts to sob quietly.

"That was good of you, Matthew," I tell him, handing him a wad of tissues. "It really was. In fact" — I can't think of what to say to comfort him — "you've really taken on more than your share." He looks up at me, suspicious, grateful, scrubbing at his eyes. "I can see now how much you've worried about what to do, and how much you've done. You've worried a lot, haven't you?" I ask him, and at least he gives me a slow nod before we go inside.

Waiting for us in the living room with the other kids is Darwin, home early from work. He knows Wednesday is the afternoon I take Matthew to see Dooley, and he is wearing his betrayed expression, betrayed but today perhaps willing to forgive me for plunging into one more project with what he calls my congenital zeal for reform.

I can't sort everything out. The image of my father afraid and regretful, Matthew's handsome face swollen with sadness, and now Jeremy, Benjamin, and Rachel grouped attentively around their father — these are not exactly familiar portraits. Beside Darwin on the couch there is a flat purple box, the reason why his righteous look gives way to eagerness, excitement. As though they have been waiting for the moment of our appearance, he plucks off the lid with a flourish and begins to pull out costumes, one after another, magically shaking them out before us, letting them expand, fill up the chair, cover the table, all from the one box. The children are stunned silent, incredulous.

There is a cloud of pink tulle for Rachel, a halo headband, foil wings, and a child-sized body stocking so she won't freeze. She tries to take this sudden extravagance in stride — she has never needed anything from us, it would have been fine with her to walk the neighborhood as the hobo, bearded with burned cork, that she assembled a week ago in a dry run. But soon she is hugging the dress to her chest and twirling around the living room. Benjamin, always easily satisfied, grabs his rather generic-looking jumpsuit with LUKE SKYWALKER written across its

back, yanks his shoes off without untying them, and starts climbing into it, as though nothing else in the world mattered beside
that probably flammable bag of blue and white rayon. I help him
tuck everything in, venture a few tickles, always grateful for his
blatant pleasure, his comic relief, though as I hold his trembling
undersize body between my hands I feel a twinge of guilt — he is
always so quick to act happy, to plunge all his formidable energy
into playing happy little brother within happy family, hoping the
rest of us will play too.

Maybe the rest of us are hoping also, trying harder. Maybe
everyone's looking at all those masks and costumes and thinking,
Maybe we aren't who we think we are. Matthew gets a one-piece
monkey suit, King Kong, Jr., Darwin tells him as he zips him in
from the top of his head to the base of his curled tail. It is a step
up, anyway, from that gory mask — is that how Matthew pictures my father's ghost, I wonder? My father's corpse — I blot
the too-fresh image from my mind, make myself focus on Matthew, who is doing a funny little hunched-over dance in Rachel's
footsteps. We all laugh. He galumps out to the kitchen dragging
his arms.

Darwin offers Jeremy the baggy white body and bulbous snout
of Snoopy. Then he unrolls something blue and red — a second
Superman leotard for himself, to enable him to wash his uniform
after every wearing, which will maybe take care of the itch between his legs. Matthew is back, holding high a banana; he peels
it amidst loud, snuffling monkey noises and begins to force it
through the mouth hole of his suit. The pulp is getting all over the
plastic muzzle; the snuffling and the dance grow wilder. In a
matter of minutes it's as if Matthew has drawn off all the happy
energy in the room to feed his own frenzy. Rachel has edged away
from him, the delight on her face dulled into indifference. Benjamin freezes on his perch on the back of the couch while I gear
up for the inevitable, Matthew being Matthew. Then Darwin
says, "Now, all except Benjamin's and mine are rentals. So we
have to be a little careful." And to everyone's surprise, Matthew
puts the mashed banana down on the table and settles for a few
last restrained lunges around the room.

Except for Darwin, though, the rest of us are more tentative now. It is hard to rise twice to the same occasion. When he pulls the pink leotard out of the box with a snap and then with another snap pulls out the pink tights, the children look over at me cautiously. They must have assumed, as I did, that I wouldn't be included or interested in the business of dressing up. Then he raises on his fist a pink rubber mask, the kind that fits over your whole head. "May I present the Pink Panther?" he says, and begins to da-dum the movie theme.

"Dad," Jeremy says, but the word seems to defeat his voice. "Dad," he says louder, "I already have a costume."

"But this Snoopy one's fantastic." Darwin is impervious, he is enjoying the younger children's gratitude so much. "Besides, I got a great deal on these things — you know, like a professional discount."

"I prefer to be a snake charmer, Dad," Jeremy persists. "Me and Either. I plan on putting him in a basket, and I'm going to wear a turban, and that vest of Mom's with . . ."

As Jeremy's words sink in, Darwin looks nervous — they weren't in the script he studied; he can't figure out what is expected of him next. "You can't cart that thing around in the cold. It'd kill it for sure."

"I'm not going out this year. I've already made my decision. I intend to sit on the floor in the front hall. The kids'll view Either and me through the window."

"Aren't you losing sight of what's important about Halloween?" I ask him.

Jeremy clears his throat. "According to the *Encyclopaedia Britannica,* what's important about Halloween is that it opens paths between the human world and the supernatural, so the souls of the dead can revisit —"

"Christ," Darwin says, turning away and stomping out to the kitchen. Rachel flutters after him.

"Jeremy," I say sternly, "you know I'm talking about collecting UNICEF money."

"Halloween is an ancient pagan festival, Mom," Jeremy says. "Collecting UNICEF money is like a recent invention."

"Well, it's a good cause," I say. "There are a lot of needy children in the world."

"I'll send them some of my allowance," Jeremy says, who has tied up every cent he will see for the next year with Either and the mice.

I remind him that the draft from the open door may be too much for Either. He says he is going to put the heating pad in the basket.

Darwin stands in the doorway to the kitchen, Rachel's arm around his middle, his eyes wide with injury.

"Well, it's not *that* important," I remind us all.

Rachel doesn't believe me, makes one last try. "The littler kids might be scared away." She speaks slowly, looking straight at Jeremy, then rolls her eyes up toward her father above her.

But Jeremy refuses the hint. "I have no intention of being scary," he says. "I intend to be mysterious."

Later that night, when we are alone, Darwin will ask me, "Why does that kid always have to make me feel like a jerk?"

And I will remember Alvin Charles, take a slow breath, and attempt the most neutral tone. "Maybe you shouldn't jump to the conclusion that he's doing things deliberately to get on your nerves."

But he will insist, "You are always siding with him against me. I haven't got a chance."

The price of harmony is too high. It is all too tricky, too new. Right then I could have agreed with Darwin, commiserated with him, confessed that each time I stepped over the electric cord looping out of Either's basket, as I answered the door and doled out apples and dimes, I wondered why for once Jeremy couldn't have gone along with the moment, foregone his sacred bright ideas, arguments, defenses. After all, hadn't I even put aside a certain fear of nonsense and struggled into that pink leotard with its rope of tail? Why did Jeremy have to ruin everything?

But I didn't. Because old words, old alliances, came easier. "Maybe if your interest in him could be a little less conditional," I said, my voice flaring with indignation. "I mean, you expect him to get into the same things you're into, at the same moment that you are. And when he doesn't pay you immediate and absolute homage, you pack up and go away."

"Earth Mother knows everything."

"He needs room to maneuver."

"I give him plenty of room to maneuver. You're the one with the one-way tickets to Ecuador."

"He's got to figure out who he is."

"So let him. Stop trying to burden him with all your stuff."

"Maybe if you weren't so scared to give him a little something yourself."

He squinted at me for a long time, then asked in a defeated tone, "So what's this 'mysterious' shit? He makes it sound like some kind of threat."

I almost did what I have always done — tried to decipher the boys for Darwin, Darwin for the boys. But then I pictured Jeremy sitting framed in the front window like an idol, pudgy face smeared with burned cork, balancing a huge knot of twisted sheet on his head, and tunelessly running up and down the scales on an old recorder, and all the old answers failed. "I just guess there *is* something mysterious about Jeremy," I conceded. Though of course from the depths of the basket in front of him, the snake never lifted its head.

12

· ·
·

IT WAS AN IMPULSE, nothing I could resist or think through, that drove me to the door of Theo Balch's cluttered office instead of home to Sugarland. I had sat through my Fundamentals of Storytelling lab in a state of distraction, only vaguely aware of the project on Aesop's fables being presented by a group of my classmates. My mind kept going back to Theo and a lecture of his that morning in which he had drifted almost shyly into the subject of his current research.

It has to do with a neurological syndrome that makes people so immune to pain that they don't protect themselves from injury, or get care if injury occurs. The bodily danger never registers. Theo has been working on preparing questionnaires to send to the several dozen reported cases of this condition (with a special plea for cooperation to their parents, since few have survived to adulthood), asking them to write down their solutions to a series of simple moral dilemmas. Although he would rather it were otherwise, he is resigned to confirming the hypothesis that if you don't experience physical suffering your moral development gets arrested.

As he talked about the basis for his hypothesis in the literature, it seemed that he was looking at me more than anyone else. I felt exposed, as if he were making direct connections not only to what I had told him about my father and the Janca but also to things I hadn't told him — that my whole family, for instance, was on the verge of falling apart. I kept thinking he was about to spill The Answer, take the step (for someone who knew as much as he did, it would have to be easy) from neatly derived theory to the muddle I was living: why, wherever you looked, was there all this hurting going on? The longer he refused to cross the gap, the stronger was my urge to pull him.

I found him in his office changed into shorts and a T-shirt and pedaling a stationary bicycle, a book propped on its rack above the handlebars; he acknowledged me with a smile that looked more like a grimace, slowed down, mopped his brow and beard with a handful of towel, but didn't stop.

"Sorry to interrupt," I said in a loud voice, though the bike was making only a faint liquid hum. Theo shook his head — *Don't mention it* — and kept on pedaling. "I just wanted to tell you, things are starting to make a little sense." He raised his eyebrows and picked up speed. "Just the way you said they would."

"I said?" He was panting heavily. "Which things?"

My blood rose at the thought of Matthew's gouged cross: it was a warning to be cautious. I had learned with Dooley how easily I could be led into confessing things.

"Is that any fun?" I asked Theo of his bike.

"I wouldn't exactly call it fun," he panted.

"What are you doing it for?"

"So I can feel good afterward."

" 'Good' as in 'moral'?" I asked.

He looked at me curiously, then dug his chin into his chest and made the pedals race for maybe fifteen seconds before he stomped them to a halt. "Whoa," he said. I watched him catch his breath. "I guess there is something moral about it. Staying in shape is sort of a responsibility." He swung one leg over the seat and dismounted.

"Please don't stop for me."

"No problem." His nylon shorts seemed very skimpy. "I've been on that thing for almost an hour. I used to run, before my knees gave out. I was just getting into marathons." He stretched his T-shirt taut for me to read MARINE CORPS '78 printed across a slightly stunted Washington Monument. "Trained a hundred miles a week for this, and by the day of the race I'd done enough Motrin to give myself a stomach ulcer. I ran it anyway, in three hours and forty-two minutes." I made noises to show I was impressed. "Now I can't jog forty yards." It was almost a boast. "And my knees ache pretty much constantly."

"But you feel good," I suggested.

He bent one leg back, grabbed the foot in his hand and pressed its heel into his buttock. "I get these cramps in my quadriceps," he said.

"But after you hurt yourself enough, you can feel proud of yourself," I repeated.

"Actually, Hannah," he said, shoving the towel up under his shirt into his armpits, "at a certain level of physical stress, the brain starts releasing its pain-killing hormones, giving you a natural high. That's really all I meant by 'good.' "

We looked at each other and then turned away, both wondering if I was going to be able to leave it at that. I took a what-the-hell breath and caught the smell of man's sweat. "But you don't really think it takes pain to turn people into decent, acceptable human beings? It seems to me that when people get hurt, all they want to do is hurt back."

"I wish it were that simple," Theo said, combing a hand through his thin wet hair, leaving the top in four ridges with wide channels of scalp visible in between. "You know I'd be the last person to endorse morality-by-threat, Hannah, but pain can lead to positive ends. If we know how painful, as it were, pain can be, we're more likely to try not to inflict it on other people."

"If we happen to know them and like them, maybe. If we don't . . ."

"Maybe if we let ourselves really get to know people," he said, pulling on his beard and watching me with round blue eyes, "we'd have to like them."

I felt a surge along my nerves, a sort of thrill that turned quickly to fear. "One of my sons," I blurted, "is, well, a little different. He's very aggressive. It's almost as if he has that neurological condition you were talking about, a mild case."

"There are no mild cases, Hannah," Theo said, settling his hips against his desk. His patient tone acknowledged that I was trying to change the subject. "At this point in your reading you are aware certainly that a wide range of aggressive behavior is considered normal in young boys."

All at once, the reason why I was in his office, talking to him that way, the confusion of reasons, overwhelmed me. There was no way back to a posture of detached curiosity, nothing to do but plunge forward. "Punishment never seemed to have any effect on him except to make things worse. I've been taking him to see a therapist. Now instead of abusing the rest of us, he abuses himself. If I only knew how the whole business started, like what I did wrong. I hate to see him hurting himself. It hurts me so much." The truth of that struck like a blow. I started to cry.

"Oh, God," Theo said.

I covered my face with my hands, and cried harder because I'd disappointed him. I felt his hand on my shoulder and sank under it into the chair in the corner. "I don't see how anything positive will ever come from this," I said, sobbing.

"A child in treatment can be hell to live with, Hannah."

"And it isn't only Matthew," I confessed.

He bent over and tried to peer in my face. "Your husband?"

I grew still.

"He wants you to get your degree but complains every time his life is the least bit disrupted?"

I shook my head.

"OK. One of your parents is seriously ill?"

I looked up so abruptly we almost bumped heads.

"I'm sorry," he said. "For a minute I forgot about your father."

"If only," I said with one more wrenching sob, "I could forget about my father." Then, as if to mock my wish, it flashed back to me — the horror I'd kept at bay since the night before, when I dreamed that I had lain with Kaewi again, in the mud of the vanishing Tiwano. He had smiled at me and made his teeth click like an alligator, and I'd been unable to understand him or return his laugh because I knew someone was watching us from the forest. I had glimpsed movement, heard cracking sounds. Then a man came wandering at the edge of the dream, shirtless, his pants torn and bloody, his pale body torn; I could see its insides.

I ran away from Kaewi, out to where the man stood, with his twisted face, eyes clouded, mouth moving, whispering wishes that he might never have taken this step, then that step, that in all the steps he had ever taken, he might have swerved just once and left the path that had led to where we were.

He fell to his knees; I reached out my arms to help him; he shook me away — no one could help him. Nimu knew this, who was all at once beside him, barely taller than him kneeling; she gathered him to her the way she did with us children. They made one figure on the soft bank, Nimu easing back on her heels, cradling my father's head and shoulders in her lap, his face a frozen mask of pain, hers gazing down, ever-moving, murmuring solace, maybe all comfort is such a lie, *masa masawi*.

I watched them and knew I was dreaming. I woke up back in the village, where there was great commotion — a knot of young men, their bodies marked with black and blood-red dyes, were dancing in the yard of the Men's House, heels pounding the packed earth, and yelling taunts at the audience they had drawn. I asked for Nimu, and someone told me they saw her take the path to the river, take it on the run. I ran back to the river, looking for her, for my father. I had run and run and woken up running, yet forgetting why.

All day I had been chasing or escaping reminders, who knows which, until I found myself in Theo's office. And he was telling me, "It's *all* right," as he patted the back of my head. "No point in holding that in. Nothing wrong with a little feeling."

I wanted to believe him. Gradually I calmed down, plucked a bunch of tissues from a box on the bookshelf, and began wiping my face. "You know," he said, taking a step back, "I get a lot of flak from my colleagues about this. My chairperson keeps warning me I'd better do more publishing and less practicing therapy without a license. She thinks I as much as invite students to dump their problems on me so I'll have an excuse not to finish what I start. You seem sensible enough, and I'm certainly not trying to dismiss your pain, but in your perception did I invite this?"

His voice was pedaling away, becoming once more the voice that quoted the literature and found virtue in pain. But still planted within reach were these two legs, something solid behind the shreds of nightmare, their coat of curly hair thinning out over each injured knee. With a sigh I gently touched the closest one, ran my fingers over its contours, then traced the vein that ran a crooked course along the ridge of shin. Then I realized what I was doing. I sniffed, cleared my throat, and peeked up at Theo, expecting indignation, but instead found again a distant, blue, beard-pulling curiosity that made my heartbeat jump. He slipped behind his desk and began moving things on its surface.

"I hope that wasn't, you know, sexual harassment," I said.

"I wouldn't have taken it that way," he said. His mouth smiled, his eyes looked sad. "My manly appeal has not been known to reduce women to tears."

"I have four children," I said. "I'm sort of beyond that."

"What do you mean, 'that'?" His eyes smiled with his mouth, a wide, pink crack in his beard.

"You're making fun of me."

"No. I just thought I might get you to laugh, cheer you up. You're always so serious."

"That's what Darwin says."

"Uh oh, your husband?"

I nodded.

"He's the happy-go-lucky sort?"

"Darwin?" I had to smile. "Not exactly."

"Hah!" said Theo. "I got you." He sat back, satisfied, and put his shoes up on an open drawer, across each instep the promise NEW BALANCE.

"Well," I said, feeling at a disadvantage now without a desk, "I guess we just forget this."

"And what is 'this'?" His face went solemn.

"Well, me touching your poor knee."

"I thought maybe you meant you grieving for your father."

In the brief clarity that follows tears, I felt I had found something I'd been looking for. The dream, the moments afterward, and now these words. "I didn't use to think it was so sad, his death. I used to be proud of it."

"It *was* highly unusual. With heroic possibilities, I suppose."

"Heroic?" I thought of Matthew and the ghost haunting his mind. All these years have he and I been dreaming different sides of the same dream? "All I can think now is, it was sad, and sort of grotesque." I was feeling very grateful to Theo for helping me see this, so grateful and close that I might have turned to him for what I could now admit I had lost.

Then the spell was broken. "According to the literature," he said, "children like to imagine fairy-tale parents for themselves. Yours almost came ready-made. I'll say it again — you and I might put together a creditable paper on some aspect of your childhood experience. Maybe we should get together next week and toss around a few ideas."

He was flying off again with his theories. Almost relieved, I told him I really didn't see how my life would fit in a paper.

"You're too close to it," he said. "By the way, I bet those Indians of yours — what did you call them?" He opened and scanned his roll book, as if they were taking his course. "I bet they didn't let your mother's Judeo-Christian preachings keep them from touching when they felt like it."

"I wish it were that simple." I plucked another tissue and blew my nose. "They also killed each other at the drop of a hat."

>> .·. <<

We are standing at the huge mirrored medicine chest in the children's bathroom, Matthew and I. The cross on his arm seems to have gotten more inflamed, and I am daubing an antibiotic jelly on it. I simply cannot stand to picture what he had to do to himself to leave this mark. Of course I want to ask him, *Why?* But I have so many *why*'s about Matthew. To ask them would be like questioning his very existence. My own child.

It takes six Band-Aids to cover the gooey sore. The Band-Aids are printed with little stars and rainbows because Rachel was with me when I bought them. Matthew says they're stupid. He says Band-Aids should be the color of blood.

"Well, no one else has to see these if you keep your shirtsleeve down." I grab him by the ears and plant a quick kiss on his forehead, then give him a lot of pats on the shoulder to send him on his way.

He doesn't move but gazes at me distantly as if trying to place my face.

"What's the story these days with Grandfather Worden?" I ask him casually. "He still bother you?"

Matthew nods, then shakes his head, then shrugs.

"You know it's not your job to fight his battles," I remind him, then tell him that I dreamed about Grandfather myself. "And in the dream he said what you said he said — that he never thought he would actually die. But he also said we shouldn't make ourselves suffer just because he suffered."

Matthew's gaze sharpens. "I like to fight battles," he says simply.

I have no words to reply. All I can finally mutter is, "No, you don't, Matthew, no one likes to fight." Who am I kidding?

"Well, I like to. Dooley said I have to tell you that. Oh, and he said I should tell you how many times I smoked marijuana too." I grab the door frame. Matthew nods with nervous satisfaction. Apparently one of the infamous Nadias can get a joint from her older sister whenever she wants one, which is often. Matthew has shared them on several different occasions on the far reaches of the playing fields. He's pretty sure he's hooked. In fact, when he pushed that girl off the bars they were both stoned.

"But you know how bad it is for you," I say. "In school they teach you all the terrible things it does."

He gives a long sigh and then reminds me, "Dad does it."

"God, Matthew, that doesn't make it right." I stop myself from blurting, *You see what it's done to him,* because maybe Matthew hasn't noticed. "He's a lot older than you, Matthew," I say numbly. We look at each other, then look away.

"Aren't you going to put me on restriction?" he asks.

"What's restriction?"

"Saying I can't watch TV or see my friends after school or on weekends. Everybody else's parents put them on restriction when they find out."

"OK, you're on restriction," I say. "For how long?"

"One month," Matthew says. "Since it's the first time you found out."

I cup my hand around his jaw, put my nose almost to his. "I don't want there to be a second time," I say. He nods sympathetically. And when I put a call through to Dooley a few minutes later, he says Matthew is only in the experimental phase, and there's every reason to think that with a little vigilance and loving discipline we will have nipped the thing in the bud, and it's very important Matthew shared what he shared with me. He calls it progress. But I don't know. I keep getting that helpless feeling of winter coming.

13

· ·

·

I WONDER IF I AM TRYING to start something with Theo
Balch. I wonder if I want to. Would I even be thinking about Theo
Balch if it weren't for what Darwin has done? I am not really
referring to the women. At least, not only the women. But the
example he's set for Matthew, this terrible business I shouldn't
even bring up, according to Dooley, because Matthew is supposed to tell Darwin himself.

I know one thing: if I can't imagine leaping into Theo's arms,
it's nothing Judeo-Christian that stops me. It's stubbornness, the
feeling that I have chosen the way our life is, arranged it just as
it should be, not necessarily the way I want it to be, but the way
it must be, advantages and disadvantages divided equitably, if
this family is to keep its balance. A random affair with whomever
happens to cross my path at a certain vulnerable moment is not
part of the arrangement. (But neither are Matthew's little drug
experiments; neither is any of this stuff that keeps happening.)

Why do I assume that Theo Balch has any interest in me other
than professional? He's going to be considered for promotion
next year. For that you need publications. So he thinks we can put
together a creditable paper — he makes it sound as if my life
could be gotten down in an hour or two. I could become a
character in the literature — a middle-aged, female Wolf Man.

I baked oatmeal cookies this morning, three loaves of banana
bread, and three dozen cupcakes, packed them hot from the oven
into my basket, and arrived at Womancenter just as Valerie was

unlocking the door. She remarked on my being earlier than usual; I didn't tell her that I had planned to catch her alone, without her band of regular feminists and the ongoing discussion group that has sprung up since we scraped together her eighty-dollar registration fee for a series of workshops in D.C. on consciousness raising. As it has turned out, I don't really fit into this group. I like to bake things; they like to brainstorm. They are in perpetual quest for the famous speaker, the perfect workshop, the ultimate fundraiser. They have plans to start various consulting firms. In their view, they must be charitable to me because I'm a fellow woman, and even though I don't say the right things in the right tone, my consciousness will probably evolve someday to their level. In the meantime, they will deign to accept the money from my well-meant but embarrassing muffins and breads, or from the cakes I stoop to decorate with colors and symbols that reinforce sexual stereotypes. Yes, I guess it makes me angry, the way they have taken things over, but I am used to being odd person out. So is Valerie, which is more than her group of disciples will ever guess.

She wears her straight hair cropped short now; her high-waisted body has grown a little stout, in jeans and one of her Womancenter T-shirts — she has about four dozen of them, having inherited most of the first batch when the logo turned out to bleed in the wash. An old tattoo of a rocket shoots up the inside of her left arm.

She set her cat down on the floor, a plump, spoiled orange tabby named Virgo, and while she started a pot of coffee, I arranged the stuff from my basket in the glass case along the back wall. I pulled out a couple of three-day-old corn muffins, set them on the butcher block table that serves as Valerie's desk, and sat down.

"I'm going to have one of these, OK?" Technically, all stale merchandise belongs to Valerie, a tiny income subsidy, but she knew I didn't need permission and didn't bother giving it.

She poured black coffee into the mug she never rinses out and settled into her chair by the phone. "Well, last night I dreamt he kicked off his campaign for president," she said. Her voice is always hoarse — I say it's roughened by her years of self-destructive wandering, she says she's allergic to the stuff that grows here around D.C. "He" is Paul, the perfect Christian man she almost married.

In the last five years Valerie has almost given up the notion that God will engineer Paul's return and has taken to falling in love with women. It is always a secret, hopeless thing because it is never one of our adjunct staff who catches her heart, never one of the regular feminists who have split from their husbands and now declare male-female relationships a dead end. No, for Valerie it is the woman in the wraparound skirt and floral blouse, whose hair still bears the ridges of rollers and curling iron, whose nail polish is chipped, lipstick smeary, whose splotches of blush stand out like fever on a face otherwise pale with misery. This woman wanders into the center terrified, a small child on each hand, and Valerie is gone, given in to a passion that will eventually interfere with everything — sleep, appetite, friendship — everything except the process of counseling and unqualified support that will finally unveil one more regular feminist beneath the trappings, those dangerous objects of desire.

Meanwhile Paul makes his nightly appearances in all sorts of dramatic circumstances in Valerie's dreams. "We're in this amphitheater type of place, like an ancient ruin," she went on today, "and the crowd is waving signs saying HONOR and DECENCY. Next thing I know I'm being arrested, but when they march me in front of him in this lineup, he says no, he doesn't recognize me, I am not the one. What do you think? Good omen or bad?" She pinched off a chunk of the second muffin and held it down for Virgo to sniff and nibble.

In the same detached, sensible voice I use on all her Paul dreams, I reminded Valerie that she didn't have to take full responsibility for what had happened with him, he had had some choice in the matter.

"You never met him," she said flatly. "You can't judge someone you never met." Paul is sacrosanct. Valerie does not have to make sense, feminist or otherwise, where Paul is concerned.

"He didn't stop you."

"That's the point. Men can't stop. They are basically creatures of instinct. Paul was trying to fight it, and I didn't respect his struggle."

"Do you really think men are always, you know, *interested?*" Here was, finally, what I'd come to ask her.

"Always," she said. "It's their hormones. They invent all these obstacle courses and detours to distract themselves, like baseball and capitalism, but they are always interested."

"And what about us?" I asked. "We're not?" I would have called Valerie pretty interested, so much so that it almost destroyed her.

"It's totally different," she said without a pause. "Sex is our distraction from other things."

"Such as?" I asked, but the elephant bells tied to the doorknob announced a visitor.

The woman, who was wearing a red wool blazer over a navy pin-striped dress with a floppy red neckscarf, answered our hello and began studying the bulletin board, a critical look on her face — wanted, rooms or roommates; for sale, baby furniture; announcements, workshops in pelvic self-examination and massage.

"How can we help you?" Valerie asked after a few minutes, keeping her back to the woman, as is her reflex when dealing with people who seem clearly not to need any help — she turns away from them and addresses them over one shoulder, her eyes on their feet. As it happened, the woman was a customer for me. She had read our little ad in *This Week in Sugarland* for cakes made to order for special occasions, and now, as though we both must think it as clever as she did, she began describing her vision of a cake in the shape of a Ferrari for her husband's birthday.

So I took down her information, put it in a folder with the pictures, front and profile, that she had clipped from some car magazine, all the while wondering, *In some far-off earlier time, wasn't I interested? Wasn't I looking for more than distraction?* Maybe sex was just another way for me to be stubborn, rebellious. Everyone around me was so captivated by chastity. My mother, Samuel, Valerie — my God, Valerie was Miss Chastity herself. She carried the pious ideals of everyone on her proud shoulders, went off to Warren Bible College, and once a month mailed back a report of her accomplishments which Samuel read aloud at the noon meal. She received commendations in Bible Studies, A's in Fundamentals of Prayer and Business Math. She was elected Fourth Class Deacon, and by personally writing 144 letters to Kansas Chambers of Commerce, she raised money to teach and feed children in central Africa.

Sometimes her envelopes included a separate but very formal note to me. She never made any reference to my history of impurity or my role in her own brief dip into its morass, but she repeated that college had inspired her to strive for perfection, that it wasn't too soon for Roger and me to start, and that we were always in her prayers. She spent that summer taking Christ's Word door-to-door in southern Illinois; in mid-August she was given a week's leave to return to New Progress — the conquering hero. Samuel invited her to lead a day-long reading of Revelation; there were pancakes and scrapple for breakfast, a picnic at the state park nearby, at which we all tried in vain to master the art of throwing a Frisbee to someone else and not have it float back and land at our own feet.

Roger and I had broken up long before. We were in the reaction phase to our passionate intimacy — his very presence made me sick, and mine probably had the same effect on him. Valerie was completely insensitive to our revulsion. She kept reaching out and pulling us to stand or sit on either side of her, as if we existed to frame her glory, as if she expected someone to take our picture for front-page news. With every breath she either blessed us or praised the Lord. Roger resented the whole performance as much as I did. He and I made a sullen pair, skulking around the edges of the celebration, whispering about false pride, hypocrisy — who did she think she was, she wasn't any better than we were. By the end of the week, we had gotten our anger and envy mixed up with reborn lust. Roger stole Samuel's key to the bomb shelter, and early in the afternoon, before Sunday dinner, we vanished into it.

I remember stepping into that first forbidden moment, leaving the bright heat outside, as if sinking into a cool bath. It seemed a world apart, silent with chances, until you made out the same old cans of tuna fish and Spam along the walls, the rifle hanging over the door, the screened toilet in one corner, the shelf of dusty inspirational books in the other, all flickering under an exhausted fluorescent light. Nothing that might suddenly, magically reveal that what lay ahead was something other than the odd joining of anatomies we had heard about from Samuel and vaguely dreaded. We were about to pay the consequences for all the wild excitement in the back of that bus.

I took off my skirt and my underpants and rolled my full slip into a bunch around my waist. Roger watched solemnly and then, equally businesslike, removed his shoes, trousers, underwear. Without saying a word, he dragged an uninflated air mattress out of a cabinet and spread it on the concrete floor. Without a word we sank onto it. God bless our young bodies, their homely shivering bottom halves (pale purple in that light, barely shaded at the groin), the way they seemed to remember what we didn't know they knew: that the whole thing could happen just the way it did, including a little pleasure for me — at least the promise of its possibility, like catching the scent of something sweet in all that bitterness of old rubber and mold — and for Roger, well, whatever pleasure accompanies the convulsive release, even when it's an angry act of rebellion, revenge.

So that time it *was* revenge, against Valerie and Samuel and the spirit of righteousness that overwhelmed us with embarrassment and revulsion afterward anyway, because revenge never wins. The next day, when I touched the bruises on my hipbones where they had supported Roger's, I wanted to throw up. We couldn't even muster the nerve to exchange a knowing look when Valerie told us good-bye and prayed that the pure love of Christ would fill us.

But by the following Christmas she had changed. She'd catch my eye and sigh when Samuel went into one of his pompous accolades; she was no longer aloof and impersonal. She wanted to talk privately with me, and also to include Roger — she kept drawing him into our huddles, which was uncomfortable for us because we not only loathed each other but couldn't trust the loathing, after last time, to keep us apart. It didn't help that all Valerie wanted to talk about was the miracle of boyfriends and girlfriends, which she understood now, since she had a boyfriend. You could tell it thrilled her to speak his name; it transfigured the simplest sentences. Paul was handsome, Paul was strong, Paul was perfect, dedicated to Christian service; with Valerie by his side Paul would conquer the world for Christ. And they were chaste, she insisted — it was their joint strength. They inspired each other to greater and greater self-control.

Those were the only hints of her loosening that I witnessed firsthand, because I didn't see Valerie again for a long time. The next autumn, our senior year, Roger took the eleven-hour bus trip to Warren College for an interview. He wasn't planning on attending that school any more than I was, but he wanted to talk to his sister. He was growing daily more miserable at New Progress. He had run up what amounted to consecutive life sentences in restrictions for smoking cigarettes, using vulgar language, failing to complete assignments, resisting the regulation haircut — he followed one offense with another. Letting him go off like that, totally unrestricted, must have been Samuel's last resort, which just goes to show how impotent his elaborate system of punishment was.

The one thing Samuel never caught Roger at (besides his sins with me) was tampering with C. W. Burpo in the Main Room. I can still see him crouched in front of the wooden console, a cheek and giant ear pressed to its round webbed window, his mouth hanging open with concentration. He fiddled with the dial like a safecracker after a combination. What he discovered was the Beatles. On Saturdays, when supply runs emptied the Main Room, he knelt there for hours, picking up Beatles songs at barely audible volume. Other times he went for walks where he thought no one could hear him and practiced his own renditions. It got so that even with people around he was singing — sort of hissing, softly and probably unaware, the same phrases over and over: *The world is treating me ba-a-ad* — *misery,* or *Chains, my baby's got me locked up in chains.*

Roger went out to Kansas to talk to his sister and never came back. There were phone calls to Valerie: yes, she had seen him, but only for a half an hour, it was all the time she had; he had seemed a little glum, a little unresponsive; well, actually, he had accused her of being a crazy bitch, but she wasn't holding that against him.

Bowed with sorrow, Samuel called the police. Sadly he answered their questions, signed their forms pronouncing Roger a missing person. As Samuel led group prayers for his return, I murmured my own: *Let him be all the way on the other side of the world by now, let him get away free.* If he made it, I could.

Then the next spring Valerie disappeared. She and Paul were in the final phase of mission training. They had one year to go before graduation, marriage, and she just walked away.

When Samuel told me about Valerie — grilled me, actually, convinced I must know something about her "secret life" — all I could think about was resisting his second agenda, my extradition to New Progress for the summer. I had my own escape to guard. I had been at Penn State almost a year, I had found Darwin, and I was dizzy with love. Maybe all Darwin was looking for was an unspoiled tablet to switch his crazy scribbling to, since he'd botched and torn his own, but he was everything I was looking for, brilliant and sexual without apology — everything I wanted to learn. I spent our moments apart counting how many were left until we could get together. If I'd had to leave him I would have died.

Valerie did show up, of course, four years later at our apartment door in Arlington, and eventually I found out that she and Paul had lost control. They had taken a walk one night into the country beyond the campus. The fields around them lay freshly plowed, waiting to be seeded with corn, soybeans. "I think I got high on that earthy smell or something," Valerie said. For she was the one who began clinging to him, sneaking her fingers inside his shirt. She was the one who pressed for love. Right afterward she had been so mortified by the sin she had dragged him into that she didn't think she would ever be able to look him in the eyes again. Much later the guilt ebbed and she tended to see her action as a cosmic sign, a summons to open her mind to the true deity. Whatever it was, she responded at the time by packing a few things and creeping out to the highway the next morning before dawn.

Somewhere I still have the letter from her that caught up with me right after Darwin came home from Chicago. It was postmarked San Francisco, forwarded from New Progress, with no return address. Everything was beautiful, she said — the people she was living with, the acid they shared, the scene on the street. Darwin lay in bed with a concussion, his left temple swollen like half an orange. He had painful, swollen bruises along his ribs, above his kidneys, on his balls. The scene on his street had been mace, tear gas, clubs, heavy boots against bottles of urine and baggies of shit — an S-M orgy, he said. Life was all games, Valerie wrote, low games and high games — she was still given to arbitrary rankings — and the Christian religion might be the highest game, but it was still a game and you had to break out of its rules, set Christ aside, in order to see God. Life was games, all right, said Darwin — low games and lower, until the bottom gave and you fell into the pit. Valerie was making a little money, tie-dyeing T-shirts and doing foot massage, and the group that had taken her in shared everything. It was beautiful.

Then why did she wander away? Why did she climb into an old station wagon with two men who were driving east, stopping when they had to along the way to pick up odd jobs or improvise car repairs with junkyard parts? Why did she arrive in Arlington with her wonderful high-bridged, haughty nose puffy and bent? And pregnant by a man she swore had a direct line to hell? I could fill up a page with questions I have never asked Valerie. These days my reasoning is, if she wants to forget, let her. Back then I was afraid of her answers. Within five minutes of walking through that apartment door into my life, she had turned it upside down.

A stranger, I thought at first, a bone-thin stranger on three-inch platform sandals, with long dark hair in need of a wash, wearing a blue workshirt knotted at the waist of a short fringed skirt of purple suede. There were mended holes in her fishnet stockings and one, above her left knee, that wasn't. Her skin was grayish; there were gray-blue shadows around her eyes. And her nose, as I have said, her nose must have been broken and then mended unset. It made me wince to look at it. What I recognized were the eyebrows, naturally dark and dramatic, fiercely angled. The eyebrows were Valerie. I asked them to come in.

"Surprised?" she asked.

I nodded. "I thought you were in California."

She shrugged as she peered around almost rudely into each corner of the living room, at Jeremy, who'd come toddling out of the bathroom with his training pants around his ankles, and at Matthew, crawling behind him. She didn't seem to notice Under sniffing intently at the hem of her skirt.

"I got your letter," I told her. "You didn't write a return address."

"We don't really have a mailbox where we are," she said.

"Have you gotten in touch with Samuel?"

"Are you kidding?"

"We never found Roger," I said apologetically, having always assumed, I guess, that her disappearance was some sort of reaction to his.

"Roger found us." She still talked in that toneless, authoritative way. "I'm going to write to him when I get myself a place. I'm headed for Florida for the winter. It's real cheap living down there. Someone told me there's food just sort of like growing along the roadside, and it stays warm enough you can sleep outdoors if you have to." She twitched her shoulders straight. "But how *are* you? You've got two *kids*. That's wild."

"Three," I said. "The baby's sleeping."

She put one hand over her mouth, gave a softer "Far out." She bent over and sort of leered at the boys. "Guess what I've got in here?" she whispered, patting her belly. "I'll give you a hint — it makes me throw up a lot." Jeremy clutched his penis, turned, and shuffled back down the hall. She looked at me and her eyes went black. "I've got to get rid of it, Hannah," she said.

"What?" I said, knowing I was stalling, but I had to take one last deep breath, get to the wall for support.

"I'm pregnant."

"That's wonderful," I stammered.

"Come on," she said. "There's no way I'm going to have it. I'm going to, you know . . ."

It was as if her body were throwing off blasts of noxious air. I shook my head. Five minutes before, the boys and I had come in from a walk; it was sunny out, Indian summer — it was just a short walk because Benjamin was still very frail and I had not yet regained my normal strength and needed to save enough to get the four of us back up the two flights of stairs. Five minutes before, I had been pure Mother, uncorrupted by the thought *get rid of a child*. Now I was trembling, no good to anyone. All I could do was shake my head.

"This kid'll never make it," Valerie said, as if there were no question about it, no need for emotion one way or the other. "It's like now, before it can feel anything, or later, after it has to go through God knows how much shit."

"We can talk after supper," I said. "If you ask me, what you need is food." In the back of my mind I was thinking that I had to get one of my milkshakes into her — a blend of ripe banana, double-strength nonfat dry milk, yogurt, and brewer's yeast — and a couple of Vitamin C's. These were my weapons against crankiness and infection where the children were concerned, and the children were my world. There was nothing else I could think of to make her well.

"Don't even say the word *food*," she begged, clomping past Matthew toward the bathroom. "I can't keep anything down."

>> ∴ <<

Darwin didn't know what to make of her. For two months of eight-hour days, five-day weeks, he had been breathing regulation at the Center for Environmental Control, tracking down radium, a newly designated danger, testing sample after sample of dust. Then at home there was the routine of three babies. Until this Friday, when he staggered in, the jacket from his early Student Union period in hand, and there was this female in a flashy skirt who'd gladly share a joint with him, who'd obviously been around, yet was still sort of prim and vulnerable — thin, pale, with a hole in her stockings and a ruined nose. I knew that nose would capture him. (Later Darwin said it was her courage, precious, elusive virtue. "She just opens herself to the whole fucked-up world and says, *I'll take what you can dish out.*" I pointed out that she didn't take all of it; some of it she got rid of. Then he said, "You know, she reminded me of you when we first met," which made me feel so sad I couldn't speak.)

Over dinner she explained that all she needed was a ride to some parking lot in D.C. and a pickup four hours later. She had the phone number; she had made the first call already. Her friends Scott and Robbie had given her three hundred dollars to take care of it. They had gone on to St. Petersburg, where they were waiting for her to join them. Oh, and if we thought she could shack up with us for a day or two afterward, that would be wild.

I knew Darwin would take her side; there was no rational reason not to. And I was clear-headed enough to realize I didn't want Valerie being anyone's mother. But I had to try one thing. I called on a person I had never believed in, in the name of something I still wanted to believe in — I mean, wasn't there something out there that was absolute and pure? We were all, it seemed, so morally grubby, so tired. "What about Paul?" I asked.

Valerie put down the fork she had been using to separate her mound of macaroni and cheese into individual noodles. "What about Paul?"

"Maybe we should try to reach him."

"This isn't *Paul's,* Hannah," she said, as if she thought I might have forgotten that human gestation never stretched to four years. "I could never go to Paul." Then she told us the circumstances of their parting, ending with her decision to put herself in God's hands. "When I have to decide what to do next, I just look

around to see which way He's left open, and that's the way I go."
She gripped the table and leaned toward me. "There's nothing
else to do, Hannah, but have faith. I mean, if God wants Paul and
me to be together, He'll help him find me."

The same intuition that warned me away from the question
made it irresistible to Darwin: "Whose is it, then?"

She sank back into her chair, covered her nose with praying
hands. "This guy in Reno." She popped straight again, palms up.
"That town is wild. It's like you talk to someone and pretty soon
they want to fuck and then they pay you. I mean, I knew there
were words for that, but I never thought that was *really,* you
know, the way it was. But it was wild," she repeated, still dead-
pan. "I mean, getting that much money for doing someone an
easy little favor like that."

Scott and Robbie did favors too, and they might have stayed
in Reno much longer because food was dirt-cheap in the casinos.
But then this crazy guy fell hard for Valerie, wanted her every
night, until after a couple of weeks he got tired of just fucking.
He wished to spank her, he wished to insert things into the openings of her body. "He was like a weird scientist or something,"
she said dully. "He kept talking to himself about what we were
doing. Once he grabbed these two hard-boiled eggs from an
all-night breakfast bar, and when we went to the room, he got off
on, oh shit, it was just all so, I don't know, wild, you wouldn't
believe." She looked from me to Darwin and her face quivered,
as if she was waiting for a sign whether to laugh or to cry. Darwin
just stared at the salt shaker he was fondling. I couldn't say what
I wanted to say — *You are terrible, crazy, get out of this house,
there is nothing fascinating about your corruption.* But there was.

I stood up and began clearing away our plates. "Sometimes it
was things like, you know, shoehorns and flashlights or his bottle
of wine. And one night he brought this little black gun, I mean
he held it out on his open hand like it was the most wonderful
surprise, and he said it wasn't loaded with real bullets — like he
was sorry. But I said I wasn't fooling around with any gun, I
mean fake bullets or real bullets, what was he, crazy? And then
he grabbed me and threw me on the bed, but I kicked out at him

and got him you-know-where and he buckled over. Then I ran up and down the main drag until I found Scott and Robbie, and I told them this guy was after me with a gun, and so they got the car started and we headed out."

"Well, you're safe now," I called to her unsurely from the kitchen. "You can put all that behind you."

"Not yet," she called back. "Soon."

I stood in the kitchen doorway and waited for Darwin to look at me so I could see what he was thinking; I was too upset to think for myself. He watched his hand put the salt on the pepper, take it down, and put the pepper on the salt. Then Benjamin's tentative waking noises called me away.

In our bedroom I lifted him from his basket and unwrapped his scrawny body. After a month he still weighed less than a normal newborn. His arms and legs moved in jerks. I rested my fingers against the soft spot on his skull where his pulse fluttered. It was too early for him to smile; he still cried without tears. His coal-blue eyes gazed through me, impersonal. For a minute his impossible weakness made me feel a little queasy. For a minute, it was as if he weren't mine, he was just a human baby, any human baby, a naked fact I had draped with all sorts of hopes and dreams, who didn't and wouldn't make any difference to anything.

I lifted his tiny feet in one hand and unbent his legs. When I let go they folded back up against his belly. A story of my mother's came to me. She had sentenced me to a day of prayer and Bible-reading alone in our hut; I was running wild, she said, I was turning into an Indian. "Thank you for the compliment," I said. "That is just what I want to do." And then she told me that Janca mothers used to bury their babies after they were born if they didn't like the way they looked or if they thought they'd been touched by evil spirits — was that what I wanted to do too? She said she had been helping the women till a new section of the garden when she had raked up a nest of miniature bones. The soil would be particularly good there, the women said, having mastered the principle of compost. They showed no remorse, though they became a little nervous after my mother explained that God forbade such killing and might himself punish by killing mothers who killed their children.

I pinned an absurdly bulky diaper around Benjamin's skinny haunches. I felt myself slipping from that odd detachment into panic. What had I gotten myself into? Suppose there was no such thing as a maternal instinct, suppose I could leave this creature by the side of the road without even looking back, suppose the grand project of having babies was completely pointless, each one got lost sooner or later in the whimpering, murderous crowd. I snapped him into a fresh gown, reswaddled him in his flannel blanket; then stiffly, as if I had never done this before, I unbuttoned my shirt, stretched out on the bed, and nestled him against me, his cheek at my empty breast. How many times had I gone over it? The heat, the trips back and forth between apartment and U-Haul lugging boxes of books, plates, and pots, the louder and louder pain. If it had been less muggy, if I had carried fewer boxes, if I had stopped the car and lay down on the seat the minute the pains began, if I had crossed my legs and simply refused to let go of him. Then he would have been spared that awful month spent wired and tubed in a glass cage, touched only when necessary. And now I would be offering him my milk.

I had the bottle of his special formula beside me for the moment he objected to having to work so hard for nothing, but he didn't object; in fact, if I hadn't stopped him after a while and replaced it with the rubber one, he might have sucked himself back to sleep on that dried-up nipple of mine, like the forgiving child he already was.

Long after Benjamin was satisfied and asleep, I lay there, braced and anxious, until I jumped at the sudden sound of laughter, Darwin laughing, fully, not cynically, something I hadn't heard him do since long before we left Penn State. I returned Benjamin to his basket and went back to the next room.

There was Darwin sprawled in the one comfortable chair, a platform rocker I bought secondhand when I was expecting Jeremy (and all the others). Valerie half reclined on the mattress. They were passing a second joint back and forth. I lowered myself beside her because I couldn't not — we were playing some scene in which I was to join them graciously, they were to acknowledge my presence by offering the joint to me, I was to wave it away, and then they could resume their exchange of funny stories. Valerie told about Poseyville, Indiana, and a deputy sheriff who'd thrown her and Scott and Robbie in jail overnight for sleeping in the car. He said he wouldn't charge them with possession if they shared their stuff, and they turned him on and he put them up for a week while they picked and crated cantaloupes at a local farm. Before they moved on, they managed to rip off about two dozen melons and stash them in the back of the station wagon, so that even with all the windows down they smelled like a garbage truck.

Darwin told about the women in watch factories whose job it was to paint the luminous dials onto the watches' faces, how sometimes they marked parts of their anatomy with the radium-laced paint so their boyfriends could find them in the dark. (He didn't mention that after every few strokes the women would repoint their glowing brushes by drawing them through their lips, and that, over the years, the little tastes of radium found their way to the women's bones, ravaged the marrow, until their legs wouldn't spread without breaking.) They were laughing more and longer at things that were funny only if you were stoned. But I kept playing my role, waiting for the moment when the day's weariness would spread from my back and limbs to my brain, and I would have to make my way quickly to bed or else spend the night wherever I happened to drop. Looking back this way, I could get furious at what happened if I didn't feel so sorry for all three of us, each thinking we knew what we were doing, thinking we had chosen what we were doing, when it was all a sort of blind plunging and groping and clutching that made Benjamin at either dry breast or bottle look like a genius.

When I pushed myself to my feet, Darwin and Valerie stood up too (she tugging at her purple skirt), as if I were the visitor, they the hosts. It was an awkward moment, because I knew they would probably seduce each other, and Darwin knew I knew — and I was wondering, how could I tell him through my expression, posture, because a speech would not make sense, that I cared enough to hope that he wouldn't do it, because in this new apartment, this new city, with this new baby, I didn't have very much to fall back on; but if he had to do it, I could see that it might give him back some of his lost vitality, and Valerie was almost a sister, and it certainly wasn't the first time, so maybe I wouldn't really care?

14

. .
.

I COULD NEVER GO BACK to those murky days when the boys
were small. I have something now — call it age, or habit, or an
adjustment to circumstances, I have something; I had nothing
then to protect me. It was as if I caught some disease Valerie
brought with her, and by the time her God waved her onto the
path to warmer, lusher regions, I was dead.

I am not blaming her. She was only the carrier, a victim herself.
Darwin had driven her to a parking lot on the waterfront in
Southwest, where she was picked up and later dropped off by a
black Buick with tinted windows and Virginia plates. At home
afterward we tried to make her comfortable on the living room
mattress. By the following afternoon, when she had expected to
be up and gone, she was running a fever that aspirin couldn't
touch, doubled up under waves of pain.

"My God, I'm dying," she kept moaning, but she objected
fiercely when I wanted to call a doctor — she hadn't the money,
she could take the pain, it was part of the deal. She was going
through a Kotex an hour, staining the bedding, the old T-shirt of
Darwin's we gave her to sleep in, pair after pair of my underpants; the trash was filling up with her blood-drenched pads. I
tried to bring down her temperature by soaking washcloths in ice
water and rubbing them over her arms and legs, folding another
over her brow. Her body cringed every time I touched it. Jeremy
peered into the living room at her agony. I shooed him back to
his room; the third time I screamed at him and swatted him as

hard as I could, after which I felt a terrible emptiness. I went to apologize and found him kneeling among the blocks of some ruined fortress. I lowered myself beside him, he toppled over into my arms, clung in silence. I remember realizing then that this would be one more thing I'd have to explain when he was older, like the baby brothers, the crowded apartment, his father's strange moods, one more thing I would have to make up to him for.

When Darwin got home, Valerie let us help her get dressed, and then we crammed all six of us into the Opel and inched our way through rush hour, trapped with her labored breathing, her groans, to Arlington Hospital. They took her right up to surgery.

I never grasped precisely what went wrong — they weren't details of the sort you wanted to remember. She had been pregnant with twins, I cannot forget that. Nor that the man to whom she paid the three hundred dollars had scraped out only one embryo, though he had unwittingly punctured both sacs. After holding her for a day in intensive care, they told us all I needed to know, that she would survive, though the damage to what the doctor called her equipment would make future conception impossible.

It was almost a month before the bleeding stopped and she regained her strength, a confusing, wretched month for me because I decided that Darwin had fallen in love with her. He got home from work promptly, never went out after dark, and once the boys were bedded down, he and Valerie would smoke and argue about the state of the nation: she still found it beautiful from shore to shore; and though he knew otherwise, and every night the news brought proof of his premise — the brutal violence at the heart of the American middle class — he never turned his anger or sarcasm on her. Her blind optimism was too valuable, something white to set off his black. I supposed he knew better than to ruin it, now that he'd seen what happened when he ruined mine.

The fact that sex was out of the question actually made it worse. Sexual infidelity I was used to; this was more insidious. Valerie owned only the clothes she had arrived in, so she had taken to wearing my jeans, my flannel shirts. When the household got moving in the morning around six-thirty, she left the mattress in the living room and staggered back to Darwin's and my bed, where she slept on until noon. She did entertain Jeremy and Matthew for an hour or so in the afternoon, telling them stories of Africa, emphasizing things like killer elephants, killer snakes, killer tsetse flies — killer anything — unscrupulously when she discovered the mesmerizing effect.

I know I should have said something, objected to the situation, but I couldn't. Caring for three babies took all my time and strength; there was nothing left for forming thoughts, much less pronouncing complicated sentences. And the message I was picking up was simple and clear: Valerie was my replacement, a new, improved me. It got so that I really didn't want to speak to anyone or make any noise at all. I imagined myself a shadow, dimensionless, flitting through our rooms, the spirit of the household — if unappreciated, at least unseen, and thus somehow free. My body, meanwhile, asleep on its feet by nine, accepted solicitous good nights from Valerie and Darwin — he must have been taking naps at work in the lab — and went off to bed. And all night my original relief that she was alive and getting well battled the wish that she were dead.

>> ∴ <<

But when she left, there was an emptiness. At first I thought it was because she had come between Darwin and me, but really, Darwin slid right back into his crazy martyrdom without missing a beat. No, nothing had changed; maybe that was the problem. After such drama — our brush with crime, a life-or-death emergency, even a romantic triangle — there I was again, used up, spirit-dead, my best years behind me and nothing ahead but the monotonous, futile busyness of three babies. Maybe Valerie didn't bring the ruin, she exposed it. Or maybe it was something of both.

Some days I lost the children behind a papery film, their voices seeming to come from a great distance, foreign, impersonal, pitiless. Other times I lost myself — what day was it, what month, where was I, in the middle of what? And then Darwin would get home and make some jabbing remark, and I would think, *I must be here, he is talking to someone.* I had fallen into such bleakness, I found myself wondering often, too often, would it have been better to have never let these children be born?

The worst thing happened with Matthew, who'd grown stiffer, more unreadable, once Benjamin had come along. The only way I could spend a little extra time with Matthew was to take him with me on Saturday mornings, which had been my time off to buy groceries. I hugged him a lot as he sat in the little seat, and sang him Indian songs, but he never cracked a smile. He stared so fiercely at the older women who tried to pat his head or chuck his chin that they blushed and turned away, clicking their tongues. While waiting at the checkout I happened to pick up a magazine and skim an article about a little-known disease that caused premature aging in children. There were pictures of five- and six-year-olds with long shriveled faces hunched beside youthful parents, and they must have gotten to me, because on the way home I kept glancing over at Matthew in his carseat and thinking he looked pale, wondering if his fine hair wasn't getting thinner, mistaking dimples for wrinkles. By Sunday, I was sure he was mortally ill.

The doctor I took him to was from the phone book, so of course I couldn't trust him when I dropped the hints about falling hair, tired eyes, crooked arms and legs, and he didn't jump to my conclusion. "This child is perfectly healthy," he told me, releasing Matthew to toddle over to my chair. And that's when I did it, I pushed him away. I turned him around and tried to force him back on the doctor. "But he couldn't be," I said desperately. "I know something's wrong with him."

I felt even worse days later when the obsession finally broke, when I had regained enough sense to worry about its effect on Matthew. And he was too young to tell me, too young for me to try to explain it away. I have got to share this with Dooley, as painful as it is — the fact that I failed Matthew, the fact that in one way or another I have failed all three boys and may still be failing them, though I've never felt as hopeless, as unredeemable, as I did the one day I actually left.

It began with just another morning — Darwin gone, me sipping instant coffee and eating Cheerios from the box. The floor was littered with Creative Playthings that never got put away. Benjamin was squawling in his infant seat after a "hug" from Matthew; Jeremy, whom Darwin had already nicknamed the Black Hole, was sulking on the stained mattress in the corner. Then as I refolded the paper Darwin had left open on the table, a headline caught me: MARCH AGAINST DEATH. Somehow it woke me enough to read on, to remember the Movement, the fervor of conviction, to think, *I have to do that again. I have to put up one last fight.*

I waited all day for Darwin to get home so that I could explain this to him. He wasn't interested. He preferred the Truth to the gimmickry of political protest, which was the new opiate of the quasi-liberal masses. He accused me of being too much a coward to gaze frankly at the horror of human greed and aggression. He also said I was abandoning my real responsibility to the children and betraying my commitment to him, seduced by some pseudo-drama invented by the media. It was quite a performance, after which he closed himself in the bathroom.

So I was about to leave three babies in the care of a man whose caring was random, who might smoke a little more that night to get back at me, who might allow some terrible accident to happen in the process of putting them to bed. It was a dreadful moment, worse than all the pointless, unloving, crazy days that pushed me to it, thinking that nothing could be worse. It was a choice: them or me. I stood for the longest time on the threshold, every part of me clenched, feeling that I would split apart if I had to move. Then I closed the door — I don't know how. Maybe I justified it this way: it wasn't fair to the children, prolonged good-byes, I would make up my mind in the hall. Maybe the first hours were just a succession of these tentative, reversible steps. I did know I couldn't not go and survive.

Outside there was death too, spreading everywhere; Darwin

could bring it in on any channel any night. My Lai had been exposed, Charles Manson identified; in a month, Altamont. That was why we had to march against it. The Weathermen were raging for the cameras in D.C., hurling bottles, stones, themselves, at the police. Darwin thought he recognized his onetime friend and mentor Clark Rathbone. "I remember his famous last words to me," Darwin said, trying to sneer. "Something about there being only one way to make the machine stop, and that was throwing your body against the gears."

But outside, I told myself, there must also be motion — why else call it the Movement, and now the New *Mobilization* Committee? Bundled in the army surplus jacket and the trailing muffler that used to be my trademark, I got on the bus to Arlington National Cemetery. With hundreds of others I sat and stood there through the night in the parking lot and waited for the signal to begin moving. At first I felt unworthy, inept, but then the magic of the dark touched me, the magic of being so awake, with such plans, while the rest of the city had gone simple with sleep. We spoke among ourselves only when necessary and in hushed tones. In one hand I carried a candle with a paper shield; around my neck a woman had hung a placard with the words VINH LINH, NORTH VIETNAM.

Toward dawn the random movements of the crowd became purposeful; on one of our fronts we were advancing. I took deliberate breaths, straightened my posture, tried to let go of the tension in my shoulders, the imagined burden. I was amazed when my own feet began moving: the sky in the east glowed pink, I gulped the morning air, cold and pure. I was rising on the sound of a thousand footfalls, and it was all I could do not to break into a run, I thought I might have to yell instead, I wanted to sign something that said, *Here I am, I will march anywhere, forever.* Behind that surge of energy came thoughts of Darwin, guilty thoughts that I was not sharing it with him, that I would never be able to persuade him that maybe purpose in life, anyone's life, didn't have to be some big change, won in the end against villainy, but only moments, bobbing up here and there when you had almost given up completely, like filing across Arlington

Bridge before dawn, in solemn step with the stranger's hiking boots in front, while behind, the human line dropped back into its milling source.

Near the White House I moved into the rhythm of drums. In a voice I had never heard out loud, I read the name on my card of the vanished Asian village, but the picture that came to mind was another village I could never revisit — it was the voice of willed memory, all that remains. The drums faded as I trudged on; others sounded as I came in range of the Capitol, lit up like a fancy cake. Drums cracked like shots beside the row of coffins at the foot of the lawn. In one I placed my card. I looked down at the flickering candle and in my mind I saw children, dark and fair, dancing in a brief clearing, a circle game.

I could not name the sorrow that touched me then, too deep for tears. I blew the candle out.

>> ∴ <<

"You sit like a man," I remember Darwin saying the morning after. My right boot was resting on my left knee. I twitched it now and then to keep Matthew from fiddling with the laces; Matthew fussed in protest. Benjamin guzzled his bottle. We were all there, of course; they hadn't slipped away while I was gone.

"Is that a compliment?"

"Observation." He was going after the French toast on his plate, sponging it around in the syrup, as if he thought someone might take it away before he was finished. "I guess you're pretty pleased with yourself."

"Look," I said. "No one's stopping you. This whole thing could be yours as much as it's anyone's. You've worked for it as much as anyone has, you've given up things." It had been only a year since Darwin had resigned from the Chapter, literally sung his swan song — "I am overco-o-ome, I am overco-o-ome" — and begun this retreat into depression. I knew Chicago had scared the shit out of him; I knew he had let himself down and thought there was nowhere else to go. If he couldn't put his body on the line, throw it nobly into the machine, he'd decided, he would have to quit. But it would be so easy to pretend he hadn't. It had only been a year, a leave of absence. He could echo what others had begun to say — that they were checking out the system from the inside. We could find a sitter, cut another armband. "And you don't have to *do* anything." He looked at me suspiciously, as if I had called him a coward. "You just have to *be* there."

"Aerial photo fodder," he said. "The good guys will get a fraction of a fraction of a point for each square inch of crowd."

"That's your problem, you know," I said, the night's wisdom pressing to be spoken. Since stumbling home at dawn, I'd felt different toward him and the children — not quite so detached, in touch with a strange, tentative appreciation: they *had* managed without me. "You're always looking down at things from somewhere in space."

We were not used to my diagnosing his problems. "You really are pleased with yourself." He put his empty fork one last time in his mouth and pulled it slowly out between his lips. "Mother of three finds self-fulfillment."

"It's History," I said.

He got up and went into the bedroom and then came out again, wedging a couple of joints into a box of Marlboros. "Hell, it's not like I've got anything better to do," he said.

>> ∴ <<

The Mall was solid bodies, stamping, smoking, shouting, shoving, waving — churning out energy, as though they knew the day would return only what they gave, maybe a little less, and they needed a great deal. By odd chance we did bump into people we'd known at Penn State, and there wasn't at all the awkwardness Darwin said there would be. They felt just as vaguely apologetic as he did now that the Chapter had fallen apart, and obviously hadn't ever dreamed of blaming it all on his defection (as Darwin tended to). In fact, Clark Rathbone, who decided after Chicago that the concept of friendship was meaningless reactionary mush, there could be only comrades in arms, in blood — Clark had disappeared underground, and Darwin's stock had risen. His were now remembered as the good old days, of flamboyant symbolic gestures — baked bean banquets and fart-ins, a giant foam rubber effigy of LBJ with a .45 fastened between its legs — when grossness not violence was the weapon of choice. Darwin lit a joint and passed it around. One earnest, dingy young man with a stale, cold smell wore glasses that slid down his nose the way Darwin's used to. Tiny spit bubbles collected at the corners of his mouth as he denounced Nixon's savage strategy of bombing Southeast Asia into oblivion. "But we're showing him today," the boy said, clenching a fist. "He can't ignore numbers like this."

"He's watching the football game," Darwin said. "Besides, you think if you get rid of this war they won't find another?"

The kid began to nod vigorously; he had had a flash of understanding. "It's too profitable," he said. "It's the imperialist system. It's all got to be brought down."

"Comes the Revolution," Darwin said. "Comes the fucking Revolution." The kid looked puzzled by Darwin's sarcasm. "Parade your imperialism in front of the mirror, and what do you see there, strutting oh so proud?" I was tugging on Darwin's arm, thinking we should move on. "Your Revolution's a system like any other system — a bunch of maniacs scrambling for power."

I caught Darwin's hand and plunged us into the mass of bodies swelling from curb to curb. The people around us were chanting, "Give peace a chance," their voices sliding like a sluggish phonograph. I joined them, tugging Darwin along for a block or two; then he jerked his arm away from me and began shouting in his nasal tenor, "Peace, peace, send Spiro back to Greece." Others picked it up immediately, and soon all around him beat the quick new time. I bumped my body into his. He jammed his glasses up the bridge of his nose, and his mouth tipped in a brief crooked smile. It was a glimpse of the old Darwin, the man I fell in love with, the man I'd been destined to meet when I said no to Warren Bible College and faced down my mother's reproach. My eyes teared in the cold air. Then he reminded us both, "Peace hasn't got a chance. They could send Spiro to the moon next time and it wouldn't change a thing. Everyone loves a good war, they just don't want to die."

I let him ramble; I was too happy to risk responding and saying the wrong thing. Through it all there sounded the undertone of feet shuffling along concrete, hundreds of thousands of marching feet. That had to mean *something,* even to Darwin, even as word traveled along the crowd that Weathermen were getting gassed over at Justice for trying to raise the NLF flag, even as someone said, "Maybe they're crazy, but they've got guts," and a bunch of marchers near us broke away to go find the action. Turning onto Pennsylvania Avenue, Darwin put his mouth to my ear and said, "We've got to stop meeting like this." Along the curb, a banner — FIGHTING FOR PEACE IS LIKE FUCKING FOR VIRGINITY. "I want to fuck you right here," he whispered. "Right in the middle of this." Though my blood rose, I pretended I hadn't heard. It has always been easier with Darwin not to expect anything.

As daylight waned and our section of the march completed its appointed loop and began to dissolve, Darwin broke into a faster pace, now dragging me by the arm. "To the Monument," he said. "To the great American phallic symbol." He began pointing out people in the crowd whose noses he could do it right under. But when we reached the Monument's trampled slopes there were too many people, and he was off in a semi-jog again along the Reflecting Pool heading toward the Lincoln Memorial. "So we'll proclaim our emancipation," he called back to me. "We'll climb up and do it right in his lap." Panting and sweating, we darted in and out among the shrubs and kiosks there, me losing him and then doggedly catching up to find him shaking his head. Then it was over the grass to the banks of the Tidal Basin. "Life, liberty, and the pursuit of happiness," he promised gamely, but he was slowing down, giving in to a hitch in his stride. His long, fine hair hung in wet strings. We stopped finally in front of the marble igloo of the Jefferson Memorial, and it was almost deserted. We had just settled ourselves behind some shrubs along its base and Darwin was reaching into his jacket for the Marlboro box when we heard the clop-clop of hooves. A park policeman appeared in twilit silhouette above us beside the monstrous, steam-snorting head of a horse.

"Sorry, folks," he said. "I can't let you camp on public property."

"We're not camping, officer," Darwin said politely. "I got this overwhelming desire to fuck my wife." I grinned and nodded.

With wet, snuffling noises, the horse seemed to be trying to lick its lips. "I'll have to ask you folks to move along," said the policeman.

We got up, linked arms, and took off, synchronizing our steps like a pair of vaudevillians. From the bridge onto Hains Point, we looked back to see horse and rider still watching.

"You practicing to be a statue?" Darwin yelled. The man yanked on the reins; the horse reared unimpressively, then ambled away.

We were both tired, and our clothes had turned icy next to the skin. A small, vaporous groan escaped Darwin every few steps. "Maybe we should go back," I offered, though I longed to draw him into my arms, to breathe encouragement into the free spirit the day had brought out of hiding.

"Not yet," said Darwin, but I could see it had become a matter of principle — Darwin against all the social forces that were working to inhibit his desires.

Along the landspit of West Potomac Park we came upon an old raised bandstand. We found a break in the trellis around the base and crawled underneath it. It was cold and dank, and we had to sit hunched to keep from hitting our heads on the rotting floor above. I said I liked the way it smelled. "You would," Darwin remarked cryptically. He was all at once nervous, squinting around as though he couldn't imagine what to do next.

As soon as I was off my feet, I felt the lack of sleep from the night before and I could have sunk right into the earth, but I felt so sorry for him, it was so like him — the bright idea, the explosion, the squandering of energy, and then the anxious doubts: action, reaction; offense, defense. I wanted to pick up where he left off, rub warmth and energy back into the two of us. I would forget the times in bed he had rebuffed me, drawn away from my touch. ("Everywhere people are dying hideously at the hands of their fellow human beings," he would say, "and you're all huggy-kissy. It's not that simple.")

He leaned back against the peeling trellis and watched blankly as I struggled out of my jeans and crawled to his side. I tried to work one arm around his shoulders and felt him stiffen away from me. "It's all right," I whispered, kissing his salty cheek. "We're alive, we're free." With one hand I worked on his fly.

"I wonder if you know what 'free' means," he said after a minute, with a mournfulness that surprised me. "It's like living in a place so empty nothing else can survive."

"We don't have to think now," I said, taking up his soft penis, squeezing it gently.

"Existentialism is shit. Radical freedom is not doing anything, not making *any* choices, because something out there has already defined and limited every one of your options." He sighed as I bowed over him. He let me kiss him, suck him, then all at once pushed my head away, drew his knees up protectively. "I hate this body," he said simply.

"I love your body," I told him. I wanted badly the warmth of holding him.

"My mother's thing used to be mind over body. I was raised in that faith, you know how that is, Hannie, but I couldn't live up to it. My mind tried, but this body said no. It whined and made excuses. Maybe it's got like an abnormally low pain threshold."

"Oh, Darwin," I said, taking his face in my hands, "you're not the only one who ever felt afraid."

"I'm the only one who quit." His hands were still cupped on his groin.

"You did what you had to. Maybe you were the smart one."

"You know you don't think that." I stopped stroking his cheeks and sat back on my haunches. As often happens when I'm tired, the dark rims of my own eye sockets seemed to close in on what I saw — his face as expressionless as his voice. "You'd be happier if I were fighting against something. War. The military power elite. That thing out there that tells us what we can and can't choose. Fighting to the death." I put a hand over his mouth. Through my fingers, he added, "Like your father."

I wanted to say, *My father was fighting for, not against,* but even more, I didn't want to continue the discussion. It was so like Darwin, too, to start an argument, to jam affection or the first waves of desire. "Do you know what I'm going to do to your cock?" I asked. "I'm going to pound it like manioc." His body jerked; his eyes seemed to darken. "I'm going to whip it with branches of nettles." He took my hand from his mouth and guided it to his penis. It was beginning to harden.

"What is it out there, Hannie," he asked, "that's always standing in my way?"

"There's nothing out there." With one of my hands helping one of his, I was wriggling out of my underpants. I knocked the boards overhead as I straddled him, causing a rain of debris.

"Maybe it's like friction or inertia," he said. "Something you can't see. Maybe it's the fifth force."

I slid back and forth on him, my knees digging into the cold dirt. "There's nothing out there but us," I repeated, rhythmic love words, over and over. "Nothing but us."

It was our first intercourse since Valerie's visit, in fact since before Benjamin was born. It had been a blessed surprise (I want to say reprieve), like maybe leaping from Hell to Heaven in less than a day. By the time we got back to the apartment, I knew the life I felt at my core was more than a good mood. And sure enough, the following August I delivered a perfect baby girl by the gentlest of methods. She cried once softly as they lifted her from the tub of warm water, and then she caught herself, contained herself, as she has ever since. She is like my mother in that respect. I see it more every day. Oddly enough, Darwin, who punched the wall and then stomped out of the apartment when I first told him I was pregnant, and who launches into vehement denunciations when my mother is even mentioned — Darwin has always brightened at the sight of his daughter, still calls her his "little old lady from Pasadena," and claims she's the only woman who doesn't try to pull his chain.

15

. .
.

IT IS VETERANS DAY on the Mall, a bright morning of ragged, mobile clouds. We are ten years beyond political protest, this is anything but. (If Darwin reminds me of that one more time, I will scream.) *What is it, then? What are we actually going to do?* Maybe I should have pushed for a definite answer yesterday when I was dressed in legitimate clothes, but I didn't want to act the spoilsport Darwin often claims I am. Besides, he never knows from week to week which monument or museum the RATS will drop in on. As missionaries of the Spirit of Play, they go where it moves them. Twice in the last month the spirit of publicity has followed, granting them an interview in the *Post* "Style" section and a three-minute spot on the local news.

Shivering out of control in spite of the thermal underwear I have on under my pink tights and leotard, I am surrounded by strangers: Darwin's troops, in costume like me, and the ones dressed sensibly, who mill about staring with a mixture of disapproval and expectation. Lurking as close as he dares to Superman is the Snoopy dog of synthetic fur containing Jeremy. He has made himself sick with excitement this morning, pushing aside his half-eaten oatmeal and muffin, responding to questions with hoarse, distracted grunts, spending so much time in the children's bathroom that Rachel, who wished to wet and blow-dry her hair, was moved to register a complaint. I almost understand his feverishness, just as I almost understand his new scorn for me. I watch him watch his father, silently begging for his attention. "Once in a while you could give him a hug," I have suggested to Darwin. "When did a hug ever solve anything?" he's asked, still adept at pushing his own father away. But today he has gone many steps better. As if finally granting Jeremy a birthright, Darwin has chosen him first for this RATS happening, while the younger children must wait.

What I still can't figure out is why Darwin invited me. I'm beginning to think he doesn't really know either. He said he could get another deal on the costumes, two for the rental fee of one. Besides, wasn't he correct in assuming I'd sort of enjoyed getting dressed up on Halloween? And hadn't he all along promised I'd be included, and hadn't I wanted to come? All this in a noncommittal, almost distracted tone; nothing about *him* wanting *me*.

But if I always waited for him to say things the right way, where would we be? "I'll try it," I said, "what's to lose?" Plenty, I realized when his face sort of drooped with dismay. "I wasn't supposed to say yes, was I?"

"It's not that," he said. "I just hope you'll relax."

Maybe if Darwin would, I could. He has been so polite to Jeremy and me it feels ominous, complimenting us on our costumes, carefully enunciating instructions: "The plan is, there is no plan. No one tells anyone else what to do. OK?" Before we left the house this morning, he presented me with a real magnifying glass he had borrowed from one of the labs. "I know you think I'm a bad bet," he said. "Well, there's no point in arguing about it one way or the other. See for yourself. All I know anymore is what mood I'm in."

The mood he has toked himself into now is manic exuberance. He introduces me to his troops by their heroic names. At his right hand, the newly restored Spiderman, short with knotty muscles, all but his mouth and lower jaw hidden by a blue nylon helmet. His costume is the reverse of Darwin's, red with blue trunks and boots. The wealthy Miss Piggy anchors one plump arm across his lower back by tucking her fingers into the top of his trunks. She wears a rubber pig mask with inch-long eyelashes, a taut, pale bodystocking, and an oversize little-girl's dress with puffed sleeves and a sash.

Batman has a beard, King Kong, Sr., reeks of aftershave, and beautiful, blond Peter Pan is slightly pigeon-toed, with a southern accent. He shakes my hand with both of his and says he is honored, that I have waited too long to join them, that he has been looking forward to meeting me. This instant bonding makes me anxious. I have overheard Darwin on the phone: Peter Pan is not really cut out for this, his cavorting looks clumsy and premeditated, all he wants to do is stand around and strike poses.

And the other women. Maybe I was better off when I could pretend they were creatures of Darwin's imagination. How could I have thought this would work, that I would meet them and not begin wondering which one Darwin has been sleeping with (if only one)? But maybe that is why I came in the first place, to find out.

With quick, flushing glances, I acknowledge them: the Tin Woodswoman, emaciated, a silver funnel over each breast; Batman's Robin, petite and all smiles with crewcut hair, who greets me with a combination of karate kicks and chops; Wonder Woman, still bundled up in her overcoat. When I give her my hand, she scowls and looks very bored.

But Darwin is in his element. He scoots off to head up his troops, Snoopy trundling behind him. Miss Piggy comes waddling up, pulls me with her a few steps, then jabs her snout back in the direction of Wonder Woman. "Don't let her get to you," she says. "She's like that with everyone. Really."

Darwin is hitching the waist of his trunks, rearranging his cape. "Attention," he calls, and King Kong spatters some noise on a tin drum. Miss Piggy insinuates her flute up her rubber snout and begins to play "Bridge over the River Kwai." I loop my tail over one arm and hold my place next to her, behind the chivalrous Peter Pan. "The rest of you do your own thing," Darwin orders, dancing backward, conducting them with wide-swinging arms. "OK," he yells — his new red leather boots pivot frontward expertly and he gives a bold snap to his cape — "everybody out of step." And we straggle and prance, skip and lunge and hop across the lawn and up the steps of the Air and

Space Museum, while a dumbfounded father and son hold open the doors, into the warmth, where cameras begin to flash.

"Fan out," Darwin calls, and the bodies that surrounded me, concealed me, are falling away faster than I can decide whom to follow, all except Snoopy. I make a desperate grab for Superman's cape. He bends backward, cocking me an ear.

"I can't do this," I whisper. Above us the airplanes hang like trapped birds of prey — the Wrights' glider, the *Spirit of St. Louis,* a drab fighter from World War II.

"You don't have to do anything particular. Whatever you feel like." His bright boots shuffle to be gone.

"Jeremy's scared to death," I say, huddling closer.

"You're going to ruin him if you don't let go. Give him some room to breathe."

"I'm sure he thought he'd be able to stay with you."

Darwin takes a long look at Snoopy. Finally he says, "You guys follow me."

The three of us march grimly into the Solar System, Galaxy, Universe. If the latter were the size of this dim chamber, we read, Earth would be lost to sight, even by microscope. The captions abound with these disconcerting comparisons; we move stiffly from one to the next. The lighting is eerie, glowing points cluster and float in midair, glass walls reflect the same vague portrait here and there — Superman with clenched jaws, the Pink Panther, hugging herself, and silent, inscrutable Snoopy.

Soon I watch my reflection lean sideways toward the Man of Steel. "I'll be OK now," I whisper.

Superman's jaw relaxes and he turns to the ghostly dog, sets a red glove on the head barely an inch below his own. "If you don't want to work the crowd, you can walk around and look at things."

Snoopy holds himself utterly still under that hand.

"You understand that?" He scrubs the white furry scalp. "You can do whatever you want to do?"

"Dad," Jeremy says — hoarsely barks the word through his snout. "Dad, what's the difference between air and space?"

It is all I can do not to throw my arms around him and hug him, he is so earnest.

"Well," Darwin says with a nervous laugh. "Space is thinner, and beyond the earth's atmosphere, obviously. I guess it's like the difference between the known and the unknown."

Jeremy clears his throat and goes on in his halting way. "How far beyond, Dad, exactly? How many miles?"

"Oh, I don't know, ten, maybe, fifteen."

"I see," Jeremy says.

"Look," suggests Darwin, "why don't you wander around here till you find the exact answer?" There is a pause. "OK?"

"OK." Jeremy's voice cracks.

As I nod, Darwin promises to check back with us and disappears.

Jeremy and I are in the main gallery again. By the front windows, in his own world, Peter Pan is shifting poses like a fashion model. In the opposite corner outside the rest rooms, Spiderman turns backflips under the doubtful eyes of a guard. The others have vanished.

A girl the size of Rachel is squinting up at me, asking, "What are you supposed to be?"

"The Pink Panther," I say, feeling like a fraud. I lift the magnifying glass to my rubber muzzle, add off-key, "Da-dum, da-dum, da-dum da-dum da-dum da-dum . . ."

"Oh," says the child, disappointed.

"And this is Snoopy." I rest a hand on Jeremy's shoulder, which he wrenches off, but the girl has already fallen back into the crowd. I hope I don't have to explain my identity to anyone else. I lean closer to Jeremy and ask, "How're you doing?" His answer is muffled by his mask. "I can't understand you, dear."

He lifts the mask up at the throat to uncover his carefully enunciating mouth. "Would you please quit asking me that?"

Of course I will, I hadn't realized I was bothering him. "Look," I say, "we can split up too," and I prove it by taking a few steps away from him. "Is that what you prefer?" Snoopy is silent. I must assume he does, I must leave him. "Fine. How about I meet you back here in half an hour?" And I march off without looking back, down the central hall, in the shadow of hovering wings.

Tail in one hand, magnifying glass in the other, I try to look intensely interested as I stop and read the specifications of each space capsule, each satellite, the replica of Sputnik. Miss Piggy waves to me as she reels past, a bundle of clumsy arabesques and twirls. Though the charts comparing Our achievements in space to Theirs assure me that We are winning, the numbers and intricately labeled diagrams mean nothing. I am thinking about the other women — where they are, which one she is. I can imagine the appeal of the Woodswoman's starved eyes, her faltering voice. And Robin is a technician in Darwin's lab, the one who introduced Darwin to the others, friends of hers, friends of friends. A bouncing, smiling student of martial arts — is that a clue?

The hall opens into another vaulting gallery, at the center of which is a circle of towering missiles. Under the Lunar Lander to one side stands Wonder Woman, dazzling in her satin costume, authentic from tiara to the golden wristlets, which she rests along the shoulders of two young girls. Above her sequined bodice, the swells of bluish flesh rise and fall like a waterbed. She is still frowning, and I wonder if that is just the way her face is, narrow, pinched, with close-set eyes. A man has gone down on one knee with a camera, at too short a range, I think, for him to catch the children in his shot.

And there, in the middle of the ring of missiles, is Darwin, holding in his stomach and telling admirers that he flies to the moon all the time without any of this silly equipment. His current project, he explains, is to wrap all of Mars in sheets of reflecting foil and turn it into a space mirror, which, given the sluggish speed of light, would serve us on Earth with instant replays of important events. I wave my hand from the periphery of his audience. "So if there was a misunderstanding about something," Darwin says, "people could just look up at Mars and see what really happened."

Individuality, Darwin instructed Jeremy and me in the Bus coming down. *That's the name of the game. Expressing yours* and *respecting the other guy's.* I wait patiently, respectfully, for him to notice me. His audience turns to check me out, but he never breaks his jaunty rhythm. Then suddenly, out of nowhere, Robin zooms into the crowd, arms and legs flailing. She lunges at Darwin, he grabs a flying foot and makes her hop around in a circle before he lets go, whereupon she takes off back down the main hall and disappears. They were both laughing.

"Yoo hoo," I call now, once, twice, and hunched over my magnifying glass I begin to tiptoe and da-dum my way through the crowd.

"And here's my friend the Pink Panther," he says. "That was great," he whispers to me with a grin, then he takes a step back, as if to give me plenty of room.

I can't move. I peer nervously through the magnifying glass at a blur of gaping faces and in the background the fat steel spears. I am supposed to do something else. I can't imagine what it is. This whole expedition is some sort of test, a competition between me and the happily aggressive Robin, who is having an affair with my husband. I pull Darwin's ear to the mouthslit in my mask. "This place is all wrong."

He straightens his head and looks past my shoulder, bewildered. He may realize before I do what I will say next.

"I mean, it really bothers me," I begin in a loud voice, "the money that went into these things that could have been feeding hungry kids. Or curing some disease."

Now Darwin is whispering in my earhole. "You came along for the *fun* of it, remember?" he says. "Not to play Grand Inquisitor."

"It's all weapons," I announce, pointing my tail up the shafts to their cruel tips, shocked by my own accuracy. "We should all be opposing this."

"You won't lay off, will you?" he asks quietly.

I lower my voice. "It's what I feel like doing, Darwin. I'm sorry."

He looks at me sadly. "You shouldn't have to apologize, for Christsake." He starts backing out of the circle. "I'll just get out of your way."

"Can you fly?" asks a small boy tugging at his sleeve.

"All the time," Darwin mutters, stomping off. "I fly back and forth to the moon all the time."

Sweat trickles from my scalp, down my neck. Another little boy raises a foam glove whose pointing finger is a foot long; painted across the knuckles is the proclamation "#1." Beyond him, Wonder Woman is staring, but not at me, at Darwin's disappearing back, her narrow, ungenerous look transformed into one of anxious desire. That's when I finally figure it out.

Right on top of the urge to get away comes the urge to strike. Shaky with adrenaline, I stumble over to the open space where this other woman rules. How come no one dares crowd in on her? How come no one criticizes her for just standing around doing nothing?

We are face to mask. I hate the frown lines that pinch her brow. She wears stuff on her eyes and too much of some sharp perfume. In two minutes I know all about her, the frivolous gourmet frozen foods she buys, her taste for wine, her sets of lace-trimmed underwear from that shop in the mall, skimpy nightgowns. And I want her to *realize* I know everything.

She rises on tiptoe, stretches in the direction of my pointed ear, hisses, "I've got to pee." It throws me all off.

"I never thought this would be so hard," I say.

She looks at me quizzically.

"I mean, I can't figure out what I'm supposed to do or not do, I'm no good —"

"You don't look half bad," Wonder Woman says. "I wish I was thin like you. I do this aerobics class on my lunch hour, but I just *look* at food and I gain."

A girl is poking my hip. "Are you the Pink Panther?"

"I'm nothing," I snap. "I've disappeared into thin air."

"Oh," says the child, backing away, mouth open.

"Now I feel guilty."

"Don't," says Wonder Woman.

"She's only a child," I say, all at once ready to defend her like one of my own. "Children are a lot more important —"

"They ask for it," Wonder Woman says. "They nibble and nibble until you say no."

"If I know about anything, I know about children," I say. "You know, Darwin and I have four of our —"

"Grownups are the same."

"Jeremy is just our oldest. We'll probably bring Matthew next time."

"It's like you get dressed up and that makes you public property." She offers me a tentative smile. Without the bitterness her face is almost pretty.

"Well, maybe it's an honest mistake. They don't know what you're doing here." I gather myself for an affront. "The truth is, you don't either."

"But that's the point," she says. "Being random. The universe is random, Darwin says."

"And you believe him." I feel as if I'm drowning in this rubber mask.

"What do you mean?" Her eyes avoid mine.

"I know what he's like. I know how he seems to have *the* answers."

Her face has pinched up again. She is trying to look haughty, above it all.

"Look," I say with sudden conviction: I know the best thing for both of us. "I can't be sociable, much less random. I am not going to smile and ask you where you live, what you do, where you got your costume. What I'm going to do is tell you that your affair isn't going to go anywhere. They never do."

"I know *that*," she says sulkily. "I've been telling myself that since day one."

"Well, now you've heard it from me."

She is gazing at my feline mask as if aware for the first time that there is someone behind it. "I'd better find the john," she says, tugging the bottom edges of her trunks down over her buttocks.

I grab her brass wristlet. "You know it makes sense, what I said."

"It'll take me forever," she says, "to get out of this thing."

I watch her move away, her brisk strut discouraging company. Her smell fades and I can breathe again, but I am completely drained of energy. All I want to do is lie down right where I am and take a nap. I force myself to keep moving; I must find Jeremy. I wish I'd insisted on bringing the other children. I need them around me. I want all the people staring at me to see that I am not this cartoon of a detective, I am a mother, a mother who has left three perfectly good children at home for reasons she cannot now explain.

I wander back into the exhibit on the universe. I catch a glimpse of Snoopy's floppy ears and furry shoulders on the other side of the central display — The Milky Way: Home Sweet Home. His back to me, legs spread, arms akimbo, he is talking to two girls. Girls. He would kill me if they saw, if he had to answer the question *Who's that? Is she with you?* I pretend I have dropped something on the carpet, then sneak away.

Lost in the ruins of World War II, I come out upon the innocent Robin and Batman simulating a fistfight on the simulated deck of an aircraft carrier — the one takes agile leaps and falls, the other lumbers comically. "Smack, pow, bang, crash," cheer the onlookers. Across the next threshold, a cross-sectioned B-26 Marauder enshrines three olive-drab General Purpose Bombs, propped upright in a row, triplets in a grim womb. I catch my own pink-sheathed reflection in a display case, and I almost faint with disgust. "It'll blow your mind," Darwin promised about wearing a costume. "You'll feel free to do things Hannah Charles wouldn't ever do." Instead it seems to have emptied me of the ability to do anything at all.

My path leads through a doorway hung with a black curtain, into a darkened circular room, a sort of theater. Built into the curved front wall are three large glass cases containing miniature models of famous air battles. I push the button beside one display, and a B-47 goes into action, bombing an enemy target with light flashes, smoke, and the sorts of noises Matthew makes when he plays war. Another button pits two P-38's against a luckless Messerschmitt, all three spitting sparks. Another sends three planes with Japanese insignia nose-diving into the Pacific. On every stage, American goodness finishes number one until a second push of each button returns everything to its original tension.

Taking advantage of the privacy, I peel off my mask and try to wipe my dripping face on my sleeves. I restart the Japanese battle, watch the destruction, then press the button once more. The smoke is sucked away; the good Americans fly backward while the Japanese are allowed to rise again into suspended stasis. The restoration intrigues me — it is vaguely amusing, like the punchline of a forgotten joke. I start the cycle again. But then against the toy stutter of machine guns, there is rustling behind me. I know before I turn around whom I will see, what I have begun to smell, what, in trying to avoid, I have again tracked down — a shadowy couple on the highest dark-carpeted tier against the wall, Darwin and Wonder Woman.

Darwin steps down to my side, drawing one edge of his cape around him. "We were just talking about how basically right you are," he says. "I mean, how it didn't take very long for man's desire to fly to get mixed up with his urge to kill."

I look away from him, away from her, at the fringe of light around the curtained door.

"There *is* a moral issue here," he says. "We were talking about possible actions for —"

"Darwin." I make myself look at him, make myself read the silent question on his face — *Do you really want to do this, embarrass the three of us? When you know it's not a big deal, never has been?* I can feel myself blushing, I would like to pull the mask in my fist back on, but I keep looking at him, I want him to read my answer — that nobody loves anybody, nobody needs anybody, enough for this.

The *S* on his chest sags. "We got tired," he says. "We came in here to rest."

His words are bombs, blunt and ugly. I take them somewhere around my heart. Wonder Woman clambers down finally and joins us. Her hair is tangled and her tiara askew. I want to shake her, ask her how she could have gone after him this way when I expressly told her not to. "I'm sorry," she says. "I hate myself. I really do. I am *really* sorry."

"I don't want you to be sorry," I say. "I want this not to have happened." If only I could push a button, return everything to its original order. But where is it, that order? On a bus, on a rally platform, or under a rotting bandstand? In which crowded apartment, diapers everywhere? How far back do you have to go?

"What's happened?" The indomitable Darwin nudges Wonder Woman aside and places his face in front of mine again. "Maybe *you* should tell me. Heidi came to me all upset. We came in here to find a place to sit down away from the crowds. Heidi, Hannah," he continues after a pause, breaking the Clark Kent Commandment, never to acknowledge a Superhero's secret identity. "Hannah, Heidi."

Light from one of the cases bounces off his glasses, erasing his eyes. It is like a revelation. "Do you ever stop trying to hide?" I ask.

"It's my pattern, I can't help it," Heidi says. "It's like I don't see what I'm doing until something like this happens. And then I feel so rotten, so ashamed, I just want to literally die."

Darwin says, "I'm not hiding."

"I don't just mean screwing around and I don't just mean a minute ago, I mean for the last, for the last ..." Swallowing panic, I line the children up in my mind by height, touch each one on the shoulders, cheeks, hair. "I don't even know how long." Four precious lives. Then my fear slips through them into a dark confusion; my mother is on the edge of it, telling me — no, warning me — not to cry.

My hand is grabbing at Darwin. "Is this why you wanted me to come down here with you? So I would find you out?"

He gives a few vigorous shakes to his head, then slows and stops, his gaze somewhere over my head. Heidi plops down on the bank behind her, knees out, hands hanging between them in despair.

"Look," Darwin says. "I was trying not to hide. I've been working on it. I thought if maybe we came down here together, with no heavy agenda, but no, you've got to go around finding issues, threatening people, and dragging us all —"

"Why do you have to work on it, Darwin? Why does it have to be work?"

"Well, maybe I'm just not as good as you are. I mean, if the whole business comes so fucking easy to you."

"We never really did anything," Heidi says.

"For Christsake," Darwin says to Heidi. "It's none of her business."

"How can you say that?" I ask.

"I wasn't trying to break you guys up," Heidi says.

"Stop," I almost shout. I don't want to hear anything else. "I give up, Darwin." I hand him my crumpled mask. "I don't want to do this anymore." I want to unpeel my leotard and hand him that too. I want to step out of my skin. As I slide around him, I can see that he is trying to figure out what I mean, and I realize I don't know either. I punch the Start buttons for all three displays. "Jeremy and I are going home." I barge through the curtain, tiny battles raging behind me.

Then I remember where I last saw Jeremy, preening in front of two girls. I turn back, peer into the dim room. "On second thought, Darwin, Jeremy is all yours."

"What are you going to do?" Darwin asks. He sounds more curious than worried. I let the drape swing back over the door without answering. Because I don't know that either, until I find myself marching down the center of the Mall toward the Reflecting Pool, impervious to the cold, as if no one is stopping to stare at me, a gawky pink shadow, crying again, like the last person alive.

16

. .
.

I KNEW I WOULDN'T BE very good at an affair, I don't have it in me. I came as close as I'm ever going to come with Darwin, but falling in love with him was so easy and natural — it really was painless in the beginning, nothing like those books that made Valerie and me gasp and blush in Brockett's Drug Store. I didn't lose sleep or appetite, or become feverish or faint. Never did I experience such a peak of ecstasy that I wanted to die rather than come down from it to ordinary life. I simply knew he was the one, knew the two of us were meant to be joined, knew these things before he even knew which, among his admirers, his disciples, his New Left troops, I was.

After that people started calling me uptight, a prude. Sex was like a friendly handshake, they said, as healthy as a square meal, and there I was in a corner, hands folded in my lap, abstaining. Even Darwin used to tease me. "So-and-so just made a pass at you and you didn't even know it," he'd chuckle, but I wasn't *that* naive, I had known it: everyone flirted recklessly with everyone else, and some were crying for help, and some were proving a point, and some were looking for new victims for their cruelty. It was harder to tell which was which than it was to pretend I didn't understand. And all I ever had in me was Darwin.

Speeding home from the museum, I lost my muffler on the George Washington Parkway, and my car started to roar like a space launch. My tears dried up because all the other drivers were craning their necks and staring. Back home Rachel wanted me to quiz her on her Middle Eastern map, and we were out of milk. It didn't matter that I didn't believe anymore in milk or the Middle East. That was just me, my problem. And I wasn't really at the end of the road. There was that detour marked *Theo*.

I suppose I thought that maybe after all those passes I ignored, all these years of being faithful, I would have built up some sort of credit, that Fate would somehow put the right man in the right place and show me the way. It was some such reasoning that sent me off to Theo the Compassionate, Theo the Not Unattractive, alone and defenseless in his office. The next thing I knew I was barging in on him again, and the next, blurting out that I thought it would be a good idea if he and I had an affair. Once spoken, the words rang false as old slang.

"Why is that?" he asked. Already he was sitting up straighter at his desk, and the dollops of cheek above his beard had begun to redden.

"Because my husband is." If I'd bothered with grace and tact, I wouldn't have been there in the first place. "I've seen her, I met her, I caught them together. It's opened my eyes."

"At least you're honest," he said, and I realized I'd offended him.

"But that's not really it — them. Or not only it. There is more to it."

Sitting there behind the desk, his back to the wall, he tugged at the knot in his tie and seemed to look right through me. In fact I turned around, expecting to see someone peeking over my shoulder. Beside the door hung a poster in gorgeous colors advertising a race for hot-air balloons.

"As far as I'm concerned, I'm still a virgin," I said.

His blush deepened, and he forced a pathetic smile. I thought he was going to pull his beard right off.

"Really," I said. "I think that."

"After four children," Theo said, very quietly.

"I know I'm acting a little crazy." I mounted his bicycle and began pedaling slowly beside the desk. "But notice I'm not about to cry in your office today." He humphed at his hands in his lap. "How do you decrease the resistance?" I asked. The single wheel of the bike buzzed rhythmically. I cocked my head toward the pot of ivy on his desk. "If you'd pinch that back and water it, it would do a lot better."

He cleared his throat and said, "You realize I make it a policy never to get involved that way with students."

"I can see where that would be the only policy you could have."

He stood up abruptly. "I've got to get out of this office," he said. "It kills me that I can't run."

"Did you ever think about one of these things with real wheels? Of course then you couldn't read."

"I'll buy you lunch," he said, jamming his arms into his jacket, a nice jacket, bluish tweed, with suede patches at the elbows and a piece of suede at one shoulder.

"I'm ravenous."

His blue eyes looked stricken. "So am I."

After a stop in the library for Theo to drop off some books, a swing by the dry cleaner's to pick up a couple of pairs of his pants, and a dash into the post office for the roll of stamps he needed, we arrived at the Peanut Gallery. I kept thinking that I was cashing in my credit, that some cosmic human mobile was revolving slowly into that new balance. But by the time we slid into a booth I was faintly disappointed that neither one of us was showing signs of being swept off our feet. Maybe it was Theo's crisp tidiness; maybe it was the way he walked, bottom tucked under, like a scolded dog. Even when I am furious at Darwin, my eyes welcome the familiar rumpled sight of him, draw him into the empty place in my mind where he fits exactly. I kept looking at Theo: squinting, blinking, cocking my head at different angles, but he stayed right where he started — outside. He was a piece for the wrong puzzle; a stranger, of another tribe.

The Peanut Gallery was three flights up, in the renovated attic of an old county building. Scarred tables and benches covered in red plastic lined the short wall of exposed brick. Along the sloping ceiling, there was a row of skylights. The floor was slippery with peanut shells. Our waitress, Monica, was wearing a down vest that exactly matched her green eyes, the sort of eyes that seem perpetually to be rolling up. One of Darwin's early women had eyes like that, I remember; he thought she looked sexy and I thought she looked comatose. Monica warned us that they were having trouble with the heating system and suggested I put my muffler around my head. "The body loses fifty per cent of its heat through the head," she said, and plunked down a bowl of peanuts on our table. We ordered coffees, a peanut-butter-and-banana-on-raisin sandwich for me, and for him, peanut-butter-and-bacon-on-rye.

"Banana," Theo said with a shudder as soon as Monica left. "I could never understand what people see in fruit."

"What is there to understand?"

"I can see an apple every once in a while," he went on, "but all that other stuff — it's too mushy or something."

It was late for lunch, and across the room at a table on the inside wall, the only other couple in the place lifted wineglasses in gloved hands. In my army jacket and muffler, I still started shivering. Theo turned up his collar; his eyes matched the soft shade of his jacket too. He said, "The trouble with affairs," and snapped the shell from two peanuts, popped them into his beard.

"How do you know there's got to be trouble?" I asked. I had decided: Play the docile student; get the lecture. Play the long-suffering wife; get the ordeal.

"I was only going to make the general point that when one of the participants is married, the whole focus becomes sex, and when and where and how you're going to set up the next . . . encounter."

We were both cracking peanuts relentlessly, tipping them into our mouths one after the other, brushing the husks onto the floor, guarding our full mouths with our hands when we talked. I happened to notice that he bit his nails and the skin around his nails; I noticed that at times he had drawn blood. "My husband and I have no sexual relationship."

Theo's head dropped forward and wagged from side to side. Monica had come skating over the peanut shells with our coffees;

she asked if anything was wrong. *Oh yes,* I wanted to say. *Everything.* Why not tell her, who knew so much about the body's heat, her with the bedroom eyes; why not expose the fraud I have been living to the whole world? I curled my hands around my mug, but it had already cooled to lukewarm. "We wanted hot coffee," I said, and for an instant Monica's irises disappeared.

"Why are you telling me this?" Theo groaned when she was gone.

"Don't worry, I'm not the sort of person who can't live without it. For a long time I didn't even notice." I picked at the end of a piece of tape that ran along the seat beside me. I pulled up on it, and it came away from the plastic with a satisfying screech, revealing a split underneath and spilling yellowed crumbs of old foam. Then I couldn't get it to stick back down.

Theo smiled in spite of himself. "We won't be able to come *here* again," he said.

I slid over and sat on the damage. Monica was back with our sandwiches and two empty mugs, which she clunked down under our noses; clouds of spiced steam rose as she poured from a carafe into them. There were no windows to look out of, just the skylight above. The view was mottled gray.

"Are *you?*" I asked Theo as soon as she left.

"Am I what?"

"The sort to live without it. I mean, you aren't married."

"I've had long-term relationships."

"Are you having one right now?"

He bit into his sandwich, but not hard enough to bite through an undercooked strip of bacon, which pulled away from the bread and hung down over his beard. He yanked it off and dropped it onto the plate, chewing urgently. "I just broke an engagement. At the end of the summer, before classes started."

"And what about sex? You did sleep together. Was it like every night or every other, or what?"

He tucked his face down into his beard and looked up at me. In the cold the patches of chapped skin along his hairline had gotten brighter. "You realize none of this is any of your business."

"Tell me how it's supposed to work. I mean, I've been so out of it I'm just now getting around to seeing that something's wrong with Darwin and me." I rushed those last words. "I've got nothing to compare us to. I've got my friend Valerie telling me men always have fucking on their minds and I've got Darwin flinching when I try to give him a hug. Then he goes out and starts something with this Wonder Woman. I can't figure out what he wants."

"Maybe you should stop right there and figure out what you want."

"That's easy for you to say. There are a lot of people mixed up in this." A better answer came to me. "Besides, I told you what I want." My eyes dropped to his chilly red nose, to the flecks of peanut shell in the beard around his mouth, the strange, kindly mouth I was insisting I desired. Thank God he was keeping me at bay.

"It took me two years to realize that's what I had to do," Theo said, less defensively.

"And what did you want?"

He bristled again. "That's irrelevant. I'm talking about a general principle."

"Please. Maybe it would help me to know."

"I'm afraid it would give you the wrong idea because of the frame of mind you're in."

"I can handle it." I daubed with a napkin at my own cold nose.

"OK, I wanted her just once to make the first move. This isn't only about sex, Hannah. Sex was just one aspect of the whole problem." His gaze turned inward as he fondled the last corner of his sandwich. "You know, I was never sure she really needed me in that way." He snapped his attention back to me. "Or any other way except the way I suppose we all need chairs around to sit on." He looked at me curiously, almost imploringly, then his shoulders gave in. "Sex never seemed to cross her mind until it crossed mine, and how can a man tell about women in that respect, really, I mean, if they decide to hide? We can't. You women have the distinct advantage of anatomical privacy; you could put anything over on us males."

There was urgency in his voice; it wasn't the sort of deliberate excitement he manages in the classroom. I found my cold fingers gripping his sleeve. "I'm making the first move," I said. This time I thought I meant it.

He sat back into the booth. "And in three weeks I'll be in the position of grading your final exam."

"Look, I've read those articles about faking orgasms, and I never understood how it worked. I mean, I didn't even know there was this part that wasn't happening until it happened. How can you fake that?"

His face relaxed into a smile. "That's you," he said. "You led a sheltered life."

"I think we should do it," I said, a little shocked to be actually believing that.

"If you mean collaborate on a paper, I agree. Something about the impact of culture on social-sexual development."

"I'm not a female Wolf Man, Theo." I smacked my fist down right beside the half-empty bowl of peanuts, making it jump.

"Well, I'm not the cure for a sick marriage." He smacked down his fist and sent a few nuts out onto the table. Monica hustled over looking sleepily oppressed — we had been nothing but trouble. She handed us our check. Theo didn't even wait for her to leave before he added, "Nor am I interested in being your easy escape route. I'm not a case study myself."

Maybe it was hearing through Monica's ears that made me realize the truth of what he said, and it was like losing everything — my train of thought, my confidence, and this other man, whom of course I had never "had," whose appeal blossomed now beyond my reach like certain forest flowers unfolding their ripe sweet smell.

"Well," I said, adjusting the muffler around my head, gathering up my books, "you must be really laughing at me. I've obviously made a huge mistake on this whole thing. And I've got to keep on going to class, looking you in the eye."

"I'm not laughing at you."

"I don't know why not. Darwin's lost interest in me, so I come and throw myself at you, and you're not interested. Next thing you know, I'll be sneaking back into the kitchen to proposition the cook."

"You don't believe that," Theo said. "I don't believe that."

"Then what *are* you doing?" He was picking out coins from his flat palm, lining them up on the table. His open hand was trembling; maybe it was the cold.

"I'm certainly not laughing. In fact I'll tell you what I was thinking. I was thinking, wouldn't it be funny if we pretended we were having an affair. You could start acting as if you had a lover — you know, smug, secretive. Maybe stop wearing your hair tied back that way. And I could flatter myself that you put the so-called moves on me. You could experiment relatively safely with a little healthy quid pro quo and I could indulge my narcissism, which hasn't had a lot to work with lately. And —"

"Like your bike," I interrupted, because I saw him again pedaling feverishly, holding two fingers to the pulse in his neck, going nowhere. "Your exercise bike."

He flashed a resigned smile. "I'm afraid you know more about me now than I'm entirely comfortable with, enough to sit there in my class and have a little laugh yourself. I mean, what a strange, uptight fellow *he* is, he'd just as soon think about love et cetera as feel it."

"I'm not laughing either." It was hard walking on peanut shells.

"Wait a minute," he said. "Not so fast." He cupped my elbow and then lost his footing himself. "I know that pretending business sounded a little weird, I mean, it probably is some sort of neurotic displacement, but I didn't mean it that way. What I meant was, we weren't *that* far off. It could have happened. It's like if you'd hit me on a Tuesday or Thursday, instead of a Monday, Wednesday, or Friday, it *would* have happened." He halted and showed me a finger and thumb. He looked rather amazed. "We just came that close."

I went first down the stairs, gripping the banister, making sure of each step. When we were almost to the street, he remembered he let Monica take his dry cleaning to hang in a coat room somewhere. "I don't think I'll wait," I told him as he started back up. He understood. "You know what you are?" I turned and called to him before he disappeared. "You're a virgin too." He nodded modestly as if I were flattering him again.

17

"YOUR MOTHER COULDN'T FLY," says Darwin a.k.a. Superman, peering down the dark parkway through the crescent of glass his wiper almost keeps clear. "She's got to prove how humble she is by riding the bus." He has rushed home from an important RATS session, a dress rehearsal for their upcoming debut in RFK Stadium during the half time of a Redskins game. Though it is another unpaid appearance, this exposure may finally be the second chance for the RATS which Darwin had despaired of; he hadn't known that Miss Piggy's father played squash with the owner of the Redskins. To prepare for what must seem a spontaneous performance two weeks from now, the RATS have been meeting every other evening at Miss Piggy's Dupont Circle co-op; they are launching into a new phase of development. Individual identities must be subdued now; the group must learn to function as a single organism, to listen for the whisper of the collective will. They work on transmitting thoughts by telepathy, then they take turns falling backward into each other's arms or carrying one another around as pallbearers carry coffins.

"You didn't have to drive me," I say.

His heavy brow, his jaw, settle into their coming-unstoned scowl, the reality of a wife who gets hopelessly lost in D.C.

"You realize, if she'd flown," I say, "we'd be stuck right now in the traffic at National. Because normal planes never land out at Dulles, no planes from proletarian Pittsburgh, anyway. It might spoil the atmosphere for the precious —"

"You do find your openings."

"— Concorde and its handful of precious passengers, who don't give a damn about what they're doing to the rest of us as long as they can save a couple of hours of their precious time."

"Whereas with the right attitude they could have crossed the Atlantic perfectly well on foot," Darwin says. "I honestly don't know why you're so hung up on that thing."

"If you and everyone else keep calling it absurd, I can't exactly back down." He gives an ambiguous grunt. The rain streams down the windows; above the river, on our left, the city melts into falls of rippling light. "I hate that plane. I hate everything it stands for. I'm going to protest it forever if I have to, all by myself."

He looks over at me, pulls at the crotch of his trunks, then has to swerve us back into our lane.

"You know what I'm doing?" I ask after a while.

"No, Hannah, I honestly don't."

"I'm concentrating on that little piece of white line disappearing alongside the Bus. It feels like the road's moving backward while we're standing still."

I am also trying not to worry. Plenty of time has passed — years now — since the night Samuel called to say my mother had been plagued by spells of nervousness and weeping. She hadn't wanted to bother me with any of it, he mumbled gloomily, confused, as though reporting hints of life he'd detected on another planet. They were giving her pills, but the pills must have stopped working. She started to scream; they had had to take her by ambulance to the hospital in Pittsburgh.

The next afternoon I was there; at the nurses' station they told me she was downstairs receiving her first treatment. I waited, and then the metal doors at the end of the corridor swung open and a dark little orderly in crisp white marched through. Half a dozen patients in gray gowns shuffled behind him, shoulders bowed, like blind people without canes. *Mother,* I called out when I realized one of them was she, but my smile stiffened at her blank look. *It's me, Hannah,* I said. Her unbraided hair frizzed out around her face, down her back. *Hannah,* she repeated, as if the word meant nothing; then something clicked, her eyes focused, and she managed to properly introduce me to the rest of her group, which by then had all drifted away.

I stayed with her for a week, force-fed her her meals, which she spat into a napkin if she thought I wasn't looking. (She used to claim that if she could take a pill instead of eat, she'd just as soon. While we were at home in the body, after all, we were absent from the Lord.)

After the first few treatments she began to ask to go home, promising that she could forget the bad now and dwell solely on the good. I wasn't sure whose home she was thinking of — she couldn't mean Samuel's prison at New Progress, and I couldn't imagine bringing her to live with us in Sugarland, where I was still hoping we would make a fresh start as a family, a most fragile enterprise. I pretended I didn't hear her pleas. Or I repeated Samuel's parting promise: "We all pray for your recovery. In a month you will be back among us as though you never left." I was trying to protect what I am on the verge of losing now.

Darwin doesn't say another word until the neon spine of a greyhound flashes high on a corner several blocks ahead and he asks where in the fuck he's supposed to park. There are vacant meters up and down the street.

"Why don't you relax a little," I suggest. "It's not like she's coming to see you. She hasn't seen the children in nine years."

She offered to help me after Rachel was born. We were still in the apartment then, crowded and messier than ever, but she never complained — about sleeping on the mattress in the living room, or the bathroom full of diaper pails, or the illegal dog and his bin of cat litter beside the door. I remember the first morning she and the boys built a Janca village in their bedroom out of Tinkertoys and newspaper. A team of plastic astronauts was dubbed Indians, along with a boy doll, which Matthew proudly stripped to its accurate genitals and my mother promptly dressed again. Jeremy starred as Grandfather Worden wearing a real World War II leather flying helmet, complete with goggles, which Samuel had sent along for his fourth birthday.

My mother was pleased that Jeremy and Matthew knew so

much about my father and Ecuador — so much and so little, I realize now. Was Matthew even then catching glimpses of what was missing, what we had to forget in order to strengthen the moral, the pain the story makes no sense without? For that morning it was all adventure and heroic dedication. There was a simple, misguided people, frightened out of their good intentions; there was forgiveness. And when the game ended there was so much salvation, it almost made up for Jeremy's inability to recite a blessing over his peanut butter sandwich.

There wasn't the slightest portent of breakdown then. In fact it was Darwin who was acting crazy. A few months before, Clark Rathbone, the redheaded rock of a man who had first recruited Darwin to the New Left and five years later abandoned it and him for stronger stuff — Clark had blown himself to pieces in his family's summer house in the Poconos. Darwin stopped sleeping, took to wandering around the city at night and working strange hours. When my mother showed up, he lashed out at her about Ecuador, calling her and my father "a search-and-destroy mission" unto themselves, saying that the way he saw it, "fucking with a person's mind or soul is just as brutal as fucking with his body."

"Certainly words," she replied without flinching, "can be as brutal as spears." But after two evenings of such sparring, she cut her visit short.

I plunge ahead of Darwin now through the loud rain, into what may be disaster. I hesitate at the doors to the terminal; they have opened electronically. "Why don't we just let things ride," I call back to him. "That's what I'm trying to do."

"No." He comes puffing up beside me. He has flipped the hem of his cape up over his head and clutches it tight at the throat. Water drips down his glasses. "No, you're not. For two weeks now you've been giving me the bum's rush. You're trying to get me to make promises. I'm supposed to swear, Boy Scout's honor, something about never seeing Heidi again."

I close my eyes, turn my face away from him. Is that what I'm doing? I have tried to avoid dwelling on the simple fact that every other night at RATS rehearsals he *is* seeing her, avoid dwelling on the not-so-simple possibilities that "seeing" implies.

The lighted warmth of the station smells of disinfectant, carbon monoxide, and tired, damp flesh. Darwin's appearance has the effect of a loud noise. Travelers dozing in their seats, fumbling through bags, sharing junk from vending machines, sit up and stare, and he loves it; his eyes take on an odd, dreamy cast as he pretends not to know he has an audience. I head for the far corner of the waiting room. I don't want to be around when the gullible little kid shuffles up to him and stammers out the inevitable questions.

I march along the arrival gates, wringing out my hair. Darwin tags after me, yanking the soggy, clinging cape out from between his knees. "I don't see her," I say. "Her bus must be late."

"Hannah," says Darwin, trying to sound imperative.

"Where *is* she?"

"You're not answering me."

"I am not trying, Darwin, to get you to promise anything. I haven't the right." I can feel my blood rising; I am thinking of Theo's invitation to pretend. Why not? What has our life been up to now but me pretending, clutching my script for the model family, prompting us as if we were being taped for public television?

"Now what are you talking about?"

"Your getting involved with Wonder Woman. Heidi. How could I ask you to promise loyalty when I can't be loyal myself."

"And what is that supposed to mean?" he asks, voice taut, controlled.

I turn back to the waiting room and scan once more the seats along the walls, the rows down the middle. Maybe Darwin and I cannot both be happy at the same time. That is a startling thought. I have always been sure that with the right adjustments, I'd be able to make it so we were.

"Han-nah." He swerves away from me a few steps, then turns back.

We are eye to eye. I have not lied yet. My mind darts and shies at the prospect. Then, with great relief, I see her: no hospital gown, no disheveled hair, but tall and straight, in a long dark coat, crowned with a bright yellow-white braid. She is backing through a door under the prim-skirted sign for women. She is carrying a pastel bundle — in a moment I can tell it is a baby — and there is a young woman lugging suitcases right behind her.

"Yoo hoo, Hannah," she calls.

Just for a moment I want to run to her and throw myself into an embrace, I can even picture it happening, right up to the point where I fall into her arms, someone's arms, anyone's arms, but no, not hers. In an instant the pleasant memory I'd worked to revive is swept away. She expelled me from the village. She packed me onto the plane in Quito saying, *Samuel will be like a father to you,* a promise that his first words — *You will begin as Girl Private, you will find that promotion brings privilege* — cruelly broke. She came to visit Darwin and me after we were married and addressed all her speeches to me. When we told her a baby was due, she got up in the middle of supper and walked herself all the way back to the bus depot.

I cross the room like a normal human being, wondering what I have let myself in for. I wait while she returns the baby to the young woman. I am sweaty, rain-sodden; I offer hands and a cheek. Her kiss, her hands, are dry and quick. She doesn't mention Darwin's costume but reaches for his hand too. Oblivious to everything but her own will, she hangs on to us both until we squirm. "Sharelle needed someone to hold the baby while she relieved herself," she explains. The young woman eyes Darwin and giggles, undaunted by this introduction. She shifts the baby's position so as to display its pinched newborn features. Her own round, rosy brown face looks even rounder, younger under its cap of short black curls. "And I told her we'd wait to make sure she got the right taxicab," my mother says. "We are sort of in the same boat, Sharelle and I. She's going to visit her mother for the first time in quite a while. And I am visiting my daughter."

18

. .
.

ROAST TURKEY IS THE ONLY FOOD I remember liking at New Progress, religiously served three times a year, on Thanksgiving, Christmas, and Easter. The stuffing came out in one gluey lump, the potatoes were runny, the gravy pale and mostly salt, and the vegetables indistinguishable. But the flesh of turkey endured — chewy, substantial, crusted with savory skin — and on those rare special occasions brought the desperate pleasure of a prisoner's last meal.

I have prepared it again as I do three times a year as well; it is the only meat we have not given up. With great care I chose the freshest, largest bird, stuffed it with apples and raisins and nuts, set it to roast breast side down so the juices would collect there. Under has grown restless; the air is thick with that tantalizing smell he cannot quite place. Matthew and Benjamin sort of swagger into the kitchen to check on its progress, Jeremy is anything but gloomy, and Rachel is a little less aloof. It could be the anticipation of mysterious visitors. Mostly, though, I think the children think that for once we are acting the way every other family is acting, getting ready to eat what every other family would eat. We are bringing to brief life the dream that haunts them — I would like to see it explained in Theo's literature — to be exactly the same as everyone else.

And my mother is part of it. She sat through breakfast with them, the model grandmother, telling Janca tales, asking riddles, listening to indignities, ready to give her sympathy to any child who needed it. They like her. They can sense her patience, her concerned interest in them; she takes them utterly seriously. What they don't realize is that she sees each one as a little container of something infinitely valuable, something she wants, the pearl buried in the clinging oyster, a soul. She is willing to wait almost forever to deliver it to Him. *He* is where all roads lead.

When Darwin staggered in, hair matted, the buttons of his flannel shirt a buttonhole off, we all held our breath because she was sitting in his usual seat. "I didn't expect you down so early," I said when he looked at me. Then he settled himself at the end of the table under a hanging spider plant, with a bowl of shredded wheat and the skimpy *Post*.

My mother allowed him the front page. But when he snapped the paper open and folded it back, he had to look up, and she said, "Now, Darwin, what do *you* say to the idea of sharing our blessings with those who are not as well off as we are?"

"Everyone we know is better off than we are," said Darwin.

"Ah," she said. "What about Sharelle and her mother and baby?"

When my mother addresses him, Darwin likes to hunch his shoulders up and squint, as if he were expecting something to crash. A tired joke. He sputtered something now about the idea being fine but a little hard to execute.

"We know her last name is Turner," my mother said.

"Do you have any idea how many Turners there are in the D.C. phone book?" Darwin asked, taking a swipe at the baby spider tufts that floated around his head.

"Maybe it's best I don't," my mother said. "We have all morning."

Four pairs of eyes swung between Darwin and my mother and then focused on me. Darwin picked up his cereal bowl and slurped off the remaining milk.

"Rachel can be in charge of reading me the numbers. My eyesight has gotten so bad."

"Wait a minute, wait a minute," Darwin said, slapping the spiders aside and pushing away from the table. "You can't just

interrupt the lives of a couple hundred people, invade their
privacy —"

"Would you mind handing us the phone book while you're
up?" my mother asked.

It landed on the table in front of her with a smack.

"It's for a good cause," she chided, placing the book in front
of Rachel, who tried to slump small in her seat and stole a guilty
look at her father.

"Tell that to the guy who's got the day off from some shit job
and was planning on sleeping till noon. Or the guy who's in the
john trying to take a crap when the phone rings."

My mother acted as if she didn't hear. "We might as well start
right there" — she poked her large finger at the page — "Adele
A." She stood up slowly and straightened her broad shoulders,
drawing attention to the fact that she is taller than Darwin. He
backed away from her as she moved into position beside the
phone inside the kitchen door. "Just think how you'll feel if the
first person we call turns out to be her," she told Darwin. "You
might feel a little silly about all this fuss. Now." She looked at
Rachel expectantly, who rattled off a string of numbers. My
mother picked them out with a careful finger. Then she stared at
Darwin as we all waited.

"Yes," she said suddenly, her eyes going blank. "I'm trying to
get in touch with a Sharelle Turner. Is this her number?" A brief
pause, then, in her kindest tone: "Are you by any chance a rel-
ative or an acquaintance? I'm sorry to have disturbed —"

With a grotesque smile, Darwin dragged a chair away from the
table, placed it under the phone, and offered it to her with a
sweep of the hand. She smiled back as if he'd been genuinely
thoughtful.

Darwin went downstairs to his desk to update the RATS scrap-
book and redesign their brochure. Each time he came up for
coffee, he guessed at the specific inconvenience my mother had
just caused, dragging her innocent victims out of showers onto
wet tiles where they slipped and cracked their skulls; away from
stoves and frying pans that went up in flames, catching kitchen

curtains, burning whole houses down. Meanwhile Rachel called out number after number and my mother apologized to stranger after stranger, and I kept basting the turkey, mixing pumpkin pie filling, rolling pie crusts, and kneading the bread.

Then when we had all begun to ignore this search going on in the background, my mother reached someone who didn't hang up. She gasped, I saw her free hand fly to her throat, but she recovered her same calm, kind tone as the conversation opened onto a new path. "You are? The Lord be praised! This is your friend Grace Worden. You do remember who I am? Why, thank the Lord. I'm calling to invite you all to come here to share Thanksgiving blessings — the baby, your mother." My mother's lips moved as she listened: they do that now, as if she is praying you will say what she wants you to say. "Your grandmother is welcome to come too. Certainly. Everyone is invited. There is plenty of food." Just then Darwin came up the stairs. "I'm going to turn you over to Darwin now," she said, raising her voice for his benefit, "and you are to tell him how to find you, and he'll drive in and pick you up." She thrust the receiver at him in triumph.

Then she gathered the children around her on the couch in the living room to explain how Sharelle and her family are less fortunate than we are and deserve our kindness. Sharelle has lived with an aunt in Pittsburgh from the time she was Rachel's age because *her* mother was paralyzed from the chest down when a bullet hit her spinal cord and left her barely able to manage in a wheelchair.

Darwin, having received directions and hung up, paced the kitchen frantically. "This isn't the jungle, you know," he muttered. "There must be laws to protect the Sharelles of the world from people like her."

"Not to mention the Darwins of the world?"

"What do *you* care about *them?*" he hissed.

"Oh, Darwin," I said, because he sounded so injured, "she's my mother. It's time we got together."

"What bullet?" Matthew was asking meanwhile in the other room.

"The bullet from a wicked man's gun."

Matthew humphed. That was the obvious answer; he'd been hoping for juicier detail. With his instinct for such things, he'd probably sensed what my mother whispered to me earlier when Rachel was in the bathroom, that the man with the gun was Sharelle's mother's boyfriend, and he'd caught her mother stealing his dope.

"Something's on your mind," Darwin said, and I began again my spastic little dance with Theo's lie. Closing in, backing off. Giving it a quick prod to see if it still moved. All the while, pleading silently with Darwin, and him glaring back at me — unshaven jaw set, eyes full of mistrust. Neither of us happy. How long have we held that pose?

I opened the oven, bowed into the heat, squeezed up the drippings, and squirted them over the bird. "Just smell," I said.

My mother came limping into the doorway, her eyes full of questions, her mouth in the control of an aggressive smile. "Is everything all set up, then?"

Darwin sort of fell onto the counter on his elbows, head in his hands. "Let's make sure I have this straight, Grace. I am to bring back one baby, one young mother, one older mother, largely paralyzed. By the way, how am I supposed to get the latter mother into the car?"

"I guess a man of steel can manage to lift her," I said.

He didn't move; then his head snapped up. "That's *not* such a bad idea," he said, straightening. "Go in uniform. You never know." With his mind's eye he was studying a future scene, gauging the prospects for positive publicity. "OK," he said, "that still leaves the grandmother. Maybe Jeremy'd better go with me in case I need help." He threw me a warning look: *Don't make anything out of that.* "This thing is out of control."

"Out of your control, perhaps," said my literal-minded mother, missing the eagerness in his tone. "Hardly out of control."

"You people with principles are ruthless," said Darwin.

So Darwin in leotard and cape drove off in the Bus with Jeremy, exultant, flushed with father love, not even waving to those he was leaving behind. Matthew, who begged to go with them, probably thinking he'd be able to sniff out something rougher, realer, than my mother's story about the wicked gunman if he could get to the scene of the crime — Matthew tromped downstairs and has begun to pound the punching bag prescribed by Dooley Clement. Dooley says that Matthew doesn't feel safe in the family. Maybe there is too much confusion in the home, Dooley suggests; not necessarily in an absolute sense but in terms of what Matthew can handle. Getting angry is like his armor; we can't expect to strip it away overnight. Harder and faster he hits the thing now, and the rhythm resounds through the house like a heartbeat, hostile, needy. Something has to give.

In the living room Rachel hovers around my mother. The child is almost frantic with fascination now that they've been left to themselves. She asks to touch my mother's skin, so minutely wrinkled and freckled it seems to be covered with tiny scales. She examines the healed gash in the palm of my mother's hand, from the one time she tried to forget she couldn't run very well and went with the Janca women to hunt the boar; through the heavy stocking, Rachel feels the scar along my mother's shin from the same attack. She asks how long my mother's hair is, how long it takes to dry. Can she play with it? From the kitchen I watch my mother's fingers undo her white waist-length hair while Rachel trembles for the moment when she can get her own deft comb into its thickness and indulge her obsession. Patiently, her mouth moving in silence, my mother sits as Rachel's delicate hands fuss over three different kinds of braids. More amazing: she pretends to be interested in all the options Rachel is considering for her own fine dark curls — elaborate styles described half dreamily, like incantation.

I stand in the doorway, bouquet of broccoli in hand. "You should have seen the way she made me wear my hair when I was your age," I tell Rachel, who doesn't look up from her work. "I had to kneel down and spread it over this stone. Then she took a shell and hacked off these wide bangs so that my ears stuck out."

"That wasn't I, Hannah," my mother says in a soft, hurt voice that takes me aback. "It was Nimu."

"I didn't mean I begrudged it," I say. "At least, not until I got to New Progress and had to let it grow out. Talk about rats' nests."

"Nimu did that for me as well. She insisted we would never learn the Janca tongue unless we listened with naked ears."

"And now look at you," I say, because Rachel is daintily poking the last hairpins into the two fat muffs of braid she has coiled right over my mother's ears. But neither one laughs.

Instead, Rachel sinks back on the sofa and starts to comb and flip her own hair. "When's Dad supposed to get back?" she asks, combing, flipping, and before we can answer she adds, "What happened to Sharelle's father, anyway? And her baby's father?"

My mother is ready for this last. Sharelle made a mistake, she explains to Rachel. As a result she had a baby without marrying anyone. The father has run off; God, who is everyone's Father, has His ways of taking care of *him*. As for mother and child, Sharelle found Christ a few months before she gave birth. It is never too late to be saved, Christ is infinitely patient, infinitely merciful, and Sharelle is back in high school with a B+ average.

"Mother," I warn before she has finished her story. She has drawn Rachel over into the circle of her arm. I can't picture myself sitting that close to either of them.

"I am only telling what really happened," my mother says.

Rachel asks my mother how you find Christ.

I hold my breath. Nonchalantly, my mother suggests that Rachel might ask Sharelle when she gets here.

"Don't you dare," I say, too quickly, too loud. "Do you want your father to have a fit?" That gets to Rachel — she will think twice now — but my mother wears a look suggesting that she has just gotten some news about me from God.

"Hannah," she says, but I turn back to the kitchen and am saved by the opening of the front door and the appearance of Valerie, who is mildly surprised by her reception: at the sound of a new voice, Matthew comes thundering up from downstairs, and Benjamin comes down from above, where he has struggled into his Luke Skywalker jumpsuit, while I capture her in a stiff hug as though I didn't see her just the morning before, when I took six dozen cranberry muffins by Womancenter, and how many mornings before that?

My mother and she have never met. They have both heard a great deal about each other and say so.

"Nothing too awful, I hope," Valerie adds, assuming that sideways position of hers, gripping her own waist, talking over one shoulder. She means, of course, the opposite. Reform has made her vulnerable. She feels more secure once people know how bad she has been.

My mother shakes her head and smiles with that calculated reassurance — Valerie's is one more soul she has not given up on. "I heard — I still hear — you turned into a hippie."

Valerie shrugs. "I've been called worse." When she is really anxious, she has a way of building a box around herself with her eyes: they refuse to see things beyond a distance of about two feet.

"Oh," my mother says, "those are his words, not mine. And I tell you, he doesn't mean anything by them. It's what he calls anyone who doesn't go along with him. I don't know how many times I've said, 'Samuel, the word *hippie* simply does not fit the way things are anymore.' And he just gets huffy and says, 'There you go, sounding like one yourself.' "

"Not too many words of his ever did fit," Valerie says to her left elbow.

"For all his faults," my mother says in the gentlest voice, then turns my way to add, "and I would rank a stubborn pride his most ruinous — for all his faults, Samuel was . . . is a gifted man. Gifted, sometimes I think cursed — the Lord works in such unfathomable ways. Samuel's lot has not been easy. He's different. He sees things differently than we do."

" 'We,' Mother?" I try to sound playful, take some of the pressure off Valerie. "When have we ever seen things the same?"

"With Samuel there's a kind of special sight." She doesn't notice the look that Valerie and I exchange — we came of age in the shadow of Samuel's visions, learned to challenge them with some of our own. "Folks are always stopping by," my mother goes on, "and he tells them his war stories, about all those pilots who were so brave, the battles in the sky against impossible odds, with flaming plunges, crashes, heroic endings. They listen spellbound, he has such a way with his words, and he has told the stories so many times. But after they leave feeling all proud and uplifted, Samuel starts thinking the strangest things. The more these people turn to him, the more suspicious he gets. I know a visit from you," my mother says to Valerie, "would do him a world of good."

"Valerie's got enough problems," I say, "without loading on Samuel." Valerie shrugs again.

"She meant a great deal to him," my mother tells me, "she and Roger. He broods about them. He holds himself responsible," she says to Valerie's back, "for what occurred with your brother. He says he *knew* Roger was starting down the path to ruin; he *knew* the boy was struggling with Satan himself; yet he, Samuel, handed Roger the ticket for the bus to Hell, he let him go."

Rachel, wide-eyed, squirms even closer to her grandmother and cradles one large bony hand protectively in her own two small ones. I take Valerie's arm. I know she considers Roger's death *her* responsibility, don't know if she is willing to share it. She was at the same party, in the same room with her brother, though on her own trip, when he announced he had solved the mystery of flight and went out the open window before anyone understood what was happening. When the two guys from the rescue squad barged into the apartment, everyone thought it was just a raid.

"Well, you can tell Reverend Sam I said hi," Valerie says. My mother nods sadly. "Tell him Roger says hi too," Valerie adds, "because I know he does. I know Roger died happy."

The window from which Roger dove was only three stories high; it took him two days to die of internal injuries. I begin nudging Valerie toward the kitchen, claiming I need help.

"Some would say happy for the wrong reasons," Valerie says, "some who think people should all be happy the same way. So tell Reverend Sam that if he can be different, we can be different. And Roger holds nothing against him. He's at peace now, Roger. He can finally stop trying."

Her speech over, she lets me position her with potatoes and peeler at the sink, a pot of water beside her. "You handled that very well," I say, getting back to my broccoli.

Valerie lifts her head and calls to the other room, "I don't blame Reverend Sam for anything either. Because he is what this macho society made him. I mean, he's just a victim himself, I can see that. The helpless victim of the sadomasochism he calls Christianity. I'm not going to hold that against —"

I am slapping the air with my hand. I lip the words, *No religion*. Valerie sighs, because she thinks it might be interesting, taking on my mother over matters religious, and maybe it would be — for her. Valerie has devised her own faith — she has something to fight for, something to fight with. With my mother and me it feels as if I'm dodging around, naked and unarmed, trying to defend an empty plain. I shouldn't say Valerie "devised," because it's not something she sat down and worked out — pieces just come to her when she needs them, like when someone mentions Roger. She believes life is a giant body, but not a human body, not any shape or structure we would recognize. Time is its circulatory system, and we are the blood cells, one generation per heartbeat, traveling each a slightly different course, braving sudden separations and lonely excursions to remote, impoverished capillaries, to spill finally into reunion at the cosmic heart, in a tumult we will all experience as joy.

Bits of potato skin are flying everywhere as Valerie peels with quick, short strokes. It makes me wonder, *What if the cosmic body cut itself? Are those drops of spilled blood lost forever? Where do they fall?* "Another thing," I whisper, nudging her. "This afternoon's gotten a lot more complicated than I expected. We've got four other people coming — I guess you'd have to call them friends of my mother's. One's a baby." Her face and shoulders droop. "It wasn't my idea."

What in the world *was* my idea when I invited my mother? Certainly not four generations of Turners. I try to explain what happened at the bus terminal, but I keep flashing to Rachel sitting beside my mother in the next room, mesmerized, taking everything in, the look on her face of someone wanting to see the light, someone on the verge. "I just thought I should warn you." I begin processing the broccoli for the soufflé.

"You're awfully nervous," Valerie says, when I keep stopping every few minutes to check her progress. "If it's the extra people —" I shake my head. "If it's your mother, I can see it must be weird —"

"I guess I'd forgotten how hard it is to stop her once she makes up her mind. She's so damned sure she knows what's right."

"What I meant was the way she puts up a front, like she's scared someone's going to find her out."

"You're projecting," I tell her, flourishing one of dear Theo's terms. Because that is Valerie now in a nutshell — mysteriously plain on the outside, half hoping and half fearing the world will guess the intricate map of exotic suffering folded within. She's decided *I'm* normal — husband, children, normal. She's decided, or I've convinced her. "Besides," I ask, "who isn't?"

Her reckless potato peeling halts. "Projecting?"

"Putting up a front." She waits for me to go on, frankly interested, always earnest, still as trusting as a child. "Be sure and dig out the whole eye," I say. "They're poison."

She resumes her task and the impulse returns, this time stronger, to tell her something, something undisguised as advice, maybe something about us — her and me. What about those first years at New Progress, or later in the Arlington apartment, when I felt so jealous of her I didn't know who I was or what I was doing? What if I told her now? Then I think, *What did all that pain amount to?* A split second in a lifetime, so temporary it is surely better not to say anything, then or now. People change, after all, move on. I learned finally to live a little apart from Darwin, to focus on the good things, like having Rachel.

Valerie had followed her friends to Florida, sent postcards from the Keys, New Orleans, San Francisco again, and then nothing until a phone call, local, from downtown D.C. I found her in a basement room off Thomas Circle. It was cheap — a mattress, a sink, eighteen dollars a week. She didn't know how long she had been there. Long enough to have had problems with her equipment again, and undergone an outpatient procedure at D.C. General, after which she was to refrain from intercourse for six weeks. She did not refrain — could not, if she was to pay for rent, food, pills — and now, she told me with a terrible pride, she was seeing things, thanks to a spiky fever. She had had several conversations with Roger (that was when I found out he was dead) and was throwing up everything she ate. And though she begged me not to, begged me to let her die, I put her back in the hospital. Someday, she says, she may thank me for saving her life — maybe years from now, when she has finished paying off the medical bills.

From the other room come grandmotherly murmurs and the higher-pitched approval of children. I know I should interrupt whatever is going on out there, whatever she is telling them, promises that may take me months to explain away. Just as I know I shouldn't confide in Valerie — we have an efficient working relationship, why let things get all mixed up? But I'm hearing words in my head, temptingly clear. I have the eggs just at the point to be folded into the puréed broccoli. It is one of those breathless moments before the one you know you'll have to pay a long time for. "Valerie," I whisper, "I've been thinking of leaving Darwin."

"Leaving him?" she almost shouts. "How . . . you can't —"

"I can't take it anymore."

"I never thought," Valerie says softly, and I can see her mind going back over things I have said, done, could feel myself being reshaped, demoted, diminished. In Valerie's world women leave their husbands, corpuscles split and part, every day. What is amazing is when they manage to stick together.

"Don't think," I say. "I just wanted you to know. In case I seem a little spacy —" The Bus was pulling in at the curb. "Oh no, they're here." I am relieved. From the window we watch Jeremy get out on the passenger side, then heave the side door back. The egg whites are losing their stiffness, going runny. Then a baby is lifted into his arms, a baby who to my amazement has doubled in size overnight; then a young woman unbends onto the pavement, looks around with wary defiance. "They're total strangers," I gasp.

Valerie puts a hand on my shoulder. "It's OK," she says. "Stop thinking you have to take care of me. I can cope."

"But I mean stranger strangers than the ones we were expecting."

Jeremy sets the baby on the sidewalk in its furry hooded jacket and high white shoes and holds its hand while it lurches beside him up to the door. "Poor Hannah," Valerie says, and the words ring like doom as I shove the sloshing broccoli mixture into the upper oven, then take on the chaos in the living room, where everyone is standing around waiting to be introduced.

Sharelle's face was soft, a milky, rosy brown, framed with short, tight curls. The difference between her and the person before us is startling. Her skin is the color of oiled walnut; her nose, a thin, fine ridge, flares back into wide, delicate nostrils, and her straightened hair, black with brass streaks, shoots out from the crown like a thick plate. She is wearing sharply creased designer jeans, high-heeled boots, and an acid-green velour top. Anyone can see she is not Sharelle. With a swirl of his cape, Darwin introduces Cheryl Turner, accenting the first name clearly. My mother looks from him to her and back to him with a bewilderment that disturbs me and seems to please him no end.

"This here's my baby La Jette," the stranger says, lofting the child to straddle one hip, leaning away from the weight. "Capital L and capital J. She gets called Jet for short — thirteen months old on Tuesday and never sick a day in her life, not even when that stomach bug come round." She shifts from one boot to the other. "I do not attend school at the present time. But I got plans." She runs a hand over Jet's curls. She gives Jeremy a quick, pleading look. "You didn't tell me you folks lived so far out."

"It's all right, we're shy," he says, sounding a foot taller and handsome. With great formality he announces our names as we nod, then looks over at his father as if they have rehearsed this whole thing.

"We told her she didn't have to come," Darwin says, "that there appeared to be some mistake."

"But she preferred to," Jeremy says.

Jet wraps one of Rachel's fingers in her grasp; Rachel jiggles it; they both smile. The baby has a high, round dimpled forehead, the tiniest nose and chin, and appears to be, as her mother claims, in the best of health. Cheryl puts her down on the floor, and she toddles across the room, her shoes slapping the bare wood, Rachel hovering after. Under staggers over, places his snout right in her face, and licks. Jet chuckles.

"Tell them what you thought," Jeremy says to Cheryl.

"We weren't planning to fix no fancy meal or anything," Cheryl says. "Gramma's always complaining she's too old to fool in the kitchen. Mostly she just watches her programs."

"I mean the other part," Jeremy says, nodding encouragement.

She tips her head doubtfully. I realize that she is beautiful, so fiercely beautiful that you could think her looks were all she was. "You folks won't laugh?"

"They do and you get credit for a miracle," says Darwin.

"Ma'am," Cheryl addresses my mother most politely, "I figured you were a radio station. I figured when I said yes, I know who you are, the free Thanksgiving dinner was like my prize. And then when he shows up like that" — Darwin and Jeremy stifle smiles — "I figured TV, you know, 'Candid Camera,' one of those shows — I was ready for anything."

My mother's lips move for several seconds before she manages to declare, "You are more than welcome to share what we have."

"It must be wonderful," I say to Darwin when I can get him alone in the kitchen, "to be able to laugh at all this."

He nods happily. "Did you see the shocked look on your mother's face? No pun intended."

I am furious. "You don't care how awkward the situation is, do you, or how many people you use, as long as you can play a trick on my mother?"

"That's right, shoot the messenger," Darwin says.

Jeremy sidles through the doorway, puts one hand on each of us, forcing a loose huddle. "There was this old woman in the apartment and she didn't even say hello or good-bye," he tells me, full of hoarse wonder. "We told her she was invited, but she didn't even know we *existed*. She just sat there in front of the TV eating Cheetos."

"Just because things don't happen one way doesn't mean they aren't happening," Darwin says. "She clearly fits the less-fortunate requirement. Besides, I think your son here has the hots for her." He jumps back a moment before Jeremy tries a punch at him. Jeremy has to clamp his arms across his chest and look down to hide his pleasure.

"What do you mean, 'besides'? You think as his father you're supposed to bring home girls for him? You think that's what fathers do for their sons?"

"Jesus Christ, Hannah," Darwin says. "What's gotten into you?" Jeremy's face goes sort of slack and he retreats from the kitchen. "Now look — you've driven him away."

"*I've* driven," I say, trying to control my voice; then all at once I don't care. I'm tired of holding things together, I want to be in on ruining them. My anger folds up into something hard and cold. "I'll tell you what's gotten into me, Darwin," I say, coldly savoring the pun. "It's that I'm involved with someone too."

"I don't believe it," Darwin says, so quickly I can't believe he has heard what I said.

"Fine," I say. "That'll make things easier."

He doesn't like what he is thinking: *If she'd tell me a lie like that, then I don't really know her; but if she's telling the truth, I really don't know her.* "OK," he says, "who is it?"

"Is that all you can say, who is it?"

"I always told *you*."

"That doesn't make it the rule."

"When and how did it start, Hannah? You have to tell me that. If you're trying to get back at me for Heidi, it's a little —"

"You don't care, do you? It's just another news item, reported in not enough detail. You don't really care."

"If you mean, am I hurt, of course I'm hurt, who wouldn't be hurt, but let's —"

"Who wouldn't be hurt?"

"I was about to say, let's face it, I haven't —"

"Just me, I guess. I wouldn't be hurt." Darwin grimaces. "Anyone else in the world would be hurt, but not me."

>> .·. <<

The food is spread before us — the turkey, perfect as always, mashed potatoes and gravy, a gummy broccoli soufflé, candied carrots, whole wheat soda bread, cranberry–mandarin orange salad. The table, huge with its extra leaves, all but fills the dining room, pinning us against the walls. By the time the ten of us are seated, Benjamin has dripped a little of everything onto the handwoven Indian cloth. Matthew has to be stopped from picking only oranges out of the salad. My mother seems not to recognize her own hand as it now and then lifts a spoon from a serving dish to her own. Opposite me, Darwin bows over his plate like a threatened dog. Once he looks up at me and shakes his head. My secret is out: I have been hiding too. Jeremy, beside him, is constructing a sort of citadel of food, roofed with turkey slabs and drenched with gravy. Valerie, usually nose to the grindstone when putting away a free meal, is spending long minutes gazing across her barely filled plate at Cheryl, who welcomes each dish with enthusiastic praise.

I am probably staring too much at Cheryl myself, to avoid looking at Darwin and because I wonder how it feels to be beautiful, whether it affords some higher awareness, some immunity to the sort of petty mess I've made around me. As if it were the greatest tactile pleasure, Cheryl's long fingers tear a slice of turkey into bits, which she flutters into Jet's bowl. Each movement of her lips, her shoulders, her hands, is like a lesson in beauty, a complete surprise yet warmly familiar. She is the young queen in our midst, oblivious to the tensions her presence has increased. Jeremy with the diaper bag, Jeremy with a little more milk for Jet, is her willing knight. But then, when her plate is filled, she folds her arms and launches into a speech, about how she's going to get her GED, how she's going to cosmetology school, how she's on some list to get her own place, how carefully she spends her ADC.

My mother interrupts her gently with a general request for grace, and Cheryl saves us all by volunteering. "Then you are no stranger to the habit of regular worship?" my mother asks, her face brightening, a happy ending, after all.

Cheryl wags her head noncommittally. "My last foster mother was a real churchlady," she explains. "Baptist. They're big on praying all the time — before you eat, after you eat, going to bed, getting up. That was fine, long as she stuck to the same words, but no, she'd got to go and make up new ones right there on the spot, and then nod at me, like I'm supposed to keep up with her. Now, I'm not one of those mindreaders, so pretty soon I just shut up. Then she goes, 'You're lazy. You don't try hard. You think life's a free ride.' And once I found this skinny kitten. All I ever did was sneak it a little milk and bread and one night bring it inside under my coat so it could sleep on my bed. Course, I didn't have no door to my room, and it got out and peed in her old man's Sunday shoes, so she took me and it to the pound. She hands it over to the man and he looks at me like he knows it's my fault, and all the way home she goes, 'That poor cat's life is on your conscience. You're the one that brought it into the house and put it under the temptation to do wrong.' "

"Maybe a moment of silence," my mother says, not for the cat but because no one has yet said grace. But the children are completely absorbed in Cheryl's story of injustice. My mother bows her head and closes her eyes for such a long time that it crosses my mind that maybe she is having a stroke.

Jet is sitting between Cheryl and Rachel in our old high chair, scrubbed over the years down to the bare wood. "No, no," Rachel keeps saying sweetly, "no, no," picking food up off the tray, out of the pocket of the baby's bib, and flicking it back into her bowl, "no, no," shaving mashed potatoes off her round cheeks with the edge of her spoon. Every once in a while she turns to one of the small mounds on her own plate and separates off a precise forkful, and Jet takes advantage of the moment to tip her milk onto her tray, whereupon poor Rachel drops the fork and resumes her cleanup with a despairing sigh.

"That's OK," I tell her, "babies are like that. We'll take care of it later."

She sits on her hands and looks at me.

"She's getting grossed out," Matthew shouts. "A little baby's grossing her out. Isn't it, Miss Saliva?"

"Mother," Rachel moans. In the family we know the word *saliva* makes Rachel sick to her stomach. *Saliva* and *mucus,* which is what Matthew calls her next.

"Sticks and stones, Rachel," Jeremy says, as I have so often reminded him. But her whole body is clenched with distress. I am concerned. She eats so little; why is there always some disturbance at mealtime to upset her appetite? I warn Matthew that he will have to leave the table, and again and again he says he is sorry, explaining that he was jealous of Rachel because the baby is paying so much attention to her. Thanks to Dooley, Matthew has gone from refusing ever to apologize to apologizing so readily and elaborately that you suspect it may amount to the same old thing. And what can I do about my mother, who decides to come to the defense of saliva as God-given and indispensable? She tells how Janca mothers used to chew up the manioc root before feeding it to their babies so the parental saliva could make it easier for the children to digest.

"You were always finicky about food," my mother tells me, as if that explained Rachel's excusing herself now and slipping away.

"My last foster mother was some kind of eater," Cheryl offers, two fingers resting politely on the curve of her mouth to make sure its contents stay hidden. "She said she had this sickness, hy-po-gly-ce-mia. She had to eat a little something every hour or else she'd go into a coma and die. Something like a little jar of fish in cream sauce. Or a few little chocolate-covered caramel turtles. After dinner, she got specially hypoglycemic" — Cheryl's nostrils flare over the syllables — "and started in on her little somethings, and her man and me, we weren't allowed to have any. It was her medicine, she said, and she couldn't afford to share it with us. Except he knew how to get around her; with a woman like that, he said, you got to learn the practice of de-ceit."

"Hear, hear," Darwin says, then slyly draws his cape across his face.

"He's been good to me," Cheryl says, dropping her eyes. "He

still comes by to see us and bring us a few things. But her — she come by D.C. General to tell me good-bye, and she goes, 'This wasn't your first man, was it?' 'My first man, my only man, and a good man,' I tell her. And she goes, 'I believe you don't even know who the father is.' 'You believe what you want to believe,' I tell her. 'You always have.' "

Her words echo in the silence. All of us except Valerie are trying for different reasons to act innocent of their meaning. Then Rachel is back, propping up the wall with her shoulder and cheek. My mother's long arm stretches out to her, draws her to the table. "I'm going to change places with you," my mother says. "It's my turn to sit next to Mr. Matthew." She starts switching around the plates and glasses. "You are all to notice that my hair has been fixed this interesting way by Rachel." She is up, shoving her chair under Rachel and into the table. Valerie, Benjamin, Matthew, and I suck in our breath and pull in our chairs. "Rachel is a genius with hair," my mother says, struggling as she squeezes by.

"Who is the baby's father?" Valerie asks flatly from her own world.

Silence again. My mother stops in transit, grabs the back of Matthew's chair.

"I like my hair real relaxed," Cheryl says. "I put this stuff on you got to leave on all day. One night my foster mother comes into my room and goes, 'You're not putting any more of that stuff on your head and skipping school. You spend entirely too much time looking in that mirror, so I'm taking it away, and I better not see you dragging that comb through your hair except for once in the morning and once at night.' So I walked right out the house."

"I'm sure she had your interests in mind," my mother says, composing herself tentatively in her new seat. "Your schooling —"

"She had money in mind, which she don't get if they don't see me in school. It was real cold outside and I just kept on walking. Didn't know where I was going, just figured when I was too tired to move, I'd be there. But then I got real tired, and real cold, and there was no place to settle in except this Exxon station, and I didn't want to spend the night in no Exxon station, so I figured I'd go back to Gramma's, where I was before they took me away for skipping school and being uncontrollable. But I didn't know how to get to New York Avenue, and there were these three guys with this old van, and so I asked the one pumping gas where New York Avenue was. And they all laughed and said they wouldn't mind taking me there, and a few other places. I thought, I've gotta get out of here. I was so cold and worn out, it scared me. Then I saw her old man in his Pontiac. He was following along after me the whole time. Waiting for me to run out of rocket fuel, he said, so he could carry me back home."

I feel us relax, relieved to get away from those three threatening strangers back to the known territory of Cheryl's foster mother, however mean. Polite requests for seconds of this dish or that dish can begin; Rachel is finally taking firm bites of her firsts.

Valerie has stretched to hand Cheryl the stuffing. "This a lot better than Stove Top," Cheryl says. "Gramma, she loves Stove Top. We eat boxes and boxes of Stove Top."

"Were you getting around to answering my question?" asks Valerie.

"Give us a break!" Darwin explodes. "She's a guest, not a fucking criminal."

"Try victim, Darwin," Valerie says. "She's obviously trying to tell us something, but you wouldn't pick that up in a million years."

Cheryl is shaking her head deliberately, as though in response to my murmuring that I made the stuffing from scratch.

My mother, wishing to protect the children, offers what she thinks is a wonderful idea: "Maybe Cheryl would be more comfortable talking to Valerie in private."

"Who says I'm uncomfortable?" Cheryl asks. "This is nothing." Her long fingers brush us away. "Folks can say what they want to say and think what they want to think. I got nothing to be ashamed of. He was a good man."

"She doesn't mean that," Valerie insists to Darwin.

"How can you say good?" my mother asks.

"Ma'am, I don't care if you don't believe me," Cheryl says coolly. "Everyone's on her side. I'm used to it."

"But we're not on her side," Valerie says ambiguously, crowding Rachel as she reaches to pat Cheryl's fist.

"You act just like my social worker," Cheryl tells Valerie.

"You didn't mean it that way, did you, Mother?" I ask, but Cheryl's bright friendliness has faded, our efforts to be trusted are in vain — odd, that a secret lover is where she has staked her strength.

My mother is shaking her head, worried. She stands up, taller than any of us, and braced by the wall behind her, shoves the table away several inches to make room for her escape. "Why don't the children and I," she says, "take Jet downstairs to see Either?"

"But it doesn't move anymore or anything," Jeremy, wedged now in the corner, says in a thick voice.

Darwin says, "Relax, Grace. It won't kill them to get a dose of the truth."

"You still insist on calling wickedness truth."

Cheryl throws herself back in her chair. "See?" she says, triumphant. "She thinks I'm wicked."

"The *man* was wicked," my mother says grimly. "Wicked beyond words." She limps out to the kitchen.

"Was he the guy with the gun?" Matthew wants to know.

"You'll never get me to think bad of him," Cheryl says. "He's Jet's daddy. She's got his same blood."

Jet, busy squeezing potatoes, senses our sudden collective attention, looks up, and smiles winningly.

"Oh God," Valerie says, and slaps her hands over her face.

My mother returns with a wrung dishcloth and begins wiping Jet's hands, plump finger by finger, and then, careful not to catch her legs, lifts her from the chair. She turns to Darwin. "I can't think things through as well as I used to," she says. "Things I knew as well as I know my own name I've forgotten. But one thing it seems I shall never be allowed to forget is how much you dislike me."

"I don't dislike you," Darwin says reflexively. "But I do appreciate the truth. This is the truth we're hearing."

"This is a human being who has lost her way." While my mother gazes at Rachel to stress the metaphor, the baby watches every movement of her pale, lined face.

"Well, not anymore she hasn't. Hannah and Valerie just found her. And they are about to put all the formidable male-bashing resources of their Womancenter at her disposal."

Valerie turns away from the table. "Fuck off, Darwin," she spits back over one shoulder.

"And if the blind lead the blind," my mother says, "both shall fall in a ditch."

"Mother," I say.

"They're in seventh heaven now," Darwin says. "They figure they've got the closest thing to an innocent victim they'll ever see."

"God, you're a prick," Valerie says. "I hope you *do* leave him," she tells me.

Darwin is on his feet, then Jeremy, then Benjamin, shoving the table back the other way. "That does it," he yells at me. "I've had enough, OK? I want to know what in the hell is going on. Right now."

I am too terrified to think, much less speak. The children are looking at me, thoroughly confused. Valerie keeps touching me and trying to apologize for her loose mouth and I keep shrugging her away.

"You *are* amazing," Darwin is saying. "You can manage to cook and serve a complete banquet for ten and still find time to badmouth our private life to your friend. I suppose you've told *her* too." He cocks his head toward my mother.

"Hannah has never told me anything of your private life," my mother says. "Jeremy, lead Rachel and me downstairs so we can show Jet the snake."

"There isn't much to see," Jeremy says, eyeing his father with consternation — the father who might need him. "He just lies there like an old hose."

"As strange as it may seem," my mother says to Darwin, "Hannah and I have more important things to talk about than you and your" — she gropes for an undeniable word — "your quirks."

My head clears at this truth; it is the idea I had lost all morning come back: my mother and I sitting face to face, just talking to each other, who knows about what — quick, humble little things, nothing dramatic, no heroes, no moral endings.

As if mocking my thoughts, Benjamin shrieks in a tone he should save for emergencies, "But we didn't tell the story of Grandfather Worden yet."

"While they're downstairs, Cheryl," I say, calmer now, "why don't you help Valerie and me get dessert."

Quick as a monkey, Benjamin works his way, spread-eagle, to the top of the kitchen door frame. Head hunched forward, the satin crotch of his jumpsuit stretched taut, he appears to be supporting the lintel on his shoulders. Rachel is slumped in her chair, eyes downcast.

"Ra-chel," Matthew says, giving her a kick under the table. "You're supposed to go downsta-yers."

"Matthew," I say, bending to pass under Benjamin's braced legs.

"I'm sorry," he says. "I shouldn't try to control someone else's actions. I'm very sorry."

"I don't believe this," Darwin says. "I don't believe you can all just get up and run off to look at snakes or fix desserts in the middle of this."

"We've always been in the middle of this, Darwin," I venture from the kitchen. "It's just that I've stopped pretending we're not. But life goes on."

I hear a strangled version of Rachel's voice whisper, "I hate that snake," then the sound of sudden tears.

"Rachel!" I come back through the doorway in alarm, forget to stoop, and dislodge Benjamin, who lands on my back. "You never cry." I disentangle myself from Benjamin, who begins to blame me for ripping the inseam of his Luke Skywalker suit. I try to touch Rachel's hair, but she waves my hand away.

"Think positive," I tell Benjamin in an aside. "It means you've gotten too big for your britches, you've grown."

"And when can I expect to be served the papers?" Darwin asks.

"What papers?"

"Divorce papers."

With an awful scream, Rachel bolts from her chair, wraps her arms around Darwin, digs her face into his chest. My mother's eyes flinch and go blank. She hands Jet to Cheryl, as if the baby's weight has become too much for her. She just stands there alone, one hand shielding her eyes until they can recover their focus. I am pulled too many different ways to move.

"You are blowing this out of proportion," I tell Darwin.

"How can I be blowing it out of proportion? It's like pregnancy, or death. People don't get somewhat divorced."

"You are deliberately escalating things," I say, "in order to get the upper hand."

"I forgot. You wanted to let things ride."

My mother's lips have been moving, praying. "I'm sorry," she says in a shaky voice. "I don't understand what is happening. I never meant to make things more difficult for the two of you, and I'm sorry if I have."

"You know, Grace, *you've* never liked *me* either," Darwin says.

"None of this is your fault, Mother," I say at the same time. From downstairs comes the thump-thump of Matthew punching.

"Well, I'm sorry too," Valerie says, a throb in her voice. "I'm sorry I got so wrapped up in my own problems, I didn't realize Hannah had her own. We'll figure something out," she promises me, and my stomach sinks.

Darwin lifts one hand off Rachel's back, offers a palms-up to Cheryl. "Look, anytime you want to go . . ."

"No problem," Cheryl says, swaying from one boot to the other, Jet's soft, round cheek dented against her shoulder. Jeremy has worked his way over beside her so that as she sways she brushes him with her hip. She seems more composed now than ever. "We like getting out, going places, meeting people. I got a little messed up back there, but you folks had me worried, acting like you got plans for me and Jet. Like maybe you want us to do something we don't want to do, and I can't deal with that. But I see now you folks got more issues than me, you just trying to forget them by grabbing on mine. I can deal with that, I'm used to it."

"Darwin," my mother says with great effort, "someday you will stop pretending that you expect next to nothing from life, when really you expect so much."

"Say no more, say no more," Darwin says, tightening his arms around Rachel. "I can guess where I'm supposed to find it."

"You are a big step ahead of me, then," my mother says, "because truthfully I cannot."

19

MISSING UNDER'S WARMTH, I stop trying to sleep, sit up, set my feet on the floor. Behind me Darwin's body shifts, contracts. In the middle of last night he woke me up with an awful groan, the sort of sound you'd expect from a person dying, and then called out something garbled in a voice not his, slurred and pained, called out as if to someone whose help he despaired of. He hasn't done that since Chicago.

I put slippers on over the woolen socks I wear at night and my robe over the sweatshirt over the nightgown. Halfway down the stairs in the dark, I pick up a funny sound, imagine Jeremy's overcrowded mice, which have taken to snacking on each other, now chewing their way out of the cage. But it's only the sound of a spoon dipping into a bowl of dry cereal — there's the shadow at the kitchen table of Benjamin's head, the boy who'd rather starve than gum his Wheaties up with milk. Underdog, fair-weather friend, holds the spot at Benjamin's feet.

"Don't you want the light on?" I ask. In the window behind him, the palest hint of dawn.

"My eyes are used to it," he says.

"Mind if I join you?" I ask.

He shakes his head, keeps on eating, raining every fifth or sixth spoonful down on the busy dog. He is not sulking, he is just not a talker, he is more a doer, always needing to prove that he can. Somewhere in one of the nearby natural areas, removed from view of the communal walkway, he and two buddies have built a treehouse, which is against the covenants of the Sugarland Community Association, of which I am the secretary. *Don't tell,* he said; *Don't get caught,* I said, *and don't fall.* We are partners in crime. He places his bare feet in my lap; they're like ice. I make the obvious suggestion, he makes the standard negative response. According to all my children, dressing warmly enough is simply not an option, it's just not done.

He dumps the last of the Wheaties into his bowl. "Are you and Dad going to get a divorce?" he asks, almost mechanically. He doesn't even stop eating to hear my answer, as if he knows what it will be — denial, reassurance. After all, if I could turn the murder of his grandfather into a cause for celebration, I can do anything.

I slip back into that August heat wave. We are lugging boxes and plastic bags, our earthly possessions, from a student apartment onto a U-Haul. We are putting Penn State and radical politics behind us. We make it as far as Providence Hospital in Hagerstown, Maryland, the emergency room. I am awake through it all, the panic, the chaos, the pain, the delivery of Benjamin, who seemed the creature of another race, made to a different scale, terrifyingly small, like something you'd see in a jar. Looking back I have felt like a quitter. The day had been so hot, unbreathable, I was tired and afraid of what lay ahead, I gave up. I should have tried harder to hang on to him, allow him those last weeks in the womb. Why am I always trying to give everyone something back?

"I don't know, Benjamin," I say. He pauses in his munching, surprised. "I just don't know what we're going to do." He puts down his spoon and pushes away the bowl, slides his feet off my lap and crosses his arms over his chest. Poor Benjamin, he doesn't ask for much. But he does. What he wants, a happy family, amounts to everything. And it seems wrong to me now to keep hope going in everyone else when I don't have much myself.

>> .∴. <<

My mother is sipping black tea and talking about Samuel's diabetes with such emphasis that I can't help but understand it as a metaphor for marital problems, specifically Darwin's and mine. At least she isn't bringing in God.

Samuel's disease was mild in its early stages, and might have been kept under control, virtually cured, if Samuel had paid it the attention it deserved, taken precautions. But I knew Samuel, didn't I, his insatiable sweet tooth? "He'd insist that a few gumdrops couldn't hurt, but when did he ever eat a few when he didn't finish the whole bag? And then he'd be deathly sick. So finally they had to remove his leg. But that hasn't made the disease any better. It's too late for getting better. They took his leg to keep things from getting worse."

I am sitting across from her, still in my night layers, half listening, as I try to decide whether to bake. The way other people wonder whether to get up in the morning or maybe just once, just for a change, stay in bed for the day, I wonder whether to bake. Benjamin has gone downstairs and tuned in the sounds of morning television — proof that somewhere man is cordial, cheerful, amusing and easily amused. Rachel is stirring upstairs. I hear the soft roar of her blow-dryer as she polishes the appearance she will eventually make at the kitchen door.

"You'll notice too," my mother is saying, "that in the early stages, there was no question of amputation. No one even talked about that as a solution, it would have been so out of proportion to the problem at hand."

"Maybe if someone had threatened to cut his leg off, Samuel would have realized what the stakes were. You and Rachel certainly seem to have hit it off."

"She is a delightful child."

"Of course she is." I lower my voice. "I think she was born knowing things I never will."

"Sounds familiar," my mother says.

"She's a lot like you, Mother," I blurt. "The way she has to have everything under control."

"I was thinking of you."

"Me?"

"From about the age of seven on."

"I never had anything under control."

Just then Rachel, perfectly coiffed in her pink and blue rugby shirt and painter's pants, a giant chartreuse comb jutting from a pocket on the side of her leg — Rachel comes into the kitchen cautiously, as if she knows we've been talking about her. I shuffle over to the counter, run warm water for the yeast, pull out the bags of flour. If I skip one day, I'll skip two days, if two days, maybe three, and then I might never bake again.

My mother smiles at her warmly. "What interesting earrings," she says of the pink enamel zippers that hang from Rachel's lobes.

"Sometimes if I don't want to hear things," Rachel says, "I can zip them closed."

"Please don't hang on the door of the refrigerator," I say. Rachel is always hanging from handles, draping herself over railings, slumping against things, as if she hasn't the strength to stand straight without a prop.

"That was a joke, you guys," she says. She is slowly circling the table, her back against the counters, the wall, watching us with Darwin's dark eyes. "Are we going to see Cheryl and Jet again?" she asks.

"Would you like to?" I ask back, pouring a cup of buttermilk into the bowl of flours, forcing the mixture with a wooden spoon.

Rachel checks her reflection in the upper oven door. "I'm kind of worried about them."

"I got the impression Valerie was going to help them out," my mother says innocently. "First of all, Cheryl must finish her schooling."

"We'll call them in a week or so." I don't want to hear what is second of all. "We'll invite them to dinner again. Or maybe go to a museum."

My mother stretches her arm out as Rachel comes closer. Rachel takes a step back. "Are we ever going to have another baby?" the child asks.

It is my least favorite moment in bread-baking, the preliminary kneading, before the dough begins to cohere and it just sticks in little gooey peaks all over your palms, between every finger, until you could almost scream. And now Rachel is asking a question that, theoretically, she should know the answer to, I have always been frank, or at least scientific, with the children about sex — asking it in front of my mother, who doesn't know, with whom I have probably never been.

Luckily my mother's mind is somewhere else. "I have to go back to Samuel's tomorrow," she says to Rachel. A subtle plea. Ever since my mother's shock treatments, I keep feeling caught, torn, between wanting to protect her and wanting to attack.

A subtle child, Rachel sort of inches into the circle of my mother's arm, or rather arches her pliant back into it while shoulders and feet keep their distance — if my mother removed her arm, Rachel would snap back out of reach. "Maybe when you're old enough to take the bus all by yourself," my mother says, "you'll come to visit Samuel and me. Maybe next summer. Samuel's never laid eyes on you. Who knows how many summers he has left."

Sidelong I watch my mother's gaze slide over Rachel's face, taking in each feature, looking for a sign of *yes*. Her lips are moving. She would never want to pressure the child, but. It's as if a sadness, a ghost, has swept into the room, and I feel it hovering over the two of them, but my mother doesn't seem to know it's there. "I'm going to miss my Rachel," she says, firm of voice — she still doesn't feel it, though I can tell from the wary look on Rachel's face that *she*'s starting to sense its presence. And then, without warning, it's smothering me.

"Oh, hell," I say, shaking out my hands, "this dough will never stiffen up." I throw the wad back into the bowl, shove it in the upper oven. "Goddamn humidity or something. Screw it." I wash my hands with some frenzy, dry them viciously.

"Is something the matter, Hannah?" my mother asks.

"Nothing," I say. She isn't even looking at me but at Rachel, fickle girl, whose one arm is hooked now around her broad shoulders.

"Why in the hell did you ever leave Ecuador?" The question startles me as much as her. "I don't mean that I'm not glad that you came, that you're here, right now, with us. But I mean, in general, why go and change everything like that? I mean, weren't you happy with the Janca, wasn't it your mission?"

"Someday, maybe I will be able to explain it to —"

"I would have come and visited you there, I could have brought the children, maybe every other year at the end of the dry season we could have flown there, they could have seen the forest, Bai, and *her* children. Why didn't you ever let me come back to visit after I left? And why in the world did you make me leave? How could you make me leave like that? I thought I could forget that, but I can't. It wasn't fair." I stop because I have been hammering the air with my fists, and she has set aside Rachel's embrace and stood up. There is the same baffled look on her face I saw yesterday when Cheryl arrived. As if her mind is playing tricks on her, as if she's trying to remember something, or even trying not to. Rachel looks paler than usual. "I'm sorry. I don't know what got into me. I'm sorry."

My mother is mouthing silent answers. Matthew is in the doorway. In a voice straining for indifference, Rachel tells him, "Mom's losing it."

"I am not, for heaven's sake. It was nothing, a little flare-up. I'm fine."

"I know why I did it," my mother murmurs finally. "I shall never know how."

"She's just expressing her anger," Matthew says, and sets about getting his breakfast.

"Well, I'm glad you've got it all figured out," I say.

"When you were all I had," my mother says, still more to herself than out loud. "How could I have parted with you? Of course I wanted you to have much more than village life could offer. But suppose it was pride. I'm afraid I was too young twenty years ago to know the difference between pride and faith. Suppose I was proving how little I could live on, how much I could give up. If that was the way it was, God forgive me."

"God?" I ask, heading for the stairs. God?

>> ∴ <<

I am considering the ridge under our down comforter — Darwin's leg, hip, shoulder, a tangle of hair — when the phone rings once and then Rachel calls up to me: it is Valerie. I would prefer to take it in the basement, with Either, Benjamin, and the mice, but that would look suspicious, as if I have something to hide. I go back down to the kitchen.

"How *are* you?" she asks.

"Fine," I declare.

"I would have come over, but there's no one to take the calls."

"That's OK. We're pretty busy here."

"Here too. The minute they put out the trees and tinsel at the malls, I get self-destruction on the line. But I thought you should know that the next cycle of Survival Seminars begins the first week in January. It's two sessions on the legal stuff, two on single parenting, one on job training."

I thanked her, told her I'd keep it in mind.

"I thought I'd check if you wanted to sign up."

"It feels just a little premature." I glance over at my mother, who is determined not to listen, or at least not to appear to be listening, and is sort of bumbling around putting water on for more tea.

"It's never too soon to know your legal rights, is it? I mean, once you're married, it's practically too late."

"Don't be dramatic, Valerie. It doesn't help."

"You've got to be sure you're the plaintiff, Hannah. You don't want to do anything like desert or commit adultery that would let him sue *you*. You could lose everything."

I hunch over the receiver; it's like a live grenade I will have to smother with my body. "Thanks, Valerie. Thanks for your support, but what I really need right now is for you to —"

"But you could probably build a case for constructive desertion. That's like he forces you to —"

"— stop interfering." Silence on the other end. Someone is moving around upstairs now, Benjamin's downstairs, my mother's behind me, breathing in sighs. Matthew is drizzling honey all over a muffin. Rachel has slipped off her Docksiders and perched on a chair, her knees drawn up under her chin. "Valerie? I'm just not there yet, Valerie."

"That's what they all say at first." I have dropped another notch in Valerie's estimation, into the category she calls "typical women."

"Dear God," my mother says as I turn away from the phone, and she sinks into a chair beside Rachel.

"Grandma," Rachel asks, fiddling with her bare feet, "do you think my toes are deformed?"

>> ∴∵ <<

The dough has risen. It always does. Just when I'm wondering what I did wrong this time, it swells itself smooth and turns the right kind of rubbery.

"What was that phone call?" Darwin asks from the doorway, startling all four of us.

"What kind of a question is that?" I ask back.

"It was just Valerie," Rachel says, and steals a nervous look at my mother, who gives her a gentle shove under the table. Half gawky, half graceful, Rachel scampers on bare tiptoes over to Darwin. I see the whole thing; Darwin doesn't notice. She drapes herself around his middle.

I punch the swelling down, jerk the dough into four parts, slap each into a pan. "You'd have a fit if I asked you a question like that."

"Rachel's feet are gross," Matthew says amenably. "If I made the rules around here, she wouldn't be allowed to show them when people were trying to eat."

"Just Valerie, unjust Valerie," Darwin says, patting Rachel's head. She slinks back to her chair.

"Don't," I warn him.

"Don't what?" The picture of puzzled innocence.

"Say anything about her." Of all the betrayals Darwin has suffered, Valerie's was the least intentional, the least direct. Still, he can't resist slipping in his snide comments here and there. I think it scares him that he thought he was sort of close to her once and then she turned around and started falling for women. Maybe he can't forgive her for acting out the same distaste for his body that he has himself.

"But I'm curious as to what she had to say." He rips a banana from the hand on the counter, peels the top half, and bites it off. "You all do understand that, don't you" — we have turned away from the sight of chewed pulp — "I mean after yesterday? She seems to be in charge of important family announcements. When Valerie talks, we all damn well better listen."

Enter Jeremy, yellow hair and eyebrows atangle, sleep in his puffy eyes. Darwin pulls him over to stand beside him.

"Jeremy and I were talking," Darwin says in the voice he uses to tell jokes. Jeremy nods like a puppet; Darwin is turning him into a puppet. "About yesterday." He looks around, enjoying the tension, the silent promptings, *Forget yesterday, we can forget it if you will.*

"Why is everyone in the kitchen?" I ask. "I'm baking. I've got an excuse."

"And we're in here because you're in here," Darwin says. "We're in here because we want you to know that we don't believe you."

"Oh?" My pulse races. He's acting as if he knows what he's talking about, and how can he?

"Under keeps farting," Matthew says.

"It's all that turkey skin," I say. "I warned you kids to go easy."

"We don't think you'd ever leave us because we mean too much to you."

"Praise the Lord," my mother says.

"Stop that, Mother. Can't you see he's twisting things around?" The children hold their poses like statues. I look at Darwin. "Since when are you an *us*? Since when are you the defender of the family?"

Darwin rests a hand on Jeremy's shoulder, raises his eyebrows, shoves his glasses back up on his nose, and, making one of those resigned non-smiles, wisely says nothing.

>> ∴ <<

He is taking all the children, including Matthew, who looked over at me with pleading eyes — he has put in almost the full month of his restriction — and then broke into a grin when I gave him the nod. The RATS have rented the community activities room in Batman's high-rise for their afternoon workshop and hired a consultant, a graduate of Barnum and Bailey Clown College in Florida. Darwin even invited my mother, and, to really flaunt his cunning, me. I took him aside and told him I knew better than to take his invitations seriously. I was not even tempted. And he said he wasn't trying to tempt me, he was just delivering on an old promise to the kids.

After they leave, my mother and I settle ourselves in the kitchen, where I can be doing things, washing down the counter, organizing the spice cabinet, my baking supplies, things I have never seen the need to do until now, when I must tell my mother, "I don't understand where you are coming from, you have never accepted this marriage, you have always disapproved of Darwin, and now it feels like you're pushing him on me, cheering him on."

"Darwin was everything I expected, everything I was afraid of. He was the worst thing that could have happened. He was much harder than losing your father. But" — she raises a finger as though I were a resistant child — "those are feelings, not facts. It is time we concentrated on facts."

She pauses for me to respond, but I refuse. She can't expect me to applaud this sudden shift of hers. We've been too long the other way.

"You do remember the Gospel according to Luke," she says, "the story of the Prodigal Son?"

"Those aren't exactly facts, Mother. And what happened to the gospel according to Samuel? The story of You Made Your Bed and You'll Lie in It?"

She tells me she has prayed for Darwin, and she senses he wants to change.

"This isn't the rain forest, Mother. He's not as easy a mark as one of your Janca."

"What do you mean, 'easy'?" For a moment I think I have made her mad, but then her face sort of collapses in confusion.

As if she has lost her place again, and her lips are asking, *What day is this? Who is this person? Where is this house?* Her shocked look, Darwin called it, if she only knew.

"I know him a lot better than you do, and I think he's putting one over on you."

The way she looks around the kitchen, as if she can't see it is only a kitchen, scares me. "But you must ask yourself why, Hannah," she says. "Why is he even bothering to try?"

>> ∴ <<

Midafternoon, the phone rings and it is Theo. I have almost forgotten such a person does exist, real and strange, outside my own mind, my own uses.

"Just a minute, I'll have to run downstairs and check," I say, and then call my mother from the living room to take the receiver. "Would you hang this up? After I'm on the extension." She looks as if she has questions. "It's someone in one of my classes who needs something," I say, blithe as Rachel when she makes the same kind of escape from me.

"You're right," Theo says when my mother is off the line.

"About what?"

"I need something."

"How was your Thanksgiving?"

"All you can eat for five ninety-five at the Hot Shoppes. And now it's Friday and I don't want to be a virgin."

He is being funny to disarm me. What he really wants is my story, for his publication, his tenure. "In two weeks you'll have to decide whether I deserve an A."

"Meet me somewhere for coffee. We could talk."

"I can't, Theo. I'm sorry. Darwin has the Bus."

"I'll come pick you up."

"My mother's visiting until tomorrow. I can't leave her."

"If she weren't there, would you let me?"

"What?"

"Pick you up."

I realize what he is asking. I haven't the courage to say either no or yes. "On a Tuesday or a Thursday, maybe."

Theo laughs longer than seems necessary. "Hannah," he says. "I'm still here."

"What do you think of this phone call?"

"This phone call?"

"Well, me. I'm working on being more spontaneous. But it's hard. You have to try to forget what you're going to do next and why, and how other people will react, and why, and so on. It's hard to make room for surprise."

I can't resist. "How about this? I told Darwin about us."

Silence, and then, "Us?"

"Well, the pretend us. What you said."

"Hunh," Theo says.

"What's the matter?"

"I guess I'm surprised."

"Isn't that what you wanted?" I have just noticed that Either after weeks of immobility has somehow shifted from one side of his cage to the other, leaving behind what looks like a transparent ghost of himself.

"Is it what *you* want?" asks Theo.

"Which?" I am wondering whether I should try to describe for him what has happened with the snake.

"Damn it, don't you even realize when you've made a decision?"

I'm confused. I don't answer.

"I'm sorry," he says. "All I meant was, you would not have told your husband about *us* if you were planning to, if you thought you and I were ever going to in actuality do anything."

"I wouldn't have? I would think I would have, I mean how could I not have —" I am growing less confused, more wary, as I talk. "Wouldn't I have to tell him if I wanted to be with you?"

"I see."

The long pause and then his flattened tone makes me a little panicky. "What do you see?"

"As I recall, your invitation made reference to an affair."

That is all he is going to say. He will wait now for the implications to unfold in my mind. "Affair" meant you didn't actually tell your husband, you couldn't be thinking about actually leaving your husband, and if you did, you couldn't expect the other man's interest to weather such revisions. "So now you're worried," I guessed. "About what I'll do next."

"Maybe a little concerned."

"Don't think you have any obligations here, Theo. The whole thing was pretend anyway, remember?"

"This has nothing to do with you, Hannah. There'll always be this piece of me that tries to avoid messes. I mean I can't help looking ahead and thinking, *Careful. Slow down. Maybe a little discomfort now is preferable to major heartbreak months from now.*"

"How lucky for you that you have any choice."

>> .∴. <<

"Guess what," I tell my mother, showing her Either's old skin draped across my open palms like a tube of crumpled clouded cellophane.

"Maybe you will have good luck," she says in a dull voice that reminds me how many years she did battle against pagan superstition, tried to force light into the forest of spirits and signs, where snakes bore their special power. In their quick and deadly bodies, the souls of your ancestors waited for rebirth. The sloughed skins somehow promised this.

>> .∴. <<

The afternoon sky has darkened and the wind has grown audible, whipping down the communal hill behind our cluster, bending the bare trees along the creek at its foot. My mother and I sit across from each other in the dim living room; we have been reminiscing about Ecuador for over an hour, and it's like we've forgotten we can turn on an electric light.

It's funny, but for once it isn't bothering me to hear her stories of Janca life, versions designed to gently amuse and/or commemorate another victory for Christ. After so much confusion maybe I welcome their familiarity — I chime in with helpful details and try to get her to laugh at the silly, random things those treatments have burned from her brain.

In this respite, a wish occurs to me, and I begin to tell it to her — "First of all that Father was alive, just for one day, and then that he and you and the children and I could all fly to Ecuador and be —"

The Concorde interrupts us with a deafening crash, and my mother goes rigid with fright. I roll Under off my feet, slide next to her on the couch, and grip her hand till it passes. "What happened?" she gasps.

I explain how we are victims of these invasions, how my plans to protest them have rallied no one. I start to enumerate the threats to the quality of our lives, but I see that her attention has drifted. She's gazing at her hand, which I stop kneading with both of mine. "But just imagine," I go on, trying to restore our mood, "all of us entering the village and seeing Nimu and Bai. Darwin and Valerie and Samuel could come too. Why not? Just for one day."

My mother retracts her hand. "I don't see what that would accomplish."

I don't see why she sounds so sullen. "It probably wouldn't *accomplish* much. But we would all get to meet each other. And just, I don't know — see who we were."

"And what would you have to say to this father of yours?"

"Well, plenty of things. I would —"

"He had a passion for flying, you know. He might very well have sold his soul for a chance at the controls of one of those fast things you're talking about. And don't forget, he is seven years younger than you and fatally taken with his own strength of body and mind."

"What do you mean?"

"I mean he will look at us but not see us. He will probably not even notice we are older. 'So it is Hannah and Grace,' he will say with a smile and an embrace that just assumes it is welcome. He will tell us he loves us, but with his every gesture, every intonation — it is written all over him — we will realize how incidental we are. And nothing will ever stop him from going too far."

"Sometimes a person can't not," I say. And isn't *she* the one who taught me the next question, posed reverently, rhetorically:

"Where would things be with the Janca if he hadn't been willing to go as far as he did?"

"That is what we will never know."

"Mother," I say, the way I might chide Matthew for a nasty remark.

"If he hadn't played his part, they wouldn't have been forced into theirs." She looks hard at me, then drops her face into her hands. "And maybe you and I would never have been caught in the middle."

I ask her again what she means, but she starts gasping for breath in loud coughs and her shoulders rise and fall. I have never seen my mother cry. I am not sure that is what she is doing now. A little frightened, I clamp an arm around her shoulders. I have to stop her should she try to run out into the night.

I don't know how many minutes pass of this labored breathing, but eventually her shudders calm, I can feel her muscles relax some. She lifts her head and adjusts her braided crown. It seems darker inside now than out, but as I withdraw my arm, I let my hand brush her cheek and it is dry. "I'm sorry, Hannah," she says.

"Don't be sorry."

"No, it is wrong to despair. And arrogant to assume that if I have failed, He has failed, or that our one little piece of things is the whole picture."

Then it occurs to me, and I bounce away from her on the couch so I can see her better. "Look, we *could* go back. You and I, and maybe the children, if we could scrape together enough for their fares. I mean for a month or so, long enough for us to get the feel of it again. It would be such a great experience for the kids. Imagine seeing Bai again and —"

"Please, Hannah," my mother interrupts. "I don't think you understand. Everything you remember is gone."

"I meant the *new* village, wherever it is. It's the people I want to see, not some particular spot in the jungle."

My mother reaches out and grasps my arm, she bows her head. "For months before I left, Hannah, the young men had stopped speaking English or coming to God's House. Naemwi, Kaewi, the others. They burned a fire away from the clearing, all night. Sometimes they came to my hut and danced wildly around it. Sometimes when I left the hut at night to use the facilities, a pair of boys would rise up suddenly in the middle of the path, whooping and rolling their painted eyes. There were rumors that Jiwaro was hiding just a day upriver. And it really didn't matter if it was true or not because his memory had filled the boys so, they were all images of him." She looks up into my face. "And there were rumors that Naemwi fought with his wife and struck her."

I shake off her hand and sit back, try to picture Bai hanging naked among the women, given over to the grinding, bearing down. Beyond the bark-cloth screen, Naemwi preening. As if the memory would refute my mother's words. "But you went to them," I tell her. "You said something."

"When I tried to speak to Bai, she denied it. Just as she denied there was anything wrong with the way Naemwi and his friends were acting. One day I made her come with me beyond the garden, Bai and half a dozen little ones who had to go along, of course, skipping behind us along the trail, scrambling and pawing through the brush, pulling up short when we reached the hidden clearing. Three columns of balsa were planted in the center, with horizontal crosspieces tied near the top.

"I *thought* they were supposed to be crosses, Hannah, when I first came upon them, but that didn't make sense, and then I realized they were supposed to be men. Men with arms and charred-out eyes, and halfway down, a short peeled twig sticking out. And their balsa bodies were all splinters where practice spears had been plunged and then torn away.

"The children began to dance around, poking at the ragged figures, delighted to have found something safe to taunt. Bai's expression never changed. 'You know they have fallen to this, then?' I asked her. And she said, 'There must be revenge for Nimu.' She didn't hesitate, she didn't try to justify or apologize, she simply looked at me and said, 'There must be revenge.' "

"So we're back to Nimu."

Her head jerks around and she looks down her nose at me.

"How did you know I was thinking that?" she asks with a sharpness that is vintage Grace.

"Lately I've wanted to remember things," I tell her. "A lot of the same stuff I think you're trying to forget."

"And never will," she says bitterly, turning her shoulders away from me, looking out past our reflections into the dark. "I may forget a name, a birth, a species of palm. But a hundred of those treatments won't help me forget that woman. I can't let go of her, Hannah, in my mind I'm always trying to make her listen. I can't stop telling her how much she's to blame, how she ruined —"

"Don't," I say with surprising force, as if Nimu were still alive, listening from the next room, deciding whether to stay with us or leave.

"But Hannah, she's the one who got the boys started when she realized her illness was killing her. She told them it was the work of evil spirits sent by some enemy to gnaw at her chest, to choke her when she tried to sleep. She asked me what she had done wrong; when had she not followed God's teachings, that He would allow this attack? Maybe He wasn't strong enough to prevent it. What could I say?

"I offered to stay with her, to help her pray when she had trouble breathing. I reminded her that Christ would fill her heart with perfect peace. And meanwhile, at night I'd hear her racking coughs and think, *She is dying for no reason, she is dying unnecessarily because that one intruder had a cold her body couldn't resist.* I was angry myself at everything, resentful, and completely out of contact with my Lord. When your father was taken, I knew I would go on — in fact it freed me to find my own way. But I must have known that when Nimu died it would stop me short. Even before I noticed the boys slipping under her roof. I knew my work depended on hers. My life. Yes, Hannah, I want to blame her. And in the same breath" — she gives one more gasp — "I should beg her to forgive us all.

"The afternoon came when she was strangely agitated. I asked her what was wrong, what I could do to ease her discomfort, and she said, 'Make me a bed in the earth. It is time for me to sleep in the earth.' I assured her that her mortal body would be taken care of just as she wished, once her soul had passed on to Life Everlasting, after the Sacrament had been spoken. But that wasn't what she wanted." My mother's voice is thin with failure. "She wouldn't be satisfied until she had thrown away ten years of Christian teaching. She wanted to be buried while she was still alive, so her body couldn't fall into her enemies' hands. She had to be sure it became the food for worms. As if her whole lifetime had come down to that.

"I tried to explain that the body was nothing, it didn't matter *what* happened to it, it was her soul that would enter Eternal Life. Stubborn old woman. She said if I would not make this earthbed for her, she would do it herself. She was barely able to walk, but she got up from her hammock and groped for two of her largest shells and staggered like a drunken person to the edge of the garden. Not far in she fell to her knees and began tearing vines and digging frantically. She was obviously calling up every bit of energy that remained in her body. And I couldn't do anything but stand and watch." My mother stops and stares as if she is seeing it all again, as if it is her punishment to repeat this helpless witness.

"It seemed to go on for hours, the digging on hands and knees, like an animal. There was something about her determination — I couldn't bring myself to try and stop her, but I couldn't help her either, how could I help her, my hands were tied to help her, and when the boys saw what was happening and moved to help her, I had to order them to go away. Finally she had scratched a hole that was deep enough for a body as wasted as hers; she barely had the strength to roll into it. Then I watched her arm rise above the hole and claw at the earth piled at the rim, scrape it back where it belonged. By the time the sun set, there was only the ring of loosened ground. And all night those boys must have sneaked out to it, piling it high with her store of special stones."

>> .·. <<

"How come she's so down?" Darwin whispers after he and the children have been home only a few minutes.

"I don't think she is down," I whisper back. "I think she's just not pretending to be up."

I feel different too. My mother's story left me aching with vague regret, but I don't feel alone in it. Her loss and mine are the same. And I keep thinking, there are all these things we can share that aren't lost — they are floating around us like all the subjects that get left hanging in an intense conversation. They are there to go back to when our situation calms down. Because the story itself is not really the truth, the truth is something we can begin living, as soon as all the stories are told.

The children are certainly different. During a break in the afternoon's more strenuous work with slapstick and mime, the clown consultant gave all four a special lesson in make-up. At the dinner table their white faces and large, notched eyes turn to me patiently. My mother is refraining from her usual cheerful question — who will say the grace? Three creamy red mouths curve up in smiles; Benjamin's frown matches the tears he has penciled at the corner of each eye. I pick up my fork and we begin.

Benjamin stays in his seat and Matthew does nothing that requires an apology. Jeremy doesn't gorge and Rachel cleans her plate. Darwin goes ahead and talks about his plans for the RATS, even though after my mother's first night here he swore he was never going to mention the group around her because she hadn't commented on his uniform or shown any curiosity or even interest in the RATS. And lo and behold, my mother asks him a question — what does he mean by the Spirit of Play?

"Riding the moment," he says. "Letting it move you. Giving up all the habits and hopes you were taught to resist it with. Doing it without trying, because if you make it a goal, you know, write it in on your calendar and everything, you'll never get anywhere."

My mother looks down at the hot turkey sandwich she has hardly touched, then rolls just her eyes back to Darwin. "Redemption through Jesus Christ, our Lord, almost sounds easy next to that."

"What have I been trying to tell you?" Darwin says, miraculously undefensive, somehow having picked up in my mother the improbable willingness to play.

"I suspect the Janca women possessed a little of your Spirit," my mother says, with the briefest wistful smile, "though it was sadly no use at all against the Spirit of Revenge that possessed the men."

"What is?" Darwin asks, still uncontentious. "Nothing is any use against that. That's History. If you bother to fight it, you've surrendered."

"Perhaps," my mother says. "Yet if you give up the struggle against wickedness, it grows and gains strength." She raises one hand to stop Darwin's rejoinder. "The Lord's work is accomplished by many means, Darwin. Can we grant each other that?"

Darwin presses his lips together; for a moment — who knows his motives — he will accept her terminology.

"I'm a fighter," she goes on. "I've made terrible mistakes. I've failed. But I'm too old now to change paths."

Her unexpected confession makes him silent, and for a moment there is peace. As if all of us have found something we wanted, or at least enough of it to relax our grasping at one another. Which is why I am completely unprepared for Darwin's old mistrust to erupt out of nowhere as we are fumbling around each other in the bathroom, getting ready for bed.

"I just want to know," he says, pulling out the stub of a joint, "if you put Jeremy up to it."

"Up to what?" I have to ask.

"The perils-of-pot lecture. Straight out of some program I bet they're pushing at school." He cracks the lid down onto the toilet and sits.

I tell him I haven't put Jeremy up to anything. He attaches a clip to his tiny roach, twists his face to light it, takes one long drag, which pretty much wipes it out. I ask him what he is talking about.

Well, neither Spiderman nor Miss Piggy showed up for the session that afternoon, and Miss Piggy came rushing in an hour and a half late and announced in front of everyone that Spiderman was, even as they spoke, being detoxified.

"And I guess I put them up to that too," I say. "You know, to sort of set the stage for Jeremy's lecture."

"Rich, self-important bitch," Darwin says, ignoring me. "Thinks a man is on the level of an apartment — something Daddy will buy for you and pay to have remodeled before you move in."

Apparently Spiderman's idea of Thanksgiving was to smoke so much hash and drink so much wine that he passed out, whereupon she decided to help him do what he had been claiming for months he wanted to do. She loaded him into her car and drove him out to the country, to a private rehab center beyond Sugarland. He wasn't too thrilled about it when she visited this morning. He made some noise about leaving, and she threatened to start the paperwork for involuntary committal.

Her actions seem surprisingly reasonable to me. Reasonable to the point of heroic. I am in the bedroom, layering on my nightclothes, trying to conjure up her plump curves, her baby-doll pinafore, and realizing I've never seen her without her rubber pig mask. "She didn't strike me as a woman who could pull off a plan like that," I call back to Darwin.

"You can pull off anything if a guy trusts you." Darwin comes out of the bathroom seething. "He fucking trusted her." There isn't really any space for him to stomp around in, so he rips his cape off, bunches and hurls it into the corner, and drops onto the bed. "And you could see she really got off on the fact that she'd locked him up."

"Darwin," I say.

"Meanwhile, she's taken leave from her job and signed up for some sort of program where you pay, or rather, your daddy pays, three thousand bucks to live on newts and berries for a month and maybe die of starvation and exposure."

"It must be hard on you, losing them both at once," I say evenly, smothering a surge of selfish joy.

Darwin sags, elbows on knees, head in hands. "And then all this shit with Heidi."

My stomach turns; I put a hand over my mouth, nod cautiously.

"I know what you're thinking, what you've been thinking all along — the old Darwin screwing around, the quest for the ultimate lay — but it wasn't ever that, I sort of drifted into it because I thought it was just a game for her, the compliments, the innuendoes, and she could play it with anyone, it didn't particularly have to be me." He looks up, straightens his posture. "But shit. I don't see that I have to explain anything to you. You're not going to explain anything to me."

I keep nodding, conceding him that.

"All I wanted was for everything to go smooth in front of the kids today, and it was a mess — Heidi oozing tears whenever she looked at one of them, the victorious Piggy not taking orders from anybody. Then the little know-it-alls, they waited till we were coming home in the Bus and then Jeremy started in. Gave me the whole pitch, everything from lung cancer to organic brain dysfunction to something about male hormones. I mean, he'd throw out some bizarre statistic, and the others would chime in like a chorus, and all I could see in the rear view were these white painted faces with big scared eyes nodding up and down." He gets up and pokes in the closet for his old mountain parka with all the unexpected pockets, where he keeps his stuff.

"They're worried about you. Don't you think they know what you do up here in the bathroom? Or what it means that you hide?"

"What do you mean, 'hide'? I'm not trying to hide anything. If I were having a beer I wouldn't have to hide. In fact I told them that. And I said I hoped they weren't getting any ideas like those kids in California who turned their parents in just because dope is technically illegal." He has the baggie in one hand; the other searches an inside pocket. "So then they started in with their statistics on alcohol. For Christsake, what are they doing to our kids? Can't they allow kids their innocence?"

"It's not a 'they,' Darwin," I say. "It's you."

He turns and I can see the blood rise into his face, spit from his words. "Why don't you be a little more blunt?"

"Their father's a pothead."

"Sure he is. Oh yeah, sure. Do you realize there are guys who smoke ten, fifteen times more in a day than I do? People who can't control it?" He jabs his pretty little painted pipe at me like a scolding finger. "Save your judgmental labels for them. Besides, I don't see anyone coming out with a better way to salvage a little pleasure from —"

"Matthew."

"Matthew what?"

"Matthew's tried it. Enough times that he's not sure of the number."

"Matthew," Darwin says, as though to summon up all pertinent data.

"Matthew thinks he's hooked. He says he's kicking the habit with Dooley."

"Jesus Christ." Darwin puts the pipe and the baggie back in their respective pockets.

"Dooley says the dope part is not that serious. Matthew was only experimenting. But it's a symptom."

By clamping the instep of one foot over the heel of the other, Darwin removes his boots, then jams down his red trunks, steps out of them, and kicks them aside. "And when was anyone going to tell me about this?" He unzips his leotard, begins wrestling his arms out through the neck.

"When have you ever wanted to know what's really going on?" I ask warily from where I sit on my side of the bed, scratching Under's throat.

"I could ask you the same question."

"How many times have *you* talked to Dooley?"

"Dooley, Valerie. Damn it" — he has to wriggle to get the leotard off — "anyone else out there I need to consult with on my personal life?"

"What if I had told you, Darwin? You wouldn't have done anything, I mean, you aren't going to change. You'd have had that much more guilt to drag around, one more reason to feel down, but you wouldn't have changed."

"You want to know what it was about Heidi," Darwin asks, bowing forward to spit out the words, "what it really was? She never acted like I let her down. She just slogged through whatever shit happened to come down and didn't try to blame it on me or turn it into a cause for reform. You know how easy that could have been?"

I pretend to shrug off the new subject, but I am letting all the past tenses sink in. So it is over. I have to fight off relief, hope, our whole history of fresh starts.

"Well, it wasn't," Darwin goes on, his tone inexplicably softening. "It was a total mistake." I shrug again. "You don't believe me. You've got something going now and you don't want to believe me. But I'm telling you anyway" — he marches over to the bed and stands over me — "it was an eye opener. She'd start in on this 'nothing-matters-you-just-live-and-die' business, and all I could think was how she was kidding herself. Maybe she realizes that now, after Air and Space. Seeing you and Jeremy about freaked her out, you were so real, so she asked if I would hold her one more time till she calmed down. Which was what I was doing when you found us." He is bending over, trying to get me to raise my head. He looks so vulnerable, so innocently lumpy in his undershirt and blue tights. "I'm trying to tell you I *have* changed, Hannah. The thing with Heidi never got off the ground. I didn't have the heart for it."

I don't want to believe him, I'm afraid to believe him, to give in to this marriage all over again. "If we could only afford it," I say, "I'd go off into the wilderness like Miss Piggy."

"You and who else?"

"Just me. There is no one else." Darwin's gaze goes distant, puzzling, moves me to fudge that utter truth: "It never really got off the ground either."

"Well," he says, standing up, shuffling in his stocking feet. "Well, if you're thinking of going off somewhere, you ought to realize you'll find *your* share of this family's shit right there in your backpack."

"I don't deny it. But maybe I'd be able to figure things out better, out there without any distractions."

He plops down suddenly on the bed next to me. "So you really feel you have to leave?"

"Oh, Darwin," I moan, "I don't know."

His glasses are low on his nose. He throws his head back to see if he has worn me down. He looks satisfied. He pats my knee stiffly. "I'm staying right here," he says.

"I don't know," I tell him again.

20

. .
.

I HAVEN'T MENTIONED my plan to anyone. I have nursed it in the back of my mind like a sinful fantasy, something to fall back on, a temporary escape from the minor revolution taking place in our home since Darwin agreed to an appointment with Dooley and the three of us talked for over an hour among the toys.

I sat in the large reclining chair, Darwin in the smaller, and Dooley, gentle soul, on the little pedestal table with the box of Kleenex in his lap. You would not have thought Darwin had ever dismissed openness and honesty as "seventies bullshit," he had so much to say — or, as Dooley says, so much input to share: father, mother, their expectations, my expectations, my self-sufficiency, my irresponsible innocence, his own ongoing fight to stay mentally alive. In Dooley's perception, Darwin and I each make the other feel inadequate, not on purpose but on purpose, as we thrash and bumble around trying to unload the feelings of inadequacy in ourselves. Darwin appeared to understand this crazy logic better than I did, in fact it delighted him, and he said yes, he wouldn't mind coming back in two weeks. Then, flushed with such evidence of breakthrough, Dooley suggested a hug. We both dropped our eyes, swallowed, couldn't move. "I didn't mean me," Dooley stammered. "I meant the two of you." That got a nervous snicker from Darwin. "OK," Dooley said, "first you stand up facing each other," which made me giggle, and then we were all three laughing hysterically as Dooley coached us through an embrace.

In the car going home we were tense, silent. In bed that night we hung on to our separate edges of the mattress, then chose the same moment to give a deep sigh and turn face to face. It was strange to be held, touched, entered. You might imagine indescribable pleasure after how many months, years, of refraining. But no, my body was tight, wary; it gathered its nerves and took flight to a high corner of the room, left the whole business to pass like a dream. And Darwin's refused to come. "Look," I said finally — we were sticky with sweat and both struggling for breath — "it's the same for me, I'm not ready either," and we rolled apart.

"Consider that a dry run," Darwin said with a plaintive little laugh.

"A warm-up," I said, and gave him a long kiss on the mouth which he watched with open eyes.

Meanwhile, the RATS have scored an overwhelming success in the field. In front of all the Redskins fans who did not spend half time waiting in line for beer and nachos or the bathroom, the surviving Superheroes cavorted through the ranks of the Groveton High School marching band, disrupting their configurations. One half of the band was supposed to form a tomahawk and, playing warpath music double-time, rush the other half, arranged along the lines of a Dallas cowboy's hat. But assorted RATS danced right into the weapon's trajectory and dispersed it into random particles. The band had no better luck with the Christmas tree that spread its branches to the tune of "Here Comes Santa Claus," or with the school's initials. There were retaliations — trumpeters and trombonists, blowing ugly blasts, chased individual Superheroes around the field. The band director from Groveton came running into the mess shouting orders, and got his ears fondled by a seductive Wonder Woman. The audience loved it. Now Darwin is negotiating a modest contract for next season's home games. He's trying not to appear too eager.

And Jeremy is walking on air, having been granted apprentice status in RATS, not as Snoopy or a snake charmer but as Superboy. Darwin has promised the other children heroic roles as well when they turn thirteen. Two Saturdays ago he and Jeremy paid a free introductory visit to Fit Accompli, where they checked out something called weight training. They thought maybe they should look their parts more, and Darwin needed to take his mind off the pot he wasn't smoking. They came home with greenish faces and shaky limbs. They had been introduced to these machines, strapped into them. These machines had invited them to design their own bodies, muscle by muscle. No pain, no gain. They were trying to remain skeptical, but they were having to work hard at it.

Then one night Darwin and I drew deep breaths again, rolled into each other's arms, mouth seeking mouth with a sudden hunger, and came together on the first thrust. We both avowed we'd been satisfied, then confessed how terrified we were.

"We're talking progress," Darwin said.

"I hate that word," I said. "Let's say we're making repairs."

Of course it was love we were making, but it seems almost too good to be true. I watch Darwin struggle through his cravings, watch him work to believe that the stiff hugs he grabs from us will help shore his resolve. He marches off to the gym every other evening with Jeremy instead of rolling a joint. He has managed to hold a discussion of nonviolent politics with Matthew, who later removed from over his bunk the large homemade yellow poster — NUKE THE AYATOLLAH. And he has bestowed on tiny Benjamin the sacred nickname Bear.

>> ∴ <<

I haven't said a word about my plan to my mother, whom I've called three times in as many weeks since I put her on the return bus to Pittsburgh. I'm not exactly sure why, but I sort of enjoy talking to her now. I don't feel that I am interrupting some urgent business of hers, or that I have to remind her who I am, or that she's preoccupied with calculating the phone bill. She's never mentioned Samuel's ailments, physical or spiritual, instead has asked question after question about the children, Valerie's progress with Cheryl, even the snake, whose markings have brightened, who has been more or less consuming the melted mouse Jeremy dangles into its cage every Saturday. Last time I told her that Valerie had enrolled Cheryl in a course to prepare her for her GED and had even borrowed the Bus and driven all the way into town to get her to the first session. My mother said if only we all went to that kind of trouble to prepare for our G-O-D, but I just answered, "I know," and left it at that.

I keep remembering what she said about Darwin, her last words as she boarded the Greyhound after Thanksgiving: "He needs you. He may try hard to hide it, but he's a true family man."

While Rachel read the map and called out rights and lefts, my mother had spent the whole trip into town dwelling again on the Janca, on the deserted village, surprise attacks, destruction. Two employees of the State Petroleum Company have been killed; last year, a tourist. It seems the curious are paying well for the adventure of government-sponsored tours, in riverboats, under armed guards, all to catch a glimpse of one of the famous "killer Janca" among the trees and see him try to duck the bullets and throw his spear at the same time. Every once in a while the spears hit someone, every once in a while the bullets do. "It's a lovely picture, Hannah," she concluded. "You can't try to tell me anything we gave them has survived."

I was distracted by the traffic. The metered places were all filled; taxis and cars were stopping anywhere to discharge their passengers, suitcases, warped boxes, shopping bags; and my mother was being annoyingly morbid. She seemed determined to whittle away at the common ground we had found the day before. "I won't try to tell you anything," I said. "Except I have to believe otherwise."

Her gaze snapped away from me and out her side window, and she spoke under her breath. When I asked what she'd said, she replied reluctantly, as though confessing criticism, "You are your father's daughter."

"Am I supposed to apologize for that?" My mother hung her head. "I'm sorry," I said. "I guess we each have our different

memories. Our different tribes, even." Mine would flourish along
the riverbank forever, out of range.

We were almost in front of the station on our second time
around the block when a car started to pull away from the curb,
just as we were rolling into a position to take its place. My
mother perked up and praised the Lord; and the look I ex-
changed with Rachel in the rear view — something between tol-
erance and amusement — inspired me to parallel-park the Bus on
the first try.

Then we were coming out of the terminal into the monoxide
stench of the loading area, walking down the row of idling buses.
We stopped beside the one, and the driver opened the door,
leaned forward in his seat, but we just stood there, so he closed
it again.

"Well, Mother," I said, wishing that I hadn't let her get to me,
realizing she probably always would.

She looked at me, then looked off over her shoulder. Was she
reminded of all our other stiff partings, the hurt on both sides?
"You've been more than hospitable," she said finally. "I hope
you're not sorry I came."

"Next time it'll be less confusing," I said. "It really will." And
she must have heard this as the promise, the concession I intended it to be, because she patted my arm and gave her reassuring pitch about Darwin. She might have continued to pat, and
I to stand there, while the love I knew we felt played its stubborn
tricks, except that Rachel threw herself against the two of us,
wrapped an arm around each waist, drew us a stumble closer.
Rachel crying in her high, sweet voice, "I don't like for you to
leave, Grandma, I don't like it when people leave me": Rachel
melting my mother as I never could, Rachel who has never shown
signs of needing anyone — we all three hung on to each other
with Rachel's need.

>> .∴. <<

All day I have baked while my brain raced with plans. The
counters are covered with Christmas cookies piled three deep —

chocolate chip, molasses, Russian tea biscuits, sugar, pinwheels, jelly tots. On top of the refrigerator, loaves of cinnamon bread are stacked like logs. Built-up reserves.

Rachel comes breezing into the kitchen from school, her last day before Christmas vacation. She slips her pink backpack off, props it against the wall, removes her hooded jacket, pulls a comb from her hip pocket, and tries to fluff her electric hair, which flies where it wants to.

Like her grandmother, she doesn't ask for anything. The cookies everywhere could be just so much Play-Doh for the interest she shows. She kneels beside the backpack, unzips a pocket, pulls out the envelope, hands it to me — her report card. I know that she will have all O's, no S's or N's, but something keeps me from making the prediction out loud. It isn't her face — terribly nonchalant — or the way she fans the envelope impatiently as she waits for me to soap my buttery hands at the sink. It's that all at once I realize how badly she wants to astonish me. I realize how often I've praised her brothers for achievements I take for granted in her — because Jeremy is always getting picked on and Matthew can never get enough positive reinforcement and Benjamin is doomed to being small and frail. The exemplary reports from school and gymnastics and other girls' mothers, the bedroom in perfect pink order, every article in every drawer folded neatly, every shoe lined up and paired, all the parallels and perpendiculars — we take all those things for granted. The child has nothing left to try.

"How wonderful," I exclaim, opening the card. "You're 'continuing to progress toward new horizons.' That's fantastic."

She looks up at me with those dark eyes of hers, head cocked skeptically as if to say, *You don't really mean that, do you? And if you do, what difference will it make, what will it get me?* I just stand there, amazed at the density of the mistrust that has grown there between us — I have glimpsed it, denied it, thought it impossible, frivolous to worry about. How could your daughter insist on being everything you ever hoped for, yet slip away while you are playing father to your boys?

And so Rachel's the one I tell: "This is the big day."

"Oh," she says, carefully not making it a question.

"The put-up-or-shut-up-about-the-airplanes-day," I tell her. "I'm going out to Dulles. And you've been selected to come with me." She is not amused, but having lunched and snacked nonstop on cookie dough, I am riding a sugar high, I am impervious to tactful resistance. "I really would love for the two of us to do this together." In these last minutes I've become utterly certain it is the only thing to do.

She has pulled her turtleneck up over her nose like a bandit, muffling her suggestion: "Couldn't we just go to the mall or get tickets to the Ice Capades? That's what Amanda's —"

"It's not like that," I tell her, folding the neck back down. "This is standing up for something that's basically wrong and unfair."

"I'm just a kid," she says. "Other kids are going to think I'm crazy."

"Do you think *I'm* crazy?"

Her brain won't come up with something fast enough to camouflage such a painful truth. She pulls a little tin of lip gloss from her corduroys, smears some on her mouth, then offers it to me. "Strawberry," she says.

I put my hands on her shoulders, feel the bones stiffen. "Rachel." I wait for her to look at me. "Wouldn't you like to be a little bit crazy?" Her face shows not a flicker of yes or no. "You must get tired of doing everything right, *all* the time."

"Don't say stuff like that," she says, slumping.

I let her go. "You're right, you know, it is crazy. Everyone says so — why not something big, like the destruction of the rain forest, they say, or oil spills, or the plastics choking our landfills, or all the toxic stuff in our food, or some endangered species? And I don't know why not."

"Because it's right here," Rachel declares grudgingly. "We can see it every day almost, and we can sure hear it."

"But that's true, Rachel, you know it's true. How cold is it out?"

"Pretty."

"Let's go put on a couple of layers of old clothes. And I'll write a note to the boys."

I think it is the idea of the note that captures her. *Dear Boys
. . . Love, Mom and Rachel* — a new alignment. *P.S. Cookies and
bread go to Wctr. Call Val.*

Bless her heart, when Rachel reappears, she still looks very
stylish — a pink and blue plaid shirt over her pink turtleneck, a
navy sweatshirt over that. The way she wears them, clothes always match, never wrinkle, get dirty, or age. Her own winter
jacket, pink and trimmed with flowered ribbon, is no good for
this. Too visible. She lets me tuck her into an old gray jacket of
Matthew's I'd put away for Benjamin. Over long underwear,
faded jeans, and several sweaters, I don my faithful parka, olive-
drab.

We are approaching the shortest day of the year, and at two
forty-five the overcast sky is already darkening. I have been waiting for this, I have run through the first steps in my mind, not
knowing if I would ever actually take them. This last week I have
observed one Concorde landing from the airport access road and
one through the panoramic violet-tinted windows of the cocktail
lounge, sipping a two-dollar glass of orange juice. I have a general idea of the region in which these landings occur.

We get on the access road going in the only direction
allowed — toward the airport — and drive the eight miles out to
where the dazzling terminal curves up like a breaking wave; there
we loop around and start back. About a quarter mile past the
point where the chain-link fence runs out, we slow down, pull the
Bus onto the shoulder, tie a handkerchief to the stub that remains
of an antenna, grab the hunk of rope I slipped under the middle
seat the day before. An empty taxicab passes us, then starts to
brake, but I shake my head and wave it on. There are no other
cars in sight. We jump a shallow gully and duck behind the
ragged ridge of scrub cedar and leafless shrubs that grow along
the other side. We have made the first move; it floods us with so
much adrenaline we cannot even run efficiently. Half-screened,
we stumble and trip our way back to the fence.

It's much colder here looking up at the strands of barbed wire
than it was where we left the Bus. The air is odorless and pinches

our nostrils shut with each breath. I have worked up a sweat that chills now that we have stopped and makes me shiver. I pull Rachel to me and give her back some vigorous rubbing. After we have checked again for cars, I tell her, we're going to climb the fence. She nods at me numbly. She is not allowing herself to be afraid.

I make a stirrup with my hands and almost sling her right onto the barbs, she is so light. I keep one hand under her bottom as she anchors one foot on this side and finds a safe hold for her hands. When she swings the other leg up and over the barbs, she kicks my arm away. She is on her own, balanced on the fence above me in an awkward, pigeon-toed straddle, and out of habit her arms fly up into the proud V with which she finishes her stunts in gymnastics. Meanwhile I am sure she will fall, a car will come by and see us, something, but hanging on to the fencepost with both hands, she clears the barbs with the outside leg and drops, loose as a paratrooper, into the brittle grasses below.

She looks up at me through the wire. Maybe we are thinking the same thing — it won't be as easy for me, I am large and clumsy, the toes of my boots will never hold in the mesh, I can't begin to pull my body up and over with the strength in my arms, even with the rope, we will surely be seen now, arrested separately, sent to separate jails. I tie a loop in one end of the rope and, holding it hip-high, throw the other up over the fence; it dangles out of Rachel's reach. We stare at each other blankly for a minute, and then she scrambles back up the fence. Clinging to it like a fly, her face contracted with effort, she manages to weave the loose end around the wire, then knot it again and again. I have my foothold, my stirrup. I half-mount; it doesn't slip. I claw my hands up the chain-link panel, then reach the instep of my free boot up onto its top bar. Clutching the post now, I slowly pull my weight and the other roped boot up to the bar, then slip off its noose. I am crouched there, with the barbed wire digging into my shins, afraid to breathe for fear of upsetting my balance, letting the desperation gather so I can do what I must do — quickly shift one foot onto the top strand of barbed wire and spring off into a flying leap. I land in a sort of squat on the frozen ground beside Rachel. In spite of the sharp pains in my ankles and shins, I force a smile so she will realize we have come through something.

"I was wondering how we're going to get out," Rachel says. "I guess I'm not supposed to ask, right?"

I give the gray hood a couple of pats. I want to say, *Trust me, let me take care of you, I'm your mother.* But when I stand up and look around, I'm surprised at how little I can make out. Some distance away, a double lane of concrete turns a corner and stretches into a blur. Farther off, a gray strip and more signal lights suggest another runway. Otherwise, the ground is flat, dull, acres of brown-green emptiness. As we stand here with our feet upon it, the terminal and tower a modest thrust on the horizon, it's impossible to see where we are.

I check my watch and wonder how much time we'll have once we spot the Concorde, once it begins its last descent. I give Rachel the sign to follow me. Bent close to the earth, we leave the fence behind and half run, half waddle across the crunchy field. We reach the nearest concrete strip and continue along it. I am beginning to worry: this was easy to imagine — lying down in front of the thing — but how do you know where you can do that safely, when it is taxiing slowly enough to be able to stop?

I feel a little unworthy that I am even considering the risks, unworthy because I really have no desire to be run over, and I think about what my mother called me — "your father's daughter." Somehow, he has driven me here; I am still haunted by his vision of heroic sacrifice. But how could I do anything that might endanger Rachel? How could there be anything I would risk Rachel's life for?

The concrete strip turns into another. We stumble our way along it to a point where a much wider runway crosses. My lower back aches from running bent over, I can't put much weight on one ankle, and in my mind a yearning for safety and warmth is doing battle with guilt. Rachel has not yet complained. The strips are laid higher than the land around them by about a foot and a half. Here where they intersect, the slight slope makes a hollow.

I flop down into it. "That's enough," I tell Rachel in gasps. "This must be sort of the middle of things."

She collapses on her knees beside me. "Now what?" she asks, not facetiously but as someone ready to absorb the next task. Her bluish lips still tremble. The arms of Matthew's jacket are almost too short for her, and she hunches her shoulders up to keep them covering her wrists. I realize that she *is* trusting me, she has let go of all her precocious sophistication for this. It makes me want to cry.

"We wait," I say, pulling her down to lie with me, her back against my front. The gray light is fading. I bury my face in her hood, and try to force my warm breath through it as I tell her, "We're on this other planet, far from the sun. It's cold and empty. There's nothing around but these two stones on this wide open plain, you and me. I'm a boulder . . ." She is mumbling into her jacket. "I can't hear you," I tell her.

She half turns her head over her shoulder, informs me solemnly, "I said, 'You're making it worse. Think warm.' "

"I'm sorry," I say. "Let's do the jungle, Rachel. One more time. It's perfect for this. What do you think?" Her head nods against my chest. "OK. Well, you and I have finally come for a visit, and here we are in the village, I mean the very first one where I lived. And we're resting together in a hammock." I draw my knees up behind hers as if she were sitting in my lap. "And it's warm. Toasty warm. Sometimes it's chilly at night but there's always a fire burning at the center of the round house." She wiggles, presses herself harder into the curve of my body. But now it's daytime anyway, and the sun is straight overhead, and we're taking a nap, and Nimu is telling us a story. Let's see. She's telling us about her great-great-grandmother, and how she made her husband angry by giving birth to seven daughters in a row. He wanted warriors to fight alongside him and thought she was deliberately having the girls out of spite."

"MCP," Rachel announced.

"Definitely," I said. "Anyway, the moon saw the raw deal she was getting and made her an offer. She would be allowed three chances to change herself at night into anything she chose, and then change back at dawn if she didn't like it." I paused. "What would you choose, Rachel?" She heaved her shoulders, asked me what I would. "Nimu's ancestor tried the mighty jaguar first, but she found that all the forest creatures ran away from her and so the night got pretty lonely. Then she chose the parrot for its gorgeous feathers, but she didn't like having her head filled with other people's words. Maybe I'd try the kinkajou. They're graceful, and sort of appealing, and I always thought they seemed content. A kinkajou certainly wouldn't have had any trouble with that fence back there."

"I'd never pick an animal," Rachel says. "I'd pick a person, like a singer or a queen."

"Nimu's great-great-grandmother thought for a long time before she made her third choice, because if it didn't work out she'd be stuck with her husband's abuse. Finally she decided to become a drop of water." Rachel says that was pretty silly. "Well, she plunked herself into the Tiwano River, and by morning, when it was time to decide whether to go back or not, she had met the Amazon, and she realized that she loved always moving and that as a drop of water she would go everywhere and become part of everything, so she kept right on flowing, down to the sea."

Rachel sits herself up, looks at me almost accusingly. "I don't like that story," she says. Surprised, a little hurt, I ask her why. "It makes me think about you leaving," she says.

"Nobody's leaving, Rachel. We told you that."

"Dad says he's cleaning up his act. And I almost never do anything bad."

"I wouldn't leave you, even if you did do something bad."

Her face perks up into a smile I have never seen before, mischievous, a little reckless. "Tell me a story about you and Dad," she says. "How you fell in love and had us." She flops back down in a ball against my body, and I am realizing what a clever little tactician she is, and wondering, if I even could, how and where I would start, when in the distance something vibrates, low and dull. Grows gradually louder. Rachel rolls onto her back, we look at each other in silence, and then I say, "I guess it's time."

Still we just look at each other, wondering what in the world we are going to do, refusing to raise our eyes, refusing to acknowledge that tapering, much-admired body, paler than the sky, the arrogant arch of its nose. As if it was outside our world and then a door opened and all of a sudden it was let in, the dull whine explodes into a lung-rattling roar, so loud I can't think, can't even feel the beating of my heart, only a thickness in my throat. I raise my head and scan the horizon. It is still farther away than I expected, and floating there head-on in midair, it doesn't look as if it's getting closer, only growing a little bigger. I open my mouth and scream as hard as I can, "Go back, we don't want you," and Rachel stares at me curiously, because we can't even hear my voice. Inside the precious cabin, in warm, womb-like silence, the passengers sleep on. Time has stopped for them; bodily functions have been suspended; when they wake up, they will remember nothing.

Outside, the cold open space is boundless. Distances can't be gauged, everything is happening at once, and I have to pee. It is clear that the plane is heading for some other landing strip, nowhere near where we have pitched our little camp. I grab Rachel's arm and drag her up onto the broader of the two runways we were resting against, the one parallel to the course of the incoming plane, and take off in the same direction.

It is like forcing your way through something solid, that thunder, it affects your sense of balance, and as the plane hangs behind us and then roars past far to our left, Rachel stumbles and falls. I help her up, and we stand there peering off into the distance as it takes one delicate, playful bounce and is down. We must limp on, but we're sort of in slow motion — my back, my ankle, and now my bladder hurt with each step, and I am squandering my breath screaming things like *Get out, Go home, Leave us alone.* I shake Rachel's shoulder and point to my lips, which form the invitation, "Scream. Scream all you want." Her mouth flies open, much to the surprise of her eyes, so I assume she is trying it.

Minutes later the Concorde makes a right turn, and its slender silhouette rolls across the horizon in the direction of our runway, teasing us on. I can hear Rachel yelling that she has to go to the bathroom, I yell back that I do too, there is no one around, we can go right here in the grass. Rachel is appalled. She jabs a mittened finger three, four times toward the plane moving against the pink-tinged sky in the distance. "Who cares?" I ask. I get my mouth right down beside her ear. "They can't really see us any better than we can see them. All they see is some blobs in an empty field, I told you, like stones or something. They don't see *us*."

Rachel folds her arms around herself and turns away. I hop down off the concrete on the side away from the plane, undo my pants, and squatting back against the ledge, let the crampy pain pour out of me, steam up the ground. When I look up again, there is more to the world than me and Rachel, hunched over her crossed legs, and a plane. Two boxy trucks, the size of toys still, are bouncing along the narrower runway, headlights blinking, toward the intersection where Rachel and I had waited; I can make out figures riding their running boards, somehow hanging on along the sides. So there is no going back, no undoing what is yet to be done.

I yank one of Rachel's hands from her pocket and we're off again. Looking back after a minute or two, I catch the trucks stopped and the bodies popping off. The trucks are painted sort of dark purple, the bodies wear uniforms of the same color. I can't see faces.

I can't tell how much our head start is worth, I'm no good at time, distance, and I'm lost now, disoriented — the cold, the noise, the purple crew, the responsibility for Rachel, who must be miserable. I'm not even sure whether we aren't running away from the purple guards instead of running toward the SST. But I am starting to understand with this dead cold certainty I've never felt before that we cannot stop the progress of that plane, it has already happened. Just as my father has died, just as the Janca have changed. No matter how desperately I wish other-wise, no matter how far I'm determined to go. The whole issue finally appears to me the way others have seen it all along — an absurdity, some obsession of mine, cranky and inexplicable. It aches like a cold dead weight in my chest, and though my legs keep stumbling forward, all I want to do is give up. I don't understand why I feel so much worse than silly or ashamed, why it seems as if everything around me is falling apart, and I can't stop any of it, I can't save anything — not the air, not the oceans, or the earth, or our bodies upon it.

There are six or seven purple uniforms coming across the field now, trying to cut us off, taking long, mechanical strides, not even running. Behind them are the toy terminal and the toy trucks; still ahead, the pretty plane. I am deathly worried about Rachel, staggering beside me. My own throat and chest feel seared by the freezing air.

"We're almost there," I yell meaninglessly, and Rachel stretches her mouth into a smile. Then all at once the concrete begins to quiver under our feet. The perfect creature has turned one more time, and it is rolling toward us, shimmering in the haze of its own heat and fumes. It is rolling slowly for it, but way too fast for us. It is getting bigger, closer than it's ever been before. My legs falter and then they stop. I am too stunned by this new vantage, the enlarging scale of the thing, the air-splitting power. We are so destructible, Rachel and I. I try to make out a face, a friendly wave, some flicker of human life in the slits of glass above its nose, but they are black.

It can't be very long that I stand there like that in the middle of the runway, with Rachel tugging my arm on one side and the purple guards closing in on the other. Maybe it is that damned sound, but it's as if some spell holds me there, some last-ditch crazy test: do I have what it takes to keep the plane from advancing, or this whole thing from happening, or myself from having to decide whether to move or die?

"I'm starting to go now," Rachel is shrieking. "I can't hold it anymore, I'm starting to go."

And that is it — I whisk her off into the grass, drag her jeans down without even undoing them, and as Nimu once did for me, I make a sort of seat for her with my clasped hands while she relieves herself. By the time the first of the purple squads reaches us, she is all pulled up and tucked in again, with a defiant edge to her composure that I've never seen before. She glares into their identical, almost childlike faces and insists with violent shrugs on walking by herself. I on the other hand almost welcome the nervous, reassuring smiles, the pressure of those purple gloves on both arms. Maybe something is finally over, and they are leading me away, guiding me to what's about to begin.